The rain had  above the fie
The stems of v
already full to
come early thi
tinued. It had
with only a fe~~~~~~~~~~days and autumn
had seen little improvement. No wonder the
labourers were up in arms, but what could
they do? Like her, they had nothing with
which to fight.

She did not understand why they would
not accept her; she could not see that she
was in any way different except that she
lived in a caravan instead of a cottage and,
judging by some of those, she was better
housed in the wagon. But, without Pa, even
that would be cold and uninviting, not really
a home at all, just a few bits of wood held
together with love and faith. She dawdled,
delaying her return, trying to make herself
think objectively, to plan what she would
do if Josiah were not restored to her. But
she could not; without him her life stretched
before her, a great dark void of nothingness.

Born in Singapore of a Dutch-South African father and an English mother, Mary Nichols came to England when she was three and has spent most of her life in different parts of East Anglia and now lives with her husband in Ely, Cambridgeshire. Beside being an author of short stories, articles and novels, Mary Nichols has been a radiographer, school secretary, industrial editor and information manager. Now she divides her time between writing novels, gardening and the golf course. She has a son and two daughters and four grandchildren.

By the same author

The Stubble Field

The
POACHER'S
DAUGHTER

Mary Nichols

ORION

An Orion paperback
First published in Great Britain by Orion in 1995
This paperback edition published in 1996 by Orion Books Ltd,
Orion House, 5 Upper St Martin's Lane,
London WC2H 9EA

A CIP catalogue record for this book
is available from the British Library.

ISBN: 0 75280 183 X

Printed and bound in Great Britain by
Clays Ltd, St Ives plc

Prologue

*J*osiah Brough pulled the green and yellow tinker's wagon to one side of the narrow street as hundreds of yelling men, women and children raced past him. Some of them carried axes, others pitchforks; one had a firebrand. 'To the mill!' they shouted. 'The devil take all millowners!'

The big black carthorse was not used to people and noise at that volume and showed every sign of wanting to bolt. Josiah jumped down and went to its head, as more and more people crowded along the street, threatening to overtopple the van. 'Steady, old fellow,' he said, stroking its nose. 'We'll soon be out of it.'

But he could not move against the flow and stood there, calming the horse, waiting patiently for the mob to pass, for it was a mob, intent on mischief, of that he was certain. He was beginning to wish he had never ventured into the town; the place was a powder keg. 'Luddites,' he said, addressing the horse. 'As if we hadn't had enough of war, they must wage it on their own doorsteps.'

At the end of the street, he could see the object of their hatred, a large brick-built building, three storeys high, its rows of windows winking in the sunlight and reflected in the water of the river running along one side of it. Newly built, it housed hundreds of looms, made, according to the mob which was even now battering at its doors, to put honest weavers out of work. As he watched, he heard the sound of hooves on the hard cobbles and the next minute a troop of militia came into sight, sabres drawn. They galloped into the midst of the crowd, slashing this way and that, scattering the screaming rioters, who fled in all directions. 'Time to get a move on, Brough,' he said to himself. 'This is no place for you.'

There were casualties, he could see that; the cobbles were red with their blood and the still air echoed with their shrieks. Their comrades were dragging them away and there was nothing he could do to help them. He climbed back onto the high front seat of the wagon and resolutely turned his back on the carnage. It was not that he was a coward, nor that he did not feel for those who were hurt; he had spent years in uniform and distinguished himself on many a European battlefield and he had never failed to do all he could for those who had been wounded. But that was all behind him now. All he wanted was a little peace to nurse his own wounds.

Twenty-four he had been when he enlisted, newly married and out of work. He had needed the regular army pay, especially when the child came. What he had not envisaged was that two years later he would be sent abroad and his wife would be unlucky in the ballot to accompany the regiment. He had left her behind. Ten years he had been out of the country, ten years in which the only news he had of his family was through his wife's infrequent letters, and they told him little enough for they had followed him across a continent and she was no scholar. When he returned after Waterloo, war-weary and recovering from a wound to his knee, he came back to nothing but two mounds in the churchyard, one smaller than the other. Carried off by a fever, he had been told, made worse by near-starvation. He had raved and cursed and drunk himself insensible, but even that had come to an end and he was left bereft and lonely and without work. He had taken to the road to become a travelling man, a tinker, a loner.

By evening the wagon had reached the open moors and he was thinking of stopping for the night. Looking around for a suitable place, he spotted something on the side of the road which made him jerk on the reins and call, 'Whoa! Whoa there!' It looked like a bundle of rags and rags could be useful; there might even be something wearable among them.

He jumped down and bent to stretch out one gnarled brown hand towards the bundle. 'Why, bless my soul!' he said, pulling aside the hood of a blue woollen cloak to reveal pale cherubic features and blonde curls. 'Bless my soul, it's a babe.'

She must have been asleep because she knuckled a dimpled fist into her eyes and regarded him with a mixture of surprise and curiosity, as if she could not understand how her nurse had transformed herself into this funny man, with his dark curly hair and matted beard.

'What are you doing out here, alone in the wilderness?' he asked. He scanned the narrow potholed lane along which he had just come. It wound back over the heath until it disappeared over the hills towards Caspertown, where a plume of black smoke rose on the windless air; there was not a cottage or dwelling of any sort in sight. He looked forward; the view was the same, except there was no smoke. To either side the moors were bleak and unfriendly. There were a few sparse bushes, a tumble of rough boulders, a single leafless tree on the horizon and heather and bracken everywhere. There was no sign of anyone out searching for her. And yet she was warmly clad in petticoats and woollen dress and her feet were in tiny soft leather shoes. 'Where's your folks?'

She was no more than two or three years old, he judged, too young to answer him. Gently he lifted her; she was as light as thistledown. 'What's your name?'

She smiled up at him with wide blue eyes which held no sign of fear and put up a plump hand to touch his tangled beard. 'Kate.'

'Kate,' he repeated, captivated. 'Kate and what else?'

Her answer was to give his beard a tug, making him laugh aloud. 'Kate,' he said, holding her close against his chest. 'What'll we do with you?'

He took her to the caravan and climbed back onto the seat, then, supporting her in the crook of his left arm, picked up the reins with his right hand and guided the horse off the road. 'It's late,' he said. 'We'd best stop here tonight and see what's to be done in the morning.'

He put her down on a soft patch of grass. 'Sit still, my lovely, don't run away now.'

She stayed contentedly where he put her and watched him unharness and tether the horse, then light a fire and cook a meal. He had little idea what babies ate but she took a little of the gravy from the stew he offered her and drank some milk, chattering in a baby language he did not understand. The only coherent word she said in answer to his questions, was 'Kate'. He made a hammock cot with a bit of canvas he had tucked away and put her to bed. Not once did she cry. He took it as a sign, a sign he was meant to have her. Why else had she been on the roadside just as he came along?

By morning he was convinced of it; he would not turn back to Caspertown, that was asking for trouble, and although he made enquiries at the next village he passed through, no one had heard of a lost little girl and he knew she was his.

'My little Kate,' he said, as they left the village behind. 'My little gift from heaven.' She had been sent as a recompense for the injustices he had suffered; she was God's gift to him.

She nestled at his side, her head against the roughness of his coat, pointing podgy fingers at things as they passed, while he talked. He talked of the countryside, of the stars, of his life before she had come into it, of the wars with the French and Napoleon's defeat at Waterloo the year before, of the revolution in France and his fears for the peasantry of England, who might even now rise up and take the law into their own hands; the mob in Caspertown were not the only ones driven to violence and repressed by armed force.

To feed and clothe them both he took whatever work was available – mending pots and pans, minding sheep, hoeing, harvesting, fruit-picking, moving on when the work ran out and the parish overseer began to look at them with a suspicious glint in his eye and hint that paupers without settlements were not welcome in his parish. When that happened, they simply took to the road again.

And though he intended a different life for her, as he told her often enough, he saw no harm in teaching her to be as independent and self-sufficient as he was. He taught her the ways of the traveller, to love the clean, fresh air of the countryside, the brightness of spring, the beautiful colours of autumn, the song of the birds and the smell of burning wood drifting up from their camp fire. He taught her to catch fish from the rivers by whose banks they stayed, to pluck and draw a pheasant, to skin and cook a rabbit, using wild herbs gathered from the hedgerows, how to keep a fire going in the rain and how to survive the winter out of doors. But for all the rough simplicity of their life, he made sure she spoke properly and instructed her in the rudiments of reading and writing, for he had been educated to a fair degree before he had fallen prey to the blandishments of the recruiting sergeant.

As they journeyed on, covering the length and breadth of England, the weaker became his resolve to turn back and try to find her family, and as year followed year, it faded completely.

Chapter One

*K*ate, swatting the corn midges which flew in a black cloud about her head, followed the wagon containing the last load of the harvest as it pulled off the field, crossed the wooden bridge which spanned the dyke and turned onto the road. Silas Gotobed, who had been appointed Lord of the Harvest, sat on the topmost sheaf with a gotch of ale into which he was already making inroads, singing lustily, 'We've toiled all day and itched all night, we've cut and tied with all our might, and now the last is gathered tight. Horkey! Horkey!' And the children, running alongside the decorated cart, echoed 'Horkey! Horkey!' Behind it the women in their floppy white bonnets walked more slowly, not because they stood on their dignity but because they were weary. There had been no rest for anyone during daylight hours for the last three weeks, but at last they had finished, later than some, for William's fields were on the east of the village and more exposed than most and his was the last harvest to be brought in. Today it was done and they would all go home early because tonight was Harvest Horkey.

The wagon turned into the lane which led to White Poppy Farm. It was bordered by hedges of buckthorn, alder and bramble, its verges scattered with the flowers which had given the farm its name, intermingled with yellow rape which had seeded itself there, teazles and white cow parsley. Two minutes later they pulled up before the barn, where some of the men had already begun on the threshing; you could hardly see across it for dust. Silas, carefully holding his ale jar aloft, slid down the sheaves and jumped to the ground just as William Chapman came out of the barn. 'Thass the larst, Master,' he said.

'Unload it and then come to the barn for your wages.'

With so many to lend a hand the task was soon done and all the workers, the men who had scythed down the growing wheat, the women who had tied and stooked the sheaves, the children who

5

had made the ties for the sheaves and frightened off the birds, lined up at the table in the doorway of the barn to receive their pay.

Kate, when it came to her turn, looked down at the four shillings and sixpence which lay in her palm and then up at the burly farmer who had put it there. A week's wages, he had said, half a man's; she was worth half a man to him. The injustice of it rankled. She had worked from dawn to dusk alongside the men, bent and straightened her aching back as often as they had. By her own reckoning, she ought to get three-quarters.

'What's up?' he demanded. 'Count it, if you like.'

'It doesn't need counting,' she said. 'I can see what I've got and it's little enough.'

'Make the most of it, for it's the last. I can't keep women working, the men are grumbling.'

She knew that. The men were often to be seen huddled in groups, muttering and gesticulating, but they always fell silent when she approached. 'Life's as hard for me as it is for them,' she said. 'I need to eat too.'

'They're breadwinners, they've got families.' He paused, softening his voice. 'Kate, you know how it is. We had hoped for a good harvest after last year's disaster, but it hasn't happened; this year is nearly as bad. The threshing will all be done by Christmas. Leave what work there is for the men.'

She knew he was right and he was a good man; he could have got rid of one of the men and kept her, it would have been cheaper for him. Unlike some of the wealthier farmers, the squire included, he had not yet invested in one of the new threshing machines which threatened to put more men out of work. She closed her fist over the coins and stood uncertainly. 'You're standing me off?'

'You've still got Josiah,' he went on. 'I'll not put him off 'til the barn is empty.'

She turned to look at the man in the line of workers behind her. Josiah, like the others who had been threshing, was covered in a white dust which clung to his beard, filled his eyes and nostrils and caked on his lips. Yes, she still had Pa. She could not contemplate a life without him. He loved her dearly and she returned his love with a single-minded adoration, trusting him implicitly to do what was best for them.

'Go on home, Kate,' he said. 'I'll follow bye and bye.'

'Where are you going?'

'I've a little business to attend to, nothing you need bother about.'

'Don't forget the horkey,' William Chapman said, as if they could forget the reason they were being paid early and there would be no work that afternoon. 'Four o'clock. You'll bring your fiddle, won't you, Josiah?'

'Aye,' he said.

The supper, provided by the farmer, meant a really good blow-out, food such as they never had on their plates at home. Kate smiled, not because food and drink bothered her, but because there would be gaiety and laughter and music and she loved that.

Pulling her shawl closer about her, she left the warmth of the barn and set off along the lane towards the common, musing as she went. As a child she had not understood her Pa's fears for the labourers, but she was beginning to now, when the farmers couldn't afford to pay them for their work and hunger nipped their bellies. Next week there would be a big hole in the housekeeping money and soon after that, a bigger one, because once the heap of corn in the barn had been bagged up and sent to the miller, Pa, too, would be without work. More and more of the men, who would once have been assured of round-the-year work, were being employed on a casual basis, by the day or by the week, or contracted for the task in hand. It was cheaper for the farmers, who could stand them off when the weather was bad or the work ran out. Then there was nothing left for them but parish relief. Parish relief was something that her proud, independent Pa would never contemplate.

To avoid it, he would resume his nightly forays into the woods. Josiah, whose creed of honesty was peculiar to him, was not above a bit of poaching; pheasants, rabbits, fish, they were all God's creatures, there for the taking by those in need. He would admit of no other owner in the shape of the squire, no law in the person of the bailiff or the parish constable. He maintained that poor people only took game because they were half-starved and it was the landowners who made them hungry in the first place; poaching, and getting away with it, was only justice after all. She guessed that the mysterious errand he had mentioned just now was something to do with that; he had a few rabbits to sell and he was not such a fool as to risk that in the immediate neighbourhood.

At the crossroads, where the lane joining Middleacre and Lowacre was dissected by the main highway from Peterborough to King's Lynn, Jack Watson, the Glebe Farm shepherd, was sitting idly on the milestone. She wondered if he, too, had been put off. She felt very sorry for him if he had, for he had a wife and several children and taking parish relief would come very hard; like all fenmen, he was proud and fiercely independent. It was the ever-present threat of being without work which made him such an ill-tempered man, she decided, bidding him a cheerful good-day.

He muttered a gruff response and then turned his attention towards the afternoon stage which was approaching from the direction of Peterborough. She could not safely cross the road and continue on her way until the coach had passed, so she stood and watched as it drew up and Jack Watson greeted the man who stepped from it.

Watson was a tall man, but the other was taller, and against Watson's sturdy bulk he seemed slim-hipped and self-contained. He had thick dark hair, she noticed, as he doffed his hat to someone sitting in the coach, and his complexion was bronzed, as if he led an outdoor life. He was in his early thirties, she guessed, and although he was dressed as a labourer in heavy fustian trousers and waistcoat and a collarless shirt beneath a rough tweed coat, she knew instinctively he was no ordinary labourer. He wore the clothes with an air of distinction and held himself with an upright bearing which made her think he was accustomed to giving orders. This was borne out by Watson's greeting.

'Cap'n Tolley?'

'The same,' he said cheerfully, extending his hand. 'But we'll forget the captain shall we? Call me Matthew.'

Jack wiped his hand nervously down his smock before taking the proffered hand. 'I'm Jack Watson, sent to meet you.' He took the Captain's bag from him and the two men began to walk towards Middleacre, with Kate just behind them. She was not deliberately following them or listening to their conversation because she was, after all, going in the same direction, but she had to admit the arrival of the stranger had aroused her curiosity.

'I've taken a room for you at The Ferryman,' Watson went on. 'I'm sorry there's nothing better in the village, but it's clean and comfortable.'

'I'm sure it will do admirably.'

'Farmer Chapman do say he will give you a job if you need it, but he bade me tell you he don't want open involvement.'

Kate was astonished. William Chapman had put her off not fifteen minutes earlier on the grounds that he could not afford to pay her and yet he was going to employ this total stranger. It wasn't fair and it wasn't as if the man looked as though he needed the work. Without realising she was doing it, she crept closer behind them.

'I understand, but I don't plan to stay above a few days.'

'You'd best hev a job,' Watson said. 'It don't look good to have an idle furriner in the village.'

'What kind of job was he thinking of?'

'Cowman.' He paused and laughed. 'Hev you ever milked a cow, sir?'

The captain chuckled. 'No, but I'll learn if I have to.'

Kate stifled an angry gasp. If William Chapman needed an extra cowman, which she doubted because he had only a small herd, then why didn't he choose an experienced man, one of the many without work in the area?

'Word hev gone round about the meeting,' Watson went on. 'Howsummever they're a hully careful lot and I don't know how many will turn up.'

'If even a few attend it would be something. The news will spread.'

'It'll do that all right. It's a blessing the squire's away. Don' seem to spend much time at 'ome since his mother died, leaves it all to his bailiff.'

'Yes, I know,' the stranger said. 'I saw Sir John in London at the offices of the land commissioners. He is planning to return fairly soon, I think.'

Sir John Haddow had been away nearly a year, leaving Haddow Hall in the hands of a couple of servants and the estate in the care of his bailiff, an idle gamekeeper and an old gardener. The game-keeper, unsupervised, had neglected his duties; the poachers had been almost blatant in their activities, striding through Haddow wood, filling their sacks without hindrance. How many birds had been quietly pulled from their perches in the middle of the night and silently passed to waiting buyers, it was impossible to calculate, but if the squire were to come back and wanted some sport, there would undoubtedly be a shortage of game and the keeper would find himself without a job. But Kate wasn't troubled by the problems of Sir John Haddow and his inefficient servants; her only concern was for her Pa. If Sir John really was coming home, there would be a concerted effort to catch all poachers, Josiah included.

She was so immersed in their conversation she had unconsciously quickened her pace to close the gap between them and, when the captain suddenly stopped and turned, she walked straight into him. She found herself in his arms with her face against the roughness of his coat. She could hear the firm beating of his heart and felt the warmth of his breath on her forehead before he took her wrists in his hands and held her at arm's length away from him. He had a firm, clear-cut jaw and brown eyes which were looking down into hers with ill-concealed annoyance. 'Whom have we here?'

She faced him out, though inside she was shaking and that was something she did not understand; Josiah had taught her to fear no man. But it wasn't fear which made her tremble, it was something caused by the depth of those brown eyes, as if they could see right into her, could unravel her muddled thoughts and untangle her mixed emotions. It would be hard to have secrets from such a man. 'Let me go, you are hurting me.'

The timbre of her voice made him release her immediately; he had been expecting the broad vowels of a fen child and she had spoken with careful enunciation. Seeing her gently heaving breasts, he realised she was not the inquisitive youngster he had at first thought, but a woman, a petite, angry and disturbingly attractive woman. He shifted his gaze to her small feet, planted squarely in front of him, up over her dust-covered peasant skirt and blouse, topped by a knotted shawl, to an oval face, blonde curls and clear blue eyes. Her manner and her dress were definitely at odds and he was intrigued. 'Why are you dogging our heels?'

'I am not dogging your heels,' she retorted. 'I am on my way home. The road is free, is it not? Anyone can walk on it.'

'True,' he said. 'But do you usually walk so close behind people you fall over them if they stop?'

'You did it on purpose.'

He laughed. 'Perhaps it will teach you to keep your distance.'

'Oh, I shall keep my distance, never fear,' she said, tossing back her blonde curls, so unlike Josiah's thick grey locks. 'I have no wish to be close to you. And I'm surprised at you, Jack Watson, encouraging someone to come here and take a job one of our own men might have.'

'Hold you tongue!' Watson commanded. "Tin't none o' your business and you shouldn't ha' bin listenin'.'

'Is it my fault you talk so loudly?'

Matthew Tolley smiled and the smile, reaching his eyes, softened the hard look; she found her anger abating as quickly as it had risen. 'She's right, Jack,' he said, speaking to Watson, but keeping his eyes on the spitting kitten who faced him. 'Let that also be a lesson to us to be more careful in future.'

Watson was becoming impatient, shifting his weight from one foot to the other. "Tis of no consequence,' he said. 'She's only the poacher's daughter, ar'er all, she don't belong to the village.'

'Only the poacher's daughter,' Matthew Tolley repeated softly, still looking at Kate, as if committing her features to his memory. 'Is that all your father has to commend him? A dubious character and nothing more?'

'That's not true!' she flared at him. 'Pa is no more dubious than you are. Less so, for you are the one doing the scheming, not him.'

He threw back his head and laughed. 'Well said, poacher's daughter.'

For a moment she was non-plussed. What was so funny? Why was he angry one minute and laughing at her the next? She was not sure she liked being laughed at. How dare he liken whatever he was plotting to the innocent activities of her Pa and the poor people of the village who took game because they were hungry? She felt the heat flaring in her cheeks, unaware that her heightened colour added an allure to her already clear complexion which he found unaccountably disturbing. 'What you have heard, you keep to yourself,' he said.

'Why?' she demanded, unwilling to admit she had not understood what they were talking about. 'If you are plotting to break the law, you will find no friend in me or in Pa. He is a good man.'

'What makes you think I am plotting to break the law?' he asked.

'Aren't you?'

'I would rather alter it.'

'Then you are scheming against the villagers and I shall tell them so,' she said, not understanding his somewhat ambiguous reply. 'You're a stranger in this village and yet you would take the bread from the mouths of the little children.'

'Be silent, girl!' Jack Watson commanded. 'You hen't any notion what you're a-sayin'.'

'I know there's little enough work for the men who are here, without calling in outsiders ...'

'You be a bloody outsider y'self,' he said. 'So git you gone and keep yar mouth shut.'

'Why shouldn't I go straight to the constable and tell him what I heard?' she demanded.

'If you do ...' Watson's tone was menacing and he raised a clenched fist. 'It will fare ill with you and that precious pa o' yourn. He ha' more to hide than most ...'

'Leave it, Jack.' Matthew Tolley's voice was quietly authoritative. 'Enough said.' He turned to Kate. 'We don't wish you or your father any harm, but it would be better if you held your tongue and he stayed indoors tonight.'

'Why should he take any notice of what you say?'

He shrugged. 'It's up to him. Just take it as a friendly warning, that's all.'

'And who are you to be giving warnings?' she retorted.

'Who I am is of little importance,' he said, taking her arm again as she attempted to pass him and continue on her way. His grip was firm and she knew he would tighten it if she struggled, so she stood still, looking straight ahead, aware of his powerful physique, feeling his closeness, afraid and yet not afraid, wanting to be gone and yet wanting to stay. 'Just stifle your natural woman's curiosity and forget you have seen me.'

He released her and she pushed her stubborn little chin into the air and marched on past him and didn't look back, although she was eaten alive by curiosity. Who was he? Why had he come to Middleacre? And how did two people as far removed as Jack Watson and William Chapman come to be allies in whatever it was they were scheming? William Chapman was a tenant farmer, not wealthy by any means, but certainly not impoverished, and Jack Watson was a shepherd, living in a tied cottage, and not even one of his own employees. They had nothing in common that she knew of.

She walked on through the village. It was a long straggling hamlet, which had grown up on a roddon of high ground between two waterways, one the natural river, which wound alongside the road, and the other a man-made cut, meant to help drain the excess water which came down from the uplands every winter. Both were higher than the road, their waters kept at bay by high banks, but sometimes even these were not enough and outlying parts of the village were prone to flooding in severe weather, and because the top soil was so peaty and subject to shrinkage, many of the cottages were built on stilts driven into the clay subsoil.

In the centre of the village there was a patch of green with a tiny church on one side, a brick-built vicarage beside it and, a few yards further on, The Ferryman. The inn was a handy place of refreshment for travellers and villagers alike; it was bright and lively every evening, even in bad times – especially in bad times. It dispensed beer and forgetfulness if that was what the customer wanted, but it was also a meeting place for dissenters, everyone in the village knew that, a forum, under the guise of the Middleacre Friendly Society, for all who had something to say. Was there to be a meeting there that night? And if so, what about? And did it involve the stranger?

There were a few people congregating at the open door of the smithy; it was warm there and a good place for gossip. Children played on the green, women stood talking in groups, but Kate felt they were all watching covertly for the arrival of the newcomer. They took no notice of her as she went by, crossed the river bridge and turned onto the narrow lane which led to the common.

On the right it ran alongside the high flintstone wall of Haddow Hall. On the left, edged by buckthorn and brambles, was a stubble field belonging to Glebe Farm, part of the living of the Reverend Mr Cox. His land was sheltered by the wall and he had managed to harvest early; now the field contained a single stook of cut corn standing sentinel in its centre. Until that was removed, the gleaners knew they must not enter the field, but once it had gone, they were free to pick up what they could of the dropped ears. The early autumn had been so wet that already some of it was sprouting and would be useless. Daily, the village women watched for the ritual removal of the guardian, fuming with frustration that something so fundamental to their way of life was being denied them.

Kate stopped when she saw someone moving across the field and recognised Charlie Barber who, at seventeen, endeavoured to support his widowed mother and a host of brothers and sisters. He was a tall lad, but had not yet developed the breadth of shoulder and thickness of neck of the older labourers and was, therefore, considered three-quarters of a man when it came to paying wages, just as women and boys were deemed half. She watched as he picked up the sheaves, one by one, broke open the binding and scattered them about the field before running back to the gate where she stood.

'Kate Brough!' His surprise at seeing her was laden with guilt.

She smiled; he was one of the few villagers who treated her as if she were a human being. 'What are you doing?'

'What the parson should ha' done long ago.'

'You'll be in trouble if he finds out.'

'But he won't, will he?' He looked anxiously into her face. 'You'll keep squat, won't you?'

'Me? I'll not say anything.'

'Thank you. Tomorrow we glean.'

'Won't the reverend try to stop you?'

He laughed. 'He'll hatta be up betimes if he hev a mind to do that. We'll be in and out afore he's had his breakfast.'

'Why did he leave the guardian there so long?' she queried. 'That field has been cut for weeks.'

'It's jes' one more way of bringin' us to our knees,' he said and there was anger in his usually cheerful voice. 'But we won't hev it. We'll beat them yet.'

She knew he was referring to all the local employers including Sir John Haddow, as well as the cleric, whose living was in the squire's hands. 'Good luck to you,' she said, as she continued on her way.

The wall continued on her right, enclosing not only the Hall itself but a small wood, planted by Sir John's ancestors to shield the house from the bitter northeast wind. On her left were dark cultivated fields, separated by dykes. They were so contourless you could see for miles and the horizon was so low the great bowl of the sky filled the eye whichever way you looked. Sometimes it was a cloudless cobalt blue, but that had not been evident for weeks; sometimes clouds built up like mountain ranges, one above the other, from fleecy white to palest pink, from grey to deep mauve and black. And when the wind blew, as it often did, the clouds scudded along like breakers on an ocean. Beyond the fields was the fen itself, a large stretch of open water, teeming with fish and fowl, all of which were the property of the lord of the manor. How long that would survive she did not know; the draining of the fens, begun with the Romans, was still going on and digging channels to change the courses of rivers and canals, or scouring out old ones, left waterlogged land high and dry and dry land inundated. The country was both bleak and magnificient; it made you feel like a tiny ant battling for survival one moment and a giant the next, able to stride over the ground a furlong at a time. Distance meant nothing; that group of farm buildings she could see beyond the fen looked almost near enough to reach in half a dozen quick steps, but she knew they were all of five miles away. It was strange that of all the places she and Pa had visited in their fifteen years of wandering over the length and breadth of the country, they should end up here, in this spot.

The old caravan had been, and still was, a good home, but the time had come when all the nails and bits of wood in the world could not keep it rolling and one dusky evening three years before – 1827 it had been – when they were pulling off the road onto the common, it had fallen sideways into the ditch. Kate, about fifteen then and blossoming into womanhood, had only just managed to prevent herself being thrown violently from her seat as the horse stumbled and fell to its knees.

They had both jumped down, she to help the horse to its feet and Josiah to assess the damage. One wheel had been completely broken and the axle twisted; the back wheel on the same side had lost its iron rim and several spokes. They had levered and pushed and urged on the exhausted horse until, at last, the wagon was dragged up the bank and onto the common. But it stood so crookedly, with the furniture inside all tiptilted and the contents spilling onto the grass, it was useless as a home.

'There's nothing for it, but to take off all the wheels,' Josiah had said, stroking his beard. 'Let's be thankful it got us to this place, for here we are and here we stay, for it'll not move again.'

If she was surprised by his untypical acceptance of their immobility, especially in so bleak and inhospitable a spot, she had not questioned it as they propped the wheel-less wagon up on boulders and settled down to become part of the village, albeit living some distance from the main group of buildings, the church, Haddow Hall and the inn. But they had never really been accepted by the villagers, who looked down on their humble home with contempt and treated Kate warily, almost with suspicion. And they laughed at the way she spoke, for Josiah always insisted she express herself in a ladylike fashion. 'Hoity-toity,' the village children called her.

She left the lane, crossed the wooden bridge which spanned the dyke surrounding the common and almost fell over a post hammered into the ground in the middle of the well-worn path to her door. 'What madman put that there?' she asked aloud. 'I could have broken my leg.' She knocked it loose with a stone and flung it away, then went up the few steps into the wagon.

It was roomier than it looked from the outside. There was a table and a bench which served as Josiah's bed, a shelf full of books, a cupboard, an oak chest and a pot-bellied stove which they lit only in the winter; when the weather was fine, they cooked on a campfire out of doors. At the end of the wagon was a curtained-off section which was Kate's bedroom, containing a narrow bed and a chest of drawers. Josiah had rigged that up when she left her babyhood behind, so that she could have a little privacy.

She washed and changed out of her dusty skirt and set about lighting a fire in the lea of the wagon, using sticks gathered from Haddow wood and peat flags dug from the far side of the common. Once the fire was burning, she put a tripod over it, from which she suspended a cooking pot. By the time Josiah arrived, the meal was cooked and water she had fetched from the brook was heating in a kettle over the embers.

'Wash first,' she said, taking the kettle into the wagon and pouring the warm water into a bowl. 'Supper's near ready.'

They ate mutton broth and rabbit pie, after which he reached for his fiddle and began to play a quiet ballad and she sat beside him, mending one of his socks and singing softly. 'You've a splendid voice,' he said.

'I wonder who I get that from,' she mused. 'Do you think . . .'

'Now, how should I know that, my love?' His reply was swift, as if he did not like her probing the past. 'It is God given, just as you are.'

She smiled, not wanting to upset him; he had told her how he had found her, how much she meant to him, over and over, but any further questioning always seemed to irritate him and so she accepted what he said along with what he did not say. 'I heard the squire is coming home,' she said.

'Who told you that?' he asked sharply.

'No one. I overheard Jack Watson talking to a man who came

off the afternoon coach. The man said he'd met Sir John at the land commissioners and Sir John was coming back to Middleacre.'

'Land commissioners?' Josiah's dark brows came together in a frown. 'That means more enclosures. Do you know who the man was?'

'No, but I heard Jack Watson call him Captain Tolley and they said something about a meeting.'

'I guess he's one of the commissioner's men, come to spy out the land. The meeting will be to try and win over the men so they don't cause trouble.'

'Pa, who are the commissioners? Where do they come from?'

'London, usually. It's their job to sort out the holdings and allocate land to those who have been dispossessed by the enclosures.'

'But the villagers don't own any land.'

'No, but some have a little ground with their cottages and they use the common for grazing cattle and cutting peat, don't they?'

'But surely they won't agree to give that up without a fight? Is that what the meeting is about?'

He shrugged. 'Mayhap. Oh, they'll grumble and curse, but they won't do anything because they know they can't win. Besides, they need so much ale to work themselves up, they'll drink themselves insensible before they find the courage to act. Talk's cheap and hurts no one. By morning they'll have sore heads and red faces and nothing will be done. We need not concern ourselves with them.'

'But we are concerned. We live on the common and we are part of the village. Where will we go if we're turned off?'

'We'll cross that bridge when we come to it,' he said philosophically. 'It may never happen.'

'They warned me not to let you go out tonight.'

'Who did?'

'Jack Watson and the man who came off the coach.'

'What I do is none of their affair and they should never have spoken to you of it.' Normally very placid, he sounded unusually snappish. 'I'll do as I think fit.'

'What will I do if the squire's men catch you?' she asked, voicing her ever-present fear. 'I couldn't bear it if you were taken from me.'

He leaned over and pinched her cheek affectionately. 'They won't, they're too fond of their beds.' Then, as if to change the subject, he began to play a lively dance tune. 'Do you think they'll like this one at the horkey?'

'Oh, yes, they are sure to.' He was a fine musician, better than anyone she knew.

A little after three, she tidied away her mending and went to change into her best Sunday-go-to-church dress. It was made of very light wool in a clear blue, patterned with tiny flowers. It had a pointed bodice and tiny pearl buttons. Over it she wore a precious silk shawl with a fringe all round it, which Pa had bought her one day when he had been affluent over some deal he had done. It was always the way; if he had money to spare it was always spent on her. He put on his best shirt and a cravat and brushed his unruly locks and combed his beard, so that she was as proud of him as any daughter could be, as they set off down the lane to William Chapman's farm.

They could hear the sound of revelry coming from the open door of the small barn almost as soon as they turned in at the gate. All the farmworkers, men and women, regulars and casuals, were crowding round the long table which was laden with food – roast pork, chicken, ham, potatoes, puddings and fruit pies. The farmer's wife and Betty Watson, Jack's daughter and their maid-of-all-work, had been busy for days cooking it all. Everyone had a glass of ale in their hands and were toasting each other, determined to forget their troubles for a couple of hours and make the most of the feast. William Chapman presided at a side table on which stood a barrel from which he refilled their glasses. Seeing Josiah and Kate arriving, he crossed the floor to draw them into the circle. 'Come and sit down. Eat your fill.'

He drew a chair out for Kate beside Charlie Barber, who smiled shyly at her. 'I'm glad your Pa ha' brung his fiddle,' he whispered. 'If there's to be dancing, will you dance with me?'

'Gladly,' she said, tucking into a plateful of food.

'Blind Cally ha' said he'll gie us a toon on 'is penny whistle an' all. Will you sing?'

'Oh, no, I couldn't ...'

'Why not? It's a lovely voice you have ...'

'When have you heard me sing?' she demanded. She only sang when she was doing her chores at home.

'In church. And when you milk your old cow.'

The cow was kept on the common along with several others

belonging to the villagers, but she had not been aware of anyone listening to her. She laughed. 'She isn't so critical as humans.'

'I shall tell Farmer Chapman you've said you will. 'Tis no good bein' shy, for everyone must do somethin'.'

'What are you going to do then?' She became aware that Josiah was watching her from the other end of the table and there was a frown on his brow. She smiled at him and the lines disappeared as if by magic.

'I'll give 'em a ditty, if you will.'

When the meal was finished, the farmer stood up and thanked everyone for their hard work, then Silas Gotobed replied as Lord of the Harvest, but he was already very tipsy and slurring his words; Nathaniel Green tugged at the hem of his smock and forced him to sit down again. 'Yew is too long in t'wind, Silas. Dew yew save yar breath for suppin'.'

When the laughter had died down, the tables were cleared and Josiah's chair set up on a table so that he could play for the dancing. Kate, whirling round with Charlie, forgot everything in the pleasure of the moment; she laughed and teased, her eyes alight and her slim hips swaying. Josiah, loving her as he did, could not begrudge her whatever happiness came her way, but he was suddenly afraid. She was growing into a very desirable woman and that Charlie Barber was looking at her like an adoring puppy. It would not do.

He told her so, as they walked home. The wind was whipping the clouds across the sky, like charging horses, and fitfully obscuring the moon, but it also held the rain at bay. 'You know, Kate,' he said, when they had been walking for a few minutes in companionable silence. 'You are growing so fast, you're a woman now, and I hardly noticed it until tonight.'

'Why tonight?' She was not exactly sure how old she was; she and Pa had always celebrated her birthday on the anniversary of the day he had found her and he had said he thought she was three at the time. If he were right, she was eighteen now.

'You looked beautiful in that dress, so much the lady, but you know, you must begin to behave like one. It does not do to pay too much attention to one young man. People might think you were leading him on ...'

'Pa! What do you mean?' Her singing had been well received and the applause, led by Charlie, was most gratifying. She was glowing with happiness to think that, at long last, the villagers might be coming to accept her; it was all down to Charlie and she was unprepared for her father's criticism.

'You were a might too friendly towards that Barber boy,' he said. 'He might think ... He might start thinking of you as ...' He paused. It was difficult to put into words the unease in his mind. 'He is not for you, my child.'

'But Pa, he was only being friendly. In fact, he is the only one who is well disposed towards me, the others only tolerate me because they can find nothing to say against me. It is the same for you, you know it is.'

'Yes, but you were born for better things. One day, you'll have a proper home and fine clothes and servants and you'll ride in a carriage. And when it comes to finding a husband, you'll have the pick of all the gentry for miles around, you wait and see. Until that time comes, we are all right on our own, company for each other. Be patient ...'

His attitude was difficult to understand. How did he know she was born for anything better? He knew no more about her birth than she did; she was a foundling, abandoned by her parents to be picked up by whoever came along. It had been her good fortune that it had been Josiah and she would be forever grateful to him. She didn't wish for the moon, even if Josiah wished it for her. But she sometimes found herself wondering what it would be like to live in a proper house made of brick, with windows and chimneys and good solid furniture, and occasionally she would wish a little wistfully for the company of other young people. She had seen them in the village, laughing and joking together, even when times were hard as they were now. And sometimes there was a wedding and she could not prevent herself envying the delight of the young couple in each other as they stood at the lychgate after the ceremony, receiving the congratulations of their families and friends and being showered with rice and rose petals.

She knew what was expected of every woman when she became a wife, Josiah had told her that in his blunt, down-to-earth way and she, being a country girl and used to the ways of animals, thought she understood. 'Mind you, humans are different,' he had said. 'They fall in love with each other and when love comes in the door, reason flies out of the window. There's no accounting for that.' He had laughed in an embarrassed way and added, 'You will come to understand in the fullness of time, when you're a woman grown.'

She had listened to what he said, as she always did, but now she was a woman, she still did not understand. All she knew was that the man she chose would be handsome and strong and dependable, someone like Pa himself, for Pa was the yardstick by which she measured all men.

She took his arm and smiled up at him to reassure him. 'Of, course, Pa,' she said. 'But if he speaks to me, I think I should answer, don't you? It would be very rude to ignore him.'

'Of course, child, I did not mean ... Oh, I am such a bad hand at explaining myself ...'

'No, you are not. You have always explained things very well.'

'Then you do understand?'

'Yes, I think so.' She didn't though, and she ought to tell him that Charlie had asked her to take a walk with him one day, but something held her back. It was the first time she had not been entirely open with him and it worried her a little.

'I have been remiss,' he said, after a long pause. 'I should send you away to a seminary for young ladies ...'

'Send me away! But why, Pa? What have I done wrong?' There was anguish in her voice. 'If I have displeased you, I am truly, truly sorry. Please don't send me away. I couldn't bear it.'

'Bless you, child ...' There was a huge lump in his throat which prevented him from going on. He swallowed hard. 'You have done nothing wrong, Kate. You are my joy, my life, but I have been selfish, keeping you so close. Here I have been saying you shall have the best of everything and the pick of the young gentlemen and I've done nothing to teach you how to conduct yourself in that kind of company.'

'But Pa, do I not conduct myself well?'

'Of course you do, but there are things you should know ...'

'About myself? About when ... when you found me?'

He did not answer for a full minute, covering the silence with a search in his pocket for the key to the caravan. 'No,' he said gruffly. 'I meant about young men.'

'I do not need to go away to learn that, you can teach me, can't you? And if any gentleman does not like the way I have been brought up and educated, then he is not worthy of the name and I shall scorn him.'

He laughed suddenly and, unlocking the door, ushered her inside. 'You'll do, my love, you'll do. And just you remember, your Pa loves you no matter what.'

'And I love him.'

He became just as quickly serious. 'I pray you will never have cause to change your mind.'

'Oh, Pa, you are becoming sentimental, it must be all that drink Mr Chapman gave you. Ale always seems to have that effect on you. Now let's go to bed, it's getting late.'

He smiled and dropped a kiss on her forehead and watched her as she went through to her own bed, dropping the curtain behind her. 'Goodnight, my dearest daughter,' he said softly.

He ought to have taken Kate's advice and gone to bed, but he knew he would not sleep. He laid his violin up on the shelf above his bunk, took off his best jacket and his cravat and carefully put them in the bottom drawer of the chest, then he wound a dark scarf round his neck and reached for his old coat from the peg behind the door.

With a last glance towards the curtain to satisfy himself that Kate was asleep, he picked up an empty sack and let himself out of the van, closing the door softly behind him.

Chapter Two

Sir John Haddow had returned home in a great flurry of cantering horses, his carriage so heavily loaded with trunks and boxes there had been no room for his manservant, who had been left behind in London to follow by stage. Indeed, the squire had been so uncomfortably squeezed into a corner of the usually roomy coach, he had arrived in a very grumpy frame of mind. His mood had not improved when he discovered the letter he had sent announcing his return had gone astray and the few servants he had left to take care of the house were loafing in the kitchens. His bed was not made, the fire hadn't been lit in his room and dust covers hung over half the furniture. What was worse, the extra staff he had ordered the housekeeper-cum-cook to hire had not been taken on and he was left to manage as best he could without valet, butler or footman. He lost no time in summoning Mrs Bunny to the dusty withdrawing room.

Grace Bunny was in her fifties, as round as she was tall, with bright cheeks and pale eyes. Her hair was grey and arranged in corkscrew curls, which became even more curly in the damp heat of the kitchen. The only way she could control them was to stuff them unceremoniously under a white cap, so that hardly any showed. She had been in service at the Hall since she had been a gawky girl of twelve and had made her way up to housekeeper, simply because she was prepared to stay when others would not. She had known Sir John throughout his growing up and always maintained she knew him through and through, and in her opinion he did not get any better with age. 'He was always spoiled by his mama,' she often said. 'If he couldn't have his way he threw a tantrum. He's no different now.'

'Mrs Bunny,' he said, running his finger over the polished table, leaving a trail in the dust. 'You have been negligent in my absence. I want this house cleaned from top to bottom.'

'Yes, Sir John, but how am I to do it? You dismissed all the staff before you went away.'

'Round them all up and engage them again.'

'But Sir John,' she ventured. 'Most of them have found other situations. They might not want to come back.'

'Nonsense, woman. Offer them another pound a year, extra tea or small beer, think of something yourself. That's what I pay you for, isn't it?'

She wished she dare argue the point. Instead she said, 'Yes, Sir John.'

'And I want you to turn out my mother's room, get rid of all the knick-knacks and have it cleaned and redecorated. Blue, I think ...'

Mrs Bunny's mouth had dropped open when he first mentioned his mother and it stayed open until he became aware of it and stopped to say, 'What's the matter, woman? Do I not make myself clear?'

She gulped. 'Your mother's room, Sir John?'

'Yes, that's what I said. I want it made ready for a lady.'

'A lady, Sir John?' The housekeeper could hardly believe her ears. The dowager's room had been sacrosanct ever since she had died two years before; it had been locked on the day she had left it for the last time and Sir John kept the key on the chain that held his gold hunter. The servants had speculated about it, commenting aloud how strange it was that anyone could come and go into his dead wife's rooms with impunity, but no one dare put a hand on the knob of the dowager's chamber door. Not that the old lady wasn't the most beautiful, the most loving and indulgent of mamas, for she was, and her son had been cast into melancholy for months, before taking himself off to the continent. Something must have happened in the last year to bring on this change of heart.

'Yes, Mrs Bunny, a lady,' he said, unfastening the key and handing it to her. 'She will arrive in a few weeks' time. In the meantime, the boxes I brought with me are to be taken to Lady Haddow's sitting room and unpacked. Carefully, of course. If anything is broken you'll pay for it out of your wages.'

'Yes, Sir John.'

'Mrs Wisdom will naturally be bringing her maid with her, so prepare a room for her too.'

He was intensely put out by the absence of his personal servant who had always attended to his clothes; he felt ill-dressed, his cravat was creased and his boots lacked their usual shine. He wished he had left some of the baggage behind in order to accommodate Johnson in the coach but Laura would have none of it. 'Take my valuables with you,' she had said. 'I'll follow when I have settled my affairs in London.'

'What valuables?'

'My collection of porcelain and the gilded dinner service my dear husband bought for me when we were married. I can't trust them with a carrier.'

'Why not bring them yourself when you come?'

'How can I do that, when I have to come by the mail? Is it so much to ask?'

'No, of course not, my love,' he had said. 'But what about my manservant?'

'He can follow by the morning coach.'

He was beginning to wonder what he had let himself in for, marrying again after being so long a widower, but it was the only way out of his fix. He had been procrastinating ever since his dying mother had urged him to find another wife. 'Someone strong and young enough to bear children,' she had said. 'An heir will nullify that impossible agreement you made with that upstart millowner who married your sister. He's not even gentry, let alone family.' She had died before he could follow her counsel, but he knew it for good advice and sooner or later, he would have to find another wife. He had put off the search while he travelled the world, spending his inheritance like sand running through an hourglass until there was little left except the house and land, and his creditors were becoming more and more vociferous. He had been obliged to return to England to do something about it. Friends had introduced him to Laura Wisdom in London. She had been widowed for a couple of years and had been left wealthy enough to be choosy about a second husband, her main requirement being a title and the freedom to please herself in what she did. He had used all his considerable charm to woo and win her, but it had left him and his coffers exhausted. Now, all he wanted was to get the wedding over with and settle down to getting himself a son, which was something his first wife had never given him, though she had died trying. A son would oust Andrew as his heir, an arrangement that he had been forced into a few years before when he had been threatened with bankruptcy, but which would end when he paid his debt to his brother-in-law and produced a son of his own. Sending Andrew off with his tail between his legs would give him no end of satisfaction.

Mrs Bunny, who had not been dismissed, interrupted his thoughts by asking, 'What about dinner, Sir John?'

'What about it?' he said irritably. 'I'll take it at six in my room, you will hardly have prepared the dining room by then.'

'Oh, but the dining room is usable, Sir John,' she said. 'Mr Carrington-Haddow arrived yesterday. We opened it up for him and he asked for dinner at three.'

'The devil he did! And what's he doing here, throwing his orders about?'

She did not answer, knowing he did not expect her to. Instead she repeated, 'What about dinner, Sir John?'

'I said at six in my room. Do I have to give all my orders twice?'

'No, Sir John.' She bobbed and hurried off to begin her mammoth task, leaving him pacing the room.

'Poachers,' he said, suddenly remembering why he wanted to see Fiddy. Game seemed to be on every menu in every inn he had visited on his way home and he wanted to be sure none had come from his woods, nor would in the future. He wanted to be able to offer his wedding guests a little sport. He strode out of the house and across the park towards the clearing where the gamekeeper nurtured his pheasants and where he confidently expected to find his bailiff.

Mrs Bunny returned to the kitchen and called the scullery maid, who was the only other member of staff in residence. 'Bertha! Move yourself, girl. Sir John wants the house springcleaned, so you make a start on the drawing room while I go and make up his bed ...'

Bertha, fat and lazy, went reluctantly, grumbling about having only one pair of hands, but it made no difference; they spent the rest of the day rushing from one once-elegant room to another, sweeping, dusting, polishing, and were glad that Sir John had taken himself off and left them to it, though they didn't envy the bailiff.

'He'll not be hully pleased to see the squire,' Bertha said in her broad fenland accent. 'Not arter last night. I could hear them there pesky poachers from my room ...'

'Don't talk through your bonnet, girl. Poachers don't make a noise or they'd never take the birds.'

'I towd you I heard 'em.'

''Twas more likely the combination men.'

'An' what would they be a-doin' in Haddow woods?'

'Plotting some mischief, what else?' Mrs Bunny paused to flick a feather duster under Bertha's nose and added, ''Tisn't for the likes of us to ask. If Sir John knew we'd even been talking about it, we'd be out afore we could draw breath.'

'Why d'you reckon Mr Carrington-Haddow be here?' Bertha asked, taking her advice and changing the subject. 'There's no love lost 'tween him and t'squire, I'll lay.'

'I've no doubt he's looking after his own interests like everybody else.'

'What d'you mean by that?'

'He's Sir John's heir, seeings Sir John don't have a son of his own, that's why he added Haddow to his name. That rankles with the squire.' She paused to run a finger over the edge of a bookcase, grimacing when she found her finger black with dirt. 'You'd better make a better job of it than this, my girl, or you'll find yourself out on your ear.'

Indifferent to the reprimand, Bertha gave a half-hearted flick with her duster. 'Did Mr Carrington-Haddow know Sir John wor comin' home, d'you think?'

'How should I know?' Mrs Bunny snapped. 'But he is back, more's the pity, and just as contrary as ever. Now I've got two separate dinners to get, so I'd best get on with them.'

She left Bertha to finish the cleaning and returned to the kitchen. How Sir John thought she could manage to cook and clean with no one but that idle Bertha to help her, was a mystery. And as for re-employing the old servants, that was a laugh. Sir John had summarily dismissed them when he went away. Did he imagine that they had hung around waiting for him to come back and take them on again? If he wanted good servants he needed to treat them better than that. And why he could not have his dinner with his nephew at a civilised hour, she did not know.

She had just served Mr Carrington-Haddow with his meal and was leaving the dining room with an empty tray, when she met Sir John in the doorway. He ignored her as he brushed past her and advanced on the young man.

Andrew was in his late twenties, a fair-haired, handsome young man, dressed impeccably in country breeches and frockcoat. He looked up and smiled agreeably. 'Hello Uncle John, I heard you were back. Did you have a good journey?'

Sir John didn't bother with the preamble of a greeting. 'No, I did not,' he said.

'I'm sorry to hear that, Uncle.'

'Indeed!' He stood looking down at the young man, who continued to eat his meal with every appearance of enjoyment. 'I notice you have made yourself at home, though I must say I consider it a little premature. In spite of the journey, I am in the best of health.'

'Why, you asked me to come, Uncle, don't you remember?' The young man refused to be rattled, knowing it would only make Sir John lose his temper. 'Keep an eye on things, you said . . .'

'And have you?'

'I only arrived yesterday, but I came three months ago for a se'nnight and all was well then.'

'It isn't now. It is very far from well.' He paced the floor impatiently. 'But since you are here, you might as well make yourself useful.'

'Of course, Uncle, anything.' Andrew helped himself to more food from the tureens. 'Why don't you sit down and join me? There's far too much for one.'

'Then Mrs Bunny is becoming wasteful and I shall have to speak to her about it. She knows when I want my dinner.'

Andrew shrugged; the man was becoming meaner by the day. 'Is it money you need? I could write to Father . . .'

'No, it is not,' Sir John snapped, turning to face him. 'Your father's money is neither needed nor wanted. This estate will be made to pay its own way and my debt to him will be cleared. Until it is you will have no hand in the running of it except under my direction. Is that clear?'

'As a bell,' Andrew said cheerfully.

'I mean to improve the farming with more advanced methods,' Sir John went on. 'The first thing to do is to put more land under the plough. The only large area still uncultivated is Middleacre Common and while I was in London I spent some time talking to the land commissioners with a view to enclosing it. I mean to grow rapeseed; I can sell us much as I produce to the Wisbech mills.'

'How can you think of enclosing the common? The villagers have been using it for generations for their livestock and fuel. And isn't there someone living on it?'

'They are obstacles easily overcome. The villagers can take their cattle to Lowacre Common and as for that gypsy, cluttering up the countryside and paying no rent, I shall be only too pleased to see the back of the fellow.'

With Sir John in his present mood, Andrew thought it unwise to argue. 'What is it you want me to do then?'

'Fiddy tells me he's got wind of a meeting tonight . . .'

'What sort of meeting?'

'Labourers. Friendly Society, they call it. It's not the name I'd give it. They're talking about combining and other such treasonable nonsense. I want them caught redhanded and punished.'

'Combining is hardly treasonable, Sir John, considering it's been legal since 'twenty-four. And they can't do much harm talking.'

'It's what happens when the talking stops, that I'm concerned about. I want it nipped in the bud. Fiddy's not sure who's involved, but some of the estate workers can be trusted to go with him and round them up. I want you to go too, it needs someone with authority to take command.' He noticed Andrew's amusement and added, 'I only need you because I have other things to do. Go and see Fiddy as soon as you've finished, you'll find him staking the new boundary.'

'Isn't that a little premature? Surely the commissioners haven't finished the survey yet?'

'They'll do as they're told and I haven't got time to waste while they dither. I want to marl the common before I plough.'

He turned to leave the room and Mrs Bunny, who had been listening outside the door, just managed to disappear in the direction of the kitchens, before he came through it.

'What d'you know?' she said breathlessly to Bertha who was making up the fire in the cooking range. 'The squire's got wind of a meeting tonight . . .'

'What's 'e a-goon' t'do?'

'Catch 'em redhanded, that's what he told Mr Carrington-Haddow.' She took down her shawl from the peg behind the door. 'I'm going out. You get on with those vegetables and if anybody asks, you don't know where I am.'

*

Head down against the strengthening wind, Josiah cut across the common, skirted a meadow and made his way down the deserted drove road which, a week before, had been black with highland cattle, shuffling along like a mighty river, then crossed a shallow brook on stepping stones and plunged into the wood. It was mainly planted beech and oak interspersed with the native alder, buckthorn and sallow, which gave it a particularly dense undergrowth. Kate hurried after him, every muscle taut, her nervousness heightened by the wind howling in the tops of the trees. Quiet as he had been, she had heard the click of the latch as he left the wagon, and fearing for him as she did every time he went out late at night, she had left her bed, put on her old wool skirt and blouse, taken her shawl and followed him. He was no longer young and no match for the youthful stalwarts employed by Sir John to patrol his woods and riverbanks at night, but he would never admit it. Tonight, because of Captain Tolley's warning, she was more than usually anxious.

Oblivious of her presence not far behind him, he scrambled into the undergrowth and a few moments later emerged with a rabbit in a trap. He released it, put it in his sack and reset the trap. A scattering of dry beech husks tumbled on her head and she nearly cried out, but Josiah was moving on again and she hurried after him. It was difficult to see him, but beneath the sound of the wind, she could hear his feet scuffling the dead leaves and his heavy breathing. Suddenly she heard a crack like a branch breaking and then his muffled oath. She began to run towards the sound, unheedful of the noise she was making as she pushed her way through the undergrowth. She almost fell over over him as he lay on the ground with a great iron mantrap biting into the flesh of his calf. 'Pa!'

He looked up, surprised at her sudden appearance, but said nothing; he could hardly speak for the pain which clearly told him his leg was broken. He bent again to tearing at the jaws of the trap with his hands, while she searched about, found a stick and pushed it down beside his leg in an effort to prise it open. Blood was oozing through his breeches where the heavy jaws were clamped to his leg and though she could not see it, she felt its warm stickiness. Realising she was adding to the pain, she stopped.

'Go on, girl, push it down. I can bear it if only you'll be quick ...'

She tried again and the stick broke, making a noise like a pistol shot. He swore. 'Come on, Katie, fetch something to use as a lever. We've made enough noise to wake the dead and the varmints who set this can't be far away.'

She fumbled among the fallen leaves for another stick. 'I'll have to go for help.'

'There isn't time and, besides, who'd come? Here, take my knife and cut something green, and make haste, the pain is killing me.'

She hacked at the branch of an alder. 'Couldn't we get you home and take it off there?'

He had lost his senses and did not answer, but she knew that was impossible. He was a heavy man and she could not support him and the trap, even if he managed to get to his feet.

A sound along the nearby path startled her but there was no time to retreat and, in any case, she would not have left Josiah helpless. She heard shouting and footsteps, noisy on the undergrowth, cracking twigs, rustling leaves, dogs barking; whoever it was they were making no attempt to keep quiet. She tried to heave the injured man further out of sight, but he was no light weight and groaned with pain. Half a dozen men passed uncomfortably close but they were obviously intent on other quarry, a gang of poachers perhaps. She breathed a sigh of relief as the woods became quiet again. The only sounds were the soughing of the wind, Josiah's heavy breathing and her own half-controlled sobs as she bent again to help him. But it was no good; the spring on the trap was just too strong for her and Josiah, weakened, could not help himself.

A rustling close at hand startled her and she whipped round to see the shape of a man pushing aside the branches of a low buckthorn and stooping towards them. Her heart missed a beat as he straightened up and looked down at them. She thought at first it was Captain Tolley simply because, like it or not, his warning had been in her thoughts ever since Josiah had left the wagon. It was not the captain, but a stranger, though he was about the same build and he must have been every bit as strong, because he wrenched open the trap in one quick movement, released the battered leg and hauled Josiah over his shoulder. He bade Kate support the injured limb and strode off through the woods with his burden, while she stumbled beside him, too thankful to have help to wonder if he were friend or foe.

'You are from the wagon on the common, aren't you?' he asked, and his voice, though breathless, was cultured.

'Yes.'

He said no more as he hurried under Josiah's weight, back along the drove, across the windswept common and up the steps of the caravan. She lit a candle while he put the unconscious man on his bunk and called for something to bandage the wounded leg. She fetched some scraps of cotton material and a bowl of water and stood uncertainly as he began to dress her Pa's wounds.

'I'll do that,' she said, because somehow it didn't seem fitting that gentry should kneel at the bedside of a poacher. She was glad Josiah was unconscious; he would have been mortified if he had been aware of it.

'It's done now.' He didn't appear to notice the incongruity of the situation and carefully covered Josiah with a blanket before standing up to face Kate.

She found herself looking into a pair of startlingly blue eyes. He was about ten or eleven years older than she was, slightly younger than Matthew Tolley, and fair where Matthew was dark, although they were of the same height and build. But his clothes were very different; he wore country buckskins and a frockcoat, both of very fine quality and well cut, though by no means dandified, and they must have cost the equivalent of a whole year's wage for a labourer.

'Why did you help us?' she asked bluntly because he was clearly gentry and, because of that, was unlikely to condone trespassing or poaching or, indeed, law-breaking of any sort.

'The old man is hurt and mantraps are illegal.'

'That doesn't stop the squire's gamekeeper setting them.'

'No, I know.'

'Were you with Sir John's men tonight?'

'And if I were?' he countered with a hint of amusement.

She shrugged. 'I was just thinking that if it hadn't been for the trap, Pa would never have been caught, you were making enough noise to wake the dead. Gamekeepers don't usually crash about like that, soft-footed they are, like cats . . .'

He laughed. 'As it happens, we weren't looking for poachers.'

'What then?'

'Rebels, upstarts, combination men.'

She wasn't entirely sure she knew what a combination man was, though she had heard the word frequently of late. Josiah had been vague when she asked, but she guessed it had something to do with the labourers combining in unions to improve their working conditions. Pa would never have anything to do with them; he maintained they were all troublemakers, out to foster discontent for their own selfish ends. 'In Haddow woods?' she queried.

'Why not? It's as good a place as any.'

A picture of Captain Tolley, standing in the lane with his feet apart and head thrown back in laughter, flashed into her mind. If the quarry had not been poachers, did it mean his meeting at the inn had been a failure? Were the men less easily persuaded than he had hoped? If so, Pa had been wrong; they had turned from drink to action, though what they were trying to do, she had no idea. 'If Pa being in the wood turned you aside, then I'm glad,' she said. 'I hope the rebels get away, that I do.'

He smiled, impressed by her spirit. She was nothing like his notion of a gypsy girl. She was fair, for a start, and well spoken and though her clothes were plain, they were clean and neat and her hair was brushed into shining strands which gleamed golden in the candlelight. 'I advise you to be more circumspect in what you say. You never know who's friend and who's foe.'

That was true. She put a hand on his arm. 'I'm sorry, I should not have said that. I am grateful for your help.'

'It's little enough. The old man ought to be seen by a doctor.'

'He doesn't hold with doctors. I'll look after him and he'll do.'

He turned to leave. 'Fiddy will be mad as a March hare if chasing after combination men loses him his poacher. He'll go back to the mantrap and when he sees it's been sprung, he'll be looking for someone who's injured, so take care.'

'We can't hide, we've nowhere to go,' she said flatly. 'We'll just have to take our chances.'

'Then good luck to you.' He paused. 'If you really want to thank me, then I would appreciate it if Sir John did not learn I was here tonight.'

She smiled. The squire would certainly not approve of anyone helping a poacher, but the chances of him hearing about it through her were remote. 'I'm hardly likely to tell him,' she said.

'No, of course not. Look after your father and make sure that wound stays clean.'

He went down the steps, looked quickly about him and strode

off in the direction of the village. She shut the door and went back to Josiah, her head full of questions she had been too shy to ask. Who was he? Why had he helped them when he could so easily have left them to fall into the hands of the gamekeeper?

Two mysterious men had come to the village on a single day, two men with something to hide, both handsome, strong, self-possessed men, but so very different in every other way. Something was happening in the village, something important, something that would affect all their lives. She felt a quiver of excitement run through her. Or was it fear?

She shut the door and returned to Josiah, who was conscious again and obviously in great pain. 'Who was that?' he asked.

'I don't know.' She sat down on a stool by his bed, prepared to stay there as long as he needed her. 'A stranger. He found us in the wood and carried you back.'

'Then I'm beholden to him.'

'Yes, for I could not have managed it.'

He stirred a little, trying to make himself comfortable. The pain caught at his breath and it was a minute or so before he could speak again. 'Why did you follow me? We could both have been caught.'

'I was afraid for you, especially after what Captain Tolley said, but we can talk about it in the morning. Go to sleep, I'll sit by you.'

'No, go back to bed, Kate, I'm as comfortable as I can be and it would be better if we were both in bed and asleep if anyone comes.'

'Do you think they will?'

'I don't know, but sitting up all night waiting for trouble will not help. Go to bed, there's a good girl.'

She kissed him and went to her own bed, but she hardly had time to scramble between the covers, before the sound of barking dogs and men's voices came to her as they moved across the common. She held her breath as they approached and began to bang on the caravan door, shaking the flimsy woodwork until she thought it would tumble about her ears.

'Open up, gypsy!' one of them shouted. 'Open up if you don't want the door stove in!'

Josiah stirred. 'Hold your hosses,' he muttered, trying unsuccessfully to obey, while Kate pulled a skirt and blouse over her head and went to open the door.

'What's all this hollering in the middle of the night?' she demanded, pretending to rub sleep from her eyes. 'What's so important it can't wait 'til morning?'

'We want the old gypsy.' The biggest of the three men pushed past her into the wagon and she recognised Fiddy, the squire's bailiff. He was carrying a shotgun, which he waved about in alarming fashion. Behind him hovered the village constable and the gamekeeper.

'We're not gypsies,' she said. 'And we object to being called it.'

'Not you,' Fiddy said, turning to look at her pale complexion and blonde hair. 'Him. We want him.' He prodded Josiah with the barrel of the gun. 'Up you get, old man.'

Before Josiah could answer, she said, 'He can't, he's not well ...'

'I'll wager he's not. I'll wager a week's pay against a hazel nut he's not able to stand. You can't, can you, old man? Come on, let's see you on your feet.'

'No,' she said quickly, patting the blanket which covered Josiah, warning him to lie still. 'I told you, he's not well. Come back tomorrow.'

'And give you time to slope off? The devil we will!' He reached for the blanket and Kate put herself between him and Josiah, but she was roughly pushed aside. 'Keep out o' this, m'lady, or you'll be took alonga him.'

'Took where?'

'To the beak, that'll do for a start. After that a few years in Bridewell, if he's lucky. If not, there's a fancy neckcloth, or maybe a nice long sea voyage.' He pulled away the blanket to reveal Josiah's bandaged leg, already stained dark red. 'Aha! Come in, mates, here's our poacher and no mistake. Let's have him out.'

'He can't walk,' she said, while Josiah glared at them from beneath thick dark brows. Not for him protestations of innocence. They would be useless, he knew, and neither cursing nor pleading would do any good. The game was up, he realised that, and he was stoically prepared to take whatever fate dealt out to him. His only concern was for Kate. He eased himself into a sitting position and nearly fainted with the agony it caused.

'Kate,' he began, grabbing her hand. 'Go to ... go to ... the Hall for help. Tell them ...'

''Tin't no good a-goon' there, now, is it?' Fiddy jeered, while Kate wondered why Pa should suggest such a thing. It was the last

35

place she'd go to for assistance. 'She'd be thrown out on 'er ear the minute she set foot in the place.' He turned towards Kate and leered at her. 'Though there are some perhaps who could put her to good use.' He laughed. 'But then you'd know all about that, wouldn't you old man?'

'Shut up!' shouted Kate, trying to put herself between him and her Pa. 'Shut your filthy mouth!'

'Kate,' Josiah murmured. 'That's no way for a lady to speak.'

'Lady!' scoffed the gamekeeper. 'Lady, he says! Why, she's no more'n a . . .'

Anger lent Josiah strength and he struggled to his feet to try and bring the gamekeeper down, but the effort cost him dear and he collapsed back onto his bunk in a faint.

Fiddy prodded him with his gun. 'Get up! Get up and come alonga us. You're under arrest.'

Kate looked down at Josiah, who lay still and white as a ghost. 'For God's sake, have some mercy,' she said. 'You can see he's lost his senses and he can't walk.'

'And why can't he walk, eh?'

She started to say something about the mantrap, then thought better of it and said, 'Someone put a post in the ground outside the caravan and he fell over it.'

Fiddy laughed. 'A post! Well, that will do for me, but that don' alter the fact that the post, if you want to call it that, was in Sir John's woods and the injury happened in the dead o' night.' He turned to the constable. 'Arrest him, man, that's what you're here for, in't it?'

The constable looked doubtfully from Fiddy to the injured man. ''Tis plain to see, he'll hatta be carried,' he said. 'I'll go and fetch a litter and a cart.'

He was gone twenty minutes and in that time the other two, without his restraining influence, ransacked the caravan, looking for evidence in the shape of dead birds or rabbits or blood-stained poaching sacks, but they found none, because the rabbit in the sack had been abandoned and forgotten in the woods. They vented their frustration on flimsy tables and chairs and the chest of drawers containing Kate's few clothes. Kate screamed at them and beat her fists against Fiddy's arms and back, but he laughed and continued strewing her petticoats about the floor.

'Such finery for a strumpet,' he said. 'Such fancy frills for a gypsy's plaything. How come you to be travelling with him, I should like to know; you're no kin of his, a blind man could see that. Steal you, did he? Take you in the dead of night, just as he takes the squire's game?'

'Shut up!' she yelled at him, stung to fury and thankful that Josiah was unconscious and could not hear him or her either. 'Shut your lying mouth!'

He grabbed her angrily, but she was saved from further violence by the return of the constable with a litter and a horse and cart to transport them all to Wisbech; all that is, except Kate. They had lost interest in her now they had caught their poacher and for that there would be a reward, but to claim it Josiah had to be delivered safely to gaol and a magistrate fetched first thing in the morning. The law would have its man and the squire would have a scapegoat, someone he could hold up as a dreadful example to anyone tempted to poach his game. The girl could wait; they could always return and have some sport with her later.

They dumped Josiah none too gently onto the litter and carried it to the cart. Fiddy pushed Kate to the ground when she tried to follow. 'You can go tomorrow,' he said. 'See what you can do for your dark gypsy friend then, with prison bars between you.'

She sank onto the grass and watched them go. 'Oh, Pa! Oh, Pa!' Covering her face with her hands, she wept, there on the windy common with the door of her caravan home banging back and forth behind her until it threatened to come off its hinges.

But it was no good wallowing in self-pity, she told herself sternly; tears did not help. Drying her eyes, she picked herself up and went back to the wagon, where she spent some time repairing the havoc their unwelcome visitors had caused, before going back to bed and trying to sleep.

At dawn, having slept not at all, she made herself eat a little breakfast, then took a pail and a milking stool and went to find their cow. The horse had long since been sent to the slaughterer but the cow had been retained for the milk and butter she provided. She had been a good and faithful asset, a last bulwark against pauperism, a reminder of better and happier days when the wagon had been on the road, but if Kate could sell her now, the money might pay Josiah's fine or furnish a bribe for his freedom.

'I'm sorry, Daisy, old girl,' she said, settling herself on the stool and putting her fair curls into the cow's side. 'But you and I must part. I have to think of Pa.' The warm milk began spurting into the pail beneath her fingers and in spite of her worries about Josiah she found herself thinking of Matthew Tolley and wondering if he were engaged on the same task and speculating if he had anything to do with the men in the woods and her father's arrest. She dismissed the thought as unworthy; she had no evidence at all that he had anything to do with it and the mantrap was almost certainly set by the squire's gamekeeper. If only Pa had listened to her fears and stayed at home. He didn't need to poach; they still had their wages, for this week at least, but it was a habit with him, a compulsion, as if he had to pit his wits against the bailiff in a kind of game. And this time he had lost.

'Prison is a cruel place,' she said, deriving some comfort from talking to the cow. 'And Pa'll go mad kept indoors. I've got to get him out.' She would not allow herself to voice the worse horror of transportation, for that, as sure as there was heaven and hell, meant parting with him for ever. No one found their way back home to England after a term in Australia. It couldn't, it mustn't, happen to her Pa for what would she do without him? The milking done, she made sure the fire was out and then wrapped a woollen shawl about her shoulders and set off to walk the four miles to Wisbech, leading the animal by the halter.

A handful of women and children, sacks tied about their waists, were gleaning in the Glebe Farm stubble field as Kate passed, but they paid her scant attention; their concern was to be in and out again before the parson saw them. And Kate was too worried about Josiah even to bid them good morning.

She passed through the village, crossed the bridge and onto the road to Wisbech, which followed the line of the river Nene. The waterways were the highways of the fens. It was by water, rather than by the potholed roads, that people and goods were moved. At almost any time of day fenlighters could be seen, often in strings of half a dozen or more, headed by the lighterhouse, which was home to the crew and hauled along by a sturdy horse on the towpath. There was one coming along the bank now and she moved aside to let it pass, answering the greeting of the boy who rode the horse. On the opposite bank there was a woad mill and beside it the racks for drying the pulp, before it was shipped to Wisbech for export. A woman worker lifted a blue-dyed hand in greeting, but Kate, engrossed in her problems, hardly spared her a glance. Nor did she pay much attention to the changing scene as the wide acres of farmland gave way to smallholdings which produced fruit and vegetables for the London market. She was wondering how much the cow would fetch.

By the time she reached the grand new mansions at the entrance to the town, dark clouds were piling up, threatening rain, but undeterred she made her way along the South Brink towards the centre, passing the Sessions House and the gaol on the way, and though she knew Josiah would be held there pending a hearing, she did not stop; her goal was the market. Wisbech as a port had been in decline because of the silting up of the river which led to the sea, but in the past couple of years a great deal of work had been done to deepen the channel and the town was, once again, a flourishing seaport. The quayside was crowded with tall-masted ships, wherries and fenlighters, as dockers and seamen scurried about loading and unloading cargo from the warehouses, mostly imports of timber and coal to be carried upriver to inland towns, and grain, rapeseed oil and garden produce being exported, but Kate did not think the apparent prosperity of the town was doing much to help the agricultural communities on its doorstep.

Today it seemed unusually busy and she remembered that there was a fair taking place and though the population grumbled about the weather, they were bent on enjoying themselves. Street musicians vied with jugglers and acrobats; Morris men danced for a few coppers thrown on the ground and children watched, entranced. If Kate had not been so concerned for Josiah, she would have stopped to enjoy the spectacle, but as it was, she hurried along to where the serious business of the day was being done. Sheep, pigs, cows, chickens, garden produce and implements of all kinds were being bought and sold alongside new corduroys, smocks and boots, tin kettles and framed pictures, hot chestnuts and sticky sweetmeats. There were sellers of ballads and flysheets with news of rick-burning and machine-breaking by discontented labourers in Kent, Surrey and Norfolk and some even closer to home, which was a worry everyone seemed determined to put aside for a day.

Beside the market a hiring fair was taking place, for Michaelmas was also the time of year when annual contracts of employment ran out and servants looked for new masters. Kate paused to watch as labourers and servants paraded up and down displaying the symbols of their trade – a shepherd with a crook, a carter with a whipcord in his hatband, a milkmaid with her pail, a molecatcher with a moleskin waistcoat, men and women, mostly young, waiting for someone to give them a year's work and the security that went with it. Pa had never stood in line like that, being too proud and also unwilling to tie himself down for a whole year to one employer. Kate wondered what sign she could display because she would have to find work for herself; when Pa came home – and she would not allow herself to think of any other possibility – he would not be strong enough to work for a bit, she would have to be the breadwinner. But what could she do? She had no trade, had never been in service and knew little of the skills that most girls learned at their mother's knee. She could not keep house, could not sew, did not have enough of learning to teach. She could weed and hoe and cook on a campfire, but what good was that? Only now, when it was important, did she realise how strangely limited her education had been. But she would not think of that today; it was more important to find a way of setting Pa free.

She led Daisy from one farmer to another until one agreed to buy the cow for five pounds, bemoaning as he paid for her, that 'times is hard'. Putting the money in the purse she had tied into her skirt pocket, she hurried back to the prison, determined to do all she could to free her Pa.

Chapter Three

*W*hen Kate pushed open the door into the anteroom of the gaol, the town's custodian of law and order, in the person of Ben Carter, the Superintendent of Watchmen, was lounging in a cane-bottomed chair with his feet, in muddy boots, resting on the table beside a plate containing the remains of his breakfast and an empty beer pot. His top hat, though still on his head, was pushed so far back as to defy gravity and looked as though it might be glued to his greasy black curls.

'I believe you have Josiah Brough here,' Kate said.

'That we have and not afore time.'

'I should like to see him.'

'Is that so ? And what for, may I ask ?'

'I want to arrange for his defence.'

He laughed. 'He hen't got one and 'sides, you in't no kin of his, you in't entitled to see him.'

'I am his daughter, you know that very well, Ben Carter. And I've got money to pay.'

He removed his feet from the table and leaned forward, his interest aroused. 'How much ?'

She hesitated, wondering how much of the precious five pounds to offer. 'A sovereign.'

'Let's see the colour of it then.'

She took a coin from her purse and handed it to him. He pocketed it and reached for the bunch of keys on the desk, glancing out of the window as he did so. Whatever he saw out there seemed to make him change his mind. 'No,' he said. 'That's bribery and I'll have none o' that. Get you gone.'

Kate's heart sank; she had been counting on Josiah telling her how to proceed, where to go for help; she was sure he hadn't really meant her to go to the Hall. 'But you took my money.'

'Evidence,' he said, standing up. 'In fact, I oughta tek you in.'

He leaned towards her to shake his finger under her nose, making his hat fall off and roll under the table. He bent to pick it up. His backside was too much of a temptation to resist and she gave it a sharp kick which pitched him onto the floor on his nose. His yelp of fury gave her a certain amount of satisfaction but it didn't make up for the loss of the sovereign. She was tempted to try to fight him for it, but quickly realised it would be more prudent to make her escape before he carried out his threat to arrest her; she could not help Pa if she was in gaol herself. By the time he got to his feet, wiping blood from his nose onto his sleeve, she had fled.

Once outside she realised what had caused his change of heart; a carriage had drawn to a stop outside. The tall man who was at that moment stepping down from it was in his forties and might have been handsome if his features had not been spoiled by a scowl. He was dressed immaculately in a grey frockcoat, a lilac shirt and mauve silk cravat in which sparkled a diamond pin. Even without the crest on the door of the coach, Kate would have recognised Sir John Haddow. Her first reaction was to shrink out of sight but then, for Pa's sake, she took her pride in her hands and went towards him. 'Oh, Sir John, please help me. Pa's been took for poaching. He's not a bad man and he only took a rabbit.'

'A rabbit!' he repeated, looking down his nose at her with ill-disguised contempt. 'Are you asking me to condone poaching?'

'He didn't mean any harm,' she said. 'And we were hungry. Everyone's hungry.'

'Is that my fault?'

She would have liked to say 'yes', but impudence like that would not help her Pa. She swallowed her bile and lifted pleading eyes to his. 'Please help him, Sir. He'll promise not to do it again.'

'Aid a poacher! I'd sooner help a murderer. Now, out of my way girl, I've no time to waste with you.' He pushed her roughly to one side. 'See a lawyer if you want help, though I doubt even he could save your ill-gotten parent.'

She stood and watched him go into the building she had just left, wondering if he would be the magistrate to pass sentence on her Pa; Josiah could expect no mercy if he were. And would Ben Carter report her attempt to bribe him? And her assault on him? If she stayed where she was, she might be arrested herself and that would help no one. What ought she to do now? Where could she go for help? She knew no lawyer and could not have paid for one if she had. Wearily she began the trudge back to Middleacre in pouring rain, every squelching step a step away from her beloved Pa.

Sir John entered the gaol and, ignoring Ben Carter, who had hastily tidied the desk and put his breakfast plate and the beerpot in one of the drawers and was bowing almost double in his effort to be noticed, he strode through into the adjoining room where his fellow magistrates were gathering for the weekly petty sessions.

'Sir John! Good to see you again,' the elderly Crispin Lawson greeted him. 'Did you have a good trip?'

'I did until I got back on these confounded East Anglian roads. You'd think with all the unemployment there is, there'd be enough labour to fill the potholes, wouldn't you?'

'It appears they would rather be idle,' Sir Giles Manning put in. 'And the devil makes work for idle hands, isn't that what they say? It's true enough in Lowacre, I can tell you. Having meetings and making demands. Demands! Did you ever hear such a thing? There's a dozen of 'em on the list today. Causing an affray, threatening behaviour, that kind of thing. I hope you intend to be severe with them. It don't do to be soft . . .'

'No one could accuse me of being too soft,' Sir John said. 'And I've caught me a poacher. Been a thorn in my side for years.'

'Caught in the act, was he?' Lawson asked.

'Near enough. Let's be hearing them.' He led the way into the adjoining courtroom and took his seat on the bench. 'You'll join me for nuncheon in the Rose and Crown afterwards?' And to the hovering Ben Carter. 'Put up the first case, and be quick about it, man.'

It was easy to find people guilty when there was no one to defend them and the business of the day was soon done. The three men, thoroughly satisfied with their morning's work, repaired to the Rose and Crown for a hearty meal and to talk over the news of the day. It was well into the afternoon before Sir John called up his coach to return to Middleacre, feeling decidedly more mellow than when he had arrived. It was a feeling which would not last out the day.

'They found out about the meeting,' Matthew said, watching William Chapman milking one of the half-dozen cows he had lined up in the shed, while the rain drummed on the roof. 'We had a warning, so we changed the venue to the drovers' hut.'

'Why there ?'

'It was Watson suggested it. It seemed a good idea at the time.'

The shelter was built, as so many of the local hovels were, of blocks made with a mixture of clay, chopped straw and cow dung, and roofed with sedge thatch. It stood on the corner of the meadow between Haddow woods and the drove road at the head of the lane that led to the fens. Long ago it had been the home of a fen slodger, a man who lived from what he could harvest from the water, but as more and more land had been drained, it was left four hundred yards from the bank and its owner had moved on. The drovers had taken it over to use as a stance, somewhere for them to sleep when they came through, driving the herds from Scotland to Norfolk, where they were fattened for the London market. It was not really large enough for a meeting, but they had crammed themselves in, leaving a lookout to patrol outside. 'Even then we weren't safe; the bailiff was out with a band of estate workers and it wasn't poachers he was looking for.' He smiled suddenly. 'Fortunately the fellows made so much noise, shouting to each other and making the dogs bark, we couldn't fail to hear them. We scattered in the woods.'

'A narrow squeak.'

'I've had narrower,' he said laconically. 'We'll have to call another meeting before the men start taking matters into their own hands.'

'I think they already have,' William said, as the milk gushed into the pail. 'The guardian was removed from the Glebe Farm stubble yesterday. It had been left there for weeks. The parson probably forgot about it, but it was just one more thing to add to the villagers' grievances.' Although he was not directly involved and could not openly side with them, he was, nevertheless, concerned, not only because he was sympathetic, but because any action they might decide to take could affect the working of his farm.

'Damnation !'

'It's only a small thing and not aimed directly against Sir John.'

'All the same, we had better meet again tonight.'

'In the drovers' hut ?'

'Why not ? They will hardly expect us to go back there so soon.'

'How do you suppose they found out you were there?'

Matthew shrugged his broad shoulders. 'The girl, perhaps. Watson called her the poacher's daughter. She was on the road when he met me and overheard some of what we said.'

'Poacher's daughter,' he repeated. 'That's what they call Kate Brough. She lives with an old gypsy on the common.'

'His wife?'

'No, he calls her his daughter, but she's no gypsy, you have only to look at her to see that.'

'Do they live in an old caravan without wheels?'

'Yes. Have you seen it?'

'Yes, and what I saw makes me believe it was the girl. When the men scattered, I stayed to make sure no evidence of the meeting had been left behind and then waded along the ditch to put the dogs off the scent. I left it half a mile further on and struck off across the common. I was passing close to the wagon when I saw a man leave.'

'Brough perhaps, off to do a bit of poaching.'

'I thought you said he was an old man.'

William laughed. 'He looks older than he is, the outdoor life perhaps, but I know he served with Wellington in the Peninsula. I reckon he's around fifty.'

'The man I saw was younger, but I could tell little else in the dark, though he seemed well dressed, better than a labourer.'

'It could have been Andrew Carrington-Haddow.'

'Andrew Carrington?' Matthew repeated in some surprise.

William looked up sharply. 'Do you know him?'

'I knew an Andrew Carrington at Cambridge. I never knew his name was Haddow. Is there a family connection?'

'His father married Sir John's sister, so I suppose you could call him a step-nephew. They're close enough for him to have added Sir John's name to his own. About five or six years ago, it was. He lives up north somewhere and visits from time to time, though I didn't realise he was in Middleacre now. Does it make any difference?'

'It might.'

William got up from his stool and moved along the line of animals, followed by Matthew. 'You think Kate Brough told him about the meeting?'

'She might have done. If they are travelling people, they would have no loyalty to the village, would they? She could have done it for money or immunity for her father.'

'It's possible I suppose, but it doesn't sound like Kate.' William set the stool down again. 'Here, you have a go. This old girl's fairly gentle.'

'You think I need this job?' Matthew asked, laughing.

'I don't know about that, but I reckon you'll not be leaving for a day or two now.'

'No, damn it.' Matthew sat down, put his head into the cow's side and took hold of her teats. For a moment nothing happened but, as he found the rhythm, the milk started to flow. 'If it hadn't been for the poacher's daughter ...'

'What are you going to do about her?' William asked, standing with his head on one side, watching Matthew's long brown fingers at work.

What was he going to do? Matthew did not want to believe badly of the girl; what he had seen of her, he admired. She had a simple beauty which was refreshing, but when he had spoken to her, the lovely blue eyes had been angry and the red mouth and small chin defiantly set. Dressed like a peasant, she was also neat and well spoken, but surprisingly strong, he had discovered, when he tried to hold on to her. How could he make sure she never betrayed them again without hurting her? He did not want to hurt her. And from there, it was an easy step to wanting to protect her. 'I don't know. Warn her, I suppose. Or threaten her.'

'You'll have Josiah to answer to, if you do that. He guards her well.'

'Tis a pity he didn't guard her against Sir John's nephew, then,' he said pithily.

Leaving the regular dairyman to finish the milking, they turned up their coat collars against the rain and ran across the yard to the farmhouse. As they passed through the kitchen, William called to Betty to bring them ale in the parlour, where they settled down before a good fire. 'The poacher's daughter must not be allowed to pass on anything else,' Matthew said, as he made himself comfortable in one of the armchairs and stretched his long legs towards the flames. 'We must warn everybody to be on their guard.'

William Chapman smiled. 'If you and Jack had not been so careless, she would never have heard enough to pass on, would she?'

'Then I have only myself to blame.' Matthew paused. 'But someone should talk to her, find out what she does know and if she has said anything and to whom.'

Betty brought in two brimming glasses of ale on a tray and set them on a small table between the men. She was a buxom girl, dark-eyed and dark-haired, with full breasts and sturdy legs. Matthew smiled at her and was rewarded with a beam of pleasure and a broad wink. Startled, he looked away.

She turned to William. 'Kate Brough is outside. She wants a word with you.'

'Then you had better show her in,' he said, glancing at Matthew with raised eyebrows.

'I'll stay, if I may,' he said.

Kate followed Betty through the farm kitchen, warm and comfortably furnished and big enough to contain her wagon three times over, along a carpeted hall to a door at the far end. She could not remember being in a house before, certainly not one as large as this was, and would have been curious had she not been filled with anxiety about her Pa.

Betty pushed open the door. 'Here she be,' she said, by way of announcing her.

'Come in, Kate.' William Chapman's voice came to her from inside the room, but she could not see him until Betty stepped aside, and then she realised he was not alone. Comfortably ensconced in one of the wing chairs which stood beside the hearth was Captain Matthew Tolley.

The sight of him set her hackles rising. If he really was a cowman, what was he doing in the house? Outdoor servants rarely set foot inside and yet he looked thoroughly at home, so relaxed, toasting his toes by a roaring fire. She hesitated on the threshold, reluctant to discuss her personal problems in front of him; he might say, with some justification, that Josiah had brought his troubles on himself and he deserved whatever befell him.

'Come in, Kate.' William got up, took her wet shawl from her shoulders and gave it to Betty with instructions to dry it by the kitchen fire. Then he drew her into the room, shutting the door behind her, leaving the maid, eaten with curiosity, on the other side. 'Come and sit down, my dear. Warm yourself.'

The captain rose and pushed his chair nearer the fire for her. She

was wet and exhausted after her sleepless night and the walk to
Wisbech and back in the rain and gratefully sank into the seat. He
knelt, as if it were the most natural thing in the world, and
unbuttoned her boots, slipping them from her feet and standing
them on the fender. He was, she discovered, no less sure of himself
on his knees than he had been when seated. She looked down at his
big brown hands as they began gently massaging the warmth back
into her frozen toes. His touch made her shiver suddenly and he
looked up and smiled. 'You'll soon be warm again.' The firelight
flickered on his face and lit his brown eyes, almost mesmerising her
into forgetting her errand. It came to her, as their gazes met and
held, that Pa must have looked like Matthew when he was a young
man; the captain had the same dark, crinkly hair that she remembered on Josiah fifteen years before, the same strong features and
dark brows and, at this moment, the same tender expression. It
was very disturbing.

'It's Pa' she said, pulling her feet away and tucking them under
her skirt in a sudden movement which left him with his hands
clasping the empty air. 'He was caught in a mantrap. They came
to our wagon and took him off to Wisbech gaol.'

'I'm sorry to hear that,' William said. 'Was he badly hurt?'

'It made a mess of his leg.'

'We did try to warn you,' Matthew said quietly.

'Not about mantraps, you didn't,' she snapped. Why was she so
angry? She had no right to be angry with him; it was an emotion
she did not understand. 'Were they put there to catch poachers or
combination men?'

'What do you know of combination men?' he asked sharply,
sitting back on his heels to look up at her.

'They're troublemakers, that's what Pa says. He says they do
more harm than good.'

'Do you believe everything your pa says?'

'Course, I do. He would never lie to me.'

'How did he get out of the trap?' William asked. 'You didn't
manage to open it yourself, I'll warrant.'

She hesitated, remembering she had promised the man who had
carried Pa home that Sir John would not learn of it from her, but if
she was to persuade William Chapman to help her, it behoved her
to be honest with him. 'I tried, but then someone came along and
set him free. He carried Pa back to the wagon.'

'One of the villagers?'

'No. A stranger.'

'He didn't tell you his name or where he came from?' Matthew asked, getting up from his knees.

'No. We didn't have time to talk.'

'Are you sure?' The captain's intent gaze made her feel uncomfortable. There was nothing ordinary about him, not his physique nor his way of speaking and looking at her. Except for Charlie Barber, the village men looked through her, almost as if she were invisible, but he looked into her as if he could see her heart pumping and her thoughts whirring.

'Of course I'm sure. Are you calling me a liar?'

'No, indeed not,' William soothed her. 'But what did you say to him?'

'Say to him? Why, I thanked him for his help. What else would I do?' Both men were looking so closely at her, Matthew from his great height by the hearth and William from the depths of his armchair, they made her feel muddled and ill at ease. They were obviously more concerned with their own problems than with Josiah's plight and she began to wish she had not come. 'Why are you asking me all these questions? Just because someone helps us ...'

Matthew smiled at her, a gentle, half-mocking smile as if he were talking to a child, and it did nothing to smooth her ruffled feelings. 'I'm sorry the old fellow was caught,' he said calmly. 'But he was breaking the law. Sir John's bailiff had every right to have him arrested.'

'He has no right to set mantraps, they are against the law. How do two wrongs make a right, tell me that?'

'They don't,' he said, standing with his back to the fire. 'But if Sir John's men were chasing combination men, they would hardly have turned aside to go after your father, would they? Someone must have told them the trap had been sprung. How do you suppose they knew where to find their poacher after you had returned home?'

'If you mean the man who helped us,' she said, realising suddenly where their questions were leading, 'why should he do that? If he had wanted us caught he would have left us in the wood; we could not have escaped.'

'You didn't talk to him about anything else?' William put in. 'You didn't, for instance, mention a meeting or Captain Tolley?'

'Why should I do that? It's none of my business. Besides, the meeting was over by then, wasn't it?'

'How do you know?'

'I heard you all, crashing through the woods, and Fiddy and his men after you.'

'How do you know it was us?'

'It most certainly wasn't poachers.'

'Why were you in the woods?' William asked her. 'Do you usually go poaching with Josiah.'

'You know I don't. And he doesn't go all that often. I followed him.'

'Why?'

'I told Pa the captain had warned me he shouldn't go out, but he wouldn't listen. I had to go to watch out for him ...'

'So, you talked to your father about seeing me?' Matthew lifted one finely arched brow.

'I don't have secrets from Pa.' She was feeling more and more annoyed. They had no right to question her like this, trying to make her feel guilty. She was not the guilty one. 'How could I tell him you had warned me he shouldn't go out if I couldn't tell him who you were?'

He smiled slowly and it changed his whole demeanour; he was a different man when he smiled. 'And what did he say?'

'You had probably come from the land commissioners to persuade the villagers to accept the enclosures.'

'And your father is in favour of them?'

'We live on the common, Captain Tolley,' she said flatly. 'Enclose that and we lose our home.' She turned from him to appeal to the farmer. 'I'm not interested in what anyone else was doing in the woods. I only want to get Pa out of gaol.'

'He is very fortunate to have you,' Matthew said quietly, wondering just how far she would go to protect her father. 'You would do anything for him, wouldn't you?' His voice had a hint of accusation which made her look straight into his eyes. There was a light in them she did not understand, something of anger, something of hurt, something of steely hardness. What were they accusing her of? And why?

'Anything,' she said.

'Why not go to Sir John?' he suggested. 'Or his nephew. Tell him all you know and he might reward you by having your father released.'

'His nephew?' she repeated, perplexed.

'Your saviour was probably Mr Andrew Carrington-Haddow,' William told her.

'A Haddow?' she queried in surprise. 'But he was kind to us.'

'He would be, if he thought he had found someone to spy for him.'

'Oh.' Her voice was no more than a whisper. 'Is that what you thought?'

'Can you blame us?' Matthew asked.

'What could I tell him, except that Farmer Chapman has a new cowman? He would laugh in my face.' Angrily she rose and turned for the door. 'I came for help, but it seems I have been wasting my time. I bid you both good-day.'

'Come and sit down again, Kate,' William said, getting up and putting his hand on her arm. 'Let's see what can be done to help you.'

Her battle between her anger and her need lasted only a second or two before she obeyed. 'I've got money,' she said. 'I sold our cow for five pounds . . .'

'Is that all?' William said, as Matthew pulled up a chair to sit beside her. 'That's a poor price for a good cow.'

'But she was old and no one would give me more.' She delved into the pocket of her skirt for the little purse containing the four remaining coins. 'But I don't know who to give it to, nor what it will buy. I was going to ask Pa what to do, but Ben Carter wouldn't let me see him.'

'Ben Carter is the Superintendent of the town's watchmen,' William explained to Matthew. 'He's a stupid fellow, full of his own importance.'

'You went to the gaol?' queried Matthew. 'Wasn't that a mite foolhardy?'

'Why? I had done nothing wrong. At least, I hadn't 'til I went to see him.'

'What do you mean?'

'I offered him a sovereign to let me see Pa. He took the money and then said he was going to take me into custody for bribery.'

'Which it surely was,' Matthew said.

She smiled ruefully at the memory of that encounter. 'His hat fell off and when he bent down to pick it up, I kicked his backside. It was too tempting to resist. He fell flat on his face.' She waited

51

until they had stopped laughing and then added, 'Will he arrest me?'

'No, of course he won't,' William said, serious again. 'If he did that, he would have to part with the sovereign. He'll keep the money and hold his tongue, though I think you may have made an enemy there.'

'Could you find out what is happening for me? Take a message to Pa? Tell him I'm doing what I can ...'

'Me?' he queried. 'No, m'dear I'm afraid not. You know the squire's my landlord.' He did not need to go on.

'I saw Sir John after I left. He wouldn't help me either. He said I should ask a lawyer. I don't know any lawyers.'

'So, he's back,' Matthew said.

Kate turned towards him, struck by the tone of his voice. There was a note of anger, of resignation, of finality, as if it were something he had been waiting for and yet dreading. 'Yes,' she said. 'He's back and no doubt more worried about his game than people who are out of work and hungry.' She paused, wondering if she had said too much. 'All I want is to have Pa home again. Will four pounds pay for a lawyer to get him off?'

'Hardly,' Matthew said, wishing it were otherwise. 'No lawyer will take the case knowing your father was caught redhanded, as it were, but the money might furnish him with better quarters and some good food and a doctor for his leg. It's all you can really hope for.'

'Oh.' Her already low spirits plummeted even further. 'Not enough to pay a fine?'

'He's unlikely to be fined,' William said. 'The bailiff will want to make an example of him.'

She had been hoping against hope, refusing to acknowledge that Josiah would get a prison sentence and to have the possibility, even the probability, forced on her was a terrible blow. She did not want to believe it. 'What'll I do? What will he do? He hates being shut up indoors.'

'It's the price he has to pay for being caught,' Matthew said. 'You would do better to look to yourself. What will you do without him?'

'What can I do except wait for him to come home again?'

'Can you manage alone?'

'Course I can,' she said fiercely. 'It's not me I'm worrying about.'

He already knew that. 'I'll go to the gaol and find out what I can,' he said.

'Is that wise?' the other man asked. 'You might be recognised.'

'Oh, I don't think so.' Matthew answered him while looking at Kate. 'And we owe the old fellow something for the diversion he created.'

Kate hesitated. He was a stranger who had arrived in the village in very mysterious circumstances and, apart from that had already issued veiled threats towards her and Pa. He didn't trust her so why should she trust him? But who else would help her? Pa had said go to the Hall, but he had been crazed by pain and had not really meant it. Besides, she had already appealed to Sir John and that had been a waste of time. She still burned with the humiliation of that.

'You can trust the captain,' William said. 'He is here to help us. He'll do what he can for you. Give him the money and I'll give you the pay owing to Josiah.'

Suddenly making up her mind, she tipped the contents of her purse onto the sofa table at her side. 'Here, take it all. I'll be forever grateful.'

Matthew picked up the coins, intending to give them back to her and use his own money, but then he realised she would not accept his charity; she would take it as just another attempt to bribe or coerce her. He took one sovereign and put it into her palm, closing her fingers over it. 'You'll need that to look after yourself,' he said gently. 'I'll see what I can do with the rest, but don't raise your hopes too high. If it is already out of the inspector's hands ...' He shrugged without completing the sentence.

She thanked him, feeling a traitor as she spoke, a traitor to all the good people of Middleacre who were out of work and whose livelihoods were threatened, but what else could she do but accept help where it was offered?

'There is a price to pay,' he went on slowly.

'Oh.' She was angry again. 'I should have known.'

'It is only a small thing.' He smiled to reassure her. 'You tell no one you have seen me here.'

'But everyone knows it, surely?'

'I mean here in the house. Very few know I'm not a labourer.'

She laughed suddenly. 'But if I can see through you, then so can everyone else.'

'Maybe, but I still want your word.'

She hesitated only a moment before giving it. He had been right; she would do anything for her Pa.

William Chapman gave her Josiah's wages, then opened the door for her and she made her way out through the kitchen where Betty was working. 'Keep outa village affairs,' she said, giving Kate her shawl, warm and dry now. 'They in't no concern o' yours. And leave Cap'n Tolley alone. He've got enough to do without worrying about you.'

It was too silly to warrant an answer and Kate left the house with her head in the air.

The rain had stopped and a misty sun shone above the fields which bordered the lane. The stems of the willows dripped into the ditch, already full to overflowing; the floods would come early this year if the wet weather continued. It had been miserable all summer, with only a few golden days and autumn had seen little improvement. No wonder the labourers were up in arms, but what could they do? Like her, they had nothing with which to fight.

She did not understand why they would not accept her; she could not see that she was in any way different except that she lived in a caravan instead of a cottage and, judging by some of those, she was better housed in the wagon. But, without Pa, even that would be cold and uninviting, not really a home at all, just a few bits of wood held together with love and faith. She dawdled, delaying her return, trying to make herself think objectively, to plan what she would do if Josiah were not restored to her. But she could not; without him her life stretched before her, a great dark void of nothingness.

In spite of her determination not to cry, her eyes were blurred by tears and she stumbled in a pothole. The next instant she felt a hand under her elbow, steadying her, and heard Matthew Tolley's voice, saying, 'It seems your Pa is not the only one who needs a helping hand.'

'I'm all right.' She did not look up because to do so would mean he would see her crying; tears were for old women and children Pa always said. 'I can look after myself.'

'I am sure you can, but you won't mind if I walk beside you? After all, you said yourself, the road is free . . .'

He was teasing and that annoyed her, but she didn't want to antagonise him in case he changed his mind about helping Josiah, so she said nothing and he fell into step beside her, taking the lane through the village which ran round the Haddow Hall estate.

She was acutely aware of his height and strength, the breadth of his shoulders, the narrowness of his hips, his self assurance. He dressed like a labourer and behaved like ... She couldn't find the comparison she needed, 'gentry' wasn't quite the right word, but he was no simple cowman; why was he here ? Had he been asked to come ? Who had asked him ? Jack Watson, William Chapman, or the squire ? And why was it so important ?

They were passing the great wrought iron gates to Haddow Hall when he halted suddenly. She stopped and followed his gaze. Strung over the entrance to the drive was a rope and hanging from its centre was a mantrap. It swung ominously in the wind, creaking like some bizarre inn sign. Below it, painted in red on a piece of rough board were the words, 'ARE WE MEN OR RABITS TO BE CORT IN THE SQUIRS TRAP ? WORKERS UNITE WITH CAPTAIN SWING.'

'What does it mean ?' she asked. 'Who is Captain Swing ?'

He had almost forgotten she was there and at the sound of her voice, turned to look down at her with only half-veiled annoyance. 'You and your precious pa have really put the cat among the pigeons, haven't you ?'

'Why blame us ?' she countered. 'We didn't set the mantrap in the first place and we didn't put that up there.'

'Who did ?'

'I do not know, but I'm glad. Let the squire see what everyone thinks of him.'

'He knows that already and things like this don't help their cause one iota.' He began striding up the middle of the lane and she had to run to keep up with him.

'What are you going to do ?'

'Get a ladder and take it down.'

'They won't like you interfering.'

Before he could answer, they heard a carriage being driven very fast round the bend towards them. He just had time to lift her bodily and jump with her down onto the bank of the ditch before it rattled past and through the gates, so close to where they crouched, they were splattered with mud from the horses' hooves. Kate was almost winded and for the second time in as many days, found herself held tightly in his arms. She was conscious of his strength, his warm breath on her neck and the quick beating of his heart, before he scrambled to his feet and helped her back onto the road.

'Are you hurt?' he asked, his arm still across her shoulders as he bent to try and brush some of the sticky mud from her skirt, but it was far too wet. 'Let's get you home and dry before you catch cold.'

She stood trembling, gazing after the disappearing coach. 'Sir John,' she said, then smiled suddenly. 'He'll see that sign now whether you like it or not, so you needn't worry yourself about it.'

'It will be the end of peace in this village,' he said, realising, with a start, that it was anger and not fear, which made her tremble. 'There will be a battle royal and one I had hoped to prevent.'

'Why?' she demanded. 'What business is it of yours?'

'I have made it my business,' he said evenly.

Unaccountably, she turned her fury on him. She was grateful for his help, but why did he treat her as if she were a naughty child he expected to be troublesome? She wasn't a child and she wasn't the one causing trouble; that was Sir John and the people he hired to do his dirty work. And what of Captain Tolley himself? Had Pa been right, was he in Middleacre to smooth the way for more enclosures? But where did Jack Watson fit into that? A battle royal he had said, but who was fighting whom?

'Who asked you to?' she demanded. 'Whose side are you on, anyway?'

'I am on the side of justice,' he said.

'Justice!' she scoffed. 'Where's the justice in locking up a poor man because he is hungry and takes a rabbit? And where's the justice in giving a complete stranger work when there's men idle in the village? I hope the workers win, that I do. I hate the squire and everyone like him, all the landowners and gentry who trample on other people's feelings, for they have none of their own, and that goes for you too, Captain Tolley, 'cos it's plain to see, you are not one of the workers.'

He turned to look down at her. Even allowing for the fact that she was upset about her father, the vehemence of her outburst was indiscreet to say the least. One minute he thought he could trust her, the next, he knew he could not. 'You would tar me with the same brush as you use for Sir John?'

'If the cap fits, you wear it,' she said, finding a metaphor of her own. 'You were angry when you saw that sign, nearly as angry as Sir John is at this minute, I'll wager.'

'Perhaps for different reasons,' he said softly. 'Do you blame Sir John for everything you don't like or don't understand?'

'He's the one putting up all the fences, isn't he? He drives the poor people from their land. He makes them into poachers. He's the one who gives the bailiff and the gamekeeper their orders and he's responsible for the mantraps. He begrudges poor people a rabbit for their stewpots.' Suddenly it was all too much for her, the arrest of her Pa, the long tramp to Wisbech and back in the rain, Matthew himself, who was gentle one minute and angry the next, and she burst into uncharacteristic tears.

He kept his arm about her, waiting for her sobs to subside, aware of an almost overwhelming desire to comfort her with kisses. He could not understand it; she was little more than a child and she had a refreshing innocence, the spoiling of which would be criminal. What, if anything, had Josiah Brough taught her about life? Loyalty, most decidedly, and courage and independence, but what of love, tenderness and passion, the kind a man had for a woman, what had the old poacher told her about those? Not half an hour before, he had been talking of threatening her and now ... Gently he disengaged himself. 'One day,' he said slowly. 'One day you will understand what I have to do and why I do it, but for now, I want you to trust me.'

She wiped the tears away with the back of her hand and looked up into his eyes. 'But you do not trust me.'

He smiled, recognising the logic of that. 'If I said I trusted you with my life, would that suffice?'

'Is it in danger? Is it because of what you are doing in Middleacre?'

'Not entirely.'

'Tell me about it.'

He found himself wanting to confide in her but that, he decided, would be foolhardy. If his true identity and whereabouts became known, his work would be brought to an abrupt end and his father and brother would suffer. And Amy; she would be appalled. Oh, why wouldn't the pain go away? 'You ask too many questions,' he said with a crooked grin. 'And one of these days your outspokenness will land you in trouble if you are not careful.'

He was right, infuriatingly right; one day her fiery temper would be her undoing and she really must learn to curb her tongue. She had no idea what he had made of her outburst and if he repeated it to the squire, she really would be in trouble and it would make things worse for Pa.

'I'm sorry,' she said, though whether she meant for her outburst or her tears, he could not tell.

'Don't be,' he said. 'Never be sorry for convictions sincerely held. Just be careful, that's all.'

They began to walk again, not touching, but each with a heightened awareness of the other, as if a cord were stretched between them and every movement tightened it.

Chapter Four

*M*atthew looked down at her marching angrily beside him and wondered how she had come to be living with Josiah. William had said he didn't believe they were related, although she always referred to him as Pa. According to the farmer there was a story that Josiah had found her abandoned and though it seemed incredible that anyone would want to part with her, it could happen; parents who were too poor to feed and clothe their offspring had been known to leave them on doorsteps. Had that been this lovely child's fate? 'Kate, what's your family name?' he asked.

'Brough,' she said. 'I thought you knew that.'

'That's Josiah's. It's not yours, is it?'

'It is now,' she said, guessing he had been discussing her with William Chapman and feeling somewhat resentful.

'What was it ... before?'

'I don't know.'

'Don't you know anything about yourself?'

'No, not before Josiah found me.'

'He found you?' So William had been right. 'When was that?'

'About fifteen years ago, a long way from here.'

'Haven't you ever wondered about yourself?' he persisted. 'Have you never thought about your real parents?'

'Why should I?' she demanded defensively. 'Pa is all the family I know, all I want to know. He has looked after me all these years and he loves me, and that is enough for me.'

Yes, Josiah loved her and he had looked after her, although ill-equipped to do so, and she returned his love with devotion of her own, but that didn't stop her sometimes trying to put flesh and blood on imaginary bones, substance on ephemeral faces. She was never sure if she had dreamed the faces or if she really had a genuine memory. Who were her parents? Why had they abandoned her in such a cruel fashion? She had asked herself those questions before, but she had never allowed herself to dwell on them, but now for the first time, she felt the urge to know the whole truth. It made her feel disloyal to the man who had brought her up.

'Brough is a very fortunate man,' he said softly. 'To be able to command your love and your trust so implicitly. Anyone else would have been dying to know where they came from. You do know babies are not found under gooseberry bushes, don't you?'

She laughed. 'Of course I do. But my parents must have been dead or not caring or they would not have left me.'

'Supposing they were not? Supposing you were simply lost.'

'Pa didn't think so.'

He was intrigued, wondering what grounds Josiah had for that. 'What were you wearing when he found you?'

'What does that signify?'

'Well, were you in rags and half-starved or warmly clad and fat as butter?'

She smiled. 'I don't think I was starving, though Pa said I was very hungry and I was wearing a flannel dress and a wool cape with a fur-lined hood. He has kept them all these years in the bottom drawer of his chest.'

'Why?'

'Because he likes to remember the day I came to him, I suppose. Why are you asking all these questions?'

'You are not obliged to answer.'

No, she was not, but she found it easy to talk to him, even about personal things she had never told anyone before. 'Do you think the clothes would help to identify me? Is that why Pa kept them?'

'It's possible. Do you want to be identified?'

'No,' she said so quickly he understood her doubts. 'I'm happy as I am. Or I would be, if Pa were home and not in gaol.' After her outburst against the squire, she half expected him to refuse to go to Wisbech on her behalf. 'You will try to help him?' Her voice was quiet, almost pleading, very different from the anger and tears of a moment before.

He smiled. 'I will do what I can.'

'Thank you.' They had reached the door of The Ferryman. He stopped and turned to her. 'Go home now and change your wet clothes before you catch a chill. I don't want to be blamed for that too. Wait there until I come with news.'

'Thank you.'

He turned into the inn and she continued on her way alone. Life without Josiah would be terribly lonely. If she had had a family, someone she could turn to, it would have been so much easier to bear ... No, she would not feel sorry for herself, she would not. She was healthy and self-sufficient and ready to work hard, it would not be so bad. It would be far worse for Pa, shut away from the sights and sounds of the countryside he loved so much. And he would worry about her. Ever since he had found her, she had been his whole life; he had made so many sacrifices for her and she could best repay him by keeping cheerful and preparing for the day when he would be home again.

Deep in thought she was hardly aware of the small girl coming towards her, slowly driving half a dozen noisy geese, until she was within a few yards of her. 'You'd best make haste,' the little one said in matter-of-fact tones. 'Your house is afire.'

Kate looked up, startled. 'The caravan is on fire?'

'Yes, miss, that's what I said.'

She looked up in the direction of the common. Above the bramble and hawthorn hedges she could see a thin spiral of smoke curling upwards. She began to run, knowing the wagon would burn like tinder; in spite of the recent rain, old dry wood and worm-eaten furniture would blaze up in no time at all. As soon as she rounded the bend, she knew she was too late, the van had flared up, burned for a few minutes and then died down, and all that was left looked like the remains of a Guy Fawkes bonfire after the merriment had finished and everyone gone home; the heap of ash was unrecognisable. She stopped and stared at it for some time, unwilling to believe the evidence of her eyes.

The hate, which had been festering like a sore all day, grew in her breast until it threatened to explode into violence. She hated Sir John with every fibre of her small body, she hated him for fencing in the common, for that assuredly was what he intended to do; she hated him for begrudging the occasional rabbit or fish to keep them from hunger; she hated the gamekeeper who set the ugly mantraps, but most of all, she hated, with a fierce, almost tangible emotion, whoever it was who had set fire to her home, for she did not doubt someone had; it could not have burned of its own accord.

Numbly she began, in desultory fashion, to rake through the ashes with a piece of wood, not looking for anything in particular, for she knew of nothing which could have survived or been of use to her. She bent to pick up a blackened cooking pot but dropped it immediately, for the handle was red hot. There were other small things which she raked to one side to cool, a few bits of cutlery, a tin plate, a length of chain, a horse brass, no longer shining, but nothing made of cloth, no curtains, bedding or clothes. The child's dress and cloak were gone now and she felt as if a door had been slammed in her face. Moving slowly round the embers, her eye caught the glint of something which had escaped the scorching and, as she raked away more ash, saw that it was a little gold locket on a chain.

She picked it up, rubbed it on the hem of her skirt and opened it. Inside was a miniature of a very pretty woman, with golden hair, blue eyes and the most beautiful smile Kate had ever seen. She had no idea whom it represented, but it must have belonged to Pa and he must have treasured it, for they had often been so poor that the proceeds from the sale of such a trinket would have helped to buy them food. She cleaned it carefully and fastened it round her neck, tucking it down the front of her blouse. Then she stood up and gazed about her.

It was only then she realised that the piece of wood she had used for a rake was the stake she had pulled up and thrown away the day before, and that there were more like it, hammered into a long, straight line, stretching along the edge of the common, the last piece of open ground in the village. Angrily she flung it away and then ran along the line pulling up stakes as she went, then she bundled them up in her arms and ran across the common to the fen where she flung them in, disturbing a heron in the thick sedge which fringed the water. It took to the air, its beak and neck arrow sharp, its long legs trailing.

She stood watching the pieces of wood bob about in the duckweed on its surface, until the wind, whipping her damp skirt round her legs, made her aware of the chill in the air, and her thoughts turned to wondering where she was going to live. Parish relief! The words jumped into her head and buzzed around there. No, that was the last thing she would consider, the very last. Besides, the overseer would say she had no settlement in Middleacre and heaven knew where it really was. Parish relief was too humiliating to think about. She had a sovereign, besides her wages and Josiah's; that should last a little while. Picking up the pots and spoons she had salvaged, she took them to the drover's hut and hid them there, before turning towards the village, mentally making a list of all the things she would need to start all over again. Trudging along with her head down, she did not see Charlie Barber approaching her.

'Kate! What hev happened to you? You look like you've been drownded.'

She looked up and smiled wearily. 'I fell into a dyke.'

'Git along hoom and get you dry afore you ketch y'death.'

'I can't. The wagon's burned to the ground. I've got to find somewhere else to live.'

'Bugger me! How did that happen?'

'I don't know. I just found it like that.'

'Where's yar Pa?'

'In gaol. They caught him in the woods last night.'

'Oh.' He paused, realising the implication of that. 'You'd best come hoom alonga me.'

'Oh, I couldn't ... Your mother ...'

'She won't mind.' He took her hand. It was icy. 'You be perished. Come and dry y'self by our fire.'

She allowed herself to be led to his two-up, two-down cottage, simply because, for the moment, the fight had gone out of her and she needed someone to take charge of her life.

Aware of her son's adoration of Kate – for who couldn't be when it shone out of his eyes – Mrs Barber greeted her warily, but when she was told of Josiah's arrest and the disaster to the wagon, drew the girl towards the fire. ''Tis wicked, that's what it is,' she said. 'Who do you think could have done it?'

'I don't know. Someone with a grudge against us, though we don't do anyone any harm there, do we?' She was shivering uncontrollably now and the warmth of the fire was making her hands and feet tingle painfully.

'No, I suppose not. You ought to take them there clothes off.' Mrs Barber turned to her brood of youngsters, all gathered round in the tiny kitchen agog with curiosity; there was no privacy there, never had been, never would be. She took the kettle off the hake which hung over the fire and poured warm water into a bowl. 'Come up to my room.' She handed Kate the bowl, picked up a towel and turned to Charlie. 'Fill that up again, son, and make some tea. We'll not be long.' With that she ushered Kate from the room and up the stairs to the first of the two upstairs rooms. It was furnished with a bed, a chair, a cupboard and a small table; there was room for little else. 'Strip off and give me your wet things,' she said. 'I'll take them down to the fire.'

Kate fumbled with numb fingers at the buttons on her blouse. 'Thank you, Mrs Barber. I appreciate your trouble.'

'I couldn't leave a dog out in that pickle,' she said. 'But you can't stay, you know. I've no room and asides ...' She stopped, wondering how to go on. 'Charlie is only a boy, he's not ready to settle down yet ...'

Kate, standing in nothing but her drawers, smiled. 'I understand, Mrs Barber, truly I do. Pa said the same thing.'

'Did he now?' She brightened visibly. 'You'll be missing him, I've no doubt.'

'Yes.' What else was there to say? That she was in despair, that she didn't know how she was going to manage without him, that she felt so lonely and friendless that a single kind act was enough to send her into floods of tears. She swallowed hard and blinked even harder; she must not cry, for where was her pride?

'What are you going to do?'

'I'll have to find work and somewhere to live.'

'Mrs Bunny, the housekeeper at the Hall, was here earlier. Seems the squire needs more servants now he's back. She's taken my Maud. She's nobbut ten years old, but a good little worker and she'll be fed and clothed and that's something in these times.'

Kate's smile was wan. 'Yes, but I don't think the squire would employ the poacher's daughter, do you? And I won't go up to the Hall cap in hand.'

'You could try the hiring fair though it's a bit late in the day now, most bargains will be struck already.'

'And what could I do, Mrs Barber? I've no trade.'

Mrs Barber turned to look at her properly for the first time and realised that here was no gypsy; she had a beautiful body, her complexion, though tanned, was healthily clear and her wet hair shone with cleanliness. And the bundle of underclothes she had been handed were made of fine lawn and hardly darned at all. The old man had brought her up well, all things considered. It seemed to confirm the mystery which surrounded the girl and it made her feel uneasy. It was not just because she was the daughter of a poacher, it had something to do with the way she held herself, the way she spoke, but putting on the airs and graces of a lady didn't make her one and even if they did, she wouldn't do for Charlie. But how could you tell the son you loved that he was wasting his time? 'I'll take your things downstairs,' she said, pulling one of her own woollen dresses out of the cupboard. 'Put this on until they are dry and come down for tea.'

'I'm truly grateful,' Kate said, when she was dressed and back in the warm kitchen again, where Charlie had made a pot of precious tea.

'Hev you eat today?' he asked, taking a quartern loaf and a pot of dripping from a cupboard.

'Yes, I bought something in Wisbech,' she lied, intercepting the look which passed from mother to son, which plainly said there was little food to spare for casual visitors. She wondered if she ought also to refuse the tea, but Mrs Barber was already pouring it.

'What happened about the gleaning?' she asked. 'I saw people in the Glebe Farm field this morning. Didn't the parson stop you?'

'No, but you should ha' see his face when he saw his guardian wor gone,' Charlie told her, smiling broadly. 'He wor that savage he turned red as a turkey cock, stompin' up and down the lane with his skirts all mucky. He tell Ma that if'n they'd axed politely, he'd ha' recalled he forgot it.'

'Does he know it was you scattered the stook?'

'He might ha' figured it, cos we live nearest, but it wor done then, though there weren't a lot to pick up. Ma hardly got a bushel.'

'Not worth the effort,' Mrs Barber said.

'No, but it's the principle, isn't it?' Kate said. 'We can't go on losing our rights, one by one. It'll be the common next. There's been a lot of posts hammered in the ground round it.'

'Enclosure, do you reckon?' Charlie asked.

She nodded. 'So Pa said.'

'But we need the peat, everyone do. And Nathaniel Green do hev a cow on there. You hev too, hen't you?'

'Not now. I sold her this morning.'

'We'll hatta do somethin',' he said, smacking one fist into the palm of his other hand. 'We can't stand by and watch the fences go up. They've done it in Lowacre and their people are worse off than us.'

'No, son,' Mrs Barber said quickly. 'You'll only get yourself in trouble. Keep out of it.' She turned to Kate. 'I wish you hadn't said . . .'

'I'm sorry, I don't want to cause trouble between you. Your mother is right, Charlie. Don't do anything foolish. If you are taken to gaol, like Pa, what would happen to your family?'

He didn't want to answer that. 'Do anyone else know about them posts?' he asked her.

'Captain Tolley might, but . . .' She stopped, wondering how Matthew had fared in Wisbech. Pa could not have been released or he would have been home by now. 'I pulled most of them up and threw them in the fen.'

He laughed, then quickly became serious again. 'It won't stop them.'

'I know, but it made me feel better.' She put her cup and saucer on the table and stood up. 'Thank you for the tea and the warm by the fire but I must go now.'

She picked up her skirt and blouse and went upstairs to change and ten minutes later was out in the cold again and in some ways it was worse for the interlude. Charlie had tried persuading his mother to allow her to stay but Kate had agreed with her that it was out of the question; there was no room and even if there were, without a job she could not pay her way, not once her tiny store of money ran out. She had pressed a shilling in Mrs Barber's hand and assured her she knew exactly what she would do.

Captain Tolley would not know where to find her when he found the ashes of the caravan and she needed to have news of Pa. She set off once again for White Poppy Farm.

No one answered her knock on the farmhouse door and she stood uncertainly on the step wondering what to do. Thinking she heard voices, she crossed the muddy ground of the yard and pulled open the cowshed door. The milking had long since been done and the cows driven back into the meadow; the byres were wet and clean, although the all-pervading smell of stale milk remained. She was moving away, when she heard a sound which made her turn back and peer into the gloom. Two figures stood outlined against a small window at the far end, heads together, arms round each other, oblivious to everything except each other. They drew apart when they saw her and Kate realised with a sense of shock that the man was Matthew Tolley and the girl in his arms was Betty Watson. Her misery turned to anger when she saw the look of triumph on the girl's face and the annoyance on Matthew's. He didn't care about Pa at all; she doubted if he had even been to Wisbech. She had been fooling herself if she thought Matthew Tolley cared about her or Josiah's plight, or that he would be concerned about the wagon being burned out. He had taken her money, pretending he would help her, when he had never meant to at all. She turned her back on them and hurried away.

She heard Betty say, 'Let her go. Who cares about her anyway, she's only the poacher's daughter.'

Only the poacher's daughter! She had never really minded that name until now. Now it seemed to epitomise her problems. Born for something better, Pa had said, nodding his head sagely. It would be laughable if it did not hurt so much. Pa had taught her to be independent; so be it, she would have to find some other way. Whatever anyone said, she was on her own.

She heard footsteps behind her as she turned from the lane onto the road back to the village, but she did not turn round until Matthew caught hold of her arm. 'Kate, where are you off to in such a hurry?'

'I was looking for you,' she said, shrugging him off. 'But you seem to have other things on your mind than your promise to go to the gaol.'

'Why didn't you wait at home, as I told you to,' he countered, walking beside her and adjusting his long stride to hers. 'I was on my way to see you, when I was delayed ...'

She swallowed the retort she had on her tongue. 'I'm sorry. What happened? Did you see Pa?'

His voice softened. 'No, I didn't, they wouldn't allow it, but I've arranged for food and a doctor.'

'Thank you,' she said. 'And the ... the sentence?'

'A year.' Seeing her blue eyes cloud, added, 'It's not as bad as it might have been because they couldn't find any game in your wagon. If he had been caught out at night with a poaching sack, it would have been seven years. Be thankful you left the sack behind and managed to get him home.' He smiled wryly; it would not help to tell her a good lawyer might have got the poacher off. The only evidence there was that Brough had been in Haddow woods was his injured leg and Sir John would not have dared risk the existence of the mantrap coming to light by resting his case on that.

'A year,' she repeated, fighting back tears. 'A whole year for one rabbit and we didn't even keep that! It's not fair. How will he live through it? And he'll never find work when they let him out ...'

'He knew the odds when he went into the woods,' he said, wishing she would not waste her sympathy on the old poacher.

'But he didn't know our wagon would be set on fire, did he? Was that part of the odds?'

'Set on fire?' he queried in surprise. 'Your home?'

She nodded. 'A pile of ash. And it was no accident.'

He cursed under his breath. Kate had harmed no one and surely taking the poacher into custody was enough? 'Do you know who did it?'

'No. Probably Sir John. He wants to enclose the common and our wagon was in the way.'

'I can't believe that. He has to keep within the law.'

She laughed, though there was no humour in the sound. 'He is the law, didn't you know that?'

'He is a magistrate, that is not the same thing at all.'

She looked at him sharply but decided it would be unwise to repeat her earlier indiscretion by saying what was in her mind, and they walked on in silence.

The hedges hung with brambles, stripped of the fruit which the week before had glistened plump and black and asking to be picked. The children had gathered bushels of them in the space of a few days and every kitchen in the village had been hot and smelling sweet of boiling preserve and blackberry pies, and every larder had a summer pudding in some cool corner. The hedges belonged to the squire, but they had always picked the wild fruit, just as they had always cut turves from the common and grazed their animals there. Was that all about to end?

'It's not fair,' she said suddenly. 'Why should the squire have it all?'

'All what?'

'The land, the farms, the trees and hedges, even the water. He owns everything flying, swimming or growing. Why should it all be his?'

'It has been so for hundreds of years,' he said. 'It's part of his inheritance, just as it is for every great landowner.'

'And for hundreds of years the villagers have had their rights and he is taking them away.'

'He has his rights too.'

'Is he within his rights to build fences and turn people off common land? Someone put boundary stakes all along there yesterday.'

'Have they now? That means the commissioners' work is done and Sir John can go ahead and enclose it.'

'What will happen to everyone's geese and cows?' she asked. 'Where will they find their fuel? Without the common, they'll starve.'

She had said no more about losing her own home, he noted; her concern was for others. 'They'll be given somewhere else to take their livestock.'

'There is nowhere else, only the summer pastures and they're flooded in winter.'

'Sir John has the law on his side.'

'And what would the law say if it was known what the Squire did to get his own way, that he had set mantraps and burned down my home? They are not lawful acts.'

'I would be surprised if you could prove Sir John had anything to do with either,' he said.

'I mean to do just that,' she said defiantly. 'Somehow or other, I will beat him and no one, not you or anyone else who sides with him, will stop me.'

He smiled at her vehemence but decided to ignore her implication that he sympathised with Sir John; there was nothing to be gained by arguing. The last thing he wanted was to quarrel with her; she had enough to worry about without being upset by him. More than anything he wanted to protect her but at the moment he could not see how he could do it. 'I'm sorry, Kate,' he said softly, taking her arm. 'None of this is your fault and yet you are the one being punished ...'

'It doesn't matter about me. All I care about is Pa. You have done what you could for him and I'm truly grateful. Don't worry about me. I can manage.'

He did not answer but lifted his head as if listening to something in the distance. Then she heard it too. The sound of shouting came to them on the wind from the direction of the common and then a single shot. Without a word, Matthew set off at a sprint, with Kate behind him.

At the edge of the common he stopped. A group of workmen were endeavouring to replace the boundary posts but as soon as they were hammered in, the village men were onto them, tearing them up and using them to batter the poor fellows who were trying to put them in, some of whom were their fellow villagers employed on the squire's estate. Fiddy was standing by with a shotgun which he had just fired in the air, but without effect, the men were too enraged to heed it. Charlie was nearest; Matthew grabbed him by his jacket collar. 'How did this start?'

'Kate towd me about the boundary stakes,' Charlie said. 'I come to see for m'self, then Mr Fiddy come with the squire's men and some others what were strangers, and ordered 'em put back. I went and towd Nat Green and he fetched everyone he could find to come and pull 'em up ag'in. Thass what started it.' Although he was addressing Matthew, he was watching Kate as he spoke and had the hurt look of a puppy thrust out into the cold. 'We in't havin' it.'

'Help them,' Kate cried, when it seemed that Matthew would do nothing. 'Don't just stand there.'

They were very close to the spot where her caravan had been. The wind had blown away most of the ash but there were a few pieces of blackened wood and odd bits of iron. The sight of it incensed her to fury; there was a glow about her, a fire, the light of battle in her eyes, and she rushed impulsively forward to join in the fray. She grabbed the upraised arm of one of the estate workers to stop him hitting a villager with the post he had in his hand. 'Let him be!' she shrieked, too angry to be afraid. 'Let him be! The common must stay free!'

The man shrugged her off and she stumbled and was swallowed up by the crowd. She could do nothing but huddle on the ground and put her arms up to protect her head as they milled about her. She did not hear Matthew shouting to her, nor realise that someone else had ridden up and dismounted. Both men started towards her but Matthew reached her first. 'You silly little fool!' he said, helping her to her feet and guiding her to safety with his arm about her. 'You could have been killed.'

'Don't grumble at the girl.' Kate recognised the voice of the young man who had helped her father from the wood. She looked up to see him confronting Matthew. He was wearing buckskin breeches and a riding coat and carrying a crop. 'Look to the others,' he told Matthew. 'If you have any influence over them at all, I suggest you use it.'

'Carrington!' Matthew said, staring at him for several seconds as if undecided whether to say more. Then he turned, strode over to Fiddy, took his shotgun from his unresisting grasp and fired it into the air. There was a sudden silence and everyone turned towards them. Matthew returned the gun and strode to a hillock of slightly higher ground where he stood looking down on the throng of angry villagers, his brows drawn together in a frown. 'It's useless to knock these poor fellows about,' he said, nodding towards the estate workers who gathered a little way off. 'They're only doing the job they're paid to do. Some are not even Middleacre men.'

'And some are!' Nat Green shouted, glaring at his brother-in-law, who was a stableman at the Hall. Kate knew Nat was one of the more hot-headed of the villagers. 'Traitors, they are, ready to do the squire's dirty work for him.'

'Aye,' called someone else. 'How can we best the divil if we're not all of the same mind?'

'You'll achieve nothing like this,' Matthew said. 'You are breaking the law and Sir John has right on his side.'

'And who's side be you on?' Green shouted. 'Tell us that.'

Matthew looked across at Andrew, who held his gaze as if daring him to answer, then he turned back to the village men. 'Go back to your homes and leave me to deal with it. I will try to get justice for you.'

'You! You in't no manner o' use if all you can do is chaw. We want summat done.'

'Something will be done. Be patient.'

'Patience don' fill bellies,' Chuckley shouted. He was a huge man and could make a horse do anything he wanted but humans were another matter; he didn't know how to deal with them, especially those who were designated his betters.

'At least you've got a job,' someone from the back of the crowd called out to him. 'The ploughin' in't done yet.'

They continued to argue among themselves for several minutes, then slowly dispersed, leaving the commissioners' men to continue with their task unmolested. Andrew looked from Kate to Matthew, then touched his hat with his crop and cantered away. Matthew watched him go for a moment, wondering if he ought to have explained his presence, but decided it would have served no useful purpose and would have alienated the village men. He turned to Kate. 'Are you hurt?'

'No.' She was more than ever convinced that he was no ordinary labourer and his arrival in Middleacre, coinciding as it did with the arrival of the land commissioners and the return home of Sir John, could not be unconnected with them. He knew the young man who had turned out to be the squire's nephew, had addressed him as Carrington, without using a title of any kind. A labourer would never have done that. And Fiddy had let him use his gun. Her Pa had been right, Matthew Tolley was in sympathy with the landowners and had come to squash any rebellion on the part of the labourers, and she had better accept that fact and not dream of him as a knight in shining armour come to help her or the village. 'Why couldn't you leave things alone? The villagers would have bested Fiddy's men in the end.'

He smiled, but his smile was one of weariness. 'Not before a few bones had been broken, and there were village men on both sides. Is it good for neighbour to fight neighbour?'

'No,' she conceded.

'And with Sir John's nephew there . . .'

'You know him, don't you? You didn't have to ask who he was.'

He smiled, refusing to be drawn. 'Why are you so angry?'

'Because of that,' she said pointing to the spot where her caravan had stood. 'I'm furious enough to kill.' She laughed suddenly. 'They can hammer those stakes back in as often as they like, but the day after, they'll be out again. Who will tire of it first, do you think?'

He did not answer, having no answer that would satisfy her. 'Come,' he said, drawing her away. 'Let me take you home.'

'Home,' she said. 'I have no home.'

'Have you no friends you can go to?'

'No, we've always kept ourselves to ourselves, and, in any case, no one has room to take me in, even if they wanted to, or has the food to spare. Mrs Barber made that abundantly clear, though she did dry my clothes and let me warm myself by her fire. I'm going to stay in the drovers' hut until I can find somewhere else.'

'The drovers' hut?' he repeated in surprise. 'You can't live in that.'

'Why not?' she said, ignoring the sudden sharpness of his voice. 'It is dry and the drovers are not using it at the moment.'

'Do you know any of them by name?'

She saw no particular significance in his question. 'Not that I can recall. Pa used to talk to them when they came through and sometimes they would come to the wagon of an evening and share a meal with us.' She had loved listening to the tales of their travels; they reminded her of when she and Pa were on the road, when every day was different and contrasting scenes unfolded as they passed, hills and valleys, lakes and rivers and woods, teeming with food, and the work was equally varied and there was no time to become bored by it. 'They won't mind me being there.'

'I won't hear of it.'

'*You* won't hear of it? Who are you to tell me what I may or may not do? I shall go there if I please.'

'It's only an old shelter, you can't make a home out of it.'

'It's no worse than the wagon was. I can make it comfortable. I still have the guinea you made me keep and last week's wages, and I can live off the land and the fen, Pa taught me how.'

'Poaching,' he said. 'You'll be following in Josiah's footsteps and you'll end up the same way – in prison. Oh, Kate, don't do it. You could leave the village, go somewhere else where there is work. I could help . . .'

She stopped walking to turn and look up into his face, trying to gauge what was in his mind, but failing. 'Why should you do that?'

'Because I want to.'

'No, you don't. You think of me as a nuisance and don't try telling me any different.'

He laughed. 'I won't. You are a confounded nuisance, but that doesn't mean I want to see you in trouble.'

'Trouble? What trouble? It seems to me you are the one who's in trouble. Perhaps you should worry about that and leave me to look after my own affairs.'

He ignored the jibe, though he wanted to take her shoulders in his hands and shake some sense into her. 'Quite apart from its unsuitability, the hut stands on Sir John's land and you'll be trespassing if you use it.'

'It's not possible to walk on an inch of soil in this village that doesn't belong to the squire,' she said. 'And he won't know I'm there.' She paused. 'Unless you tell him.'

'I? Don't be foolish. But others use that hut beside the drovers.'

She laughed suddenly. 'Oh, you are thinking of the combination men . . .' She paused, looking up at him with a frank expression he

73

found unnerving. 'But perhaps you know more about that than I do, Captain Tolley.'

'I ?' he queried, wondering why, whatever he did, for whatever reason, it was baulked by this slip of a girl who had no idea of the havoc she created, not only to his plans, but to his peace of mind. Why did her life seem to have become so inextricably bound with his at this moment ? Should he tell her that if she stayed in the hut he would have to find somewhere else for the meeting, probably the inn, where no secrets could be kept ? 'What do I know of such things ? I am a simple cowman.'

She found herself laughing, although there was really nothing to laugh at. 'You are not a cowman,' she said. 'Anyone with half an eye can see that. And you are not simple either. In fact, you are very complicated. I cannot understand you or why you say and do what you do.'

'Perhaps one day, you will,' he said softly.

At the door of The Ferryman he told her to wait, before going inside and returning a couple of minutes later carrying a heavy wool cloak and a small package. 'Here,' he said gruffly, putting the parcel into her hand. 'I don't suppose you've eaten today.'

Food had been the last thing on her mind but now she realised how hungry she was and was grateful for his thoughtfulness. It was another sign of his complex character, she mused, as he walked beside her, relaxed and self-confident, matching his stride to hers. But then he could afford to be confident, he had nothing to lose. No doubt Sir John paid him well for the work he did. It was because of his intervention that the staking of the new boundary was going ahead.

When they came to a small door in the wall surrounding the Hall, she stopped. 'I'm going this way, it's a short cut.'

'It would be better to keep out of Haddow woods,' he said. 'Go round by the road.'

'No, the squire's not going to frighten me into going miles out of my way.'

'Do you have to be so obstinate ?' he demanded. 'Just like your pa, you ask for trouble.'

'Oh, don't you see ?' she cried. 'It's all I've got to hold on to, my hate for the squire and what he's done. If I go the long way round, he'll have won. And so will you.'

'If you must, you must,' he said, draping the cloak round her shoulders. 'But take this, we can't have you dying of cold and causing more problems.'

'Oh, I'm a problem, am I?' she flared. 'I'm sorry about that, indeed I am, but you need trouble yourself about me no more.'

'Would it were that easy.' He could not keep her by him however much he would like to. He fastened the cloak at her throat and lifted the hood over her golden head, before reaching to touch her cheek with the back of his forefinger. 'Don't hate so passionately, Kate,' he said softly. 'Hate feeds on itself and you are a woman made for love not hate, a gentle, caring person. Don't spoil that.'

She felt a small glow of warmth spreading from the spot on her cheek where he had touched it, almost as if his finger had left an imprint for all to see. Pa had not prepared her for anything like the tingling feeling which flowed from the top of her head to the soles of her feet whenever this man touched her. She couldn't understand it. Was she about to lose her reason, like Pa said people did when they fell in love? There was certainly no sense in the way she was drawn to the man who stood looking down at her with a quirky smile. He was arrogant and domineering and probably on the side of the oppressors, but he could be gentle and thoughtful too, more than any man she had known except perhaps her Pa. She knew her life had reached a turning point, nothing would ever be the same again. Her contented existence with her Pa was in the past and the future was uncertain, but, for Pa's sake, she would make the best of it. Before he could speak again, she turned and fled through the gate.

Chapter Five

Mrs Bunny had taken a perverse delight in her employer's anger when she heard the conspirators had slipped through his fingers and all he had caught was one miserable poacher and that without the evidence of his crime. The rabbit had been dumped on her newly scrubbed kitchen table with instructions to cook it for dinner. By that time, Johnson, Sir John's personal servant, had arrived and a butler and footman had been taken on and she was glad to hand the serving of the meal over to them; she had more than enough to do and the less she saw of Sir John the less likely was she to let slip the fact that she listened at keyholes. Even so, she obeyed the summons to the library late that afternoon with some trepidation, afraid her guilty conscience might give her away.

'Have you re-engaged the female staff?' Sir John demanded, looking up from helping himself to brandy.

'No, Sir John. They all said they were suited and didn't want to change.' She dare not risk his wrath by telling him what they thought of his derisory offer of an extra pound a year in wages.

'Then find others.'

'But it's late. Where will I find them at this hour?'

'Where you find them is of no interest to me,' he said. 'Just engage a couple of chambermaids, a parlour maid and whoever else is necessary to keep the whole house ticking over. And someone to help with the cooking. I expect to be doing some entertaining.'

'We haven't had that many before,' she said boldly, remembering his meanness over staff. Footmen he had had in plenty, flunkeys in livery who stood about doing nothing but advertise an affluence Sir John desired but did not have, and hold out their hands for vails which never reached the kitchens. Those who did the donkey work were hard pressed and, because they laboured behind the scenes, few in number.

'We didn't need them before,' he snapped, determined not to

satisfy her curiosity, but realising this business of spending money to impress would grow like a mushroom and he would be hard put to contain it. He was tempted to change his mind and remain a widower, but the thought that if he did, Andrew would inherit under the terms of the agreement he had made with his brother-in-law, was enough to stiffen his resolve.

Mrs Bunny bobbed and returned to the kitchens where Bertha was eating her dinner. 'When you've had that, clear the dining room, she said, shrugging herself into a brown worsted coat. 'I'm going into the village. The master wants a whole lot of new servants, so the first girls I meet will be taken on. They won't be trained, but if he expects to find trained servants at a moment's notice, he'll have to expect otherwise, for it can't be done, not on the wages he's prepared to pay, that's for sure.' Her last words were uttered over her shoulder as she went out of the door. Five minutes later, hurrying along the path through the wood, she encountered Kate.

'Kate Brough!' she said, eyeing the girl from top to toe. She could not see much for the huge black cloak that enveloped her. 'What are you doing here?'

'I'm out for a walk.'

'In Sir John's woods? I would have thought you'd learned your lesson after ...' She paused, as if unsure whether to say what was in her mind, then went on, 'I heard about your Pa and the fire. I'm sorry, girl, you didn't deserve that.' Her unexpected sympathy made Kate look into her face and she was surprised by the genuine concern she saw there.

'Thank you.'

'What are you going to do now? About somewhere to live, I mean.'

'I'll manage.'

'Do you want a job? I need a scullery maid.'

Kate was so taken aback she could only stare at her with her mouth open.

'It will be a roof over your head and food in your belly,' the housekeeper went on. 'And I reckon you could do with both. The pay's not good, eight guineas a year and your keep, but it's better than nothing.'

Kate found her voice at last. 'Do you think I'll work for that fiend after what he's done to Pa and me?'

'You don't know for sure it was Sir John, do you? But if it was him then it's only right he should house you and feed you, isn't it?' The idea seemed to amuse her, for she smiled broadly.

'If he sees me . . .'

'He won't. You'll work in the kitchens and Sir John never comes down there, but if you should meet him accidentally, all you have to do is make yourself scarce, and if it's too late for that, just bob a curtsey and keep your eyes on the ground. He won't even notice you, he'll look straight through you.'

'What about the other servants?'

'Apart from Bertha and little Maud, there's no one from the village, and they're no more likely to speak to Sir John than you are.' She paused, searching the girl's face. 'I need some help, so you'll be doing me a favour.'

Kate was reminded of the last words her Pa had uttered before being taken away on the litter. 'Go to the Hall,' he had said. Did he know Mrs Bunny would be sympathetic? 'Very well,' she said, deciding it would do until she could think of something else; it would certainly be better than a cold and lonely night in the drovers' hut. She followed the housekeeper along the path, across the stable yard and in at the kitchen door of the great house, wondering what Matthew would make of her lack of steadfastness. 'Now let's have a proper look at you,' Mrs Bunny said, when she had taken off her coat and hung it on the hook behind the door. 'Have you worked in a big house before?'

'No.' Kate obeyed the beckoning finger and allowed herself to be inspected in the light from the lamp hanging over the kitchen table. 'I've never even been inside a house as big as this.' She looked round at the huge kitchen. It had a long table down its centre, a dresser containing plates and tureens, a great many cupboards and a few chairs, but the focus of her attention was on the huge black kitchen range which glowed red in the gloom and on which kettles and saucepans boiled, giving off a delicious aroma which made her mouth water.

Mrs Bunny sighed. 'No matter. Bertha can take over upstairs seeings she's had experience and you can work down here with little Maud. There'll be others coming just as soon as I can find them. In the meantime we'll manage. You'll begin at five in the morning. While Bertha does the fires in the family rooms, you clean out the kitchen grate and give it a good blacking, light the fire, put some water on to boil – you'll find a big pan in the scullery – then scrub out the pantry and when you've done that, you can have your breakfast.' She had a breathless way of speaking, as if she had been running, and had to stop frequently to regain her breath. 'Now, let's find you a uniform.' She opened one of the cupboards and pulled out a pile of washed-out blue dresses and white aprons. 'Here, this one should fit. Put it on and the apron and cap. Then you can help with the washing up.'

'Yes, Mrs Bunny.' Kate, as she obeyed, was not at all sure she was going to like this mode of employment but, as Mrs Bunny had pointed out, it was better than nothing.

According to the housekeeper the washing up was a great deal less than usual. 'Only the two of them tonight,' she said, referring to Sir John and Mr Carrington-Haddow, but it took Kate two hours to see the back of it and by then she was more than ready for bed.

There was no time that night for her to see any more than a glimpse of the house on her way from the kitchen up the back stairs to the attic room and iron bedstead she was to share with Bertha, but what little she did see impressed her with its size and splendour. It dwarfed William Chapman's solid farmhouse and she wondered if she would ever find her way round it. But then she did not want to because of the risk of encountering Sir John; she would rather hide herself in the back of the house where, according to Mrs Bunny, the squire never ventured.

Getting up at half past four was no hardship, she rather liked it, especially as the weather was fine again and she was able to leave the kitchen door open and breathe the crisp air from outside and hear the starlings singing and twittering over the crumbs she threw out to them. She sang too as she blacked the grate, her clear voice filling the empty kitchen. It was a happy sound, for what was the sense in being miserable? True, Pa was in gaol, but he wasn't far away and he had medical treatment and special food for as long as the sovereigns lasted, thanks to Matthew Tolley. And she would send more. Things could be much worse.

She was grateful to the captain, but he still puzzled her. He had said he was on the side of justice, but his actions seemed to bely that, for how could enclosing the common be justice? If he agreed with the gentry in the matter of enclosures, why had he helped her, especially when she had been so indiscreetly outspoken? It didn't make sense. She could not stop thinking about him, not only his reasons for being in Middleacre, but the way she felt about him. Whenever he was near, she found herself trembling, felt her colour rise and her heart beating in her throat. And his touch was like fire. But he seemed such a cool man, so self-possessed and controlled. She could not imagine him doing anything impetuous, and yet she sensed there was a lurking anger in him, a hidden power which might erupt at any moment. Sometimes it showed itself in his impatience, sometimes in the hardness of his eyes, even when he was smiling. Then there were times when those same eyes were like velvet and his voice was gentleness itself and she wished he would always be like that. Perhaps he was when he was with Betty Watson. She stopped singing suddenly and the hand that held the blacking brush paused momentarily, as her mind's eye saw again those two figures entwined in each other's arms, then she deliberately shrugged her thoughts away and went back to her task with renewed vigour, returning to her song where she had left it, heedless of the irony of the words. *'Mid pleasures and palaces though we may roam, Be it ever so humble, there's no place like home ...'*

Mrs Bunny smiled as she came into the kitchen, tying a large white apron round her plump waist. 'It's a fine voice you have,' she said. 'But I'll be surprised if you have energy for singing by the end of the day.'

Kate stopped in mid-note. 'Good morning, Mrs Bunny.'

'Good morning to you. Where's Maud?'

'I let her sleep. Poor mite was so tired after last night ...'

'She'll have to get used to it, Kate, we can't mollycoddle her. I'll go and wake her. Have you finished that grate yet? It's time to get the servants' breakfasts and we mustn't dally, we've a busy day ahead of us.'

She was right. By the time the day was out, the whole household had been turned topsy-turvy and the slow, almost languorous, methods of the old servants had been swept aside in a bustling activity with everyone rushing hither and thither and getting under each other's feet and Sir John issuing orders and then countermanding them as he thought of something else that must be done and done immediately.

'Is it always like this?' Kate asked, when at last the work was finished for the day and they were all sitting round the embers of the kitchen fire, too tired to rouse themselves to go to bed. 'Doesn't anyone ever stop?'

'It's worse 'n usual,' Bertha said. 'For two pins I'd give notice.'

Mrs Bunny ignored Bertha's last remark; the girl threatened to give notice at least twice a day, even on good days. 'It's on account of the lady what's coming,' she told Kate. 'Mrs Wisdom her name is, though more than that I do not know.'

'She must be someone very important to have the squire in such a state of anxiety.'

Johnson, who had just come into the room, carrying a silver tray on which was an empty port bottle and two used glasses, set it down and smiled knowingly. 'She is Sir John's intended,' he said.

'Intended!' Bertha exclaimed. 'You mean he's going to be married again?'

'That's about the way of it.'

'Why now?' asked Mrs Bunny. 'Why after all this time?'

'He's hard up,' said Johnson, joining them at the fireside and tapping the side of his long nose. 'He's over his head in deep water and the only way he can swim is to marry a rich widow.'

She laughed. 'Mrs Wisdom is to pay for the privilege of being Lady Haddow, is that it?'

'You could say that.'

'She may live to regret it.'

'So might he, but needs must when the devil drives ...'

'Why is he hard up?' Kate asked. 'He's rich, isn't he? He has everything he wants and if he hasn't, he just takes it.'

'What do you mean, girl?' Johnson asked, turning to her.

'What I say. The enclosures ...' She smiled. 'How does it go? *The law doth punish man or woman that steals the goose from off the common, but lets the greater felon loose, that steals the common from the goose.*'

While Bertha and Hetty, the new parlour maid, giggled and Johnson glared, Mrs Bunny stood up and ordered Kate to follow her into the scullery. Mystified, she obeyed.

'Now, girl,' the housekeeper whispered when they were alone. 'You don't know Johnson, so it's best you be told. It don't do to question what Sir John does, nor repeat those seditious sayings in front of him, not if you want to keep your job, that is. He may seem friendly, but he's the master's man for all that, and he'd soon tell on you if he thought it would curry favour. Keep a still tongue in your head and you'll do.'

'I only said what was in my mind,' Kate said, realising she had been saved by the kindly housekeeper; another minute and she would have blurted out just what she thought of her employer. 'I didn't think Johnson would tell . . .'

'No, I didn't suppose you did, but be warned. Now let's get back before they wonder what we're talking about.' She returned to the kitchen with Kate just behind her. 'And just you make sure you do a proper job on them pots tomorrow, my girl,' she said.

The others were laughing together and Bertha turned towards them. 'Hark at this. Someone hung a mantrap o'er the main gate with a Swing message on it.' She turned back to Johnson. 'Goo on, do you tell 'em.'

'Sir John saw it hanging there when he came back from Wisbech,' he said. 'According to the coachman, he got out of the coach in a rage but he couldn't find anyone to take it down because all the outside staff were helping to stake the new boundary. It hung there all night.'

'I'll wager it wor the one the poacher got hisself caught in,' Bertha said. 'They do say it took his leg clean off.'

Mindful of Mrs Bunny's warning, Kate forced herself to remain silent as Johnson went on, 'Wherever it came from, it's lying in the harness room now. The master's damning everyone to hell fire and saying he'll punish the whole village, if they don't hand over the culprit.'

'Who do 'e reckon it might be?' Bertha asked. Then to Kate. 'Do you know?'

'I've no idea,' Kate said. 'It was nothing to do with me.'

'He's your Pa.'

'And he's in gaol,' Mrs Bunny said quickly. 'So how could he have put it there?'

'I reckon there'll be a rare ol' bang afore long,' Bertha said. 'Like there's bin in other places, fires and breakin' troshin' engines and such like. There's to be another meeting . . .'

'Who told you that?' Johnson demanded to know.

'Thomas.'

'Who's Thomas?' Kate asked.

'One of the under-gardeners,' Mrs Bunny said with a smile. 'Bertha's walking out with him.'

Johnson turned on the maid. 'I hope you are not associating yourself with the troublemakers. It would be the worse for you.'

'He in't no troublemaker. He jes' heard it, thass all.' She laughed nervously. 'Supposin' Cap'n Swing wor t'come to the meetin', wouldn't that put the fat in the fire?'

'Captain Swing wouldn't concern himself with Middleacre folk,' Johnson said. 'He's nowhere near here.'

'Who knows where he is,' Mrs Bunny put in. 'Or even who he is.'

'They do say 'e's a jin'leman,' Bertha said. ''E goes round the country in a green gig givin' out money and axin' about wages and troshin' machines ...'

'Gentleman, my arse!' Johnson said. 'More like a Frenchie, trying to start a revolution here like they had in France. And look what happened there.'

Hetty gasped and her hand went to her throat. 'You don't mean they're a-goon' to cut off the heads of all the gentry, do you?' she said with a shudder. 'I shan't sleep a wink for thinkin' on it.'

'What have you to fear?' Johnson queried, with a sneer. 'You aren't gentry, are you?'

'No, but ...'

'I'll tell you one thing,' Mrs Bunny put in before Hetty could finish what she was saying. 'Neither Captain Swing nor any Frenchman will stop me from sleeping tonight and it's time you all went to bed.' She shooed the girls from the room towards the back stairs. 'Work isn't going to get any easier, I can tell you.'

Mrs Bunny spoke the truth. For the next few days Kate found herself confined to the house, caught up in the whirlwind of activity involved in preparing for the arrival of Mrs Wisdom and there was no time to dwell on her own life and how it had so suddenly changed. She worked dutifully, but inside she was seething like a cauldron on the boil. Extravagance and ostentation were everywhere; new carpets, curtains and furniture arrived every day and rooms which had been locked up for years were opened up and made ready for guests. And what was worse, the wasted food could have fed all the hungry labourers for a month. The staff ate what was brought down from the dining room but there was too much even for them. Kate began parcelling some of it up and hiding it at the back of the pantry – a half-finished roast chicken, some slithers of ham which had not been carved evenly enough to take to the dining room, cold rabbit stew which only needed reheating, salmon pâté, sweet pastries. Somehow or other she would smuggle it out and give it to those who needed it, though how it was to be achieved, she had no idea.

By the evening of the third day, her movements had become mechanical and she helped to prepare the last meal of the day, only half listening to Mrs Bunny's grumbling. 'It wouldn't be so bad if he had his meals at a civilised hour,' she was saying, referring to Sir John. 'But no, he must eat at six and it don't matter that we have to spend half the night clearing up after him. It's all got out of hand, if you ask me.'

No one did ask her, least of all Sir John, who would undoubtedly have agreed with her. He only hoped all the outlay of money and energy would be worth it.

'I mean to catch all poachers and dissident labourers,' he said, addressing Andrew whom he had come upon in the dining room reading *The Times* which had that morning arrived from London. 'People like that pestilential gypsy fellow and his impudent daughter must be wiped out. Do you know she had the audacity to accost me in the street? Me, the squire of Middleacre! Expected me to set her ill-gotten father free. The effrontery of the girl left me speechless.'

Andrew did not believe that for an instant; it would take more than a peasant girl to deprive Sir John of speech. 'It's not just Middleacre, is it?' he said, trying to divert Sir John's attention from Kate. 'Captain Swing is everywhere. Seems the fellow has finished with the south and moved to East Anglia. Now his target is Suffolk and Norfolk. The paper reports riots all round North Walsham and they're moving south and west and it appears the farmers are at the bottom of it, encouraging the labourers to mob the parsons over the tythes. The magistrates of Tunstead and Happing have issued a public notice saying it's their opinion the trouble is caused by the use of threshing machines and insufficient wages and they recommend the landowners and occupiers of land to discontinue the use of the machines and increase wages to ten shillings a week or two shillings a day for task work. They say that although they intend to enforce the law, they think no severe measures will be necessary if landowners give proper employment to the poor and encourage their tenants to do the same.' He paused. 'You see, even the magistrates are in sympathy.'

'Then they are fools,' Sir John said, glaring at the young man. 'And don't change the subject.'

'I was not aware that I had. You were talking about the problems of the labourers, were you not?'

'No, I was talking about *my* problems. Squatters must be cleared off my land.'

'I thought you had already done that.' Andrew said. 'I was on the common earlier in the week and there was no sign of the tinker's van.'

'If you were down there,' Sir John said irritably. 'you will also know the boundary stakes were pulled up and I had to send every man I could spare to make sure they were put back.'

'Did you expect anything else?'

'I expect obedience.' He paused, surveying the young man with the satisfied air of a man who knows his own power. 'I'll offer a reward for the apprehension of the ring leader. That should bring them to heel.'

'They are men, not hounds,' Andrew said, the mildness of his tone belying the intensity of his feelings. He couldn't win an argument by being as angry as his host. 'You can't train them like puppies.'

'And if you have no better contribution to make to the conversation, you had better remain silent,' Sir John said.

Hetty picked up an empty tureen and hurried back to the kitchens to add it to the pile on the table where Kate was washing up, helped by Maud and the skinny little back'us boy. She could not wait to relay the conversation she had just heard in the dining room. 'The squire's a-goon' to arrest all the poachers and lab'rers what cause trouble and e's givin' a big reward for the capture o' the men's leader,' she said. 'I jes' heard 'im say so.'

'Then he'll hatta arrest the hull village,' Bertha said. 'They hen't got no leader.'

'I wouldn't mind earnin' the reward,' Hetty said. 'It'd pay the doctor for me ma, she's that sick ...'

Kate looked up sharply, but before she could speak, Mrs Bunny came between the two maids and put a large serving dish heaped with succulent slices of duck in Hetty's hands. 'Here, take this up to the dining room and make haste before it gets cold.' And, as the girl obeyed, added, 'Bring back some of the dirty plates from the sideboard. We'll be here all night if we don't get on with the washing up.'

'Would she?' Kate enquired of the cook. 'Would she betray the men for the reward?'

Mrs Bunny shrugged. 'What does she know? I fetched her from Wisbech hiring fair; she don't know the village, but best mind your tongue when she's about.' It was almost as if she and Kate were part of the conspiracy, though Kate herself knew nothing and she doubted if Mrs Bunny was privy to any more. But she felt she had an ally in the house and it made her feel better about her position.

Most of the new servants went off to bed as soon as their duties were done, until only Kate, Bertha and Mrs Bunny remained and Kate had still not devised a way of smuggling out the food she had hidden. Free time was something no one seemed to have and she was not used to that. She and Pa had always worked hard, putting in long hours, but when the day's labour was finished, the evening meal cleared away, they could please themselves what they did. Sometimes they read to each other; the novels of Jane Austin were her favourites because they depicted a way of life which was far removed from her own and yet they were peopled with characters that were totally believable. And she read the adventures of Ivanhoe and wept on Rebecca's behalf because Rebecca, like her, was an outcast and could not have the man she loved. Sometimes she had done a little simple mending while they talked – or more often Josiah talked and she listened – and sometimes he accompanied her singing on his fiddle. Here, at the Hall, it was very different; there was no recreation and she could not call her soul her own. It served to demonstrate the great divide between the haves and the have-nots and that angered her too. Pa had hinted that one day she would live in a fine house, wear good clothes and ride in a carriage. Did he mean like this? If so, she was not at all sure she wanted it, not at the expense of the less fortunate. What she could not understand was why he should covet it for her. In every other way he was a man of the people, a labourer, in sympathy with the workers; he had no time for tyrants.

And there was Matthew Tolley. What would he think of her when he heard she had not gone to the drovers' hut as she had said she would? He would come to the conclusion she was fickle; he might, if she did not explain how it had come about, think she had changed sides. She had hoped to have time to go to the village to find him and tell him of the reward but she hadn't been able to get away from the eagle eye of the housekeeper. His reaction might reveal just how he stood on the issue and knowing that seemed more important than anything to her at that moment. But it was too late now; most working folk went to bed when daylight faded in order to save candles, quite apart from the fact that they had to rise at dawn to go to whatever work they had, even if it was only picking stones off the fields at tuppence a bushel.

Do good by stealth, Pa always said, so that was what she would do. She did not go to bed when the others went, saying she had some work to finish, but as soon as everyone had gone upstairs, she retrieved the food she had hidden and took Matthew's cloak down from the peg behind the door. A minute later she was speeding through the woods to the little gate in the wall, revelling in her freedom.

It was a fine night with a few blustery clouds and a fair wind rippling the water in the dyke and bending the giant reeds, so that their outer sheaths blew out like pennants. After the stuffy heat of the kitchen it was blissful and she filled her lungs with the sharp air. Once on the lane, she turned towards the village, going from cottage to cottage, leaving little parcels of food on the doorsteps, smiling to herself as she imagined the pleasure they would give. Not for a moment did it occur to her that the gifts would be resented, or even frighten the timid.

She was just leaving the last package containing the ham at the Watsons' home when the door opened and Jack stood on the step. 'What are you a-doin' here, girl?'

'Leaving this.' She put the parcel into his hand. 'I thought your little ones might like it.'

He turned towards the rushlight coming from the interior in order to see what it was she had given him.

'It's best ham,' she said.

He thrust it back at her. 'I don't need no one's charity.'

'It isn't charity. It would only have been thrown away and there's nothing wrong with it.'

'No, except it come from up there.' He jerked his head in the direction of Haddow Hall. 'I heard you'd been took on there. Fallen on yar feet, hen't you? What did you undertek to git the job?'

'I don't understand,' she said, puzzled. 'They needed servants and I was available.'

'Available!' He laughed harshly 'An' you think I can be bribed as easy as you were?'

'I haven't been bribed and no one's trying to bribe you, certainly not me. I simply thought you could use the food . . .'

Mrs Watson appeared behind her husband. 'What's going on out here. Oh, it's you,' she said when she saw Kate. 'What do you want?'

'She's brought leftovers from t'squire's table,' Jack told her. 'Thinks we'll be grateful for them . . .'

'And so we are,' she said. 'I ain't too proud to tek it. 'twould serve the divil right if he hatta feed the hull village.' She took the ham from Kate. 'Thanks for thinkin' on us, girl. Now, do you get on back afore you're missed.'

Jack struck the food from her hand. 'You'll not tek it, Mother. Wages is what I want, not hand-outs.' He kicked the ham with the toe of his boot and his dog fell on it hungrily. At least the animal had no pride to get in the way of a good meal.

'Do you know where Captain Tolley is?' Kate asked.

'Why do you want to know?' he asked warily. He did not approve of the captain's partiality for the poacher's daughter; it made him vulnerable and the men would not trust a man who succumbed too easily to a pretty face, especially one that didn't belong to the village.

'That's my business,' she said.

'Well I don' know where he is,' he said. 'At hoom in bed, I dessay. An' thass where you oughta be.'

She turned away without speaking.

'Keep outa village affairs,' he called after her and the next minute the light was gone from the path as he closed the door.

Undaunted she made for The Ferryman. Although it was near ten o'clock, light still spilled from its open door and she could hear talk and laughter. As she hesitated, wondering if she ought to go any nearer, Matthew himself came out. He stood looking up at the drifting clouds as if gauging the weather for the morrow. Unseen, she watched him for a moment. He was self-possessed, as if nothing could shake his faith in himself, and because she was so filled with doubts herself it made her hackles rise. 'A fine night for skulduggery, captain,' she said.

Startled by her voice he turned sharply towards her but then relaxed and smiled. 'Kate, what are you doing here?'

'Looking for you. I wanted to return your cloak.'

He smiled down at her; she was swamped by the garment, all he could see of her was her shoes peeping out from beneath it, and her golden head because she had thrown back the hood. 'Keep it. I don't need it.'

'You don't mean that, surely? It's too good ...'

'I am not in the habit of saying things I do not mean. It will keep you warm.'

'Thank you. But I didn't go to the drovers' hut after all. The squire's housekeeper gave me a job.'

'Good.' He had followed her to see her safely through the woods and had seen the encounter, breathing a sigh of relief as he watched them disappear along the path towards the Hall. He could not have slept easy in his bed at the inn, let alone left the village, knowing she was housed in that hut. Quite apart from the fact that it was draughty and probably not watertight and she would have caught a chill if not the ague which carried off so many of the fen people, it was too much a part of the villagers' struggle to be a safe haven for her.

'You don't think I should have turned it down?'

'No, I do not. I am delighted you have a proper roof over your head and I advise you to do nothing to jeopardise it. Go home, out of harm's way.'

'Oh, how can you call that place home!' she exclaimed. 'Besides, why should I?'

'It's late. You could be hiding heaven knows what under that cloak. You would not want to be accused of poaching, would you?'

She laughed suddenly. 'No. Would you?'

He chuckled and fell into step beside her. 'No, so let us walk together and keep an eye on each other.'

'It's all gone now anyway,' she said.

'What is?'

'The food I took. Do you know Jack Watson threw it on the ground; he'd rather see his children starve than take it.'

'You mean you stole from the Hall?'

'How can you call it stealing when it would only have been wasted?'

'Kate, it wasn't a very good idea. If you are caught ...'

'I won't be.' She stopped suddenly, remembering she still was not sure where he stood. Was he friend or foe? For master or man? 'You wouldn't ...'

'No, I'll keep your secret, but don't do it again, will you?'

'Why not?' she demanded, walking on. 'No one else complained.'

'No one else! For goodness sake, how much did you take?'

'Only what would have been thrown away. I took it round the village – to Mrs Barber and blind Cally, the Chuckleys and Nat Green, the Watsons and that row of cottages at the end of the village where there are so many children. I only wanted to help ...'

'Kate, it doesn't help, it only inflames the men and makes it even more difficult to keep the peace.'

'And keeping the peace is more important than helping the villagers, is it?'

'It's the same thing.'

'No, it is not. Peace for the sake of peace is a betrayal ...'

'What do you expect me to do?'

'Talk to Sir John, or Mr Carrington-Haddow, you know him, so don't bother to deny it. Make him understand how cruel the squire is being. The poor people cannot live on the wages they receive now, they'll starve ...'

'Sir John does not pay their wages.'

'I know that but he makes it difficult for the farmers, doesn't he? And what with losing the common ...'

'Why do you concern yourself with them?'

'Because I care.'

He acknowledged that. In spite of her own troubles, she cared about others. He wished there were more like her, especially among those who had the power to alleviate the problem. 'I'm sure you do,' he said gently. 'And believe me, so do I.'

'Then you had better make up your mind whose side you are on,' she said. 'You cannot sit on the fence forever.'

'Sitting on the fence, am I?' He chuckled. 'No, Kate, that's too uncomfortable a perch.'

'There's something else,' she said, unwilling to admit that she did not understand him. 'The squire's going to give a reward for the capture of the men's ringleader.' She looked up into his face but could see no sign that he was either anxious or glad. 'There's talk of Captain Swing ...'

He threw back his head and laughed aloud. 'And Methodist

preachers and gentlemen in green gigs, not to mention peers of the realm and witches on broomsticks.'

She did not like him laughing at her when she was deadly serious. 'It won't be funny if Sir John has someone arrested.'

'No, you are right,' he said, suddenly sombre. 'But let us hope common sense will prevail.'

'You mean Sir John or the people?'

'Both. But it's nothing for you to worry your lovely head over. Go back to the Hall and for everyone's sake, please keep out of mischief. It's bad enough holding the men back without having to worry about what you are up to ...'

'That's not fair!' She was too exasperated to notice the compliment. 'You men are all alike, too proud and independent for your own good. Why can't you accept that women can play their part?'

'Oh, I do, believe me.'

'If I were a man ...'

'You would be far too hotheaded,' he said, trying to imagine her as a man and failing utterly; she was all woman. 'Keep your pretty little fingers out of it.'

'You don't trust me,' she said.

'I've said I do, isn't that enough?' His tone was sharp. Stubborn, that's what she was, he thought, stubborn and proud. Why couldn't she see that he was trying to protect her?

'Now, please go home. You are safer under the squire's roof than anywhere else and Mrs Bunny will look after you.'

They were approaching the little gate in the estate wall and he stopped and turned towards her. 'I must leave you here.' He smiled and reached out to touch her cheek with the back of his fingers. 'I have to go away for a while. Promise me you'll do nothing to upset Sir John while I'm gone.'

'Going away?' She was dismayed. Though they seemed always to be arguing, he was the one person she felt she could turn to in trouble, and now he was leaving. 'Why? Have you given up on Middleacre?'

He smiled. 'No, I have not given up, but there are other places, other people who need me.'

'Is it bad everywhere?'

'I am afraid it is.'

'You will come back?'

'God willing.' He bade her goodbye and watched her out of sight, then turned on his heel and went back to The Ferryman to pack his bag, ready for the morning stage.

She had bewitched him, this little homeless waif and he had no idea what he was going to do about her. But do something he must. She deserved a better life, someone who could give her a loving home and security. Could the old poacher do that, even if he were not in prison? He doubted it. As soon as this business with the labourers was over, he would try and find out who she really was and where she came from, and, if it were in his power, find her real family for her. He did not believe that anyone would willingly abandon her. He knew he could not.

Chapter Six

*T*he threshing was finished, far too soon for most people, the ploughing was done and the winter wheat sown. The leaves drifted from the trees and a cold northeast wind blew down from the Wash, rippling the reeds along the riverbanks. Already some of the fields were partially flooded and were now no more than shallow sheets of water interspersed with hummocks of marshy land. The duck hunters were out on the fens and the noise of their huge punt guns carried for miles. Kate, working in the great house, was warm and well fed, but she would gladly have given it up if she could have had her Pa back. Every day she thought about him, wondered how his leg was mending, whether he was well. If there had been any hope of being allowed to see him, she would have begged a few hours off and gone to the gaol and braved a confrontation with Ben Carter, but she knew he would not let her in, or if he did, would certainly not let her out again, not without charging her with some offence which would only draw attention to her and it would certainly not help her Pa. Her only consolation was that every day that passed was a day nearer being reunited with him.

She had little communication with the local inhabitants, even though she still supplied them with leftovers, creeping about the village at dead of night, a ghostly benefactor. She had no idea how their campaign for better wages was progressing; she guessed not at all. And the common had a fence round it now, and a gate to keep people out. The workers from Home Farm were out on it every day, spreading clay from carts which came loaded with it. All trace of the caravan had gone. It made her sad.

But her life was not all hard work and gloom; she had a little time off every Sunday and she made the most of her freedom, wandering along the banks and droves wrapped in Matthew's cloak, as often as not in the company of Charlie Barber.

He had caught her up one day as she came out of church and

fallen into step beside her, his Sunday boots creaking. 'May I escort you home, Kate?'

'I'm not going home. I'm going for a walk.'

'Can I come?'

For a fleeting moment she remembered Josiah's warning, but decided a little walk would do no harm and it was comforting to know she had a friend. She smiled. 'If you like. I'm only going down to the fen.'

He walked beside her, speaking occasionally, but mostly in silence, because he did not know how to put his burgeoning feelings into words. He wanted to tell her she was beautiful, that she was different from all the other village girls, that if she would let him hold her hand, he would die of happiness, but he said none of these things. Instead he told her that Farmer Chapman had praised his straight furrow and might put him in for the ploughing match the following year if he continued to improve. 'Not that it do mek any difference to my wages,' he said. 'I'm three-quarters 'til my next birthday.'

'When is that?'

'In two weeks' time. Mayhap then, when he do hev to pay me a man's wage, he'll stand me off.'

'Oh, no, Charlie, Mr Chapman will not do that, I'm sure.'

'How's a feller a-goon to git on and wed, when he can't earn enough to call his soul his own?' he demanded.

'You want to get married?' she asked.

He blushed crimson. 'One day, mebbe. But there's Ma. She'd niver stand in me way, but she'd feel it, wouldn't she? There's five at home now Maud's up at the big house and only Georgie who's next to me is bringin' aught in.'

'Yes, but there's plenty of time, isn't there?' she said, shuffling through the dead leaves which had blown across from Haddow woods, as a child might do, enjoying the scrunching sound they made. 'You are young and things are sure to get better.'

'I hope you'm right,' he said, gloomily. 'Troshin's all done, ploughin' too. There's casual work marling the common, but we've all decided we won't do that.'

'Have you? Whose idea was that?'

'Nat Green brought it up but we're all agreed.'

'You had a meeting about it?'

'Yes, but it wor secret, so don' you go a-tellin' on us.'

'Course I won't. I thought it had all gone quiet when Captain Tolley left.'

'Thass how it do seem, but underneath ... Under the touchin' of caps, and the 'Yes, sir,' there's a bomb waitin' to go off. 'Tis the same all over the country, only others have done summat about it. And we mean to when the time is right.'

'Captain Swing,' she said, but she was thinking of Matthew. 'Are you going to combine ?'

'Don' ask me that,' he mumbled. 'I in't at liberty to tell you.'

'I understand.' She ran ahead of him to the edge of the fen, standing with her skirt blowing against her legs, gazing out across the water as a great cloud of wildfowl – mallards and widgeon – wheeled in, filling the air with the sound of their wings. The sharp pop of the fowler's guns echoed over the ruffled water and they saw two men who had been lying prone in a punt, sit up and take the oars to collect their catch. 'They are so beautiful,' she said. 'What a pity they had to die.'

'They fetch a good price in London and it do help to feed us an' all.'

She acknowledged the truth of that as the men gathered up armfuls of birds. 'Pa used to go punt gunning, but he'd never take more than was food for us. He used to say the animals only take what they need to live and we should be the same. You wouldn't think he'd be like that, would you, considering he was a soldier ? He fought with Wellington at Waterloo ...' She stopped her memories from surfacing; they only made her sad.

'I'm sorry about your Pa,' he said. 'But you're all right now, aren't you ? The squire do treat you right ?'

'I never see him and that suits me fine.'

The setting sun tinged the reeds with gold and spread its blood-red light, fan-like across the rippling water, as the punters rowed to the far shore with their catch. Twilight came early now and soon darkness would claim them. She turned to go. 'I must get back or I'll be for it from Mrs Bunny.'

They turned and walked back the way they had come and he had still not told her that she was beautiful and that he wanted to hold her hand. He didn't tell her the next time, or the time after that, when he took her out in a little rowing boat belonging to a friend of his to show her the spot where a monster perch lurked in the reeds. 'He's a sly one,' he told her. 'But we'll hev him one day.'

It was an outing which had to be kept secret; Mrs Barber did not approve of such activities on a Sunday.

His shyness was not helped by his mother's nagging. 'Let her be, son,' she said. 'She's not for you. She's too different.' Different! Wasn't that one of the reasons he loved her? She was so bright, like a star, and she lit up his drab life. If only he had the courage to tell Kate what was in his heart!

Kate enjoyed his company, but she was too ingenuous to realise where it was leading and she continued to see him, to chat to him about the doings of the village, grieving with him over tragedy and sharing his joy when something good happened, laughing when he told her that someone had destroyed one of the bridges over the dyke that surrounded the common so that Sir John's men could not get onto the land until it had been rebuilt. And she told him of life at the Hall, made him laugh over the silly things that happened there and did not tell him of the drudgery.

'The Squire is getting married again,' she told him one day. 'He's having the house done up from top to bottom. You can't move for fear of falling over ladders and paint cans and rolled up carpets.'

'I had heard something of the sort. Mayhap it will mek him a mite more cheerful.'

But it didn't. Mrs Wisdom arrived post chaise one afternoon in the middle of December, bringing her maid with her and a huge load of bags and boxes. Kate, who had been commanded to take hot water to her room, went reluctantly, afraid of being questioned. But she need not have worried; Mrs Wisdom paid her no attention at all, except to direct her to fill the bath from the jugs of water and to return in an hour to empty it.

She was a tall woman, angular almost, but handsome in a dark kind of way. Her features were even, her brows well drawn and her chin prominent. She removed her huge-brimmed, feather-bedecked bonnet and undid the buttons of her fur-trimmed pelisse, revealing a green satin gown with a pleated bodice and wide puffed sleeves. Kate, who had only ever seen pictures of clothes like that, was lost in admiration, though the practical side of her nature which had been constantly nurtured by Josiah, fell to wondering how much the outfit cost and how long one of the labourers would have to work to pay for it. Years and years, she decided.

In no time at all, Mrs Wisdom had taken over the household, changing routines, altering the way things were done, demanding this, refusing that, entertaining lavishly, until the resentful Bertha and Mrs Bunny were ready to explode. It was a feeling shared by Johnson who saw Sir John's coming nuptials as an obstacle to his good relations with his master and that gentleman seemed to have gone completely off his head since he had made the acquaintance of the widow.

She may have firmly established herself as the driving force behind everything that went on in the house, but Sir John took comfort from the fact that his bride had not yet started to interfere in the running of the estate; he was still master there and he intended to show he was. The labourers were rumbling with discontent again and if what the parson had told him was true, this time the farmers were behind them. A laden wagon had fallen into the dyke beside the common when the wooden bridge had collapsed. It had been made to look like an accident but he had examined it himself and there were definitely signs of an axe on the broken support. And the bank above a field sown with winter wheat had mysteriously collapsed allowing the drain to flood the whole field. It was the sort of thing the fen people had done during the great fen drainage of the seventeenth century. They had been against the drainage, just as they were against his enclosures, and their efforts to prevent it had become part of their folklore. Fen tigers, they had been called. Well, he wanted no fen tigers in this parish. He would call a vestry meeting and let them know exactly how he viewed their behaviour and if the farmers didn't back him, he'd put up their rents. That should make them understand which side they ought to be on.

'There'll be no rebels in this village while I am master,' he said, addressing his dinner guests as they sat, a captive audience, around his table about a week after Laura's arrival. She was sitting on his right hand and Felicity, his sister, on his left. He was thankful that her husband had found pressing reasons for not accompanying her. He always found it difficult to be civil to him and it was enough to be obliged to entertain the son. Andrew sat on the other side of her, infuriatingly self-assured. Further along there was old Crispin Lawson, bumbling on about nothing as usual; Sir Giles Manning with his wife and two daughters from Upwell, and Walter Gardiner, a neighbouring landowner who also had a stake in keeping the peace, although he differed from Sir John in how it was to be achieved. Their host looked round the table at them, the men dressed in elegant tailcoats, linen shirts and fastidiously tied cravats, the women in full-skirted silk gowns with necklines which revealed rather more of their anatomy than the working classes would have deemed proper and at whose throats gleamed diamonds and pearls enough to feed and clothe the whole village for a decade or more. All were attentive, but none, except perhaps Andrew, dared interrupt. 'They won't dare defy me.'

'No?' Andrew queried mildly. 'I can think of several defiant acts recently.'

'The villagers weren't responsible. It's that outsider, leading them on and causing trouble.'

'You mean the fellow they call the Captain?' queried Walter Gardiner. 'He was in Chatteris not so long ago, talking to the labourers about unions. I doubt he has given up.'

'We'll soon silence him if he dares to show his face here again,' Sir John told him. 'I'll have him inside before I leave on my wedding trip.'

'Wedding?' Lady Gardiner queried. 'Are we to offer you felicitations?'

'Yes, it's one of the reasons for this little celebration, to introduce you to my bride.' He turned to take Mrs Wisdom's hand and raise it to his lips, smiling at her. 'Laura and I are to be married on the Saturday after Christmas. We both hope you will all honour us by attending.'

The exclamations and congratulations came at the end of the meal and the ladies rose and left the men to their brandy and cigars and repaired to the withdrawing room, where they quizzed Mrs Wisdom over the teacups about how she had come to meet Sir John, what she was going to wear for her wedding, where they were going for their wedding trip and if she intended to make any changes to Haddow Hall, all of which she found extremely gratifying.

As soon as the men had finished their cigars and brandy, they rejoined the ladies, but soon afterwards Sir John, who had been ruminating on the problem of the villagers, left them and went to the library, shouting for Johnson as he did so.

Johnson who had been waiting at table and was still in the dining room, abandoned the clearing up and hurried to obey. He did not like serving at table; it was not his designated task, but Sir John was determined to impress and had recruited all the servants who looked halfway presentable and dressed them in livery to receive the guests when they arrived and wait at table. Now the meal was over, all the valet wanted to do was to change out of the blue satin knee breeches and white stockings into his customary black cloth.

'I want a letter taken to the parson,' Sir John commanded him. 'Immediately.'

Johnson had no intention of going himself. He went down to the kitchen where Cook was dozing in front of the fire with half a glass of beer in her hand, Bertha was in the scullery muttering to herself and Kate stood, as she had done all evening, at the kitchen table, up to her elbows in washing up water. 'Where is everybody?' he demanded. 'Sir John wants someone to take a letter to the parson.'

Mrs Bunny, startled into wakefulness by his voice, only just managed to save the contents of her glass. 'They've all gone to their beds,' she said. 'There's only me and Bertha and Kate. You'll have to go yourself.'

'I can't. Sir John needs me.'

'I'll go,' Kate said, already drying her hands. Any excuse to go out would do and with luck someone might have finished her chores by the time she returned.

'Very well,' Mrs Bunny agreed. 'Bertha will finish off.' She rose and yawned. 'I'm off to me bed.' And with that she disappeared in the direction of the back stairs.

'Come and wait outside the library,' Johnson told Kate. 'Sir John is just finishing it off.'

Reluctantly Kate followed him through the door which divided the kitchens and servants' quarters from the family rooms, hoping fervently she would not encounter her employer.

She was in luck; Johnson bade her wait in the hall. It was deserted but she could hear animated conversation and the sound of a pianoforte being played badly on the other side of the withdrawing room door. Mrs Wisdom was obviously intent on continuing the conversation begun over dinner; her refined tones were loud and clear above the notes of the instrument, as if she were determined that if she spoke everyone should pay attention.

'It's all very well to say the peasantry need the common,' she was saying, as if countering some remark made by one of the others. 'But what use is land to them? Can't they see how necessary the enclosures are, that a prosperous estate is vital for their own sakes, providing them with work? How can they expect a living wage if the farms don't pay?'

In spite of her nervousness, Kate stopped to listen.

A voice she did not recognise said, 'My dear, I quite agree.'

Mrs Wisdom sailed on, ignoring the interruption. 'After all, who pays most of the poor rates? Sir John must delve deeper into his pocket whichever way you look at it and, surely, it's better to keep the labourers usefully employed than loafing away their days in idleness, which is what they always do, given the chance.'

Kate, standing in the hall, boiled with indignation and wanted to rush into the room to defend the villagers, but mindful of the likely consequences, she stood clenching her fists at her sides and clamping her jaws together until they ached.

'I feel sorry for them, they are so poor.' A new voice entered the conversation, the voice of a woman not given to making forceful statements, a gentle voice.

'It's their own faults,' Mrs Wisdom retorted. 'They spend their time and their relief at the alehouse and then complain they're starving. I've no patience with them.'

'I'm sure they would lead better lives if something were done for them ...'

'Mother, what do you know of the labourers and their problems?' Kate recognised Mr Carrington-Haddow's voice. She wondered what his mother was like. Was she really as sympathetic as she sounded?

Mrs Wisdom laughed harshly. 'The peasants haven't the sense they were born with. I've said so to Sir John more than once. He's been far too easy with them, but now you'll see a change. A shilling cut in their wages will bring them to heel ...'

Kate, out in the hall, gasped. Most of the riots in the surrounding counties had been over low wages and here was this woman suggesting a cut! It was beyond belief.

'Surely the labourers' wages are the business of the farmers who employ them, not Sir John.' Andrew Carrington-Haddow seemed to be more cautious than the rest of the company.

'Perhaps,' Mrs Wisdom said. 'But if the rents went up, the farmers would have to lower wages in order not to lose by it, wouldn't they?'

'There'll be trouble if Sir John adopts that tactic,' Andrew went on. 'You know what has been happening in other areas with riots and rick-burning, not to mention the destruction of the threshing machines and that as close as March and Chatteris. It could happen here.'

'Sir John will ensure that it does not.'

'How? By starving them to death?'

Kate smiled; it sounded very much as if Mrs Wisdom and Mr Carrington-Haddow did not see eye to eye. Was it really because he had some sympathy for the labourers or was it that he resented the lady being at Haddow Hall? After all, he would be the loser if she gave Sir John an heir.

'It would be better to find the ringleader and make an example of him,' one of the other men said, obviously trying to placate them both.

'But do you know who the ringleader is, Mr Gardiner?' Mrs Carrington asked. 'Does anyone?'

Kate held her breath, expecting Andrew to tell them how he had met Matthew on the common, but for some reason he remained silent.

'No,' the gentleman admitted. 'But how many of the labourers can read and write, I wonder.'

'If you mean that monstrous sign over our gate and those impertinent missives which have been appearing everywhere,' Mrs Wisdom said sharply. 'Why, they are illiterate, anyone could have penned them. And as for Captain Swing, whoever he is, he must be found and brought to justice. He's the one causing all the trouble, they'd never do anything without him. He must hang and then the peasantry will settle down to work as they always have in the past.'

'I believe he has already been apprehended,' Andrew said. 'I read a report of his capture in *The Gazette*, two or three days ago.'

Kate put her hand to her mouth to stop herself crying out and crept nearer.

'I don't believe all the trouble is the work of one man,' another of the guests joined in. 'Each place has its own Captain Swing. They just copy each other, there's nothing organised about it.'

'I'm not so sure.' This was one of the women. 'It's made to look that way, but you can't tell me that every village for miles around does the same thing on the same day without any planning?'

'It could be coincidence,' Mr Gardiner said. 'In every village there's a natural leader and when there's trouble, he comes to the fore. He's the one you have to deal with, by negotiation, not by intimidation. These are proud people . . .'

'That's ridiculous,' Mrs Wisdom retorted. 'They're nothing but ignorant rabble, what have they to be proud of? Sir John can best anyone who tries to cross him and if they really are starving, as they say they are, they'll soon come for the reward.'

Kate heard no more because Johnson came out of the library with the letter in his hand. 'Take this to the Reverend and wait for a reply, then come straight back. I'll be in the butler's pantry.'

Kate took the letter, hurried back to the kitchen, plucked Matthew's cloak down from its peg and wrapped it about her, then she left the house, thankful to be out, if only for a short time. Being confined indoors for long stretches made her feel as if she couldn't breathe and, cold though it was, she revelled in her freedom.

At the vicarage she was kept waiting on the step while the maidservant who had answered the door took the letter to the Reverend Mr Cox. As soon as his reply was in her hand she turned to go back, but then changed her mind. She was out, wasn't she? And there was nothing to go back for except unending toil and the snoring Bertha. She turned towards the common, but she could not go onto it for the fence that surrounded it, although there was a brand new bridge to the gate. Already the area had changed; part of it was turned over into long straight furrows, the rest was full of heaps of clay, waiting to be ploughed into the peaty soil. Soon it would be just another field. She turned away, walking along the river bank back to the village. The wash between the two rivers was inundated by flood water as it was every winter and a low mist hung over it, pricked here and there with the ghostly lights of the willow-o'-the-wisp; many a hardened traveller had been terrified out of his wits by those. If the winter was a hard one, the water would freeze and then there would be skating. Everyone from the smallest toddler to the oldest fen slodger could skate in Middleacre; sometimes it was necessary in order to move about, but for the most part it was done for amusement. Not that she thought Mrs Wisdom would allow time off for anything so pointless as enjoyment.

She had almost reached the village green when she saw Charlie Barber come out of the inn and turn towards home. He had a rolling gait which suggested he had been imbibing freely. When he came abreast of her he stopped. 'Kate! What are you a-doin' here?'

'I felt like a walk.'

'At this time of night? Git you on hoom, afore you git wrong.'

'I shan't. I've been allowed out to deliver a letter to the parson.'

'What about?'

'I think it might have something to do with Captain Tolley. They were talking about him up at the Hall. Do you know where he is?'

'No.'

'He told me he would come back, do you think he will?'

He shrugged. 'Who's to tell? Come on, I'll walk you home.' He seemed more assured than usual, as if he had suddenly matured and this time he did take her hand. She did not withdraw it, knowing he would be hurt if she did and she had so few friends it was comforting to feel the warmth of his hand in hers.

'He could be in trouble if he returns,' she said.

'Why?'

'He helped you, didn't he?'

'Did he?'

'Is he Captain Swing?'

'Now, whatever did gi'e you that notion?' He was irritated by her interest in the captain. The man was a stranger and, in Charlie's opinion had done nothing for the villagers except stop them doing what they wanted to do and then left them to carry on as best they could. Half the men had listened to him and decided against action and that had made it more difficult for the others. Charlie didn't want to talk about Matthew Tolley and he wished Kate would forget him. How could he say what he wanted to say if she kept on about the man?

'I heard Captain Swing had been arrested,' she went on. 'Is it true?'

'Aye, I heard something of the sort. But it don't mek no matter. What we do in Middleacre in't no concern o' his.'

'No, of course not,' she said, testing him. 'And I'm glad. He seems to be a troublemaker.'

He looked sharply at her but said nothing and they walked on in silence until they were approaching the gate in the wall of the estate. 'You were right about one thing,' he said. 'Farmer Chapman hev give me a man's wage.'

'Oh, it was your birthday last week! I had forgotten. My felicitations. And I am so glad about your pay.'

'It in't exac'ly a fortune, but it do mean I c'n think of the future a bit more.'

'Oh,' she queried teasing him. 'Are you still thinking of marrying?'

'If she'll hev me.' He was terribly serious and she had a sudden feeling of apprehension and wished she had not mentioned it. 'Course, it'll be a time afore I c'n afford to make a hoom of me own, but if ...' He gulped and went on. 'If you was to say yes, it would be official-like and we could walk out whenever we liked and start to git our bits and pieces together.'

'Me?' she queried, though she knew the answer and it put her in a turmoil. 'Are you asking me?'

'Yes, Kate.' He stopped and turned towards her. 'I do love you ...'

'Thank you, Charlie,' she said so quietly he could hardly catch her words. 'You honour me.'

'No, it is me that's honoured, if you'll say yes.'

'I can't, Charlie.' Even in the moonlight, she could see the disappointment in his eyes and she wished she didn't have to hurt him.

'I'm not good enough for you, is that it?'

'Oh, Charlie, it isn't that, truly, it isn't. How can you think that? It's just such a big step to take and we are both so young ...'

'Ma was married when she wor seventeen. Lots o' girls are. And I'm a man now.'

She was almost in tears. 'I know you are and I am very fond of you, but don't you see, I could not make a decision like that while Pa is still in prison. I have to talk to him about it.'

'Can't you go and see him?' He was clutching at straws now, knowing, deep in his heart, that she was trying to let him down lightly.

'They won't let me see him and if I make a nuisance of myself, they'll arrest me too. Besides ...' She paused. 'Charlie, I am not the wife for you. I don't belong to the village and you don't know anything about me. I could be anyone, a gypsy, a bastard even. I am what you fen people call a furriner, aren't I? Maybe I have some fatal flaw ...'

'Oh, don't talk squit, Kate. It don't mek no matter, anyhow, not to me, it don't.'

'Thank you, Charlie,' she said. 'But I know your mother would not approve.'

'She'll come about.'

'No, Charlie, please do not speak of it again. Let's still be friends, shall we?'

He took her shoulders and tried clumsily to kiss her. Gently she pushed him away. 'No, Charlie. Go home. I'll go the rest of the way by myself.'

She turned and hurried along the lane and through the gate into the grounds of the Hall, not looking back, though she had a feeling he was standing in the middle of the road, staring after her. Why did she suddenly feel so old, years older than he was? Poor boy, he had been so dejected, but she had been right to say no, not only because both her Pa and his mother had said it would not do, but because she could not see herself as his wife, struggling to make ends meet for the rest of her life. Did that mean Pa was right and she was destined for something better? She could hardly envisage that. But she did not love Charlie Barber and she would wait for love to come, in the confident hope she would recognise it when it did.

Johnson was not in the butler's pantry when she returned and she hesitated outside the door, wondering what to do about the parson's reply. The last thing she wanted was to take it to the squire herself. She was about to slip it under the door, when she heard an imperious voice demand to know why she had taken so long. After a moment's indecision in which she was sorely tempted to flee, she turned to face Sir John who had come from the library further along the hall. He recognised her at once as the girl who had accosted him in Wisbech, the poacher's daughter.

There was something about her cool, blue-eyed gaze which made him feel uncomfortable; he had felt it when she stopped him outside the gaol and now he could hardly trust himself to speak. They stared at each other in silent hostility until, at last, he said, 'And how did you wriggle your way into my home?'

'I didn't wriggle my way in,' she retorted, not even pretending to be subservient. 'Mrs Bunny fetched me.'

Sir John turned to Johnson who hovered behind him. 'Run and fetch the constable.'

'What for?' she demanded. 'What are you accusing me of?'

'Poaching,' he said, then as an afterthought, 'Conspiracy.'

'I have not been poaching and as for conspiracy, I don't know what you mean.'

'It means plotting with others . . .'

'I know the meaning of the word,' she said tartly. 'I simply do not understand what you are accusing me of.'

He took the envelope from her unresisting fingers. 'You have been gone hours on an errand that should not have taken above thirty minutes and at this time of night . . .'

'Perhaps she is courting.' Andrew's voice came from the door of the withdrawing room where he leaned against the jamb. Kate had not heard the door open, nor noticed him there. 'She is young and beautiful and I am sure there must be a young stalwart . . .'

'Mind your own business!' Sir John snapped at him, unaware of the colour which flooded Kate's cheeks, though she felt sure Mr Carrington-Haddow had noticed it. 'I'll deal with this in my own way.'

The young man would not be silenced, although he did not shift his relaxed attitude. 'If you arrest the girl, you'll only martyr her. Do you want a riot on your hands?'

'Let them riot. I'll show them who's master, if they do.'

'Beware they don't show you.'

Sir John glared at the younger man, too taken aback to speak. Looking from him to Kate, standing her ground in the middle of the hall, he was struck by their likeness, not so much their features and blue eyes, but their cool arrogance and refusal to be bowed. Yet what had that peasant to be arrogant about? And Andrew, the son of that bourgeois millowner, had he anything to be proud of? Sir John was more than ever determined to go through with the wedding, even if it meant refraining from anything which might precipitate a riot among the villagers. Guided by expediency, he turned to Kate. 'I'll not harbour the daughter of a poacher under my roof, so pack your things and leave now, and if I ever set eyes on you again, you will be in Bridewell before you can blink. Do you understand?'

'Oh, I understand all right,' she retorted. 'I am condemned without trial, just as Pa was.'

Moving off down the hall, she heard Andrew say, 'The girl can hardly be answerable for the misdemeanours of her father, Sir

John. Besides, she works hard, who will you get to replace her? It's only a week to Christmas and then there's your wedding, you'll need all your staff.'

For all his defence of her, Kate was not sure where Andrew's sympathies lay. He had spoken languorously as if the whole subject of poachers and conspirators bored him and he was only arguing with the squire because it amused him to see him in a rage.

'Wait!' Sir John's imperious voice stopped her just as she reached the door to the kitchens. 'Come back here.'

She stopped but kept her back to him.

'Your father is in Wisbech gaol, I believe.'

She turned to face him, angry now. 'You know he is, you put him there.'

'And I could also get him out.'

She looked at him in surprise, but before she could frame a reply, he went on, 'You would like him freed, would you not?'

'Course I would.'

'Then you can do a small service for me and I will see what I can do.'

'What service?' she asked warily.

'Tell me, who hung that mantrap over my gate?'

'I do not know.'

'And who is leading the rebels?'

'Rebels, Sir? I know nothing of rebels.'

'Do you think I am a fool, girl?' He paused, unable to take his eyes from hers, blazing at him in defiance, and was strangely disturbed by what he saw. There was pride there, and courage and a confidence he would never have expected in anyone so beneath him in the social strata. She made him feel impotent, unable to pierce her self-assurance; he could not humble her as he did all the other minions and sycophants who surrounded him and he hated her for it. 'You lived on the common long enough to know what was going on. Who put the men up to it, that's what I want to know.'

'Up to what?'

'Pulling up those boundary stakes and refusing to work on the land. If they think they'll be given poor relief when they turn down gainful employment, they'll soon realise how wrong they are.'

'I have been working here in your kitchens for two months now, Sir John. I know nothing of the villagers.'

'I am sure you could find out.'

'Why should they tell me anything?'

'You are one of their own kind.'

'That I'm not,' she said with spirit. 'Pa says ...'

He laughed harshly. 'I care nothing for what your father says; you are a peasant, nothing more. But if you were to pretend to be in sympathy with the labourers, you might learn enough to help me and your father into the bargain.'

'Spy on my friends, you mean? You must have a poor opinion of me if you think I would do that.'

He surveyed her from her black working shoes up over her coarse uniform to her golden hair peeping out from beneath her starched cap. Cheap and shapeless it was but she managed somehow to give it dignity. 'I believe your father was injured.'

'Caught in a mantrap set by your gamekeeper,' she retorted quickly.

'That can't be so.' His voice was bland. 'Mantraps are illegal. I do believe he tripped over a tree stump in the dark.'

She was about to answer angrily but caught sight of Andrew slowly shaking his head, and decided against it, instead she bit her tongue and contented herself with defiant looks.

'The old sawbones at the gaol is a trifle heavy handed, so I'm told,' Sir John went on. 'And your father's condition is not good ...'

'How do you know that?' she demanded, suddenly afraid for Josiah. 'Is he ill? Has his leg not healed?'

'He could be freed,' he went on, choosing not to answer her directly. 'He could have the best of medical attention ...'

'He's already had that,' she said. 'I ...' She stopped in confusion. Had she been about to tell him of Matthew's hand in the affair? 'I left some money with the gaoler ...'

He laughed. 'Do you think that found it's way to its proper destination? I doubt it. But I could make sure the poacher is freed and all for the price of a name ...'

For a name her tormentor would restore her Pa to her, just a name. Whose name? Watson, Green, Chuckley? She didn't think any of those could be called a leader, although they were always to the fore when there was any grumbling to be done. There was

Captain Tolley, of course. Was that the name Sir John wanted from her? But Matthew hadn't led the men, quite the reverse. He had broken up the riot on the common, he had not led it. He was also an educated man, he would not have written anything so badly spelled as that board over the gate, and, besides, he had been angry about it and wanted to take it down. If Matthew really was the one the squire wanted, surely Mr Carrington-Haddow would have told him so after they met on the common? Unless it was Andrew himself. The thought struck her as funny and she could not resist a wry smile.

'Your father is ill in prison and it amuses you?'

She was immediately serious again. 'No.'

'Gangrene is a killer,' Sir John went on implacably. 'It is a painful and messy death.'

In her mind's eye, she could picture it, the gloomy prison cell, no sight of sky or earth, trees or animals, her Pa in agony and no one caring for him. She couldn't let him die like that, she couldn't.

'I'll give you a week,' he said. 'Now, be off with you and think carefully about what I have said. You may remain at your post for the moment.'

Thankful to escape, if only temporarily, she returned to the kitchen to finish the chores which had been left for her to do, before toiling wearily up to the attic room with its bare boards and the iron bedstead she shared with Bertha.

The maid was on her back, snoring loudly, and Kate, creeping in beside her, knew that sleep was out of the question, even without the problem which filled her mind. She could not rid herself of the mental picture of her Pa dying in prison, nor the equally strong image of Matthew jerking on the end of a noose. He had been kind to her, soothing her and easing her anxieties, but more than that, he had kindled in her feelings she could not understand, of joy mixed with a kind of wild excitement as if something extraordinary was about to happen. The thought that she could be instrumental in crushing that proud figure was unbearable and it wasn't fair to burden her with it.

Pa was strong and had never been ill in his life, she told herself, he wasn't dying, and the idea that Matthew was the leader of the rebels, was just plain silly. Why couldn't she make herself believe it? He had been involved, she knew, but how? Whose side was he really on? Where did her loyalty lie? With Pa, of course, there could be no question of it, so why was she even hesitating? If only she could find out how Pa was faring, it might help. Was he really as ill as Sir John said? Or was that just a bluff to make her do as he wanted? And even if she did agree, what could she tell him? What did she know? The ringleader could just as easily be Andrew Carrington-Haddow as Matthew Tolley, William Chapman even, or any one of the more vociferous labourers and there were many of those. Would it be better to remain in ignorance or try and find out the truth so that she knew what she was up against? She tossed and turned in the bed, just as her thoughts tossed and turned in her head.

'Fer Gawd's sake, Kate, lie still,' grumbled Bertha. 'You'll ha' me outa bed.'

Kate lay on the edge of the hard bed, trying not to disturb her bedmate again, and eventually she subsided into an uneasy sleep.

She was no nearer a solution when she rose next morning and half expected to be sent for immediately after Sir John had had his breakfast, but he went out early and she breathed freely again. She decided her best course was to do nothing. Sooner or later something would remind him he had had no answer from her but until then she would let sleeping dogs lie. She was half glad Matthew had left the village, though she missed him almost as much as she missed her Pa.

Chapter Seven

*M*atthew reined his horse in on the brow of the hill and sat a moment looking down at the small village of Garforth set in a fold of land below him. Frost glittered on its roofs and sparkled on its church spire; the trees in the churchyard, bare now of leaves, stood as they had all through his boyhood and his father's and grandfather's before that, reminding him forcefully of what he most missed when he was away. He turned slightly in the saddle towards the west where Garforth Manor stood on a slight rise, its mullioned windows reflecting the winter sun, smoke curling from its tall twisted chimneys. Home. How many times in the heat of an Indian summer had he dreamed of it? Always he thought of it in terms of his boyhood; more recent memories were too painful. It was where he had been born, where he had spent his youth, playing happily in its meadows, fishing in its streams, learning to shoot and ride and hunt, cosseted and protected. It was where he was loved and where his love dwelt. And that was the trouble.

Impatient with himself, he put spurs to his horse and cantered down the hill, across the fields and along the bank of the river where, as a child, he had fished for tiddlers in the company of his elder brother and the village children. There had been no distinction in those days, rich and poor played together; it was only later, after he and Daniel had been away to school that the differences manifested themselves. They no longer played for playing's sake; their leisure pursuits were organised and they dressed for the occasion. They had become young gentlemen, their nankeen breeches and stuff jackets had become tailored trousers and tailcoats cut in the best superfine money could buy, while the clothes of the village boys hardly altered at all. In truth, they were probably the same garments, lengthened and let out for as long as possible. What had happened to those boys, he wondered. Had they become rebels, resorting to violence because landowners and employers like his father and brother could not be made to listen in any other way? He had left home twice before; should he have returned this time? But he had to come; it was time to take stock of his life and the best place to do that was here, where he had grown up.

It was Kate who had made him see the tangle he was getting himself into. She had said he was sitting on the fence. He wanted to find out how true that was. And she needed help, the sort of help that a labourer could not give her, but a gentleman of means might manage.

He left the bridleway and crossed the park, trotting up the incline to the Manor and going into the paddock through a five-barred gate and thence to the stables at the side of the house.

Daniel was standing in the yard talking to Burgess, the head groom, as Matthew rode up and dismounted. He turned almost idly to see who the newcomer was. 'Matthew!' he shouted and strode towards him, a big broad-shouldered, ruddy complexioned man in riding breeches and muddy boots. 'By all that's wonderful!'

'Hallo, Daniel.' Matthew grinned, as his brother clapped him on the back. 'Someone is pleased to see me at any rate.'

'Of course I am. Here, give me that.' He reached to take the cloak-bag Matthew had unfastened from his saddle. 'Is this all you've got?'

'It's all I needed.'

'No matter, you've plenty of clothes in your room, no one has touched them since you left.' He put his arm about Matthew's shoulders and drew him towards the nearest door of the house. 'Come on in. Amy will be delighted. I was only saying to her this morning that I hoped you'd come home for Christmas and here you are. How are you old fellow? Wound not troubling you?'

'No, not at all.' It was not his physical wounds which troubled him; his hurt was in his heart and mind.

'I must change out of these muddy breeks before dinner,' Daniel said, leading the way along a passage and into the well-furnished hall, where a huge fire blazed in a grate large enough to take a small tree. 'I expect you're used to London manners and dine late but we stick to the old ways. You do not mind?'

'No, of course not.' Matthew smiled, wondering what his brother would say if he knew what and when he had been eating lately. Soup and bread and cheese and, if he were lucky, chicken which was so old and ill-fed as to be almost inedible and that at almost any time of the day. Since leaving Middleacre, he had travelled hundreds of miles, speaking on platforms, in hostelries, barns, out of doors in market places and clearings in woods, visiting farmhands and employers, putting the case of one to the other, suggesting possible solutions, and all the time, questioning whether what he was doing had any relevance. Had he been able to do any good at all ? Was it so little it was hardly worth antagonising his family over ? And whatever he had been doing he found himself thinking of Kate. Who had abandoned her and why ?

He put his bag down on a chair and took off his hat and riding cloak. A door opened further along the hall and a rustling of skirts behind him told him that his sister-in-law had heard him arrive. He took a deep breath and turned to face her, a fixed smile on his lips.

'Matthew, how good it is to see you.' She ran into his arms and lifted her face to his. He dropped a brotherly kiss on her cheek and then took her hands to hold her at arms' length. 'Amy, as lovely as ever,' he said, straining to keep his voice light.

She was petite, no taller than his shoulder; she had a small round mouth, blue eyes and golden hair pinned up into a knot at the back of her head with tresses falling into ringlets on either side of cheeks that had never been scoured by the wind or burned by the sun. Her hands, in his, were narrow and as smooth as baby's. Her dress, of some soft fabric in a delicate pink, could only be worn by someone who had nothing to do all day but look decorative. And she was certainly that. He suddenly found himself thinking of Kate with her tanned complexion and work-worn hands, Kate angry, Kate laughing, Kate in tears, and he knew that something had happened to him in Middleacre, something important and irrevocable, though he did not, as yet, acknowledge what it was.

'Flatterer !' Amy's teasing voice brought him back to the present. 'But why have you not been home before now ? Where have you been this past twelve-month ?'

'Oh, here and there,' he said vaguely.

'Could you not have written to tell us where you were ? One letter, we had, just one, from some outlandish place in the fens. I am disposed to give you a very great scold.' She stopped prattling to look at him. 'I would too, if you were not so thin. You have not been ill, have you? You haven't had the ague? I believe everyone has it sooner or later if they live in that desolate place.'

'No, I am perfectly well and the fens can be uniquely beautiful as well as desolate. Watching the sun come up over the water at dawn, bathing the whole horizon in a pink glow, is a sight never to be forgotten.'

'And, pray, what were you doing up and about at dawn?'

'Duck hunting,' he said quickly. That was something she would understand. 'It is the favourite sport of the people there.'

'You shall tell us about it over dinner. It won't be long. Father-in-law is somewhere about.'

'How is he?' Matthew's question was directed at his brother.

'Not so good, though he won't admit it. He ought to rest more, but he spends most of his time riding round the estate. Things are bad, Matt, what with the poor harvest and the labourers rising. Did you hear about that to-do they had in Belford? Some fellow rode in and settled everything. Stranger he was. Some say Captain Swing.'

'I don't believe there is any such man,' Matthew said carefully. 'He is a myth, someone the labourers have invented to hang their arguments on.'

'Then he has not served them very well,' his brother commented. 'What have they achieved? Nothing, except to cause a great deal of unnecessary expense to property owners and even more grief to their families. Thank goodness, it all seems to have died down now.'

'Oh, do not let us talk of such unpleasant things,' Amy said. 'I am sure Matthew has far more exciting things to tell us. Hurry up and get out of those awful country clothes, Daniel, you look like a peasant. Then we can all have dinner and a long cosy talk.'

'I must change too,' Matthew said, made uncomfortable by Amy's derogatory use of the word peasant. It was the first time he had ever found the slightest fault with her; to him, she had always been the embodiment of perfection. 'I've been on the road since dawn.'

'Why did you ride? Why not come post chaise or at least by the mail?'

'Riding helps me to think.'

She gave a little trill of laughter. 'How profound! What were you thinking of? A young lady?'

He was about to deny it, but then smiled slowly. 'That's my secret.' She had never known how much he loved her, nor that it was because of her he had left home. Amy had been a part of the boys' lives ever since he could remember. She had lived less than ten miles away and their respective parents had been great friends; it was inevitable that she would be encouraged to marry one of them. Daniel was the heir, so what could be more natural that her choice, guided by her parents, should fall on him? And she had made the right decision; they were ideally suited to each other. He told himself a dozen times a day that he did not begrudge her a moment of her happiness, that he had had nothing to offer except an inheritance from his maternal grandfather which ensured he would never be in want, but it was not large and she could hardly be blamed for choosing the heir. But it wasn't just money, he knew that. She loved Daniel and that hurt as much as anything else. Unable to bear seeing the two of them together, he had left home, bought himself into a cavalry regiment and gone abroad.

The fire had burned in his heart all the six years he had been in India; even the army and active service could not quench it. He had been wounded, taking a sabre thrust in his shoulder, and though it had mended remarkably well, he knew his fighting days were done and he had come home to England, to Norfolk and Garforth Manor. Just over a year ago that had been. He had arrived to find Daniel and Amy blissfully content with each other and the parents of two sturdy children who were idolised by their grandfather. They had welcomed him and fussed over him, worrying about his wound, calling in the best surgeon in the county who had simply confirmed what he knew already – the wound had healed and all he needed was a period of recuperation and he would be as good as new.

He had spent two weeks in pampered idleness, eating, drinking and riding round the estate with his father and brother. It gave him his first inkling of how things stood with the labourers and how far his own position had drifted from the accepted standpoint of the family. Not that he had any idea of doing anything about it then; it was simply a feeling of unease, of injustice that he had so much and they so little. But he used it as an excuse to leave, not openly for that would have caused an irreparable rift with his father and that he wanted to avoid. The true reason he had been unable to stay had been Amy. It hurt to be under the same roof, to watch her happiness and know he had no part in it. If he had stayed, sooner or later, he would inadvertently have revealed he loved her and he could not do that, too many people would have been hurt. He had left again, pretending he had business in London.

Her voice, light, affectionate, untroubled, brought him out of his reverie. 'Then you shall tell it to us over dinner,' she said.

But somehow he managed to avoid it. How could he tell them about Kate without also revealing how he had come to meet her? A poacher's daughter! They would be appalled. His father, the fifth Lord Thorsborough, belonged to the old school, which had many contemporary adherents, that a man's place in society, and a woman's too, were preordained, that it was the duty of those who had been born to privilege to order the lives of the lesser mortals under their protection, to reward and punish as they saw fit. He would most definitely be on the same side of the divide as Sir John Haddow, though more benignly so. And Daniel and Amy, brought up with the same values, would concur. He was the odd man out and he felt it keenly, as he enjoyed a repast such as he had not had since leaving home, followed by brandy and cigars and a comfortable lounge in the warm glow of the fire and servants hovering to satisfy his every whim.

'So!' his father said from the depths of his armchair, with his gouty foot propped onto a stool. 'The prodigal returns. What have you been up to?'

'I had some business affairs . . .'

'So you said. What business, I should like to know. What is so important it keeps you from your family and even prevents your putting pen to paper?'

'I have been travelling.'

That was how it had started; this crusade of his. Leaving home he had looked for something to help him forget that he had loved and lost. His years abroad had made him into a wanderer; he had to be continually on the move. If he had to put his mind to where he was going next and how he was going to get there, there was no time to brood and the more remote and difficult the journey the better. And because he did not want to make it easy for himself, he had called himself Captain Tolley. Tolley had been the name of his sergeant who had died in the scrap in which he had been wounded. To begin with he had ridden all over East Anglia, learning about the harsh lives of the working people, doing what he could to help them. His active involvement had come about almost by accident when he had trotted into the middle of a riot in an Essex village. He had been instrumental in bringing the two sides together, using his experience of commanding men to restrain the rioters and tactfully approaching the local magistrates who were all for calling in the militia. Acting as a go-between, he had obtained some justice for the labourers. As a result, others had asked for his help and he had gone where he was needed.

Believing the ownership of a thoroughbred horse would set him apart from the people he was trying to help, he had stabled the animal at Tattersalls and travelled by public coach, returning to the family mansion in Piccadilly from time to time to collect mail, have a bath and renew his clothes. He had become two men in one, two very different beings, an out-of-work soldier turned labourer and a gentleman of some consequence and he had to keep the lives of both entirely separate. How long he could continue to do so, he did not know, especially as Andrew Carrington had seen him with the labourers. If he had known Carrington was in Middleacre he would probably never gone there. But, whatever the outcome, he was glad he had.

The fen people particularly attracted him. They were a dour lot, hard as nails, stubborn as mules and suspicious of those they called 'furriners', which was hardly surprising considering their history; war, plague, famine and flood, they had defied them all. And if nature could not defeat the fenman, how could a mere mortal expect to better him? He wondered why Sir John, who had been born in the fens himself, did not realise that. Fenmen were individualistic; they only worked together when they were threatened by outside forces as they had been nearly two centuries before when most of the fens were drained and it had been difficult to make them see that the troubles they were experiencing now came under the same heading. They needed to combine, not in raggle-taggle groups intent on destruction, but in organised unions. Organising fen people was like trying to organise a flock of starlings.

Kate, who was one of the so-called foreigners, had the same attributes of stubbornness and refusal to be beaten. He admired her for it at the same time as he appreciated how different she was. Unlike the fen people who were dark, raw-boned, heavily built, she was tiny and fair, but not delicate as Amy was delicate. She had a healthy bloom which his sister-in-law would almost certainly condemn as common. Again that slight whisper of criticism which made him feel guilty.

'Thought you were going into politics,' his father said.

'I have yet to find a suitable seat.'

'Find you one here, if you like. The sitting Member is a bumbling fool. He's a Reformist. He could be persuaded to step down for a consideration.'

'You do not agree with electoral reform?'

'No. They'll be franchising the peasants next.'

'And if he did step down, how can you be sure I'd be elected?'

'That's easily taken care of.' His father was typical of those people who thought nothing of buying off any man who stood in his way or paying for a man's vote and he would vehemently deny it was wrong. 'What about it?'

'I'll think about it.' What would his father, a lifelong Tory, say if he knew his son had Whig tendencies? What would be his reaction to his son's belief that there should be universal suffrage, that the population as a whole and not just those who owned property, should have a say in how they were governed? He did not need to give it any thought; he could neither hurt his father by telling him nor betray his own convictions, but this sitting on the fence was becoming more and more uncomfortable.

'Do tell us what you have been doing all these months,' Amy said, picking up some crewel work and stabbing at it in desultory fashion.

'Travelling about the country, seeing how things are for myself.'

'Not like William Cobbett, surely? I have been reading his *Rural Rides*. It is all very interesting, but I cannot believe what he says about the country people is entirely accurate.'

'Perhaps not,' he said, glad to switch the attention from himself to more general topics. 'Though you cannot deny he writes from conviction.'

'Oh, Matthew, I do believe you have been won over,' she cried. 'You will be telling us next, you side with the peasants who are burning our ricks and smashing our machinery.'

He turned to his father. 'Yours too?'

'No, no, it hasn't come to that yet, but I'm afraid it might, if I do not placate them.'

'And will you?'

'Not if I can help it. Giving in to them only makes them think they can go on making demands. There never would be any end to it.'

'But if they cannot earn enough to feed their families, what then?'

'They have Poor Relief. I have never begrudged it.'

No, he could not tell them what he had been doing; they would see it as betrayal and he did not want to quarrel with them. And if he could not tell them about Captain Matthew Tolley, how could he tell them about Kate?

'I am going up to the schoolroom,' Amy said, putting down her needlework and rising to her feet. 'I usually go about now. Would you like to come, Matthew? The children will love it.'

He looked at Daniel, reluctant to be alone with her. 'What are you going to do? Is there anything I can do to help?'

'No, thank you. I've some accounts to go through and I want to see the kennelmaster. There's a meet this weekend. You'll join us, won't you?'

'Yes, of course.' He rose and followed Amy up two flights of stairs to the room where he and Daniel had spent so much time in their formative years. Their tutor had been a tyrant and they had been regularly beaten and it had been no good appealing to their father; he simply told them they had probably deserved it and if they continued to complain he would give them a taste of the rod himself. But harsh or not, the regime made men of them and had given them a halfway decent education, proof of which was that they had both done well at Cambridge.

The children were sitting at the scratched wooden desks which had stood on the bare boards of the schoolroom for at least three generations, but as soon as they saw their mother, they scrambled down and ran to her with shrieks of delight, while the schoolmistress stood smiling benignly. It was never like that in their father's day, but he would not have wished the old days back for this pair. Seeing Amy with the three-year-old Angelique, who perfectly matched her name, and five-year-old Thomas, next in line for the baronetcy after Daniel, he was reminded forcefully of what he had lost.

'Look here,' Amy said, squatting down and putting an arm round each. 'Who do you think this is?'

'Uncle Matt,' they chorused, laughing with delight.

'Then greet him properly.'

Angelique made a wobbly curtsey and Tom an attempt at a leg, pointing his foot forward and bowing low, but as soon as it was done he stood up and tilted his curly head up at his uncle. 'Are you going to take us out in the curricle like you did before?'

'You remember that, do you?' he asked. He had taken them for a ride on his last day at home, gone into Norwich and bought them sweetmeats and a toy each. He had been somewhat melancholy, he recalled, wishing the children had been his, wanting to be gone so that he did not have to be continually reminded that they were not, wanting to stay because they were part of Amy and were so easy to love for their own sakes. He had driven too fast, until, coming round a bend he had almost run down an old man in a shepherd's smock, who was weaving his way erratically up the road, the worse for drink. The man had hurled abuse and shaken his crook at him, making the children laugh, but the episode had brought Matthew to his senses and he had driven more carefully after that. And it had precipitated his decision to leave. The next day he had ridden away and his second life had begun.

'They talked of nothing else for weeks,' Amy said. 'Tom said you drove like the wind.'

'He did! He did!' Tom insisted.

'I'm older and wiser now,' Matthew said solemnly, squatting down and sitting Angelique on his knee. 'If we go, I shall drive like a zephyr.'

'Zephyr, what's that?' the boy asked.

'A gentle breeze.'

'Oh.'

'There!' Amy said. 'That's a new word for you to learn. Now you must carry on with your lessons. You may come down to the drawing room for a little while before tea.'

Matthew stood the little girl on her feet and ruffled Tom's hair before leaving the room with Amy.

'They love you, you know,' she said.

'And I them.' He led the way downstairs again.

'You would make a good papa, Matthew. I cannot understand why you have never married. How old are you now?'

He laughed. 'You know very well that I am thirty.'

'And likely to remain a crusty old bachelor if you are not taken in hand.' They reached the first floor and turned towards the drawing room. 'Don't you want a family of your own, Matthew?'

'One day, perhaps.' It was not a subject he was comfortable with, but he did not know how to tell her so. 'I have not yet found my ideal.'

'And how can you find her if you persist in riding about the countryside on horseback? Did you even have a change of clothes with you?'

'Yes, of course. As much as I needed.'

'As much as would go in a cloak-bag, you mean. Clean linen and little else. Matthew, you cannot expect to meet the right young lady if all you have to wear is a riding coat.'

'That was not all I had.' He smiled to himself, imagining her horror if she could see the rough trousers and fustian jacket in which he had spent most of his time recently. 'Sometimes I wore trousers and a jacket.'

'Jacket!' She sat on the sofa and patted the seat beside her, indicating he should sit there. 'No frockcoat or evening clothes?'

He chose to misunderstand her invitation and sat in an armchair opposite her. 'There was no call for them.'

'That is precisely my point. Did you go out and about at all?'

He knew that it was her way of asking if he had been to any social gatherings. 'I was out and about all the time,' he said, smiling. 'And I met a great many people.'

'Evidently they were not the right sort,' she said tartly. 'I shall have a little dinner party next week to welcome you home and introduce you to one or two delightful young ladies and their mamas. Someone as eligible as you should not be allowed to hide his light under a bushel.'

'I am not all that eligible, a second son with an income that is hardly adequate for a married man, at least not one which will allow me to aim at the higher echelons of society.'

'Oh, do not be so obtuse, Matthew! Five minutes at home and already you are being difficult. I am not talking about duchesses. You have enough to offer for a young lady of gentle upbringing. Pleading poverty will pay no toll with me.'

'What will?'

'Only if you say you have already spoken to someone. And if you have, why have we not been told of it?'

'There is no one.' He found himself thinking of Kate, Kate standing in the lane at Middleacre, dressed in a rough wool skirt and homespun blouse, Kate in sturdy boots, Kate in William Chapman's parlour, cold and wet, with her bare foot in his hand. He smiled. What would Amy make of her if she were ever to meet her?

'There *is* someone! You are smiling.'

'Oh, that is because you are so determined to have me shackled ...'

'Now, that's not fair! No one wants to shackle you. I am sure Daniel does not think he is in chains ...'

'Delightful chains,' he said softly.

She caught his mood. 'Matthew, is something wrong? Are you unhappy?'

'Not at all. There is nothing wrong.'

'Then why do you spend so much time from home?'

'Business, only business. And besides, Garforth Manor is not my home any more ...'

'Not your home? My dear Matthew, of course it is. Just because Daniel and I have married does not mean you may no longer think of this as your home. I should be very miserable indeed if I thought my coming made any difference to that.' She was close to tears, but he dare not reach across to her; he could not trust himself. 'Surely that is not why you left?'

'No, no,' he hastened to reassure her. 'I needed to find myself, to find out what I was meant to do, my destiny, if you like.'

'I never heard such nonsense. This is where you belong until you marry and set up your own establishment.' She dabbed her eyes with a scrap of a handkerchief and smiled suddenly. 'But when that happens, I do hope it will not be far away.'

He had no answer to that and was glad that his father came in at that point and joined them.

His Lordship was plagued with gout and rheumatics and had recently had a mild seizure which had left him breathless and unsteady on his legs and although he still took an interest in the estate and rode whenever he could, he had been forced to hand over most of the active work to his elder son. It galled him to be so disabled but father and son were very close and rarely disagreed about what should be done. He would have been happier if Matthew could settle down, but the boy seemed to be always on the move, as if standing still would turn him to stone. The army had changed him. The gentle, quiescent boy had become a stranger.

'Well, Matthew, my boy,' he said. 'Are you going to stay this time?'

'I don't know.'

'Papa, he has been talking the most dreadful nonsense,' Amy put in. 'He says he needs to find himself. Did you ever hear the like?'

His lordship smiled at his son; it was a smile of understanding. 'And have you?'

'I am unsure. Perhaps I shall know when I have been home a week or two.'

'After my party,' she said, complacently.

Socially the party was a great success. The food was delicious, the wines outstanding and Amy was a delightful hostess, so that the guests were easy in each other's company. It was a great pity that Matthew found himself weighing them up, one by one, wondering how each would react to being told that he was a dissident. Not that there was anyone to tell them, but it was amusing to speculate. He was glad the conversation remained uncontroversial because argument was the last thing he wanted. His travels were touched upon but he was not required to explain what he had been doing; it was taken for granted that any research he might have been engaged upon would be to strengthen the arguments of the landowners. Perhaps it was cowardly not to enlighten them, but he could see no advantage in doing so, and besides, the longer he stayed the more convinced he became that this was not where he belonged.

The two young ladies, Miss Charlotte Makepiece and Miss Caroline Deane, whom Amy had determined would fall instantly in love with him, did not do so, any more than he did with either of them. One dark, one fair, they were pretty enough in a pale kind of way and their manners were exactly what one would expect of young ladies brought up in the very best social circles. They picked at their food, drank only a mouthful of wine each, took part in the conversation only when invited to do so and then vouchsafed no opinions of their own. They had none of Amy's flair, nor Kate's fire. Kate would have had plenty to say, if she had been there; she would have eaten with a hearty appetite and not been afraid to speak her mind. It was funny how his thoughts turned so frequently to Kate, how much he missed her. How was she settling down at Haddow Hall ? Would she be able to come to terms with service in a large house ? Her work would be very much the same as the servants in his father's kitchens. And he didn't know a single one of them by name.

'Matthew, how do you expect to make an impression when you make no push to be agreeable ?' Amy said, when all the guests had left and the family were sitting by the embers of the drawing room fire in drowsy contentment. 'I cannot think what Caroline and Charlotte thought of you.'

'Was I disagreeable ?' he said. 'Oh dear, and I thought I was being especially careful to treat them both the same and show no favourite.'

'And in that way, managed to give the impression you did not care for either.'

'It may simply have been that he did not care for either, Amy, my dear,' Daniel put in. 'You must not bully him. You will send him away again.'

'Oh, no,' she cried. 'I didn't mean to.' She turned to Matthew, who wished sincerely that the subject could be dropped. 'I am sorry, Matthew. I should hate myself if I thought I had driven you away. You won't go, will you ?'

'I certainly will not go because of anything you have said or done,' he said carefully.

Thankfully she did not pursue her questions and they all said goodnight and retired to their respective bedrooms. And the next day all was bustle and hustle as they prepared for the hunt.

His lordship had heard there was a dog fox in the spinney on the hill above the village and he was determined to ride to hounds in its pursuit. Amy intended to take the gig to some high ground where she might view the chase and Thomas had been told he could ride his pony alongside for a little way. Matthew had not hunted for years, but he was looking forward to it, as he dressed and went down to the stables where the huntsmen were congregating, surrounded by milling dogs. They trotted out of the yard and up the hill towards the spinney with the hounds barking and yelping. They had been riding for perhaps half an hour when reynard was spotted, the view halloo was sounded and everyone, dogs, horses, men, set off in pursuit.

The fox led them across the top of the hill and disappeared in a copse of trees. For a minute or two they thought they had lost it, but the dogs flushed it out and it was off again, streaking down the hill towards the village with twenty blood-thirsty hounds after it. The riders followed, thundering down the village street, trampling down hedges and gardens without a second's hesitation. Matthew, slightly behind, could see the destruction and, not wishing to add to it, began to pull up. A little black and white terrier burst out of the door of one of the cottages and rushed at one of the horses, barking furiously; his territory had been invaded and the brave little chap meant to defend it. There was nothing the rider could do; the flying hooves sent the little dog flying against the wall of the cottage, where it lay still. As horse and rider galloped on, a child hardly bigger than Thomas ran out of the cottage, followed by his shrieking mother.

'Dickie! Dickie, come back!'

Matthew was almost on top of them. He tried to turn his mount, but the stallion took exception to the violence of the command and reared up, throwing him. He landed with a sickening thud almost at the feet of the woman. She ran to help him. 'Oh, sir, are you hurt?'

Matthew sat up, grinning; it was a very long time since he had come off a horse like that. 'A few bruises, no bones broken, I think.'

'Dickie didn't mean any harm, sir. He was worried about his little dog. When I saw the hunt coming I told him to tie it up but it slipped its leash.' She was kneading her hands together in anguish. 'Please don't punish him. It was the dog, it was his pet, you see. Oh, please . . .'

He scrambled to his feet and attempted to brush the mud from his breeches. 'Madam, why should I punish him? It was I in the wrong.' He turned towards the child who was sitting on the ground, his back against the wall, with the dog's head in his lap. Tears were coursing down his face. 'He's dead,' he cried. 'He's dead.'

Matthew went over and knelt beside him. 'Let me see.'

The dog's neck had been broken. 'I'm sorry,' he said. 'But he didn't suffer, did he? It was quick and clean.'

'You did it! You killed him!'

'Dickie!' His horrified mother remonstrated with him. 'You must not speak to the gentleman so, you must not.'

Matthew smiled, trying to reassure her. 'Why not, if that's how he feels? I do not blame him.'

'But you are one of Lord Thorsborough's guests...'

'I am his son and I do not see what that has to do with it. The hunt was in the wrong to come stampeding through the village in the first place. He reached out and put his hand on the boy's shoulder. 'He was a brave little fellow, wasn't he?'

The boy nodded, sniffing.

'And you must be brave too. Now, dry your eyes and we'll see about finding you a new puppy.'

'Won't be Spot,' he mumbled, wiping his nose on his sleeve.

'No, I am afraid it won't. We cannot bring Spot back.' Gently he prised the dead animal from the child's grasp. Shall we bury him? And then you shall come up to the stables at the Manor and choose a puppy. I know there is a new litter there.'

Still sniffing the boy allowed the dog to be taken from him and stood by while his mother fetched a spade and showed Matthew where to dig. When the body was covered, Matthew gave the woman a guinea to compensate her for her ruined vegetable patch and caught his horse which had been cropping the grass at the side of the road, then he hoisted Dick up in front of the saddle and mounted behind him. 'Do not worry,' he told the woman. 'We'll send him back safe and sound.'

The boy had brightened considerably and by the time they rode into the stableyard he was chatting away as if they had known each other for years. The yard was crowded. The hunt had just returned and the riders were dismounting. Servants went in and out among them with refreshments. Amy stood in conversation with one of their neighbours. She had her hand on Thomas's shoulder. The boy's face was covered with blood, but his eyes sparkled with pleasure. He saw his uncle before his mother did and broke away to meet him.

'Uncle Matt! Uncle Matt! I saw the kill and I have been blooded.'

'So I see,' Matthew said, dismounting. 'Don't you think you should go and have your face washed? You look as though you've been in a battle.'

'Grandpapa cut the brush off and put it on my face, so.' He put his hand to his cheeks, making a wiping movement first on one side then the other. 'I'm going to keep it.' Then seeing the boy in Matthew's saddle, wrinkled his nose. 'Who's that?'

'This is Dick,' Matthew said, lifting the child down. 'And he is going to have one of Bess's pups. Would you like to take him to choose one?'

Tom recoiled at the sight of the ragged little boy. 'No. I don't like him, he's dirty. And why should he have one of Bess's pups?'

'Because the hunt killed his little dog and I have promised him he shall have a new one.'

'Why?'

'Why? In order to recompense him.'

Amy, hearing the altercation, excused herself and joined them. 'What is the matter?'

'Nothing is the matter,' Matthew said. 'I promised this young man a puppy, but Tom declines to take him to choose one.' He could not keep the annoyance from his voice. It was not so much that Tom begrudged the puppy which was not his to give anyway, but his attitude. Dick was beneath him and he was making no attempt to hide it. He didn't blame his nephew, who only reflected the manners and attitudes of those around him and that was what he found so disappointing. 'I thought Tom might befriend him and help him to overcome his loss.'

'I do not propose to force him,' Amy said, wrinkling her pretty little nose. 'The boy is probably alive with vermin. Why did you have to bring him home with you? You could have sent the puppy or better still given him some money. No doubt his mother could have put it to better use than buying a dog.'

'Mister, it don' matter,' Dick said, looking from one to the other and wise enough in spite of his few years, to realise he was the cause of discord. 'I'll go 'ome now.'

'No, you don't,' Matthew said, grabbing his coat collar to prevent him running away. 'I said you shall have a new puppy and so you shall. Come with me.'

He took the boy across the yard, making his way through the crowds towards his father, who was standing beside his brother, surveying the scene and thoroughly satisfied with the way the day had gone. 'Father, the hunt killed this young shaver's pet dog. I would like to give him a puppy from Bess's litter. May I?'

'Yes, but speak to the kennelmaster first. There's bound to be a runt among them. Give him that.'

It was the best Matthew could do. The boy was given the smallest of the litter and one of the stable lads who lived in the village was detailed to see him safely home. Matthew went indoors to change, feeling more than a little dejected. The incident was only a small thing and they did not mean to be unkind, but it only served to point out the great divide between rich and poor and he knew the problem was too great for one man or one lifetime to solve. He was right; he should not have come home. He would stay for Christmas because he had said he would, but after that he would leave again, go back to Middleacre. Back to Kate.

Chapter Eight

Christmas Day at Haddow Hall was hardly different from any other day, except that the servants were expected to go to church and Mrs Wisdom had decreed there should be a feast for all her fine friends, many of whom were to stay until the wedding. Kate, in freshly laundered uniform, went to early morning service, where she found herself weighing up every man in the congregation and wondering what would happen to his family if his wages were cut. It would finish many of them. They would either lose all hope and sink into lethargy, taking poor relief and starving little by little, or they would rebel against it, as others had done, burning ricks and breaking machinery, risking prison and deportation, even death. The authorities may have thought they had captured Captain Swing, but the inflammatory letters and pamphlets were still appearing, still signed with the name of that notorious captain, though there were fewer of those. On the other hand, the trouble was spreading to the towns; she had heard of textile and paper mills being attacked and their owners threatened and of poorhouses being burned down. It was all very worrying.

There had to be another way. That was what Captain Tolley had been trying to explain to her, wasn't it? Violence only led to more violence and did no good; he had set himself the task of preventing it. For the first time, she could clearly see Matthew's role and she wondered how she could have been so blind. But Sir John would not look at it in that light; as far as he was concerned Matthew was an insurgent. It did not make her problem any easier to solve; it made it more difficult. A hundred times more difficult. It was Captain Tolley's name and whereabouts Sir John wanted, she was sure of it now. Much as she longed to see the captain again, she hoped he would not return, not until all the troubles were over and there was peace again. But how was that to be brought about?

Her thoughts, which should have been on her devotions, tumbled about in her head and did little to cheer her. She was glad when the service came to an end and Sir John, Mrs Wisdom, Mrs Carrington, Mr Carrington-Haddow and all the house guests left the church and, after greeting one or two of the more prosperous members of the congregation who were not ill disposed towards them, climbed into their coach for the short ride back to the Hall, leaving the servants to make their way on foot.

As soon as they were all back, their coats and cloaks taken off and hung up and aprons tied on, the real business of the day began. The goose, which had been put in the oven before they left, was basted, the plum pudding put on to boil, glasses and plate polished, vegetables and sauces prepared, fish, ham, pork and chicken cooked, wine decanted. And after it had all been taken to the dining room and only half of it consumed, the remnants were brought down again and the task of clearing up began. Because it was Christmas and because everyone knew they would reap their reward in as much food and drink as they could consume at the end of the day, they worked with a will, taking a sip of beer here, a nip of wine there, until they were all laughing and joking and as merry as could be; even Bertha forgot to grumble and Johnson relaxed enough to join in.

Kate, with her arms up to the elbows in greasy washing up water, wondered what her Pa was doing. She had paid for a little extra in the way of food and bought a quart bottle of ale and asked William Chapman to make sure it was delivered, but it was little enough. If only he could have some of what was even now being thrown into the pail in the corner to be used for pig swill! Why did they have to prepare so much more than they needed? And the wedding in a few days' time, would be even worse. The preparations for that would begin as soon as Christmas was over. After that Sir John and his bride would be off on their wedding trip and perhaps they would all be left in peace. But knowing Sir John, she doubted it; he was like a dog with a bone, he would not let go. That was why there was to be a vestry meeting two days hence; he was planning something diabolical.

What kind of Christmas was Matthew having? Was he with friends and family, having a happy time? Did he have a family? She realised how little she knew about him. And how little she knew about herself. A wayside waif, that was all she was, beneath anyone's notice, except, perhaps Charlie Barber's. He was a nice

boy and he loved her; ought she to have turned him down so
firmly? Would she ever have any other offers? Was it Pa who had
made her discontent by telling her to aim for something higher or
was it Matthew's close questioning that had set her thinking about
her origins, filling her with doubts. 'Stop it!' she commanded
herself, picking up a pile of dirty plates and dropping them into the
water. 'Stop this foolishness.' After a minute, she began to sing
quietly. *'The holly and the ivy, when they are all full grown ...'*

Mrs Bunny smiled. The girl was settling down after all. 'It's not
so bad, is it?' she said. 'It could be worse.'

'I suppose so.'

'A good supper tonight and the vails box to be opened tomorrow.'
The box had stood on a table outside the kitchen door all year to
receive whatever tips Sir John's guests chose to put into it.

'Little enough that'll have in it,' Bertha said, picking up a pail of
water and pouring it into the copper beside the fire, filling the
room with hissing steam. 'What with Sir John being away most of
the year, who's bin here to put aught in it?'

'There was that dinner party last week and guests in the house
now, they will have given something,' Mrs Bunny said. 'And Mrs
Carrington has always been generous.'

''An' you c'n say what you like about Mrs Wisdom,' Hetty put
in. 'She in't mean.'

'If'n there's enough, I'm a-goon to buy myself a new bonnet,'
Bertha said. 'And something for Thomas. He bought me a linen
handkerchief. What about you, Kate?'

'Oh, I'll buy something for Pa, some tobacco perhaps.'

'You got a beau?'

'No, of course not.' But she blushed crimson as she said it, and
they drew their own conclusions, for how were they to know it was
of Matthew Tolley she was thinking?

'It's Charlie Barber, in't it?' Bertha said. 'I saw him in church,
sitting on the other side of the aisle, lookin' sheep's eyes at you.'

'He's just a friend.' She could not understand why they all
laughed. There was so much she did not understand about their
banter and there was no one she could ask. Never, since her
father's arrest, had she felt more alone. She had no right to any
man's love, when she could not even tell him her name and
birthday. Mrs Barber was aware of that and so was Captain Tolley,
so was everyone else. Why had Pa said she was destined for a

better life? Did he really know or was he simply speaking out of his deep love for her, because that was what he wished her to have?

She did not line up in the hall with all the other servants when Sir John and Mrs Wisdom opened the vails box with a great deal of pompous ceremony the following morning; she did not intend to risk him seeing her. She made an excuse to stay at her post in the kitchen, cleaning vegetables. No one seemed to have noticed her absence, for they returned to the kitchen clutching a few coins each, planning aloud how they would spend them. She hoped Sir John had forgotten her.

Johnson, returning to the kitchen after the family had been served with their midday meal, disabused her of that idea. He sank into a kitchen chair and picked up a glass of punch Mrs Bunny put in front of him. 'You'd think they'd have something better to talk about than those pesky rebels, wouldn't you?' he said.

'What are they saying?' Kate asked, doing her best to sound casual.

'Oh, Sir John still means to catch the ringleader.'

Kate's heart sank. 'Did he say how he was going to do it?' she asked.

'No, I reckon he'll announce something at the vestry meeting tomorrow.'

'What's he going to say?'

'How should I know? But if you think it's got you off the hook, you may think again because I'll wager he hasn't forgotten.'

'What do you mean?' Mrs Bunny asked when Kate did not reply.

'So she didn't tell you?' He grinned. 'The Master asked her for the name of the men's leader, I heard him. She knows.'

'No, I don't,' Kate protested. 'I don't know anything.'

Mrs Bunny looked at Kate then back at Johnson. 'Course she doesn't,' she said. 'Who'd tell her? They don't like her in the village, she's a foreigner.'

'Is that so? Then perhaps it's you he should be talking to. You know them all.'

'Me?' she asked, while Kate held her breath. 'I live and work here in this house, when do I have time for tittle-tattle? Now, I've got things to do if you haven't.' And with that she disappeared into the pantry, leaving Kate facing the valet.

'They've all gone into the drawing room now,' he told her. 'So you can go and help Hetty clear the dining room.'

That was the last thing she wanted to do; if Sir John saw her she would be in trouble again. 'I'm busy.'

'So am I. Sir John wants me. And it isn't for you to choose what you will and will not do.' He called to Mrs Bunny. 'That's so, isn't it, Grace?'

'Go on,' she said, addressing Kate over her shoulder. 'Hetty'll be all day if she's not helped and she'll never get off.' Hetty had been promised the rest of the day off to visit her mother as soon as all the work was done.

Kate went reluctantly, scuttling along the hall with her head down, telling herself what a coward she was.

Hetty was stacking dishes on a tray and looked up as Kate entered. 'You took your time,' she said. 'We're all behind hand. I told me ma I'd be home by one.'

Kate collected up the glasses and put them on a tray, wondering why they had to have a different one for every person for each wine; whoever had decided that, obviously didn't have to wash and polish them. She was about to leave the room with the tray when her eye caught sight of a newspaper, rolled up behind the coal scuttle. Its headline caught her eye and her heart missed a beat. 'Captain Swing arrested in Suffolk,' it said. So Mr Carrington-Haddow had been right! She put the tray down and bent to pick it up, stuffing it into her apron pocket.

'What do you want with that?' Hetty asked.

'I want to read it.'

'Why, what do it say?'

'They've caught Captain Swing,' Kate said, picking up her tray again and hurrying back to the kitchen where she dumped it on the table before sitting down and smoothing out the creases in the paper and looking at the date. 'This is over a se'nnight old.'

'Well, I'll swear it weren't there yesterday,' Hetty said, defending herself for it was her task to clean and tidy the ground floor rooms. 'I picked it up offa the coal box to mek the fire draw this mornin'. I reckon Sir John or mebbe Mister Andrew must ha' thrown it there.'

'Left what?' Mrs Bunny asked, crossing the kitchen to look over Kate's shoulder. 'The mystery of the identity of Captain Swing is resolved,' she read aloud, picking it up and taking it closer to the lamplight, frustrating Kate who wanted to read it herself. 'Yesterday, 16th December, a man was arrested in Stradishall in Suffolk. He is John Saville, a straw-plait merchant from Luton, a gentleman of means who is well known in his own parish for good works.'

Everyone was crowding round now, Mrs Bunny, Bertha and Hetty, Maud and the tousle-haired back'us boy, even Johnson, who had come into the kitchen a few moments after Kate. 'They surely did not arrest him for that,' Bertha said. 'Does it say what else he done? Is there aught about Middleacre?'

'No,' Mrs Bunny said. 'Why should there be?' She paused. 'Why did he call himself Captain, I wonder.'

'Perhaps he was a captain once.'

'He's been travelling about the eastern counties in a green gig,' Mrs Bunny went on.

'There! What did I tell you?' Bertha said. 'I said weeks ago it was a jin'leman in a green gig, didn' I?'

'I thought it was a joke,' Kate said, remembering Matthew had mentioned the man too and laughed at the idea.

'It's no joke,' the cook went on. 'According to this, he had five hundred and eighty pounds about his person and had been going round asking questions about labourers' wages and threshing machines. But worst of all, he was carrying a large number of in ... inflam ...' She struggled over the word. 'inflammatory notices, all signed Swing. The paper quotes some of them.'

'Let me see,' Kate said, holding out her hand.

'Read it to us,' Bertha said, for neither she nor Hetty could read and they were agog with curiosity.

Mrs Bunny passed the paper over. 'Oh, ye church of England parsins, who strain at a gnat and swallor a cammell,' Kate read aloud. 'Woe, woe, woe be unto you, ye shall one day have your reward.' It did not sound like Matthew at all; it was far too flowery and badly spelled. She read on. 'Will you parsons pay us better for our labour, if you wont we will put you in bodily fear.' That, too, was unlike Matthew.

'It's all squit,' Mrs Bunny said idiomatically. 'The man's a ranter.'

'He was given twelve months in prison and fined fifty pounds,' Kate said, looking again at the paper.

'If the man were really Captain Swing and had done all the

things the captain is supposed to have done, he'd have copped a lot more'n that,' Mrs Bunny said.

Kate admitted she was probably right. If John Saville was not Captain Swing, then who and where was the famous captain? And if he truly had the labourers' cause at heart, why had he not stopped the wanton destruction as Matthew would have done? Was there a connection between John Saville and Matthew Tolley? Could they be one and the same? If the man they had arrested was Matthew, it would explain why he had not come back, wouldn't it? Oh, how she wished she could find out. She dare not mention his name in front of the others. 'You don't think he is the captain then?' she asked, hoping Mrs Bunny would understand whom she meant. 'It's not the end then?'

'End?' The cook laughed. 'I'll lay odds it's only the beginning.'

'Will the squire withdraw the reward, do you reckon?' Hetty queried. She still coveted that.

'No, why should he?' Johnson said. 'It's not Captain Swing he wants, but the man causing all the trouble here.'

'Captain Tolley,' Bertha said.

'How do you know his name?' Mrs Bunny demanded.

'Thomas told me. He said he'd seen him in The Ferryman.'

'When?' Kate asked, trying to keep the eagerness from her voice.

'I dunno. But he did say the Cap'n was coming back for the next Friendly Society meeting.' She could tell them no more; Thomas had obviously decided he had been indiscreet enough and had given her no further details.

Kate's heart was pumping like an engine. Had Matthew already returned? If he had, he was in great danger, for Sir John would have no mercy; if he did not find out what he wanted to know for himself, he would try and make her tell. And if it meant Pa's release, could she resist? The storm cloud which threatened her peace of mind seemed to gather over her, making her shiver, almost as if it were an omen. A few weeks before life had been simple and uncomplicated; she had had Pa and a home in the wagon and it seemed as if nothing could interrupt their way of life, hard though it was, but now, without her Pa to guide her and explain things, her emotions rode a see-saw, up one minute, down the next, but clearly, through it all, she knew she wanted desperately to see Matthew again. Somehow she had to get some time off.

In the event it was not as difficult as she feared, although she had to pretend she was going to meet Charlie. 'He's got time off,' she said, the following morning when, for a few moments, she and Mrs Bunny were alone in the kitchen. 'There's little enough work to keep the labourers busy and Mr Chapman won't detain him once the animals have been looked after.'

The housekeeper smiled. 'Who am I to stand in the way of young love? You can go after the clearing up is done this afternoon, but mind you're back to wash up after dinner. It'll be left for you if you're not. Now get on or you'll not be done in time.'

Kate set to with a will and as soon as her afternoon tasks were done, she changed out of the uniform which could so easily identify her, put on her old wool skirt and blouse, flung the black cloak over her shoulders and left the house.

The villagers did not usually attend vestry meetings, but they clearly meant to go to this one; almost every man and woman in Middleacre was making for the church and Kate followed them, keeping a sharp look out for Matthew. There was no sign of him and she was half glad, half sorry, as she squeezed herself in with the crowd. There was a great deal of jostling and because the gathering was well attended by farmers and village officials, they spilled out of the vestry into the church itself and it was difficult to separate those who were supposed to be there from those who were merely spectators. Squashed between Mrs Green and Mrs Barber, Kate could not move and resigned herself to staying where she was, looking round her as more and more crammed themselves into the tiny building.

There was Bert Chuckley and Nathaniel Green, married men with families; there was Charlie pretending not to look at her, blind Cally and his son-in-law; Barny Bullock, grown old and bent like the reeds on the fen where he spent his life fishing and wild fowling; and Moss, the baker, who found it hard to pay for the flour and still harder to sell his bread once baked, the price had risen so; there was the shoemaker, the basketmaker and thatcher; Bob Hall, the publican, the smithy and the harnessmaker and a host of farm labourers, young and old. Jack Watson was there with his wife and Betty. Kate envied Betty; there was no blackmail hanging over her head, she could move about freely and she was trusted by the villagers because she had been born and bred one of them. The little green god was working his mischief; Kate could not forget that Matthew had kissed Betty, not only kissed her but held her in his arms. He would not have done that if he did not like her and trust her. Kate turned away, just as Sir John entered and made his way through the crush to the vestry, where the parish elders waited for him.

As soon as the meeting had been called to order, the parish overseer began his report, most of which was concerned with the poor rates and the relief which had been given to those who could not earn a living wage, and that seemed to be most of the village, with the possible exception of those, like the blacksmith, the baker and the shoemaker who were self-employed although they could not fail to be affected by the general depression. With only half her attention Kate heard him say that the newly installed laundry at the poorhouse was keeping the women gainfully occupied and that twenty able-bodied men had been taken on to build the fences round the new enclosures.

'Traitors!' Nat Green shouted from beside his wife. 'Traitors! Where are they?' But none of the men who had been working on the fences could be seen; they had deemed it prudent to stay away.

'Bread or blood!' Barny Bullock shouted, echoing the cry of the Littleport riots of fourteen years before, still fresh in his memory because the consequences had been so tragic, five men hanged and many more deported and imprisoned. Kate wondered why he was there and so vociferous; he was one of a dying breed of fen slodger, living off what the fen could provide, fishing, fowling, harvesting the reeds and osiers, and answerable to no one. He did not rely on Sir John and his tenants for a livelihood.

'Give us a wage we can feed our little'ns on,' someone else yelled.

'Down with rents and tythes.' This from one of the smaller farmers.

There was a great deal more shouting and the meeting was getting out of hand. Sir John, who sat at the vestry table and could only be seen by those crowding in the doorway, leaned back in his chair and spoke to the Reverend Cox in an undertone. 'Get them out, parson. If you can't enforce discipline among your own flock in your own church, send them about their business. What are they doing here at all?'

The parson looked uncomfortable. 'It is a place of worship, Sir John, open and free to all.'

'Place of worship, is that what you call it? And are the voices of that rabble raised in praise of God?'

'It would appear not, Sir John.'

'Sir John, if I could have a few words.' William Chapman rose to address the meeting and because he was well liked and respected, the word was passed and the noise abated.

'The married labourers are asking two and six a day in summer and two and threepence in winter,' he said. 'We cannot pay this while our expenses are so high and the corn yield so low, yet we believe their demands are fair . . .'

'Demands!' repeated Sir John. 'Who are they to make *demands*? And my expenses, too, are high. In order to provide more work, I have had to instigate more enclosures which will benefit the whole village. The major cost of those has fallen to me, have you thought of that?' No one ventured a reply and he added, 'Because of that I have found it necessary to increase rents by five per cent.'

There were united cries of protest from the farmers. 'We cannot afford more rent,' William said on behalf of them all. 'You'll put us out of business.'

'Nonsense! You must become more efficient. If you were to take advantage of the advances in machinery now available, you would be able to pay your rent and the wages of the men you employ without having to come begging to me.'

'Troshin' machines!' someone shouted. 'A whole winter's work done by machines. How d'you expect us to live 'til spring do come ag'in? There's more in the poorhuss than ever afore.'

'That's not the fault of the threshing machines,' Sir John said levelly. 'And those in the poorhouse are not idle, they are given work for which they are paid.' He could not go on for the derisive laughter which greeted this statement.

'We have found no advantage in using the machinery, Sir John,' Chapman went on when he could make himself heard. 'It only causes problems at the millers with all the grain arriving at once instead of being spread over the winter. And there is no cost advantage. I have undertaken not to use a threshing machine.' A great cheer went up at this and he had to wait for it to subside before he could go on. 'We, the farmers, respectfully urge Sir John and the Reverend most earnestly to consider reducing rent and tythes. We will undertake to pass on any reduction to the men in wages.'

'Those on low wages get poor relief,' Sir John said, when the cheers had died down. 'And who pays the bulk of that? I do.'

'Charity!' Watson shouted. 'We want work and a living wage, not handouts.'

'Then you must speak to your employer.'

'He do stand beside you,' Watson said, nodding towards the parson. 'And we all know whose side he's on.'

Sir John turned to look at the Reverend Mr Cox who was clearly uncomfortable. He ran his finger round the inside of his stock and cleared his throat. 'I need the tythes . . .'

'To buy hunters and pink coats,' Bert Chuckley muttered. 'He keeps the best stables in the county.'

If the villagers had hoped that Sir John would acknowledge that he was tying the hands of the farmers, they were disappointed. He was in no mood to make concessions and because of the number of villagers present, he seized the opportunity to deliver a lecture and a stern warning of the consequences of being led into unlawful acts by irresponsible troublemakers. 'Such actions do not put food into your mouths,' he said, forgetting that the vestry meeting was usually held behind closed doors, and addressing the villagers directly. 'The land must be worked and put to profitable use to provide food and work for all.'

'Don' you believe it,' said a voice from the back of the crowd. 'Profits for the landowners, you do mean. It don' seem to mek no difference to our wages.'

Sir John peered into the crowd, trying to identify the speaker but the ranks of the villagers had closed and their expressions were uniformly resentful. 'You cannot have one without the other . . .' But he could not go on for the hubbub that followed.

'Silence! That's enough!' Sir John banged on the ancient oak table with a paperweight, his red face showing the extent of his anger. When at last he could make himself heard, he went on, 'Because I believe you have been led astray by someone who does not have your interests at heart, as I do . . .' There were more jeers before he could continue. 'I have decided to offer a reward for the apprehension of this man. If he is delivered up to me there will be no questions asked, no recriminations, and we can all go about our business in peace again. I will pay fifty pounds.'

There was a concerted gasp at the huge amount and every man looked at his neighbour, wondering who might be tempted by it, but then turned back to hear the rest of Sir John's message. 'I shall be at home until Saturday afternoon to any man, woman or child bringing me the information.'

While they looked from one to the other, trying to gauge who might weaken and who stand firm, he added as if only then remembering it, 'I called this meeting to notify those who need to know, of my impending absence and to complete unfinished parish business before I leave on my honeymoon.' He paused, noting the half-concealed jeers, but ignoring them, then went on in what he considered a more cheerful tone. 'According to custom, there will be a feast for the whole village in the big barn of Home Farm on Saturday, so that you, too, may celebrate my nuptials.'

His announcement was greeted by silence and then a mixture of cheers and boos and, realising his generosity was not going to placate them, he stood up and gathered up his crop, hat and gloves. 'The business of the day is done,' he said. 'The meeting is closed.' Then he left the church, followed by the parson, the village constable and the overseer, convinced that he had handled matters with his usual firm efficiency and had nothing to fear from the villagers who were no more than overgrown children and needed to be treated as such.

In stony silence they watched him mount his grey mare and ride off. The Reverend Cox, his black robes clinging to his spindly legs, made his way along the church path and disappeared through the gate into the vicarage garden. The farmers, who had been talking quietly together, mounted horses or climbed into traps and headed for home. They looked defeated, unhappy men. The villagers knew it was not the farmers' fault, they were being pressed by Sir John and labourers alike but, for all that, some jeered and hissed at their employers as they passed and others shouted obscenities.

Kate, emerging from the church, noticed the men did not hurry to return to their homes, although it was already growing dark. A small group gathered on the village green near the pump, another at Watson's gate, and yet another by the open door of the smithy, where the clang of hammer on anvil filled the air as if heralding some great event. There was an expectant calm which was almost eery. What were they waiting for?

She dawdled, reluctant to return to Haddow Hall, although she had promised Mrs Bunny she would not be gone above an hour. She wanted to stay in the village, to find out if Matthew had really returned, to speak to him, to reassure herself that he had nothing to do with any trouble that was brewing. And it was brewing, she could feel it in her bones. Was it possible to stand on the sidelines and deliberately shut your eyes to it? She could not; she was too curious, too concerned, too anxious, to remain a spectator.

She was standing on the village green, not far from the inn, when she saw the man who filled her thoughts. Silhouetted against the great canopy of the darkening sky, he came striding down the lane from Lowacre, his head thrown back, his arms swinging, as if he had nothing in all the world to fear.

He stopped when he came abreast of her, looking down into her eyes and turning her insides to jelly. 'Well, Kate?' he said, with a quirky smile. 'How are you?'

'I'm well,' she said, hoping he could not see that she was shaking like a reed in the wind and all because he looked into her eyes. 'You came back then?'

'I came back.'

'Perhaps it would have been better if you had stayed away.'

'You are not pleased to see me?'

'Yes. No. Oh, I didn't mean that,' she said. It was unfair of him to make her feel so uncomfortable, as if she were in the wrong. 'You confuse me.'

'Why?' His voice was gentle. 'Why do I confuse you?'

'I don't know.' If he would only declare himself for Sir John it would be easy; she would know his was not the name the squire wanted. But if he did that, then she could no longer admire him and she certainly could not love him. Love him! It was the first time that idea had crossed her mind and it embedded itself there and refused to be shifted, though she was well aware how foolish it was. 'I was worried when I heard about John Saville.'

'John Saville, who the devil's he?' he asked, feigning ignorance.

'They said he was Captain Swing and arrested him.'

He roared with laughter. 'And you thought . . .'

'I don't see what's so funny.'

'My dear Kate, I'm neither John Saville nor Captain Swing.'

'But you are involved, aren't you? That's why you're here again, to go to the meeting.'

'Meeting? What do you know of a meeting?'

'There's to be a Friendly Society meeting, everyone knows that. Even Sir John, I'll wager.'

'I expect there is little he cannot discover if he has a mind to,' he said, making her quake with anxiety. Did he know? Did he know what Sir John had asked of her? 'Kate, it would be better if you went home, out of harm's way.'

'I have as much right to be in the village as you have,' she said, more sharply than she intended. 'More so, because you are not a Middleacre man.'

'And you are not a Middleacre woman,' he retorted. 'Does that make either of us care any the less?'

'And do you care?'

'Naturally, I do.' He cared. He cared so much he had left home and family to be here, but she would not understand the wrench that had been. He tried to imagine her reaction if he were to tell her what kind of home he came from. Would she hate him, as she hated Sir John? All landowners, she had said, as if they were a species apart.

'I went to the vestry meeting,' she said. 'Sir John said he'd give fifty pounds to anyone telling him the name and whereabouts of the leader of the rebels.'

'And you think I am he?'

'I do not know. But if you are, then you are in grave danger; the squire will have no mercy.'

'Kate, there is nothing he can charge me with,' he said. 'I have done nothing illegal. Do not worry about me.'

'How can I help it? And there's Pa ...'

'What about him?'

'Sir John said he was ill.'

He did not ask her how Sir John came to speak to her of her father; he could guess. No wonder she looked worried. 'Kate,' he said, taking her shoulders in his hands and speaking slowly in order to convince her. 'I have nothing to fear from Sir John and neither have the villagers as long as they do not break the law.'

'But the squire is going to put up the farmers' rents so that they have to cut the men's wages. He thinks it will make them more submissive, but I don't think it will. It will make them more angry, won't it?'

'Perhaps. Now, go and leave the men to decide what is to be done.' He bent his head to drop a kiss on her forehead. She swayed a little towards him and found herself in his arms with her head nestling on his chest.

'Oh, Kate,' he murmured, holding her and stroking her hair. 'Get you gone before I do something I'll regret.'

More puzzled than ever, she lifted her head to look into his face and was surprised to see a look of anguish, as if she had hurt him. But she had not hurt him; she would never hurt him because she loved him.

He pushed her gently from him. 'Go home, Kate,' he said again. Then he turned to go into The Ferryman without waiting to see if she obeyed. He had returned to help her find her family and instead had come back to find the people of Middleacre in more ferment. If he did not concentrate on the job in hand, they would take the law into their own hands and that could make things a hundred times worse. 'Kate, my love,' he murmured to himself as he made his way through the parlour to a room at the back, where the men, noisy, argumentative and in many cases pot-valiant, had been gathering in ones and twos for the last half hour. 'We must be patient.'

Once more in command of his emotions, he moved to a table at one end of the room, climbed onto it and turned to face them. Their reaction to the squire's treatment of them at the vestry meeting ranged from a resigned acceptance of their deteriorating living conditions, a sort of hopelessness born of helplessness, to advocating downright rebellion and tearing Haddow Hall apart, brick by brick, and hanging its owner from one of his own trees.

'That won't serve,' Matthew said, when he could make himself heard. 'That would be rioting and Sir John would call in the militia and we can't fight armed men. The only way you can better your lot is by combining in a union and negotiating from a position of strength. If we stand firm, we don't need to use violence. The farmers can't work the land or rear the animals without help.' He paused, watching their faces. 'We've got to get our heads together with other villages. I have just come from Lowacre ...'

'Lowacre!' said Nathaniel Green contemptuously. 'That there lot would blab everything all over the countryside. T'squire would hear of it in the time it takes to say amen.'

'It do seem to me,' Bert Chuckley said. 'T'squire do hear whatever we do. How'd he git to know how we wor in the drovers' hut afore? Someone must ha' towd 'im.'

'That there poacher do know more'n 'e's tellin',' Green went on. 'I reckon 'e's the one.'

'He was just bumbling about minding his own business,' Matthew put in quickly. 'And he did us a service when he distracted Sir John's men off the hunt for us. You must know he was put into the Bridewell for his pains.'

'What about the poacher's daughter. She could ha' towd.'

'No, she didn't,' Charlie called out and blushed scarlet. 'Kate wouldn' do that.'

Matthew smiled; the boy was obviously in love with Kate. Was Kate in love with him? Ought he to leave well alone? 'Anyone could have told Sir John or he could simply have used his own eyes and ears,' he said. 'But recrimination does not help your cause. The squire knows what you think of him and he knows what the increase in rents will do to his tenants.'

'We in't worrited 'bout 'is bloody tenants.' Green shouted.

'Then you should be. Higher rents mean lower wages; it's as simple as that.'

'The farmers won't pay them,' Chuckley said.

'They hen't got no choice.' This from Watson.

'Are we goin' to sit by and let it happen?' Green shouted. 'Let's show 'em now. We'll march on the farms. Wages hatta be riz or we fire the ricks ...'

There was a chorus of assent and Matthew had to shout to make himself heard. 'What good will that do? Will it put money into your pockets, food in your children's mouths? Will it give you more work?'

'No, but it will shurrly mek us feel a hull lot better,' Green said, grinning.

'You'll hang yourselves if you resort to violence,' Matthew said, smiling because he knew exactly how Green felt. 'You must combine and do it peaceably. Ask Sir John to reduce the farmers' rents and tythes or waive them altogether this quarter so they can pay you a living wage.'

'Farmer Chapman ha' already tried that at the vestry,' Nat Green told him. 'We heard him with our own ears and it made not a pin head's difference. Squire's determined on it.'

'The farmers have tried, now it's your turn,' Matthew said.

'He'll niver listen to us,' someone said.

'He must be given the chance,' Matthew insisted. 'And only if that fails should action be taken.'

'What action?'

144

'Withdraw your labour.'

'If by that, you mean strike, do you forget it,' someone said. 'We can't do that. We'd starve.'

'It would not last long if every single one of you agreed to stick it out,' Matthew said. 'There would be a fund to help those in need.'

'And where would this 'ere fund come from? Our wages, I dessay. If'n we had any bloody wages to speak of.'

'From your wages yes, but the fund will take time to build up and until it does, you have friends, sympathisers who will help you. You will not go hungry, at least no more than you are now, that I promise you. But first you must try negotiation.'

'Who'll do that? Who'll square up to t'squire? Will you?'

He would go if he had to, but if Sir John were to learn his true identity, it would be the end of any help he could offer, either to them or to Kate. It was extraordinary how she came into his mind at the most inappropriate moments. He could see her now, standing in the lane, head thrown back, eyes bright with defiance. He had to make sure she suffered no more, either on his account or the old poacher's. Sometimes he felt like strangling Josiah Brough. But that was unfair because he did not know the full story and until he did, he would make no judgements.

He became aware that his listeners were all looking at him, waiting for an answer. 'If necessary, I will,' he said. 'But Sir John will only say I am not a true representative of the Middleacre workers, it would be better if it were a spokesman from among you.'

Silently they looked from one to the other. No one was willing to face Sir John and his wrath for the personal retribution he would reap; courage was one thing in a crowd when you'd taken a drink and another when you were alone and stone cold sober. No one volunteered.

Before Matthew could speak again, a noise at the back of the room made them turn towards the door to see Jack Watson pushing Kate into the room in front of him. 'Look what I found,' he said. 'Spyin' at t'winder, she wor.'

Chapter Nine

*M*atthew frowned in annoyance as Watson hauled Kate towards the platform, and though she knew his anger was probably justified, she was determined to stand her ground. 'I wasn't spying,' she protested. 'I am one of you.'

'That you in't,' Nat Green said. 'Niver hev bin. And t'squire did gi'e you work and a hoom an' all when you in't ever been in service afore. He didn't do that fer narth'n'. What did you do fer 'im, eh?'

'Nothing. Hiring servants is not something he bothers his head with,' she said. 'His housekeeper took me on.' She wished she hadn't been reminded of the blackmail. If Sir John asked her again for the name of the labourers' leader, what would she say? She may not have known it the first time, but she had heard enough while eavesdropping to be certain of it now. Matthew had said he would trust her with his life, but had he realised how soon and how brutally it would become necessary? Could she stand up to Sir John and defy him to do his worst? And Pa, what would happen to Pa if she did? 'The Squire took my Pa from me and burned down my home. I have every reason to hate him.'

'We don't need to involve women,' Matthew said quietly, though his expression clearly said, 'See what you've done now?'

'But everyone is involved, from old Mr Bullock to the youngest babe,' she said, facing him out. 'What you're doing concerns me as much as any of you and I want to help.'

'Help,' Jack Watson said. 'What c'n you do? You're only ...'

'I'm only the poacher's daughter, is that what you were going to say?' She looked round the room of watchful, wary men. 'So I may be, but I am a worker just like you.'

'She brung us food,' put in Silas Gotobed, Cally's son-in-law. 'She didn' hatta do that.'

'An' that's like to mek matters a deal worse, come the squire finds out,' Watson said, still angry over it. 'We in't thieves.'

'No?' queried Charlie. 'And what do you call it when you go round axin' fer money off'n the houses for yar Friendly Society and threatenin' them tha' refuse ...?'

'Thass only axin' for donations to the fund,' Green said. 'Tin't the same.'

'Parson do hev a mind to hev us all up a-front o' the beak for threatenin' behaviour, after the ruction at the vestry,' Watson said. 'He ha' towd me so.'

'He do be bluffin',' Chuckley told him. 'He can't tek us all.'

'I'll do whatever you want of me,' Kate said, wondering how they would ever get anything done if all they did was argue about it.

'Thass it!' Green said suddenly. 'The poacher's daughter can be our spokesman.'

'No!' Matthew spoke sharply, wishing she had done as he had asked and gone home. Why did she have to be so stubborn? She was looking at him now with defiance in her blue eyes and yet, behind that defiance was something else. Fear, perhaps, but that was something he had never noticed in her before. What had caused it? The squire? The villagers? Had it something to do with the old poacher?

'Why not? Let her prove she's with us.'

'Have some sense man, Sir John would not take her seriously.'

'Then we put our demands in a letter and the girl c'n tek it to 'im,' Green said.

'No, it's too risky.'

'You mean she in't to be trusted? In that case ...' They all turned and looked menacingly at Kate.

Matthew was in a cleft stick. He had no idea what they would do if they thought she might betray them, but he knew it would not be pleasant. On the other hand, if Sir John found out she was in league with the rebels ... He looked from one to the other and then at Kate. 'This is not woman's work,' he said.

'Why not?' she retorted. 'Women are the ones who have to make ends meet, when all is said and done. I'll carry the letter and gladly.'

'And who's to sign such a letter?' a voice called from the body of the gathering. 'Who'd be prepared to put his mark to such a paper?'

'Cap'n Swing,' suggested someone. 'We use his name.'

'He ha' bin took to chokey,' Charlie said.

'That don' mek no matter, we c'n do it anyway.' Green laughed suddenly. 'That'll gi'e 'em summat to scratch their heads o'er.'

'I'll second that,' a dozen voices called.

'Very well.' There was a measure of relief in Matthew's voice. It was not the ideal solution, but they were in a volatile mood and if he refused, there was no telling what they would do. He wished fervently that Kate had kept her mind on her own affairs and left the men to theirs. 'But we must do it properly, swear an oath of secrecy and write it together. There'll be no going back. One way or another, we see it through.'

'Combine, you mean?'

'Yes. Do you agree?'

'Aye!' they roared.

Listening to him bringing them to order, Kate was struck by the contrast between him and the other men. He stood out head and shoulders, not only physically but because of his articulate way of expressing himself, the way he carried his handsome head, his commanding presence. If it had been an army he led and not a handful of dissident labourers, he would have been a general. Now she understood why he had been sent for; he was just what the workers needed. He held their attention and their loyalty and they obviously trusted him. Strangely, she didn't resent it, because now she felt part of the battle.

'Go outside, Kate, and wait for me.' Matthew sounded resigned as if he were giving in to the men when he did not really want to. Why not? Now she knew the truth, she would do whatever was asked of her. She wanted a fight; she *needed* a fight, something to do to make her feel she was avenging Pa. Reluctantly she left the room wondering why she was not to be allowed to take part in the drafting of the letter and swearing the oath.

A few minutes later Matthew came out of the inn with a folded paper in his hand, though he did not immediately give it to her. 'Can you leave this somewhere in the Hall where the squire will find it without knowing how it got there?'

'You don't want me to put it into his hand?'

He laughed at the relief in her voice. 'No, Kate, there is no need. We just want him to feel that nowhere is safe, not even his own home.'

'What have you said in the letter?'

'Read it,' he said, handing it to her. 'It's only fair you should know what you're doing.'

She took it and unfolded it. *To Sir John Haddow, Sqire. We, the labrers of Middleacre do rispectflly ax you to put down the rents and tell the parsin to leav off takin' tythes until times is better. We ax two shillins and thruppence a day for wages in winter and a gallon of bread for ev'ry chile til summer cum agin. We giv yew til saterday to do it or we stop all our work. Sined on behalf of all. Swing.*

Apart from the misspelling, it was written in a very spidery hand and she was puzzled. 'Who wrote it?'

He laughed. 'They all had a hand in it, a word at a time.'

'Not you?'

'No, it's their affair, I can only advise.'

'Why Saturday? It's his wedding day.'

'It's also the day he chose for his own ultimatum.' He paused and added, 'You know what happened at tonight's meeting is to be kept secret?'

'Of course. Is that why you swore an oath?'

'Yes.'

'Isn't that against the law?'

'Yes it is. It's to show our commitment to the cause, so that no one will betray any of the others ...' He had told Kate he had nothing to fear because he had done nothing against the law, but that was no longer true. Combining wasn't unlawful but swearing an illegal oath was. And so was writing a threatening letter. Because of Kate he was fully committed now; there was no more sitting on the fence. And he did not regret it.

'Aren't you afraid someone will give you up for the reward?'

'They won't break their oaths.'

'Not even for fifty pounds?' She wished she could be as confident as he sounded. 'It's a fortune to them.'

'I will risk it.'

'Why didn't you make me swear too?'

'There would have been no point, we could not hold you to such a vow.'

Did he think she would betray him? 'Then you still do not consider I am one of you?'

'Yes, you are, my lovely Kate, you have made yourself so. But it was not my wish, I would rather you had kept out of it.' He smiled and lifted her hand to his lips; she felt the warmth of it spreading up her arm and right through her, from her toes to her cheeks, which flamed under his scrutiny. She hadn't imagined those feelings before because they were with her again and this time there was no denying them. If this was love, then she loved and reason had gone by the board. If only he felt the same way about her, but she knew he did not and the knowledge was harder to bear when he was being kind to her; she would rather they were fighting, then she could mask her feelings with anger.

'Why should I stand by and do nothing when my friends need me?' she asked. 'I won't let them down or you either.'

'That's what I am afraid of,' he said. 'Your impetuosity, your stubbornness . . .'

'I'll be good. I'll do whatever you ask of me. I'll look and listen and tell you what goes on at the Hall, and run errands and keep out of Sir John's way. I will make myself useful. It is all I ask until Pa is free again.'

He smiled at her pronouncement that the villagers were her friends; he did not think they looked at it quite like that. They were using her because not one of them had the stomach to do what she had volunteered to do. To them, she was expendable. Looking at her now, he wished fervently he had not given in to them. 'No, I can't let you do it,' he said, retrieving the letter. 'I'll go myself . . .'

'Why? You do not trust me. I knew it.'

'It has nothing to do with not trusting you. If Sir John were to find out it was you . . .'

'You are prepared to take risks, then so am I.'

'You think you can stand up to him, do you? Oh, my dear Kate, you don't know what you are letting yourself in for. Sir John can be very persuasive.'

What did he mean? Did he know? Should she tell him of her dilemma? Unable to guess his likely reaction, she decided against it; she would cope with the problem herself. He smiled suddenly and added, 'But then, you are not one to be overawed by his bullying manner, are you?'

'Of course not.' Why couldn't she sound convincing? 'He doesn't frighten me.'

'And you will not be taken in by soft words and apparent sympathy?'

'Sir John sympathise! Pigs might fly.'

'There are others in the house.'

He meant Andrew Carrington-Haddow, she knew. 'I will be careful.'

'Good, because you know you are on trial? Your loyalty is being tested.' Even then he did not give her the letter.

'I know that.' She paused, trying to still the butterflies in her stomach. 'Captain Tolley, if you do not let me do this, the people will want to know why. They will cease to believe in you.' She laughed. 'Your fate is in my hands and you must trust me.'

He smiled wryly. Oh, how true that was! And she was completely unaware of the real reason. She had wound her fingers round his heart and he did not know how it had happened. More than anything he wanted to protect her and instead, he was being forced to send her into danger; if Sir John ever got wind of her involvement, Mrs Bunny could not help her, no one could. He sighed heavily. If he had known what would happen when the villagers had asked for Matthew Tolley's help, he might not have been so quick to agree. No, he contradicted himself, it would have made no difference, he would have come. Now he must extricate himself and Kate too ...

She took the letter from his fingers and pushed it down into the depths of her skirt pocket, smiling at him. He was looking down at her in such a strange way, as if he meant to say something but did not quite know how to begin. He had something on his mind besides the Middleacre troubles; he had hinted he was being searched for by others. Who? And what had he done? She felt a sudden urge to reassure him. 'I won't fail you.'

'I know that.' He bent to kiss her cheek, the touch of his lips light as a butterfly landing, then he gave her a gentle push to send her on her way. 'Off you go, my dear,' he said softly. 'God go with you and keep you safe.'

He watched her go with an ache in his heart. Whatever happened now, her destiny was bound up with his and there was nothing he could do about it.

From the window of his stepmother's room, where he had gone to bid her goodnight, Andrew saw Kate hurrying across the grounds towards the back of the house. Inexplicably he felt drawn towards her, although they had nothing in common that he knew of. He was wealthy and educated, whereas she was poor and clad only in a

rough wool skirt and a huge black cloak which reached almost to
her feet; one of Josiah's, he supposed. The poacher had made a
good job of raising and educating her; she carried herself well, held
her head up and spoke more like a gentlewoman than an illiterate
labourer. She was beautiful too; he had thought so when he had
first seen her in the caravan and again when Sir John had threatened her. Even then, she had been proud and unbowed and he
admired her for it while wondering if she would give in to Sir
John's blackmail for the sake of the old poacher. He wished he
could do something to help her. Not that she would accept it from
him; he was, after all, one of the enemy.

'Who is that girl?' Felicity asked, coming to stand at his side
and following his gaze. She was wearing a voluminous blue silk
undress gown and her fair hair had been released from the combs
and pins that held it all day and cascaded down her shoulders like
a young girl's. In spite of the great sorrow which had beset her, she
still looked a great deal younger than her thirty-eight years.

'One of the servants.'

'I haven't noticed her before.' She was regarding Kate with her
head on one side, as if trying to solve a puzzle.

'No, you wouldn't, she's new and works in the kitchens.'

'She's lovely, with the moonlight shining on her hair like that.'

He sighed. 'Yes, Mother, even the working classes have their
beauties, you know.'

'What's she doing out at this time of night?'

'How should I know?' He laughed. 'Perhaps she's been to meet
her lover.'

'Does John allow followers?'

'I shouldn't think so,' he said laconically. 'But young people will
always find a way if they are in love, don't you think?'

She laughed and tapped his arm. 'You sound like an old man,
Andrew, as if you were past such things, instead of a virile and
handsome nine-and-twenty.'

'Do I?' He turned to smile at her. 'Perhaps because I am so
frustrated.'

'Why?'

'There is so much to be done and now Uncle John is back and
going to be married, it is out of my hands ...'

'There are other areas in which you can be of use,' she said,
putting a hand on his arm. 'At home, with your father.'

'Yes, as soon as the wedding is over, we'll go, shall we?'

'Yes, then we really must find you a wife ...'

'Mother, I am quite able to find my own wife, thank you.'

'Are you? It seems to me you are being very slow about it. You have shown not the slightest interest in any young lady. There was Sir Giles Manning's two girls, Emma and Faith. Didn't you like either of them?'

'Too insipid. They were surely not invited to the house to tempt me?'

'I can't think why you are being so particular, they are both very handsome girls and will have good dowries. Even if you do not inherit Haddow – and that looks increasingly unlikely now – you still have a great deal to offer. Any girl would jump at the chance to marry you.'

'I do not want any girl, Mother. I am waiting for the right one.'

'Oh, and what must she be like?' she teased.

He smiled to himself. 'Beautiful, with fair curls and blue eyes and the figure of a goddess, but spirited and caring, not only for me but for those less fortunate ...' He stopped suddenly, realising he had been unconsciously describing Kate.

'You *have* met someone!'

'No, indeed not, I was simply painting a mental picture.'

'Of that girl down there,' she said, with unexpected insight. 'Oh, Andrew, you haven't ...' She paused, trying to find the words to express delicately what she meant.

He laughed, understanding. 'No, Mother, though I won't say I'm not tempted.'

'Oh, Andrew, it doesn't do, you know, not with the servants, not with those who should be looking up to you.'

'I know, Mother, I know,' he said, turning to smile at her. 'Have no fear. I will not disgrace you.'

'I should hope not.'

He dropped a kiss onto her forehead and left her, but instead of going to his own room, he went down to the kitchen where Kate had just entered and was hanging her cloak on the peg behind the door.

She was startled, but recovered herself quickly and moved forward with a smile. 'Do you need something, sir?'

'I felt a little hungry,' he lied. 'A piece of cake, perhaps?'

She went to the larder and returned with a slice of cake on a plate which she handed to him but, instead of leaving, he stood, plate in hand, and looked at her quizzically.

She blushed under his scrutiny. 'I haven't thanked you properly for helping Pa,' she said.

'That was my privilege, I wish it could have been more.'

'Mr Fiddy came looking for him like you said he would.'

'I'm sorry.'

'He got a year. Ma ...' She stopped and corrected herself quickly. 'I was told it was a light sentence because he was not caught in the woods and there was no evidence. We left the sack behind, you remember.'

'So we did,' he said, with a grin. 'But I hope you learned from the experience ...'

'Learned what?' she demanded. 'Not to poach? Or not to be caught with the evidence? Unless you mean I shouldn't help those I love, those who are hurt or too weak to help themselves ...'

'It's not just the hurt and weak, is it?' he said. 'You are involved with the dissidents, by all accounts, and they seem well able to look after themselves.'

'I don't know what you mean.'

'The broken bridge, the flooded field.'

'They were accidents.'

'And the mantrap over the gate? We left that in the woods too, didn't we?'

'I had nothing to do with that.'

'But it was done on your behalf.'

'Course it wasn't. Someone was clever enough to connect it with the workers' problems, that's all.'

'And what are the workers' problems?'

'Don't you know?' She was exasperated. 'Are you blind? Perhaps you should have gone to the vestry meeting, then you would have heard all about them at first hand.'

'I was otherwise engaged,' he said, unwilling to tell her he could not have gone to support Sir John but neither could he have openly sided with the labourers. 'And besides, it's not my business, I am only a guest here ...'

'You are still Sir John's heir, you should make it your business. Do you know what most of the villagers had for their supper tonight?'

'Rabbit, I would think,' he said, with a smile. 'Or a morsel of cold ham or goose. Perhaps a slice of game pie, followed by strawberry flan.'

Her face flamed; he knew what she had done, was still doing whenever the opportunity arose. Why hadn't he denounced her before? For a moment she was perplexed, wondering whether to admit or deny it. 'Such fare is totally out of the ordinary,' she said, evasively. 'It is more often bread and a scraping of dripping and perhaps a summer pudding.'

'Summer pudding? What's that?'

'Bread soaked in stewed apples and blackberries with a little honey and top of the milk poured over it.'

'It sounds delicious.'

'So it is, but it is hardly sustenance for a working man. The men have a God-given right to a living wage, surely you do not deny that?' She stopped when she realised he was laughing at her. 'I'm glad it amuses you,' she said coldly.

He became serious. 'I am not amused, not by your sentiments, they are entirely laudable.'

'Then what?'

'Your fire, your courage.'

'Because I say what I mean?'

'Yes. You know, it does not always pay to be so outspoken.'

Matthew had said almost the same thing. Impetuosity, he had called it. 'Because I do not know who is friend and who is foe, isn't that what you said?'

'Yes.'

'Which are you?'

'There you go again,' he said and heaved a great sigh, which made her smile. 'Asking awkward questions.'

'I am too lowly, too beneath you to deserve an answer, is that what you mean? You are gentry and I have no right even to address you, let alone question you.'

'Not at all.'

'Then answer.'

'I can't.'

'Why not?'

'Because it is not as straightforward as that. If there were no landowners what would the cooks and carters, maids and menser-vants, saddlers and shepherds, pigmen and poultry girls and the host of other artisans do for a living? The landowners keep them in work, just as the factory owners provide employment for the town dwellers. And everyone keeps the textile makers and shoemakers in work. It's all part of the scheme of things.'

'I know that,' she said quickly. 'I'm not stupid . . .'

'No, you are certainly not that,' he said softly. 'But just because a man has wealth, does not mean he is a bad man, any more than all poor men are ignorant yokels . . .'

She smiled, recognising the lecture for what it was, but also realising that he was treating her with a deference usually reserved for equals. 'I am too intractable, you mean?'

'Perhaps. Tell me, why are the villagers so opposed to the enclosures when they create jobs?'

'Only short-lived ones. The men may be put to planting a few hedges, making a few fences, building a road, but in the end they have nothing, the squire has it all.'

'But only to create more employment. Isn't that a good thing?'

'It would be if it were true, but when the farmers can't pay the new rents, he'll take back the land to farm himself and instead of taking on men, he'll use this new machinery . . .'

'You mean the threshing machine? He didn't use it, did he?'

'He will though, he didn't buy it for an ornament. He is simply biding his time.' Strangely, she felt quite at ease talking to him. She liked him, in spite of the fact that he was the squire's nephew and heir, and would do as his uncle told him to; in another time, another place, they could have been friends. That was if they could disregard the difference in their station; gentry and peasant could never meet on equal terms. 'And when he does, there will be trouble.'

'You think so? You believe in this character Captain Swing, do you?'

'He doesn't exist,' she said, her thoughts flying to Matthew.

'Oh, you know that for certain, do you?'

'No and neither do you. Besides, he is in prison.'

'Someone is in prison, I agree,' he said. 'But is it Captain Swing?'

'The paper said it was.' She was becoming defensive and annoyed with herself for allowing him to turn the conversation so skilfully the way he wanted it to go. She was acutely conscious of the letter in her pocket and wondered if he could possibly know anything of it. No, she decided, he was just trying to ingratiate himself with his uncle by finding out what he could about the rebels. But even that didn't ring true, because he had seen and spoken to Matthew on the common and had evidently said nothing.

'What about the battle on the common?' he said, as if he, too, had been reminded of it.

'What about it?'

'What the men did was against the law.'

'Then the law is unjust!'

He laughed aloud. 'You may be right, my fiery one, but neither you nor the labourers can do anything about that.'

'No?' she queried. 'We shall see.'

Was that a veiled threat? He wasn't sure. 'When anyone, high or low, breaks the law, then they should be punished,' he went on quietly. 'It does not matter who it is.'

'And if those who break the law are those who are supposed to uphold it, then what? Mantraps are illegal, taking away ancient rights is illegal . . .'

'And so is rioting and rick-burning and threatening people.'

'No one in Middleacre has done that.'

'No, not yet.' He reached out and touched her arm in a gesture of kindliness. 'All the same, I advise you keep out of it or you could find yourself in serious trouble.'

'You'd tell?' She didn't want to believe it; he had seemed so friendly and sympathetic. But she had been rash to speak to him as she had; it must be the euphoria of the meeting in the inn which was still with her, she was still fired up by it. Matthew had been right to say she would be too hot headed to be useful.

'No, my dear,' he said softly. 'I have no wish to see you in trouble.' He paused, then added, 'If you ever need help, come to me.'

Abruptly he put the plate with its untouched cake on the table and went out, leaving her wondering why he had come; it was obvious he wasn't hungry. Perhaps he wanted to warn her or torment her with doubts or even to let her know she had a friend in the house, she couldn't tell. She dare not do anything about the letter until he was safely out of the way and so finished the work which had been left for her, scraping the congealing mess off the plates into the pig swill and washing them up, before climbing the back stairs to her bed.

An hour later, she left the snoring Bertha and crept down again in her shift, opened the door of the passage leading to the front of the house and made her way stealthily along it in the dark. Everywhere was deserted. Silently she moved into the library, feeling her way around the furniture, and propped the letter against the inkstand on Sir John's desk. Then she hurried back to her bed, unseen and unheard.

She was at her usual station at the kitchen table, next morning when the uproar started. Sir John, having found the missive, demanded to know how it had arrived there. Johnson was accused and managed to convince his employer he had neither been out nor received callers the previous evening. Then one, by one, the footmen were sent for and interrogated; all swore their innocence.

'I want all the servants assembled in the hall,' Sir John ordered. 'Every single one of them. I will get to the bottom of this if I have to stay here all day.'

Kate, lining up with everyone else, knew she could not escape his attention. He stood in the library doorway, looking down the double row of servants and singled her out immediately. 'I want you in here,' he said, turning back into the library and ignoring the questioning look of his valet and the gaping curiosity of the other servants.

Reluctantly she followed him into the room, expecting to see him standing at the hearth with his back to the fire, or sitting at the big desk which stood in the middle of the room, but there was no sign of him and, for a moment, she thought he had gone. The door slammed and she wheeled round to find him behind her.

He stood with the offending letter in his hand and stared at her with hard grey eyes. She was dressed in the blue cotton dress he provided for all the kitchen staff and her sleeves were rolled up to the elbows. Her blonde hair clung to her cheeks in steam-laden wisps and her huge expressive eyes stared back at him unblinkingly. His workers had tried threats and defiance before but he had always brushed them aside, confident of his power, but this girl, this strangely proud peasant, upset him to the point of making him lose control of himself.

'What do you know of this?' he demanded, moving forward and waving the letter under her nose.

'What is it?'

'A letter, as you very well know. A threatening letter.'

'It has nothing to do with me.'

Her arrogance, her lack of fear, enraged him. He moved closer to her, hovering over her with menace in every gesture. 'But you did go into the village last evening, did you not?'

Instead of backing away, Kate held her ground, though her knees were knocking and her heart thumping. 'Mrs Bunny gave me permission, and anyway, half the servants went, you know they did, you were there yourself.'

'Impertinent hussy!'

For a moment she thought he would have a seizure; his face was purple and his mouth suddenly slack, but he pulled himself together and stepped towards her so close that she was obliged to tilt her head up to look at him.

'And having conspired with the rebels, you brought this sedition back with you.'

'Why are you accusing me?' she demanded, stepping back to avoid his brandy-laden breath. 'It could have been anyone.'

'True,' he said with an oily smile. 'But I am convinced it was you. You and that pestilential father of yours have been a thorn in my side ever since you arrived in Middleacre. I was glad to see the back of him.'

She laughed nervously. 'But I am not so easy to shift. I have done nothing unlawful.'

His face was white with anger. 'You have too much spirit for a poacher's daughter,' he said. 'You'll learn to be humble before I've done with you. You will tell me who wrote this letter and who leads the rebels.'

Kate remained silent.

'I thought so. Guilt is written all over your face.'

She stared him out, though she was quaking inside. 'I know nothing.'

'Is this how you repay my generosity? In spite of the fact that your father is a convicted poacher, I have given you a comfortable home, food and clothes ...' He looked with distaste at the thin cotton dress and suddenly had a vision of her in a full velvet gown with diamonds at her throat and in her hair and it took his breath away. She was lovely. He moved away to look out of the window to gather himself. She stood and waited.

'Have you forgotten your father?' he went on, turning to face her again, relieved to find she was once more in the servant's uniform. 'Do you want him to die in prison? He's an old man, not used to confinement.'

'He's strong, he'll not die,' she said, with a conviction born of desperation. She hoped fervently Pa was recovering well and would forgive her. He would not wish her to betray the villagers to have him released, would he?

His frustration and anger overcame him. He took a pace forward and grabbed her by the shoulders, meaning to shake her until her teeth rattled but looking into her angry blue eyes, he was seized by a different urge – the need to possess her and, in so doing, to hurt her so that she would never recover, would never again be able to hold up her head in that defiant way, would never be able to marry, for what man would have her after she had been despoiled? 'I'll beat you,' he said between gritted teeth. 'One way or another, I'll knock the pride out of you.' He gave a cracked laugh and bent his head into the soft flesh of her neck and kissed her, harshly, hungrily, bruising her with his teeth. 'Tell me the name of the rebel leader and you can go free,' he muttered, pulling her towards him, so that she was held tightly against his taut body. 'Tell me his name ...'

'Get off me!' she shouted, struggling with every ounce of her strength as his mouth roved over her neck and down into the cleft between her breasts. 'Get away from me! Monster! Devil!'

He laughed harshly and pressed his mouth to hers, forcing her lips to part, making her feel physically sick. He ran his hands over her back, tearing her dress from her shoulders, cupping his palms about her breasts, kneading them painfully. She continued to struggle but he was immensely strong and her attempts to scream were silenced by his mouth on hers. In any case, she knew her cries would be ignored, no one would dare to interfere.

He relaxed his grip slightly to change his position and force her back against the big desk, intending to make her lie on it and she seized the opportunity to pull herself from his grasp. His hand flew out to grab her and his fingers closed round the locket hanging from her neck. The chain broke as she darted away and ran to put the desk between them. Free of him, she wanted nothing more than to make good her escape, but she was reluctant to leave him in possession of the trinket, her last link with Josiah. Having it round her neck had given her a sense of security, as if she belonged to someone, was part of a family. She stood and glared at him with hate in her eyes, her breast heaving, ready to flee if he made a move towards her, but surprisingly he did not.

He stood and opened the locket, and she became aware that his attention was riveted on the tiny portrait it contained. For some seconds, she did not exist for him. He had gone very white, his expression a mixture of emotions she could not fathom – disbelief, vulnerability, sadness almost. But when he looked up he had recovered his composure and his voice had lost its passion. 'Where did you get this?'

'It belongs to me.'

'You stole it.'

'I did not.'

'Either you are lying or the poacher was the thief.'

Kate's thoughts went back to Josiah and the burned out wagon; surely he was not a common thief? He stole game, that was true, but was he also capable of taking other things which did not belong to him? And would he have kept the pendant if he had stolen it? No, she decided, chiding herself for her disloyal thoughts, he was too good, too honest, to steal anything except perhaps, a rabbit or two. 'It's of no interest to me what you think,' she said. 'The locket is mine.'

He smiled cruelly, holding it above his head. 'Then come and take it from me.'

She hesitated and then made a sudden move to reach it and was, once more, imprisoned in his grasp. 'You cannot beat me,' he said, breathing heavily as he tried to hold her. 'You will succumb. And no one will want you after that. You will be a tainted woman, a scarlet woman.'

This time she was prepared and managed to force her knee into his groin. He yelled with pain and she pulled the remnants of her dress about her and ran from the room and down the hall, oblivious of the double line of servants who had heard the raised voices and the sounds of a struggle without stirring a limb to help her. She didn't draw breath until she was back in her attic room and sitting on the bed.

He did not follow her; he would not have demeaned himself to do so, but that didn't mean the incident was over or forgotten. Her escape was only a temporary respite and the sooner she removed herself from the house the better.

But she was puzzled by Sir John's reaction to the sight of the locket; his interest wasn't just that the pendant was obviously more valuable than someone in her position could ever expect to own, or that the picture itself was very beautiful; it was almost as if he recognised the subject. But surely if that were so, he would have said so and claimed the locket on her behalf. Not for the first time, Kate wondered who the sitter was but concluded, as she had done before, that it could only have been some long-lost love of Josiah's. And that made her feel doubly sorry for him; being deprived of his freedom for a year was bad enough, but to lose someone he loved, as she loved Matthew, was unbearably sad. And now the one tangible thing that linked them was gone and she did not know how to recover it. She shook herself; time was pressing and she had to leave before Sir John sent one of the servants to fetch her back.

She stood up, changed into her old skirt and blouse, gathered her meagre belongings into a shawl and knotted the corners, then she left the bare room without regret; she had not felt at home there and Bertha snored louder than Pa had ever done.

Mrs Bunny was standing at the kitchen table, stirring something in a bowl. Kate took Matthew's cloak down from the hook behind the door and put it round her shoulders and, because it was his, she felt comforted a little.

'Where are you off to now?' the housekeeper demanded. 'You're not going out again, there's work to be done.'

'Yes, I am, I've finished with slaving in this house.'

'What have you gone and done, girl?'

'I'm the poacher's daughter and that's reason enough.'

'He found you out, did he? I'm sorry for that, indeed I am.'

Kate's voice softened. 'I'm sorry too, Mrs Bunny, you have been kind to me and I thank you for it.'

'Where are you going to stay? Have you kin or friends you can go to? Someone in the village?'

'They've no time for me, you know that, and I won't involve them. I'll go and stay in the drovers' hut.'

'The drovers' hut! You can't stay there, you'll freeze.'

'The hut is no different from the wagon,' Kate said. 'Pa brought me up to fend for myself and I'll come to no harm.'

'Then wait a minute before you go.' Mrs Bunny went to the larder and gathered up bread, apple pie, cold chicken and cheese and brought them to the table. 'Here, let's have that bundle.' She took Kate's shawl, undid it and tied it up again with the provisions inside. 'There, that will tide you over. And if I can find a flask somewhere, you shall have some milk too.' She began rattling round in the cupboard for a container.

'Thank you, thank you,' Kate said, heart overflowing.

'If any of the estate workers find you, they'll tell the squire, you know that, don't you? They dursn't do anything else.' While she spoke she filled a can with fresh creamy milk from a churn in the dairy, put a lid on it and stood it on the table next to Kate's bundle.

'Then I shall have to keep out of sight, shan't I?' She paused, then added, 'But you won't tell them where I've gone?' She nodded her head towards the upper regions of the house.

'That I won't, you can trust me.'

Kate dropped a kiss on Mrs Bunny's fire-red cheek and went out through the back door, concealing the bundle and the can of milk under the folds of Matthew's cloak.

Ten minutes later she let herself into the hut. It was cold and draughty, its tiny window was broken and the door half off its hinges, nothing like as snug as the wagon had been. It had a lopsided table which rocked whenever she put anything on it, two chairs with broken backs and a cupboard containing a pail, a tin bowl and the few things she had salvaged from the fire and left there weeks before. She set about making it comfortable, sweeping it out and hanging an old sack over the window, then she hurried up the drove to the lane which led onto the common. Here the peat flags which had been cut and stacked to dry before the enclosure had been piled up by Sir John's men and left for the villagers to retrieve. Most had already gone but there were still one or two which had been broken by the rough handling and a few pieces from the top layer which, being of poor quality, had been discarded. She gathered them up and returned to the hut to build her fire. Then she fetched rushes to make a bed and water from the dyke and made herself a meal. It was a little like being in the wagon again, except there was no Pa to keep her company and her spirits were at their lowest ebb. She had wanted to help the villagers, had been fired up on their behalf, but now she was alone and no one knew where she was.

'Oh, Pa,' she cried, as she settled down to sleep that night, huddled in Matthew's cloak. 'I wish you were here.' Pa would have soothed and comforted her and explained all the things which seemed so inexplicable, the emotions she felt – love, hate, jealousy, pity, despair, all mixed up together. Were they all part of becoming a woman ? Or falling in love. Was that why there was no rhyme or reason to it ? Or was there a purpose to everything, a destiny ? Then what was her destiny ? Oh, why was it so hard ?

Chapter Ten

*T*he next morning was the coldest of the winter so far and she rose stiff and cramped. The fire had gone out. She picked up the bucket and opened the door, intending to fetch more water and fuel; a hot drink would warm her. On the step lay a cabbage, a few potatoes, a blackberry pie and more milk. She looked around to see if there was anyone about but the drove road was deserted and the meadow on the other side contained nothing but a few sheep. Her benefactors had come stealthily in the night and she had not been forgotten after all. Tears rose to her eyes but she brushed them away impatiently; there was work to be done. She took the food inside, feeling a great deal more cheerful, but she did not think anyone would dare visit her.

But she was wrong. Matthew arrived in the afternoon when she was busy trying to fill some of the bigger cracks in the walls with a paste made from clay and water. He stood filling the doorway with his tall frame and smiling at her in that sardonic way of his which made her want to fling herself into his arms and hit out at him at one and the same time.

'Well Kate?'

'Well enough.' She would not complain; what Sir John had done to her was not Matthew's fault and she did not want to drive him away now he had come. She washed the mud from her hands and dried them on a rough cloth bought, along with a few other necessities, from the village store. 'Come in and shut the door, you're making the fire smoke and we'll be seen.'

'What happened at the Hall?' he said, doing as she asked. 'Mrs Bunny sent a message that you had left. Was it because of the letter?'

'No, not altogether.' She gave him a graphic account of what had happened, beginning with her talk with Andrew and ending with the squire's attempt to rape her.

'He did that?' he said, exploding into anger. 'The devil! He shall pay dearly for that, as God's my witness, he will be punished ...' He stopped suddenly and moved over to the window, where she stood, her lovely head profiled against its light, and put his hands on her shoulders. She flinched at his touch. 'Did he hurt you, Kate?'

The tension slowly drained from her and she allowed herself to relax; he was like her Pa, he would not harm her. 'No, a few bruises, that's all, and those because I struggled.' She pointed to one on her neck.

He stared at the blue and yellow mark for a long moment, trying to control his anger. 'Kate,' he said softly. 'Men don't all behave like Sir John, some can be gentle and considerate.'

'I know. Like Pa. And you.'

Damn the old poacher, he thought. If she was looking for a substitute for her father, she had the wrong man in him. 'No, not like a father,' he said abruptly. 'One day you'll learn ...'

'I want to learn now.' She looked up at him with frank blue eyes which held no hint of coquetry. There was no intention to flirt; flirting was a society game she did not know how to play. London's beauties would have put an inflexion on their words which was meant to tease, and he would have answered in like manner and meant none of it. Nor was Kate playing up to his sensuality as the girls in the village did, vying for his favours, simply because he was a well-set up man and, in their eyes, ripe for marriage. It amused him to watch them, even to play one off against the other now and again, though he fancied Betty Watson was more determined than most. He could not behave like that with Kate; she was too innocent, too unprepared. He wondered how Josiah had justified bringing her up alone, cut off from female companionship and guidance; he could not believe there had been no alternative. She was no longer a child, although there was something childlike about her, and his feelings were not those a man might have for a favourite niece, but of a passionate man wanting a very desirable woman. The temptation to accede to her wishes was almost overwhelming and he steeled himself to resist it; she could not be expected to understand. Slowly he bent his head and kissed her, first on the forehead and then each cheek in turn.

'Not like that,' she said ingenuously. 'That's how Pa kisses me.'

'It will have to do on account.'

'On account of what?'

'On account of this is not the time and place and I am not the one to teach you.' He paused, holding her against him, cradling her head on his shoulder and allowing his lips to brush her hair. Suddenly coming to his senses, he pushed her from him and his voice became almost brusque. 'Now we have important decisions to make. It's clear you can't stay in this hovel.'

'Why not?' Kate, who was not used to interpreting the words and deeds of complex young men, was puzzled. With Pa she said straight out what she was thinking, knowing she would not be misunderstood; he had not equipped her to deal with the conflicting emotions which assailed her now. She could not understand Matthew's quick changes of mood, solicitous one minute, sharp-tongued the next, as if she were a source of annoyance to him. Why should he be annoyed with her? What had she done? She was headstrong, she knew, and sometimes she did things which were not in her own best interests, like tangling with Ben Carter and defying the squire, but that did not give Matthew the right to be angry with her. She could not see that he had anything to blame her for and it did not cross her mind that he, too, might be in the grip of mixed emotions and divided loyalties, that his vow to help the labourers and to do it without violence, conflicted with his natural instinct to hit out at injustice and his heartfelt wish to protect her.

'It's not safe for you. Sir John Haddow is a very vindictive man and he will not rest until he has you beaten.'

'I'm only one of many.'

'But no one had defied him as you have, my love ...'

'You think I should have let him ...'

'Good God, no! But if you had refrained from answering him back, then perhaps you would not have angered him.'

'I do not think so. It was more than just the letter, or even the fact that I am the poacher's daughter. There's something about me that seems to enrage him ...'

'Your courage,' he said. 'But it would have been better had you told him what he wanted to know. I doubt it would have made any difference to the village in the long run ...'

'I couldn't have done that. Oath or no, I had given my word ...'

He smiled. 'You ask for trouble.'

'No more than you do, writing threatening letters.'

'The villagers have to state their case and that is the way they chose to do it.'

'Everyone knows it already, from Sir John himself right down to blind Cally. All you do is put the squire on his guard, so that he can be ready for you.'

'The men have to try and settle things peacefully, then no one can blame them later if things go awry.'

'Which they most certainly will.'

'You may be right.' He sighed, looking down into her troubled face and speaking softly. 'Kate, my love, I would rather you were not in the thick of it.'

It was the second time he had used that endearment and it raised her flagging spirits. 'Why shouldn't I be? Whether you like it or not, Captain Tolley, I am in it, right to the top of my head, and that's where I want to be. There's a fire in me burning to consume the squire and all he stands for.'

'And if you stay here and continue to provoke him in your usual impetuous fashion, you'll do more harm than good,' he said sharply. 'You'll undo all the work that's been done so far and you can be sure it will be the labourers who suffer, not the squire, who will rejoice in taking his revenge.'

He was as impatient with himself as he was with her. She ought to be living in a comfortable home, warmly clad, surrounded by family and friends, not eking out an existence in a tumbledown shanty, waiting for an old man to come out of prison. She was made for love and tenderness, but she had to be taught how to accept it and it was his misfortune he could not abandon his crusade to teach her. In another time, another place, it might have been different ... Where did pity end and love begin? He didn't know. He shrugged his thoughts from him. 'Kate, don't you see? You have become the focal point of Sir John's wrath. We must get you out of it.'

'I won't leave Pa.' The tears were very close to the surface now and she could not, or would not, see that his apparent rejection of her masked a deep concern, a feeling of guilt that he was to blame for her predicament. 'A year is not long and more than two months of that have already passed, I only have to be patient and wait and we will be together again.' Her voice faltered; whatever she said, it was a long time and it stretched before her endlessly. 'He'll know what to do, he always does.' She paused. Had she put his life in jeopardy or at least failed to save it? 'Are you sure my father is all right?'

'He is better off than you are at this moment.' He put his finger under her chin and lifted her face to look into her eyes. 'Kate, it's too dangerous for you here.'

'Where else can I go?'

'You could go to Ely or Cambridge. I could help you, I have contacts there.'

'Leave Middleacre?' she queried. 'Why should I do that?'

'You need a home and work to do and no one will give you either here, you know that, particularly after yesterday.'

'They left me food.'

'Kate, they are salving their consciences, because you did it for them. Sooner or later, they will tell Sir John what he wants to know.'

'What about you? Aren't you afraid someone will go for the reward, someone who wasn't at the meeting and didn't take the oath? It's a great deal of money.'

'So it is and I could hardly blame them if they did, but it's a chance I'll have to take.'

'Even with me?'

'Yes, my little one, even with you, but it would be better if you went away.'

'Oh, that's why you want me to go, not for my sake but for yours. Why don't you leave yourself, if that's what you think?'

'No, I must remain here, at least until tomorrow.'

Immersed in her own problems she had forgotten that the next day was Sir John's wedding day. 'You don't believe the squire will answer that letter, do you?'

'No, I don't believe he will.'

'Then what will you do? Will the men strike?'

'You ask too many questions,' he said brusquely. 'Just because they asked you to deliver the letter, doesn't mean you need to be privy to all their plans.'

He still believed she might betray him, that she might be tempted for the money. It was ironic when she considered the greater temptation Sir John had put in front of her. Matthew did not know about that and she would not tell him, or he would redouble his efforts to get her to leave. She could not go, not in the middle of a fight she considered her fight and she could not

169

abandon Josiah, but most of all, she did not want to leave Matthew himself; whatever he thought of her, good or bad, being near him was all she asked.

He stood looking down at her. She was such a mixture, strong and vulnerable, brave and yet he knew that underneath she was little more than a frightened child. He wanted to stay and knew he must not. 'I must go,' he said, though he made no move to do so.

'Where?' Even though they argued and he treated her like a naughty child, she didn't want him to leave.

He grinned, almost sheepishly. 'Back to work. Strangers without jobs attract suspicion and I need the men's trust.'

'Why do you keep up that pretence? You do not look or talk like a labourer. Who are you?'

'Matthew Tolley, late Captain of Hussars, friend of the good people of Middleacre, does that satisfy you?'

'No, it doesn't explain how and why.'

'Curb your curiosity,' he said. 'It's safer for all concerned if you think of me as William Chapman's cowman.'

Her smile was a little wan. 'But you told Jack Watson you had never done that kind of work.'

'There's no end to what a man can learn if he puts his mind to it,' he said wryly. 'And I had a good teacher.'

'You mean Betty Watson? Was that what she was teaching you in the cowshed?'

He laughed, knowing exactly what she meant. He had been referring to William but if she chose to think it was the maid, then so be it. 'Of course.'

She wished she hadn't mentioned Betty's name; it put another barrier between them, and made her wake up from the dream she had been indulging in and face reality. She had no claims on him; as far as he was concerned, she was simply a nuisance. The only person she could truly rely on was her Pa. 'You won't go into hiding then?' she asked, changing the subject abruptly to mask her hurt.

'No. I'll see it through.'

'And so will I,' she said. 'I shan't leave.'

'God preserve me from stubborn women!' He reached for the door latch. 'Have it your own way, it's clear you mean to anyway, but be sure to keep well out of sight until after tomorrow.'

The next moment he had gone and she was looking at the back

of the closed door. The tears which had been lurking behind her eyes, spilled over and ran down her cheeks. Why did they have to quarrel? She could not believe that he didn't like her; hadn't he called her his love? Did it mean anything? Apparently not. She wished she had someone she could ask, but there was no one.

She opened the door, tempted to run after him, but he was striding away along the drove road and did not look back. She went inside and shut the door. She had told him she could manage and now she had to prove it. She spent the rest of the day improving her hideout, trying to concentrate on what she was doing to the exclusion of everything else.

Disturbed in a restless sleep just before dawn the next morning, she rose from her uncomfortable bed to peer out of the tiny window. It was just light enough to see two figures moving about among the sheep in the meadow on the other side of the drove road. As she watched, they selected one of the smaller sheep and driving off the rest, slaughtered it out there in the middle of the pasture. She could hardly believe anyone would do such a foolhardy thing and, dressing hurriedly, ran out to remonstrate with them.

'What are you doing?' she asked, shocked to discover it was Charlie Barber and Nathaniel Green. 'Isn't that one of Sir John's sheep?'

At the sound of her voice, they both looked up with guilt etched on their faces, but as far as Nat Green was concerned it was only the poacher's daughter, and he returned to the task of skinning the animal. Charlie stood up and faced her. 'Kate, what are you doing here?'

'I saw you from the drovers' hut. Charlie, why are you doing this? There will be hell to pay, especially after all the other trouble.'

'It'll be t'squire what does the payin',' Nat said gruffly. 'An' you c'n keep out o' it, m'lady.'

'Go away, Kate.' Charlie put in, obviously troubled by her presence. 'Please forgit you see us.'

'But aren't you supposed to wait until Sir John answers your letter before taking action?'

Nathaniel stood up and faced her, brandishing the bloodied knife he had been using. 'He in't a-goon' to answer it, we all do know that. Letters don' 'urt 'im but this'll show 'im we mean business. He'll lose the hull lot if he don't gi'e us back the common.'

She was worried. Matthew would not approve of this wanton slaughter and heaven knew what it would do to Sir John's already inflamed temper. 'Does Captain Tolley know what you are doing?'

'It in't narthin' to do with 'im,' Charlie said.

'Nor you neither,' Green put in. 'Goo you on back where you come from.'

Charlie took her arm as if to lead her away. 'I heard about what happened to you,' he said. 'The squire's a-goon to pay for that, I'll gi'e you my oath.'

'Is that why you're doing it? Oh, Charlie, no! Not for me, not to avenge me.'

'Why not? He wronged you, didn' he?'

'He didn't ... He didn't hurt me and even if he had, two wrongs don't make a right. I don't want you to get into trouble on my account. Think of your mother.'

'I done all the thinkin' I'm a-goon to do, Kate. Now, go back to the hut and when this is all over, I'll come for you and take you hoom. Ma must learn I'm the man in the house now and I say what's what.'

He would not allow her to argue. 'You'm my girl and no one i'n't a-goon to take liberties with you, not even t'squire.'

This new obduracy was alien to his nature and she was sure Nat Green had put him up to it, playing on the fact that he loved her. She stood and watched as they finished their gruesome work and bundled the carcase into a sack, leaving the fleece on the ground. She bent to pick it up.

'Leave it be!' Nat commanded her.

'But Sir John will find it.'

'We want 'im to find it.' He grabbed the fleece from her and threw it to the ground. 'Now get you gone and do you say naught of seein' us or it'll be the worse for you.'

She returned to the hut, shivering with cold and an inexplicable excitement. There was disaster in the air, she could feel it and smell it. Matters were boiling to a head and she felt exhilarated and half-afraid, but if it meant trouble for Sir John, she would gladly be part of it. He would not take this latest outrage lying down; wedding day or not, he would be searching for the culprits as soon as he had been told of it. She wished one of them was not Charlie.

She was quite sure Matthew would not approve of the killing of the sheep; he had said they must not break the law, that they could achieve their ends by peaceful means. What they had done was neither lawful nor conducive to peace. He would be angry. In spite of Nat Green's warning to say nothing and Matthew's own admonition to keep out of sight, he had to be told. She left the hut and hurried up the drove.

The day was bright and frosty. The bare branches of the willows on the banks and the trees in Haddow Hall park glistened with iridescent beauty. The fires, lit very early in the grates of the Hall, burned with extra brightness. The kitchens, even at dawn, were hot with cooking pies and roasting game and a great boiling of this and that and Mrs Bunny was bemoaning the loss of Kate, who had been a good little worker. Hetty and the other housemaids were dusting the downstairs rooms as soon as it was light enough to see without a candle. The usually idle footmen had been up for hours cleaning plate and polishing glasses and Johnson and Annette, Mrs Wisdom's maid, were bleary eyed from lack of sleep. Gardeners were clipping hedges which had ceased to grow two months before, and pulling up the last vestige of weed in the drive and flower beds. The grooms were busy with the lovely black carriage horses and the monogrammed family coach. Exotic imported flowers, sent specially from London the day before, were arranged all round the house. The tables for the wedding breakfast were laid, boxes and trunks were packed, the wedding gown, in all its glory of silk and lace and beads was finished.

Laura Wisdom stirred from her sleep and demanded hot water for a bath. Annette, her maid, shrieked at Bertha and Bertha yelled at the new kitchen maid and the water was hauled, bucket by overflowing bucket, up to Mrs Wisdom's dressing room, where Annette waited with perfumed soaps and lotions. Mrs Wisdom was immersed, dried and anointed, before slipping into a flowing silk peignoir and sitting at her dressing table to have her coiffure arranged by a hairdresser who had arrived from London the day before and was just another for whom Mrs Bunny had to provide food and lodging.

Sir John rose reluctantly and, deciding to go without his breakfast, went in search of Fiddy; as far as he was concerned, weddings were secondary to the business of the estate. When he found him, down on the pasture near the drovers' hut, the bailiff was carrying something which, at first glance, looked like a lamb, but it was far too early for lambs. 'What have you got there?' he demanded.

'A skin, Sir John.' Fiddy held the fleece out at arm's length. 'I found it lying in the middle of the meadow, right out in the open where it couldn't be missed.'

'How did it die? Dogs?'

'Dogs who know how to use long knives.'

Sir John swore fluently. 'Where is the carcase?'

'In someone's stewpot, I'll wager.'

'Then why leave the skin behind?'

'I reckon it's meant to be a sign, Sir John, a sign they think they have the whiphand, they can steal at their leisure and no need to hide the crime. We're meant to take notice.'

'I'll take notice,' Sir John said, his voice cold with fury. 'I'll find the perpetrator and have him thrashed, that will show them whose hand holds the whip. Find out who killed that sheep and bring him to me. Get the gamekeepers and gardeners to help you. Scour the village, look for evidence of fresh-killed meat, the bones and the head; it can't all be hidden. I want the culprit found before I leave for London this afternoon.'

Fiddy hurried away with the fleece bundled under his arm, not relishing the task he had been given. The villagers would stubbornly close ranks and nothing but brutality would force the truth from them. He doubted if he would be able to obey Sir John's orders and dreaded the consequences of his failure.

'Four o'clock at the latest,' Sir John called after him. 'I shall excuse your non-attendance outside the church after the ceremony.' Then he strode back to the house, ran up the stairs two at a time, yelling for Johnson as he did so. More hot water was fetched and after bathing and dressing in what he contemptuously called his wedding finery, he set off for the church in the gig.

He was only seconds ahead of his bride and walked quickly to his place, looking neither to right nor left at the assembled congregation, who were all turning towards the back of the church, where Laura was just making her entrance behind him. She came slowly down the aisle, on the arm of Sir Guy who had been inveigled into giving her away, confident she looked outstandingly beautiful and regal. She joined John before the altar and smiled as he turned towards her; later she would have something to say about his tardiness.

The Reverend Mr Cox, beaming at them both, opened his prayer book at the marriage service and began speaking very slowly, savouring the words: 'Dearly Beloved, we are gathered together here in the sight of God, and in the face of this congregation to join together this man and this woman ...'

'Get on with it, man.' Sir John hissed.

Startled, the reverend gentleman looked up from his prayer book, took a deep breath and went on, almost babbling in his anxiety. '... to join together this man and this woman in Holy Matrimony, which is an honourable estate ...'

Half an hour later the newly married pair emerged through the guard of honour provided by the estate workers, expecting the whole population of Middleacre to be lined up on each side of the church path to pay homage and were astonished to see only those invited guests who had been present in the church. Where were they all? Where were the Watsons, the Greens, the Chuckleys, the Barbers? Where were all the children who, by custom, should be lined up spruce and clean in their Sunday best to show their servility? Where were the labourers, the miller, the baker, the blacksmith and the harnessmaker? All should be in attendance so that he could beam his good nature on them and tell them, to the accompaniment of cheers, that a feast had been prepared for them in the big barn of the Home Farm. It was a ritual whenever anyone from the Hall married.

They were defying him, they were deliberately staying away. But what bribery had been used to keep the little children away? How had the curiosity of the women been stilled? Were they not hungry? And thirsty? Did they not know that on his wedding day he would be benign to all? He shrugged his shoulders and helped Laura into the shining black carriage and climbed in beside her for the short ride back to Haddow Hall. Let them behave like spoiled children, they were the losers.

Now he must laugh and joke and pay attention to the idle chatter of his guests and show affection for that silly woman who, besides providing the life-blood of the estate in the form of money, must also bear him a son. The sooner that happened the better; he did not like Andrew's newfangled ideas and obvious sympathy with the labourers. Damn them all to hell!

There was no one about at White Poppy Farm, either at the house or in the empty barn where the floor had been swept clean and the flails hung idly on hooks on the wall, their work done for another year. The threshing was finished six weeks before time and now many of the men would be out of work and, in their present mood anything could happen; they needed a cool head to guide them, they needed someone like Matthew. She hurried to the milking shed, not really believing that he would be working there, but it was the only other place she could think of. Betty was there alone, doing the milking. She looked up as Kate approached, then realising who it was, put her head back into the cow's flank, without speaking.

'Where is Captain Tolley?' Kate asked. 'I've got to find him.'

'I told you afore, leave him be,' the girl said, without looking up. 'He ha' got enough troubles without tekin' on yourn too.'

'But I must speak to him, it's very important. Tell me where I can find him.'

'It in't no concern o' yourn where he be. And he don' want you botherin' him.'

'Isn't he the best judge of that?' Kate said, keeping her temper with an effort; it was more important to find Matthew than bandy words with Betty Watson. 'It's not for you to say what he does and does not want.'

'Nor you neither.' The girl turned to look up at Kate and laughed. 'Jus' so's you know, when he's done his work here, we're going to be wed, so don't you go pokin' your nose in where it in't wanted. Go back where you belong, wherever that is. One thing's for sure, it in't Middleacre.'

Kate stared at the girl for a moment, as if unable to take in what she was saying, then she turned slowly and left. She could hear Betty's laughter long after she had gone through the yard gate and started down the path to the road; it went on echoing in her head for fully five minutes, driving out all other thoughts. At that moment, if she had known where she really belonged, she would willingly have gone there, away from the torment of a love that was not returned, the humiliation of Betty Watson's taunts, the rejection and the loneliness.

She had been foolish, dreaming impossible dreams. After all, who was she? She did not know and, for the first time in her life, she wished she did. She wished she was someone with some standing, not, as Fiddy had so crudely put it, a gypsy's plaything. She hadn't even been brought up as other girls, though, until the last few weeks, she had not realised anything was lacking. Even now, she did not know what it could be, but whatever it was, it barred her from love. Betty knew who she was and where she belonged and how to get what she wanted. She knew how to behave towards men, how to roll her eyes and swing her hips. Was that how it was done? And was that enough for Matthew to want to marry her?

But that didn't alter the fact he ought to be told about the slaughter of the sheep. Where was he? She went to the inn but he was not there either and had not slept in his bed, according to the landlord. Had he decided the risk of being betrayed was too great and left the area, after all? She didn't know whether to be glad or sorry.

She stopped in the centre of the village to take stock of the situation, wondering what to do next. Everyone seemed to be going about their normal business though there were more unemployed men congregating on the green than usual in spite of the chill in the air. Winter was well advanced and winter in the fens could be very bleak, with bitter winds coming down from the arctic and nothing to stop them as they sped across the land, for there were few hedges and even fewer trees. There was ice on the water now, not enough to bear a skater, but enough to deter all but the most hardy from going out on the fen. The eels were gone and few labourers had guns for shooting the ducks. How were they going to keep themselves and their families warm and fed until spring?

Before she could ask anyone else if they had seen Matthew, she became aware of a commotion outside Mrs Barber's cottage and saw Fiddy dragging Charlie from his home by his coat collar. Mrs Barber, surrounded by her children, some of whom were crying noisily, was pulling on the bailiff's arm as he forced the boy into the dogcart he had arrived in. 'Let him go,' she wept. 'Please let him go. He's only a boy, he didn't mean any harm.'

Fiddy pushed her away, climbed into the cart beside the white-faced young man and drove away leaving Mrs Barber on her knees in the road, covering her face with her hands. 'What will they do to him?' she cried. 'He didn't know what he was doing, he's too young.'

Kate, who did not need to be told why Charlie was being taken, ran to comfort her but the woman shrugged her off. 'It's all your fault,' she shouted. 'Turning his head and making him want to be a big man. He's only a boy . . .'

'I had nothing to do with it, Mrs Barber. I didn't make him do anything.' Kate knew Mrs Barber didn't believe her and she turned to scan the faces of the villagers, hoping someone might back her, but no one did. They all looked strained and weary, as if they had lost the will to fight, and she realised that without a leader, their rebellion would collapse. 'It was you,' she said, spotting Nathaniel Green. 'You put Charlie up to it. Are you going to stand by and let him shoulder all the blame ?'

'You want me to gi'e m'self up ?' he demanded. 'Would that help Charlie ?'

'No, but surely you can do something for him, speak up for him. His mother needs him.'

'Shall we do that ?' Green asked those about him, stung by her accusation. 'Shall we go to Haddow Hall and tackle t'squire ?'

'What can we do there ?' someone asked. 'Charlie wor caught fair an' square.'

'We'll demand his release,' Kate said. 'If we all face up to the squire, he'll have to give in, won't he ?'

'He won't see you, it's his wedding day,' Mrs Barber said, drawing her youngest children to her side and hugging them to her. 'The poacher's daughter is only out to make trouble.'

'So what ?' Chuckley said. 'She in't the only one.'

'To Haddow Hall !' The cry was taken up by a dozen voices. 'To Haddow Hall !'

'Shouldn't we wait for Captain Tolley ?' someone asked. 'He'll know what to say to the squire.'

'We know what to say,' Green said.

'Where is 'e, anyhow ?' demanded Chuckley. 'He should be with us.'

'I don't know.' Kate said. 'I tried to find him . . .'

'It do seem to me,' said Bert Hall, 'that there cowman ha' no taste for a good fight. When all the chawin's done and we need action, he's nowhere to be seen . . .'

'That's not fair,' said Kate, defending Matthew in spite of her own inexplicable annoyance with him. 'He wasn't to know Charlie and Nat Green would kill a sheep and cause more trouble. He expected you to wait to see if the squire answered your letter.'

'Letters !' Nat Green spat on the ground at her feet. 'What's the good o' they? No one ever bested the squire with that, not with all his book-learning and fancy words. None o' us is a match for him in that. But we c'n fight, can't we, lads?'

'That we can,' they yelled.

'Captain Tolley don' tell us what to do,' he went on. 'We're free men, we do as we choose. He's not a Middleacre man an' we don't need strangers to fight our battles for us.' He looked down at Kate, a flicker of amusement on his face. 'Nor women neither.'

'I'm not leaving,' she said. 'I've as much reason to be here as any of you. It was the squire who put my Pa in prison, wasn't it? And he had my home burned down. I've nothing left. Nothing.'

'Then shut up and come you on. We're wasting time.'

They set off in a ragged column, across the green and onto the lane which led to the gates of Haddow Hall, knocking on cottage doors all along their route. 'Come you on out,' they shouted to those inside. 'We're a-goon' up to the Hall to square up to the squire.'

'If'n you in't with us, you're ag'in us,' Nathaniel insisted, when anyone dared to express doubts. 'You must tek the consequences.' He turned to the men behind him. 'In't that so, mates?'

'Aye,' they chorused.

'Join us or we'll pull yar house down round yar lugs.'

The meek joined the strong and by the time they surged through the wrought iron gates of Haddow Hall, they were over a hundred strong, men, women and even children, all carried along on a tide of mass hysteria which nothing could have stopped.

The feasting and merriment at Haddow Hall, albeit somewhat contrived, had lasted well into the afternoon and Sir John began to fidget. He had seen nothing of Fiddy since the morning and the time was fast approaching when he and Laura would have to change their clothes and call the coach to the front door. He was loathe to leave, and yet he told himself it was all show. The peasants might threaten, might take his game and kill a sheep or two, but they knew when to stop; they were like naughty children who couldn't have their own way and, treated like naughty children, they would give in.

Laura left him to go to her room to change into her travelling costume and he went to the sideboard and poured himself another glass of brandy. He was sipping it quietly, savouring the warm glow it gave him, when Johnson hurried in with the news that the bailiff was in the hall and he had one of the villagers with him. 'He has him tied by the arms,' he said, 'though the fellow is struggling fit to bust his buttons.'

'Good. Tell Fiddy to take him to the library; I'll be there directly. Then go and tell Annette to inform her mistress there will be a delay of a few minutes while I set things to rights.'

Johnson hurried to obey and Sir John drained his glass and left the crowded room to join his bailiff.

Fiddy had Charlie Barber's arms pinned to his sides with rope, one end of which he had twisted firmly round his own hand, while the frightened lad twitched and pulled, trying to free himself. 'Stand still, you varmint,' the bailiff grunted, giving the rope a jerk which nearly sent Charlie spinning off his feet. 'You'll only make it worse for yourself.'

'So, this is our sheep stealer, is it?' queried Sir John, looking down at the boy and feeling vaguely disappointed. He had hoped it would be the dissidents' ringleader so that he could make an example of him, have him transported, if not hanged; that would have stopped the rebellion instantly, but all he'd caught was this young pup who was obviously frightened enough to wet his breeks.

'It is, Sir John,' Fiddy told him. 'I found the head of the sheep thrown onto the midden heap in his back yard and his mother trying to burn the rest. She hadn't even the stomach to cook it and make something tasty of it.'

'Well?' Sir John turned to Charlie, who had become very still and was staring down at the floor. 'What have you to say for yourself?'

Charlie did not reply and the bailiff gave another tug on the rope. 'Answer Sir John, damn you.'

'In't got narthin' to say.' The boy bowed his head and stared at the pattern in the thick carpet.

'Take him to Wisbech gaol and tell the watch to lock him up,' Sir John commanded.

Before he could be obeyed, there was a sudden crash as a large stone was hurled through the window and landed, in a shower of glass, on the floor between them. Fiddy ran to the window and was caught on the side of the head by a second missile thrown from the shrubbery a few yards from the house.

'Get down, man! Get down!' shouted Sir John as it began to rain stones and glass flew everywhere. They hurled themselves to the floor and crawled behind the shelter of the desk, while Charlie stood in the middle of the room too bemused to move.

'Who is that out there?' Sir John demanded. 'Who has the effrontery to stone me in my own home?'

'I don't know, Sir John,' said the unhappy Fiddy. 'I reckon they're hoping you'll set the lad free.'

'I will not succumb to violence and threats. Go out there and tell them so.'

'Me, Sir John?'

'Yes, of course you.'

Reluctantly the bailiff left the shelter of the desk and crawled into the hall, where he stood upright and went to open the front door. He was met by a barrage of stones hurled by the angry villagers who were flocking onto the lawn, defying him or anyone else to stop them.

'What is the meaning of this?' he demanded, holding his hand over his bleeding cheek and dodging more missiles. 'You'll all go to Bridie.'

'Let Charlie go,' they shouted.

'I can't do that. He killed one of the squire's sheep.'

'So what if he did?' Green shouted, not admitting to his part of the slaughter. 'His kin are starvin' and the squire's to blame. Let him go or we'll wreck the house.'

'You'd never dare.'

'Try us.'

Sir John joined the bailiff at the door. 'Go home, all of you,' he shouted. 'If you leave peaceably now, I'll take no action against you.'

'Let Charlie go and we will.'

'No, he has broken the law and must be punished, He'll go to Wisbech gaol and be tried in a court of law. Say whatever you have to say on his behalf then,'

'Lot o' good that'll do.' They bent to pick up more stones, advancing slowly, step by step. Sir John noticed with surprise that there were women among them and Kate was well to the fore. His problems seemed to be crystallised in her; she was, for some reason he could not fathom, the symbol of his frustration. But he could do nothing, either to her or the mob, because the wedding guests,

181

hearing the commotion, had streamed out from the drawing room and were standing behind him.

'What's happening?' they asked.

'Nothing of importance,' he said, without taking his eyes from the advancing mob. 'Please go back and enjoy yourselves. I'll settle this in a minute.'

'Oh, no, you won't,' called Kate. The sight of him had roused her wrath to such a pitch, she was hardly responsible for her actions. 'You'll settle nothing until you let Charlie go and give in to the men.'

'Be quiet, girl!' he snapped. 'Go away and take the other women with you before I have you all locked up.'

'All on us?' someone shouted, as one or two of the women tried to retreat but found they could not, the press of bodies was too great. 'How are you going to do that?'

A stone hurtled through the open door and landed at the feet of Mrs Carrington, making her jump back in alarm. Kate was horrified; although she was quite content to watch the men throw stones at the windows and even at Sir John himself, she didn't want Andrew's stepmother hurt. But Kate could not stem the tide and she was suddenly afraid of what she had started. If anyone was hurt it would be her fault for egging them on; she had used the villagers to get at Sir John for reasons of her own and she did not like herself for it. She was relieved when, after a moment's hesitation, he had the good sense to see that it was not the time and place to face up to a mob.

'Because today is my wedding day,' he said, his face taut with controlled fury. 'And in deference to my guests who might be hurt, you may have your man. But make no mistake, you have won no victory, the price has yet to be paid for this day's work. Take him and go.'

He signalled to Fiddy to release Charlie and that young man, once free of his bonds, ran out through the door and joined his friends, giving a whoopee of jubilation. Singing and shouting, they carried him shoulder high to the lodge gates, where they lowered him to the ground and allowed him to walk.

'What now?' asked Green, still too fired up to be content with this minor victory. 'We can't just go home. We hatta make sure the squire has learned his lesson. We're not going to crawl away and wait for him to make the next move, are we?'

'No,' they chorused.

'To the Home Farm!' he shouted. 'There's a troshin' engine there!'

'The barn's laid out with the wedding feast,' Moss said, recollecting that he had not yet been paid for the bread the squire had ordered for it and probably never would see the money after this.

'All the better. We can eat and drink while we work.'

The crowd hesitated, looked from one to the other and then followed, many stopping on the way past their homes to collect pitchforks, spades, beckets and even pots and pans, anything to use for tools or weapons.

Chapter Eleven

*T*he mob stormed into the wooden building and began breaking up the squire's new threshing machine, which someone had been unwise enough to leave in the barn close to the tables laden with bread, cold meats, chicken, cheese and fruit. If they had not been sufficiently roused before, they were incensed now. They used the implements they carried, working noisily, without restraint, hacking at the metal and wood and tearing the canvas, throwing the pieces wildly about, ignoring the food. All but the children, who fell upon the loaded tables with cries of delight and stuffed themselves until they were too full to eat any more.

When the threshing machine had been reduced to fragments, they stood breathlessly surveying their handiwork. 'That'll niver work ag'in,' they said with satisfaction.

Someone, no one could remember afterwards who it was, threw a firebrand into a pile of straw at the end of the barn. Dry as dust, it blazed up immediately, the flames leaping feet into the air and touching the timbers of the roof. In no time at all, that too, was blazing fiercely. Everyone retreated into the yard to watch and, when the heat became too intense, moved further away, but no one made any attempt to put it out.

The barn was an inferno by the time the squire arrived on horseback, followed by Fiddy, some of the braver wedding guests and all the menservants he could muster. The first person he saw was Kate. She was standing on the open ground in front of the barn, her woollen skirt torn from hem to knee, her blonde curls sticking to her cheeks, the reflection of the fire dancing in her eyes.

'You again!' he said, looking down at her from the back of his hunting mare, whose nostrils twitched and eyes dilated in terror at the flames. The horse sidestepped restlessly, threatening to rear up and throw her rider off, but Sir John was a good horseman and held her firmly in check while he glared down at Kate. 'Why do I always find you wherever there is trouble?'

'Because to you I am trouble,' she retorted. 'Wherever you are, whatever you do, I'll not rest 'til you're beaten.'

'How dare you, you brazen ... harlot ...' He knew that bandying words with her would lose him the advantage and yet he could not help himself. And she was smiling, actually smiling at him. Furious, he raised his crop and brought it down across her shoulders. The end of it flicked across her face causing a little spurt of blood to run down her cheek. He felt the sadistic triumph he always enjoyed when the hounds had caught the fox after a particularly good chase. It was almost primeval, man's mastery of the wild. She was wild but he would tame her. 'I'll teach you to defy me.' Again he raised the whip, but before he could bring it down, it was snatched from his hand and he was dragged from his horse. It was a moment or two before Kate realised it was Matthew who had rescued her; she had not seen him arrive.

She watched, with her fist to her mouth, as the two men fell to the ground, rolling over and over, exchanging blows, getting up and being pulled down again. No one interfered. Around them the fire crackled and the old timbers of the barn creaked and groaned and finally toppled, sending a shower of sparks over everyone; intent on the fight, they hardly noticed. Nearby animals snorted in terror and the squire's mare bolted back to the stables. Men were shouting encouragement and children crying, running hither and thither searching for smoke-blackened parents. And then, above it all, a gun was fired.

It was enough to distract Matthew so that Sir John was able to extricate himself. He scrambled to his feet and went to stand beside Fiddy, who was calmly reloading his gun. Matthew went to Kate. He looked a sorry sight in torn trousers, the shirt half ripped from his back and with bloodied nose and bruised cheek, but he was unbowed and watchful, like a lion temporarily deprived of its prey. The mob became silent, unmoving, waiting.

Kate turned to Matthew. 'Are you hurt?'

'Never felt better.' He laughed and wiped the blood from his nose.

'Go to your homes, all of you,' Sir John shouted. He was every bit as dishevelled and bruised as Matthew. His new coat of blue superfine was caked with mud, his silk cravat had become untied and hung like a limp rag beneath a swollen chin. Blood dripped from a cut above his eye. 'Mistress Green, take your young ones to their beds, and you, Barny Bullock, have you not yet learned sense? All of you, go home, before I have the whole lot of you taken to Wisbech gaol. And don't think I can't do it, because I can and I will if you have not left in two minutes.' He drew his watch from his waistcoat pocket but it was so obviously broken, it raised a roar of laughter. 'You will be laughing the other side of your faces, if you do not do as I say,' he went on. 'I'll send for the militia and we'll see how amusing you find that.'

Fiddy lifted the reloaded gun to his shoulder and Sir John drew a sheet of paper from his pocket and began to read aloud, swiftly and without inflexion: *'Our sovereign lord the King, chargeth and commandeth all persons being assembled, immediately to disperse themselves and peaceably to depart to their habitations, or to their lawful business upon the pains contained in the Act made in the first year of King George, for preventing tumults and riotous assemblies. God save the King.'*

The villagers, the spunk gone out of them, began drifting away. They didn't want to be picked out as Kate had been and they didn't trust the bailiff not to fire.

'Come on, let's go,' Matthew said, taking Kate's hand.

'Not you.' Sir John grabbed her arm, making her wince. 'I want you. And him.' He pointed to Matthew. 'You two I mean to make an example of.'

'But he wasn't even here,' Kate cried. 'He's been away all day, he had nothing to do with this.'

'Hold your tongue, girl!' Sir John snapped and then, turning to Fiddy, 'Take them back to the stables and lock them in the harness room until morning.'

There was nothing they could do in the face of Fiddy's menacing gun. Hand in hand they preceded the bailiff across the fields to the Hall, followed by the squire, who had retrieved his crop from the ground where Matthew had flung it. When they reached the stables they were pushed roughly into the harness room and the door locked behind them.

'Rest easy 'til morning,' the squire called as he walked away. 'Tomorrow you go to Wisbech gaol and that will be a mite less comfortable.'

The temporary prison was more than adequate for its purpose.

It was a small room with a tiny barred window and a hard earth floor. Matthew tugged at the bars but they were firmly embedded in the brickwork and the door was solid and securely bolted. There was nothing in the room heavy enough to force it, only bits of harness and brasses hanging on hooks round the wall, a couple of old saddles and the discarded mantrap.

Kate found herself looking at that in the meagre light coming from the window as if mesmerised; she could almost see her Pa lying there, held by its iron jaws. That was how it had all begun, the trigger that set it off, and she wished she knew how it would end. One thing she was sure of, the squire would do nothing to help Josiah now, and she could not tell him anything he did not already know. In some ways it was a relief she no longer had to make the impossible choice, but if it meant Pa would die ... She refused to believe it; Sir John had just been trying to frighten her.

'I can see no hope of escape from here,' Matthew said, breaking into her thoughts. 'We'll just have to take our chances on the road to Wisbech tomorrow.' His voice was hard, practical, angry even. 'It's our only hope. Once in gaol, we'll not get out and I, for one, have more important things to do than languish behind bars.'

'Matthew,' she queried. 'Are you very angry?'

'Of course I'm angry,' he said, turning towards her. 'I'd got the men round to my way of thinking and the silly fools had to go and storm the Hall. It's ill-considered actions like that which ruin it for every farm worker in the country. Breaking the law does nothing to bring about justice for the people. Sir John has every right to charge them all with riotous behaviour and destroying his threshing machine.'

'But Mr Fiddy had taken Charlie and his mother was so upset, we had to do something.'

'Charlie knew what he was risking when he killed that sheep. Who's crazy idea was that?'

'I don't know, but I saw him and Nat Green do it. I searched everywhere to tell you about it, but you were nowhere to be found.' If he could be angry, then so could she. 'You can't blame the men for acting on their own if you are not there ...'

'I was busy elsewhere.'

'Doing what? You hadn't been to your work, I know, because I went looking for you. No one would tell me where you were. They still don't trust me.'

'I expect they think it has nothing to do with you.'

'Of course it has. And I can keep secrets too, you know.'

He laughed suddenly, thinking of the mystery surrounding her and wondering if she was as ignorant of her background as she maintained. 'I don't doubt it.'

'Matthew,' she said, touching his arm lightly, wanting some physical contact with him, but fearing a rebuff. 'Why are you so prickly, like a hedgehog ready to curl up into a ball all the time?'

'Because you have no business involving yourself in all this. Now Sir John has singled you out ...'

'I have been involved right from the start, and you know it, so don't you go taking your temper out on me, Matthew Tolley. You should have been here when you were needed, though what you could have done to help Charlie, I don't know.'

He sighed. 'No, I don't either, and now the damage is done, I doubt if I can restore the situation.'

'Who wants it restored?' she said defiantly. 'The squire would never have listened to combination men anyway.'

'Kate, it's not just Middleacre, it's everywhere. Middleacre is only one small village. Don't you realise the implications of what is happening, of what we are trying to do?'

'Implications?' It was a strange word to use, but then, he used a lot of words which weren't the normal vocabulary of a labourer. Just who was he? And was it because of the mystery surrounding him that she felt drawn towards him? Was that what they had in common? Or was it his physique and masculine good looks? Could her judgement of him be clouded by that? But love had nothing to do with judgement, Pa had told her that, and what she wanted most was for Matthew to love her as she loved him. But thinking of Betty Watson, she knew that was too much to hope for. She blinked back her tears; he must not see her cry.

'The old order of things is changing,' he said softly, looking out of the grimy window at the star-filled night. Across the fields, the barn still smouldered, throwing an eerie glow over the landscape. 'It is already changing. Here in this village, in Lowacre and Wisbech and Ely, from north to south over the whole country the labourers are asserting themselves. Soon they will no longer be the underdogs, but free men, able to choose the work they do and for whom they do it, able to bargain for their services instead of bowing down and accepting the crumbs thrown to them by the landowners.' He was aware of his disloyalty to Daniel, but it couldn't be helped. He had ceased to sit on the fence, although he was no less uncomfortable.

'But you don't approve of them fighting.'

'It is not the way to win. They have to negotiate from a position of strength and they can only do that if they combine.'

'I don't understand.'

He smiled. 'My lovely Kate, you do not need to understand, just trust me.'

'Of course I trust you. But you are angry with the wrong person. Vent your temper out on Sir John Haddow, not me.'

He smiled. 'I just did and look what happened.'

'Why did you do it if you don't hold with fighting? You could have stayed hidden.'

He took her face in both his hands and tilted it up so that he could look into her eyes. The moonlight, coming through the barred window, lit the bright, unshed tears on her lashes and he knew there was no hope for him. It was not pity, but love, he felt, and nothing could change it. 'Could I?' he whispered softly, kissing her tear-wet cheeks, then her arching neck and soft lips. 'I think not.'

She felt his strength flow into her, making her feel warm and safe. His lips on hers sent shivers all through her, from the top of her head to her toes, as if there was a hidden life in her waiting to be discovered. She clung to him, returning his kisses, forgetting everything else in her desire to discover more about this big, passionate man. Their surroundings faded from her consciousness; there was no one else in the whole world but the two of them. She wanted it to go on for ever.

He drew away at last and stood looking down at eyes which sparkled in the gloom and tore his insides worse than any wound he had received in battle. He had no right to kiss her like that. 'Your Pa has not equipped you to live in the real world of men and women, has he?' he said thickly. 'He hasn't told you the difference between love and desire, jealousy and hate. It is something you will have to learn ...'

'And I suppose it's still not the time and place,' she said, some of her spirit returning.

'Perhaps not,' he said, pulling her to him again. 'But if I'm to have any peace of mind, you will have to learn soon.' He kissed her again, exploring her mouth with his, and though she had no inkling of what he meant, she responded instinctively.

He thrust her from him suddenly, disgusted with himself. 'This is madness.'

'Why?' She was perplexed. 'What is wrong?'

'Everything.' He looked about him. 'This place, this situation, your innocence, my weakness. I never intended it to happen. Please forget it ever did.'

'Forget it?' She was hurt and puzzled. 'How can I?'

'Then put it down to anger or frustration, or just plain stupidity, put it down to anything you like, but dismiss it from your mind.'

'Are *you* going to forget it?'

'Yes,' he lied.

Her spirits sank like a stone dropped into the deepest hole in the fen, and ripples of misery spread right through her. 'I'm sorry I do not please you,' she said stiffly.

'I didn't say that.' He cursed himself for a fool. 'Oh, Kate, try to understand. There is no future for us together.'

'No, because there is someone else, isn't that so?'

He was too surprised to answer and she went on as if she were determined to hurt herself even more than he had hurt her, to punish herself for even daring to hope. It had been only too easy to dream, but she would not let it happen again. She put both her hands on his broad chest and pushed him away from her. 'I feel sorry for her, if this is how you behave when you are away from her.'

'Who?' he asked, genuinely puzzled; she could know nothing of Amy.

'The girl you are going to wed,' she said, not wanting to put a name to the object of her jealousy. 'You are not free to kiss anyone you fancy just when the fancy takes you, are you?'

'No,' he said, morosely. 'I'm not free, nor ever will be again, and perhaps, when all this is over, I will marry, but she won't be getting such a bargain when all's said and done. Until then I will keep faith with those who have put their trust in me.' He sat down with his back leaning against the rough wall opposite her and patted the ground beside him. 'Let's talk of it no more. You should rest. Come and sit down.' He was once again the cool-headed leader of men; their moment of intimacy had gone and she wanted to weep. She slid down the wall where she was and rested her head on an old saddle; she could not bring herself to sit beside him.

He peered through the gloom at her, but decided that if she chose to keep her distance, then perhaps she was more sensible than he was; he had been weak and selfish. He had no right to her love.

'Matthew,' she said, after a moment. 'Why did you come to Middleacre?'

'I was asked to.'

'But why was it such a secret?'

He hesitated, wondering whether to tell her about himself, about his home, about Daniel and Amy, but decided against it; the less she knew, the less she could pass on. It wasn't that he didn't trust her, but he was unsure how she would view the fact that he was himself one of the hated upper class. 'Because if the law gets its hands on me, then I could no longer help the labourers, could I?'

'I thought you didn't hold with breaking the law.'

'I don't, at least, not by the villagers.'

'But it's all right for you to flout it?'

'It's too late for me now.' He meant it in more ways that one. In defending her he had passed from negotiator to lawbreaker and shut the door on his old life; there was no going back to it. This was not simply a passing phase, an episode in his existence in which he could do some good for his fellow men and then take up the ways of a gentleman again as if nothing had happened. Kate had seen to that.

'Yes, but why you? You are a soldier, not a farm worker.'

'True, but I fought alongside ordinary men, good men, who had enlisted to escape the rigours of life at home where they could not earn enough to support their families. Their army pay, little though it was, helped to keep them from starving but separation from their loved ones was a high price for that and I wanted to see why it had been necessary.'

Kate remembered Josiah telling her something of the sort had happened to him. 'And have you?'

'Yes, I believe so.'

'Have you been able to change anything for the better?'

'Only in a very small way. I discovered I had a facility for negotiation, seeing both sides of the argument, bringing people together.'

'Pa said you had come to talk to the men and stop them causing trouble over the enclosure.'

'In a way, that was true. I simply hoped to persuade Sir John to change his mind without having to resort to the tactics of Captain Swing.'

'But you did in the end.'

'It was forced on me by circumstance, as you well know.'

'Because of me, because I could not keep my nose out of it.'

He smiled in the darkness. 'Only partly. Please do not blame yourself.'

'How can I not? You can't help them if you are in prison, can you?'

'We aren't in prison yet,' he said gently. 'Try to sleep now. Nothing more will happen until the morning.'

But he was wrong. Long before dawn they heard shouting in the distance and knew the villagers were mustering again. Not entirely sober, they made no effort to move silently and stumbled across the moonlit fields carrying long-handled torches and farm implements. Their numbers grew as they approached the stables, shouting and thrusting their brands into every rick they passed until the landscape was dotted with burning stacks and smoke drifted on the wind across the park and obscured the moon.

Kate stirred, but Matthew was already up and at the window. 'What's happening?' she asked, scrambling to her feet and joining him.

'They're mad,' he said, peering through the grimy glass. 'Do they think Sir John will let them unlock this door and set us free without lifting a finger to prevent it? He'll have Fiddy and his men on watch, there could be bloodshed.' He tried to shout, to tell them to leave, but the rabble, for that is what it had become, could not or would not hear.

The sound of Fiddy's gun sent them scampering for the cover of bushes and outhouses. 'Do you git along home,' he shouted. 'Go home. I know every man jack of you and you'll not escape. It's chokey for the hull lot o' you if you don't pack up and go home this minute.'

'You can't shoot us all at once.' This was Watson's voice.

'No, but one at a time I can, so who's to be first.'

There was a moment's silence. Matthew and Kate, their noses pressed to the window, tried to make out what was happening.

'I wish they'd go away,' Kate said. 'I don't want anyone killed on my account.'

Matthew smashed the glass and shouted, 'Go home! Go away, all of you!' They recognised his voice without hearing what he said; it goaded them into further effort and they stormed into the open. Fiddy's gun went off again and then other guns. The prisoners looked at each other in dismay, then turned back to the window in time to see about a dozen blue-coated militia riding into the yard in front of the stables.

'Oh, God!' Matthew said as the two sides confronted each other, severity on one side, doubt on the other. 'It should never have come to this.'

Reluctantly the villagers admitted themselves beaten; standing up to Fiddy was one thing, facing armed soldiers another. Slowly they backed away, and then they turned and ran as fast as their legs would carry them. After a short conference with Fiddy, the militia left and Matthew relaxed suddenly, his whole body going limp as if it had been a mighty effort of will on his part which had avoided the confrontation. He turned away from the window and sank once more to the floor, where he sat with his chin on his chest. Kate did not speak because his attitude did not invite intrusion on his thoughts. He had revealed a vulnerability she had not known he possessed, and somehow it made him more human. She wanted to comfort him, to tell him that she loved him, that he had done his best and no one could ask for more, but she could not frame the words. She sat down beside him and put out a hand. He grasped it without speaking. They were still sitting hand in hand when dawn came.

Daylight, coming through the tiny window, woke Matthew. He eased himself carefully away from Kate and moved his cramped limbs. Then he stood up and went to the window, where she joined him. The ground was littered with bits of burnt wood, overturned carts, uprooted bushes and, over it all, a pall of black smoke.

'It's all my fault,' she said. 'All of it. If I'd kept out of it like you said, you wouldn't have had to rescue me and you could have got away. This would never have happened.'

'You can't be sure of that,' he said. 'Perhaps it was inevitable, perhaps it was written in the stars ...'

She did not have time to answer because a sudden noise, followed by the grating sound of a bolt being drawn, made them both jump and turn towards the door. It was flung open and Andrew stood in its frame. He was immaculately dressed for riding and carried a crop, as if he had been out for an early morning canter. Kate looked from him to Matthew, still in the tattered clothes of a labourer who had been in a scrap. The silence stretched as the two men stared at each other. She could not bear it. She stepped towards Matthew and took his hand.

Andrew smiled; so that was the way of it. So be it. He stood aside to allow them to pass. 'Go quickly,' he said. 'Get right away before Sir John wakes.'

They hesitated only a second, then with Kate breathing their gratitude, they ran past him, through the stables and out into the yard. Across the park they sped and through the woods, not daring to pause until they were in the shelter of the trees. Here they stopped to regain their breath.

'Why did he let us out?' she asked as they moved off again, towards the drove road.

'Perhaps he thinks of himself as Sir Galahad,' he said with a quirky smile. 'Rescuing a damsel in distress.'

'Me?' She laughed. 'No, I just think he is trying to be fair but if his uncle ever finds out what he's done ...'

'He can look after himself,' he said. 'What we have to decide is what we do next.'

They had arrived at the door of the drovers' hut. He stopped and turned to face her, taking both her hands in his own. 'Kate, I have to go back to the inn. I've left some papers in my room and I must destroy them before they are found.' He looked more exhausted than one night's loss of sleep should have caused. She was not entirely convinced that he was not still angry with her and now she knew a little more about what he had hoped to achieve, she didn't really blame him if he were.

'You mean to leave me here?'

'How can I?' It was unthinkable but he was in a dilemma. He could not leave her and yet he could not take her with him. He cast about him for the answer but all he saw was a broad swathe of grass and a tumbledown hovel. 'Wait here,' he said. 'I'll come back. Keep out of sight and don't wander off and get into more trouble ...'

He *was* still annoyed with her. She didn't want them to part in anger and she didn't want to face another lonely day in the drovers' hut, but she could not complicate things any more than she already had. She put on a brave face and smiled at him. 'I'll be good.'

He took her shoulders in his hands and bent to put a kiss on her forehead, then he turned abruptly and ran up the drove to the lane, leaving her to shut herself in the crude building.

He was not sure at what point curiosity, pity, compassion, had become love, but that's what it was. He loved Kate. He was no longer in love with Amy; he doubted now if he ever had been, not in the same way. He had been a fool, but if he had not been such a dunderhead, he would never have met Kate. It was fate, destiny, call it what you like, but it was a fact. Now he had to do something to extricate them both. Could he take her home, make up a story which would convince everyone she was anything but an impoverished nobody? Could she portray the kind of young lady his father would approve of and would Amy welcome her? Would Kate agree? No, he decided, she would never leave the old poacher. He was the key.

The wedding night had been anything but satisfactory, Sir John decided as he went down to breakfast. It had been difficult enough placating Laura over the fact that they could not leave for their honeymoon as planned, without the added distraction of the noise outside, shouting and guns going off and fires in the fields which had lit their bedchamber in an eerie glow. How could a man be expected to rise to the heights of passion with all that going on? And his thoughts had been with the girl in the harness room, the girl with fire in her eyes and venom on her tongue, and he could not keep his mind on the painted shrew who lay beside him in the big four-poster, though she had used all her not inconsiderable talents to rouse him.

He meant to have the poacher's daughter in the end. She had angered him by stirring up trouble and she was a little thief, but there was more to it than that. It had something to do with the way she looked, the proud, almost arrogant set of her head, her defiant attitude, her beauty, so fragile, so perfect, so out of keeping with her role in life. It disturbed him and it had nothing at all to do with justice. He rose early, much to Mrs Bunny's annoyance, and summoned Fiddy to the breakfast room.

'What was all the commotion last night?' he asked, when his bailiff appeared.

Fiddy stood, looking down at his hands, nervously turning his hat round and round. 'The villagers tried to storm the stables, Sir John. They fired all the ricks on the way.'

'The devil they did! And what did you do?'

'Waited for the militia, Sir John. There weren't narthin' I could do single-handed. They sent the rabble packin' as soon as they rode up.'

'Good.' He helped himself generously to ham and eggs from the serving dish in front of him. 'Now fetch those two out of the harness room. I've a notion to ask them a few questions myself before I send them to Wisbech. The man is a stranger to the village and he's no peasant, I'll warrant. He's a rabblerouser and I mean to find out what his little game is.'

'Sir John, I can't.' Fiddy looked miserable. 'Not right now, I can't.'

'Can't what, man?'

'F ... fetch them, Sir John.' He was almost stammering in his agitation. 'The prisoners. They've disappeared into thin air and the door of the harness room still bolted on the outside.'

It was a full minute before Sir John could control himself enough to speak. Then in a voice of icy calm, which Fiddy knew presaged a storm of thundering proportions, he said, 'Then someone let them out. Did you stay on guard as I instructed you?'

'Indeed, I did,' the man lied, not daring to admit that he had delegated that unpleasant task to an under-gardener and that young good-for-nothing had obviously fallen asleep in the hay of the stables or gone off home after the militia left, believing the prison to be secure. 'It's witchcraft.'

'I'll thank you not to insult me by lying to me.' The anger was building up in his eyes, but he was cool enough on the surface. 'They must be recaptured before the day is out; I'll not rest until they are safely put away. And neither will you, because if they are not back in custody by this evening, your head will roll, do you hear? You will take their place in Wisbech gaol. Until those two have been recaptured and all desire for rioting has been stamped out, neither you nor I will rest. Is that understood?'

'Yes, Sir John.'

'Get all the outside staff and as many footmen as can be spared to search every corner of the village. And if anyone is foolhardy enough to hide them, they will find themselves in the dock beside them. Tell them that. And check the stage.'

'Yes, Sir John.' The bailiff sped away, thankful he still had his job, though if he failed in his task, he was not at all sure of having it by evening.

'I'll have him if it's the last thing I do,' Sir John muttered. 'I'll make sure he hangs. And as for that thieving strumpet ...' He paused to conjure up a fate for Kate, but because he could think of nothing but a proud golden head and blazing blue eyes, words failed him and he contented himself with stamping about the house and barking orders while his bride sulked in her room because he had delayed their departure yet again and Mrs Bunny grumbled that she didn't know if she was coming or going.

'First they were going yesterday,' she said. 'Then it was this morning and now I don't know when it is. How'm I to cater if I don't know who's going to be here?'

By the late afternoon, the only person who remained calm was Andrew. Sir John found him in the library when he went there to fortify himself with brandy.

'Six months in Bridewell, that's all he gave him,' he grumbled. 'I don't know what Gardiner is coming to, getting soft in his old age.'

'You mean the fellow you locked up last night?' Andrew said, putting down his newspaper. He was sorry that Matthew had been caught again, but more concerned about Kate. 'What about the girl?'

'No, not those two, they've disappeared or someone is hiding them.'

'Then who ...'

'That youngster. Barber I think his name is. I had him arrested and taken into Wisbech this morning. Six months, Gardiner gave him, and a sermon on mending his ways. A fat lot of good that will do.'

'It's long enough, specially when you think that Barber is the family breadwinner and without him they will have to rely on relief.'

'And who pays the relief?' Sir John said irritably. 'I do.' He emptied his glass at a gulp and filled it again. 'I told Gardiner he had better be ready to treat the other two with maximum severity. I mean to make an example of them.'

'But you said they had disappeared.' Andrew's lazy voice did not betray his interest.

'So they have, but I'll find them and when I discover who let them out, they'll wish they had never been born.'

Andrew put the paper down and rose to his feet. 'I must go,' he said evenly. 'I promised to take Mother for a drive.'

'Speaking of my sister,' Sir John said. 'I don't wish to be inhospitable, but I do think you should take her home. She is having one of her bad turns and would be better at home among her own people and servants who know how to deal with her.'

Andrew's lazy look turned instantly to one of alarm. 'She was all right this morning.'

'That's as maybe but I've just seen her and she's addlepated now.'

'Uncle, I wish you would not use that expression when referring to my stepmother.'

'What else should I say ? Heaven knows I am very fond of my sister, but there's no denying she's mad.'

'She is not mad, nor ever has been. Sometimes her mind becomes a little muddled, that's all.'

'Her mind is certainly muddled now. I found her wandering about the ruins of the barn, getting covered in smuts and crying that she had seen the child. Take her home, Andrew, before I have her constrained ; the barn is dangerous in its present state.'

Andrew sighed. Most of the time his stepmother was perfectly rational but, every now and again, something triggered off a memory of the child she had lost and then the intervening years disappeared ; she was young again and relived the torment of that time. Once she had tried to take another woman's infant and on other occasions she had accused mothers of stealing her child. He and his father had usually been able to soothe ruffled feelings and just lately she had been a great deal better, but the tragedy was never far below the surface of her mind and they had to be forever watchful. For once, he agreed with Sir John; she would be better at home.

He found her sitting in the window seat of her room, staring out at the barn, just visible between the trees. She was still wearing her outdoor clothes, a warm wool pelisse and a pleated silk bonnet. She had not even taken off her walking boots. Her face was dirty and tear-streaked and her hands were nervously playing with a trinket, twisting the chain round her fingers and opening and closing the clasp. He pulled the bell-rope for her maid. 'Why are you sitting here like that, Mother?'

She stirred. 'I was thinking.'

'Where is Susan?'

'I sent her to help Mrs Bunny. There is so much to do after yesterday.' She shuddered suddenly. 'Such a happy day to start with and then it was spoiled.'

He touched her shoulder and spoke gently. 'We'll go home, Mother.'

'I can't leave her.'

'Who?' he asked, knowing the answer and dreading it.

'My child.' She turned a tear-streaked face towards him, her eyes pleading to be believed. 'I know she's out there somewhere.'

'No, Mother, she is not,' he said firmly, moving to the fireplace to give the bellrope a tug. 'She's been dead and gone this many a year. And it happened a long way from here. Please don't make yourself sad thinking of her.'

'She is, I know she is. The fire ...'

He went over to her and put his arm about her to persuade her to leave the window, just as Susan arrived in answer to his summons. The plump, motherly woman, who was more companion than maid, hurried over to her mistress. 'I knew you shouldn't have gone out without me, just look at the state you're in.' She looked up at Andrew, afraid he would blame her. 'She insisted, Sir, said she wanted to walk alone. I should have known ...'

'It's all right, Susan,' he said. 'But I think she would be better at home, don't you?'

'Indeed I do, sir. This is not a happy place.' She put her arm round her mistress and raised her to her feet. 'Come, ma'am, let me help you out of that coat.'

'How soon can you be ready?' Andrew asked. 'Can we go tomorrow?'

'Whenever you wish.'

'Good.' He left Felicity in her maid's capable hands and went to the stables to order the coach to be harnessed and sent round to the door immediately after breakfast the following morning.

He would not be sorry to leave the fens. As a boy he had loved its wide expanses of flat green meadows dotted with cattle, its acres of fields divided, not by hedges or walls, but by ditches, its quietly lapping water, fringed with reed and willow, as often as not clothed in a mist which gave it a shivering kind of mystery. He had often been out in a boat, so shrouded in fog that nothing could be seen but the craft itself and there was nothing to hear but the cry of the wild fowl and the whoosh of their wings. It was a world that did not seem to belong to the civilisation of the nineteenth century and it was easy to imagine oneself way back at the dawn of history, when man battled against the elements for survival. You were very close to the elements in this part of the country and perhaps that was why the people were so hardy, so difficult to subdue. Nothing could be further from the crowded streets of the town where he had been born and brought up, with its overshadowing mills which swallowed up humanity at daybreak and spewed it out again at dusk. The one survived in isolation, the other in crowds. But now the countryside had changed, it was a bubbling cauldron and the proud, independent people were seething. He wished he knew how to help them.

Thinking of the villagers reminded him of Kate, so concerned for others, so proud and independent, so typical of her kind. No, he decided, she was far from typical, she was different, she was someone very special. And suddenly he knew he loved her. The realisation came as an overwhelming shock and he mused on it for some time before concluding the idea was preposterous and he had better put such thoughts firmly out of his head. He spent what remained of the day and the sleepless night which followed half regretting the impulse which had led him to set her free and feeling damnably jealous of Matthew. On the one hand he was sorry to be leaving her to her fate, but on the other, he knew he must put her from his mind and that was easier done away from Middleacre, where every blade of grass, every dancing reed, every stunted willow reminded him of her.

As soon as he had supervised the loading of their luggage the following morning, he went in search of his stepmother and found her picking at her breakfast, her eyes swollen with weeping. 'Come, Mother, it is time we were off.'

'I don't want to go. I have to find out . . .'

'No, Mother.' He would brook no argument; this was the worst she had been for a long time and he had to be cruel to be kind. 'There is nothing we can do here. We are going now.' He called Susan to fetch her hat and cloak and bring one or two hot bricks to keep her feet warm, and when she had said goodbye to her brother and the new Lady Haddow, he escorted her to the coach, putting a brick at her feet and wrapping a warm rug round her.

The journey was a long one, not made any easier by the dreadful state of the roads, and involved sundry overnight stops in widely differing accommodation, and even more changes of horses. They went northwest to Spalding and on to Nottingham and over the Pennines, where they several times had to dig their way out of snow and by then he was wishing they had never set out. It was not until the third day, when both he and Susan had exhausted all the subjects of conversation they could think of to keep Felicity's spirits up, he noticed the trinket she had been playing with at Haddow Hall was again in her hands.

'What have you got there, Mother?'

'A locket.' She held it out to him and he took it and examined the portrait it contained.

'It looks like the Dowager Lady Haddow.'

'It is. It was lost and now, by a miracle, it's been found.' She took it back from him. 'I was wearing it that day when ...' She paused unable to speak of that time. 'You know when. I never saw it again until the day before yesterday. I went to the library to ask John about something – I've forgotten what it was now – and there it was, lying on his desk.'

'Perhaps you left it behind the last time you visited Uncle John.'

'At first I thought so, but then I realised I couldn't have done. I didn't have it. The last time I saw it was that day ... She was tugging at it and I was afraid the chain would break, so I took it off and gave it to her to play with. I'd forgotten about it until I saw it on John's desk and then I did not remember when I last had it. It came to me in a flash when we stopped last night.'

'How did it get on the desk?'

'John said he had taken it from a gypsy who must have stolen it.' Her eyes were bright with excitement.

'When?'

'He didn't say. When I asked him about it, he said he had too much on his mind with the wedding and the trouble over the labourers to worry about such matters. I don't think he realises how important it is to me.'

He was inclined to agree with her. Sir John Haddow was too self-centred to think of anything or anyone but himself. 'It could have been years ago,' he said flatly; it would do no good to let her hopes rise. It had happened before and led to disappointment which had made her ill for weeks.

'And still been on his desk?' She turned pleading eyes towards him. 'I know everyone thinks I'm mad, perhaps I have been in the past, but I'm perfectly sensible now.'

'Of course you are,' he soothed.

'I wish we could turn back.'

'Mother, you know we can't. The road will be soon be impassable.'

'I want to meet this gypsy,' she said. 'I want her to tell me herself how she came to have it. Perhaps the gypsies took my baby, perhaps she is still alive ... Perhaps the gypsy ...' She gripped the locket until her knuckles showed white.

'But how do you find a gypsy. They do not stay in one place, do they? She could have moved on long ago.'

'I know. But don't you see? We have to try. Andrew, you will go back, won't you? When I am safely home, you will go back and question John about her? Find her and bring her to me?'

It was snowing again. The road behind them was blanketed; he could not return until spring. By that time, she could have gone anywhere. 'If it will please you, I'll go as soon as the weather clears,' he said. He had no reason to think Sir John had taken the locket from Kate but he could not get the idea out of his head. And he had set her free to go ... where?

Chapter Twelve

*I*t was bitterly cold in the cabin but Kate dare not risk a fire for fear of being seen by the small army of estate workers who were out searching for the runaways. She could hear the sound of dogs and shouting in the distance and cowered even further into the corner, wondering how much longer it would be before she was found. But mindful of Matthew's instructions, she stayed in her hiding place. She hugged the memory of his arms about her, his kisses on her face, his tenderness; surely that meant he loved her and would not leave her to her fate? But he had also been angry with her, so perhaps it meant nothing. Where was he? Had he gone back to Betty Watson? Had he left the village to return whence he came? She told herself sternly that even that was preferable to having him recaptured; heaven knew what Sir John would do to him if he caught him. She lay on her bed of rushes with Matthew's cloak about her, and dozed fitfully as the long day, and an even longer night, dragged on. By morning, she was in despair. If he did not come soon, she would be discovered because she could hear Sir John's men coming closer and they would be bound to come to the hut. She looked around but there was nowhere to hide in it.

She lifted her head to listen as a low, distant sound was borne on the breeze. It was not the searchers she could hear but the lowing of cattle. She rose and went to the window. They were coming up the drove road in their hundreds, filling the air with noise and dust, covering the pasture with a moving mass of living beef. They were being driven by three men who called out to the animals and shouted to each other across their backs, herding them into the meadow on the other side of the drove. The drovers were back and they would certainly come to her hiding place. They were rough, dirty men and would feel no particular loyalty to the village or to Matthew and, once they heard about the search for her, she would be lost.

She dressed hurriedly, grabbed up her shawl and Matthew's cloak and dashed from the hut, doubling low so that she was hidden from the men by the bulk of the animals. She forded the stream by the stepping stones and crossed over into the shelter of Haddow wood. Once there, she stopped to catch her breath; either they had not seen her or, having spotted her, were not interested. Thankfully she sank onto a log to take stock of the situation and decide what to do. No one in the village would give her shelter and she would not ask them. Matthew had been right; she ought to leave Middleacre. But she could not go without seeing him first. She stood up, intending to make her way to The Ferryman, because that was where he said he was going. Eyes down she turned along the woodland path towards the village and found herself imprisoned by steel-hard fingers digging into the flesh of her upper arms. Startled, she looked up into the triumphant face of Fiddy.

'So! The wench was right. The drovers' hut, she said and the drovers' hut it was.'

Kate was too concerned with trying to free herself to ask what he meant. 'Let me go! Let me go!'

'Oh, no, me fine lady, you might as well stand still, for you'll not escape again, that I promise you.'

The cloak dropped from her shoulders as he began to pull her along the path towards Haddow Hall, making light of her spirited resistance. 'Oh, this will please the squire no end.'

'Let me go. I've done you no harm.'

'No? If I find myself without a situation because of you, it'll be harm enough. Stop your struggling, will you? I in't a-goin' to let you go.' He had her by the hand now and was dragging her along the path.

'Why is Sir John picking on me?'

'Because of who you are, I suppose.'

'But I don't know who I am.'

Surprised, he turned to look at her. 'You are the poacher's daughter, aren't you?'

They came out into the open, crossed a paddock and went through the kitchen garden and in at the back door. The kitchen staff left off what they were doing to stare as Kate was dragged through the kitchen to the passage that led to the front hall. She knew there would be no help from that quarter; Mrs Bunny looked sympathetic, Bertha curious and Hetty so triumphant that Kate knew who it was had suggested the drovers' hut; she must have overheard Kate talking to Mrs Bunny. 'Where's Sir John?' Fiddy asked.

'In the drawing room,' Hetty said.

Sir John had been pacing the drawing room ever since he finished his breakfast, eaten by indecision and an obsession to recapture his prisoners, regardless of cost. The man, Tolley, was more than just the leader of a handful of dissident villagers. He wasn't even a labourer, anyone could see that; he was deliberately causing trouble. What he could not even guess at was why. As far as he knew he had never met him before and the name Tolley meant nothing. The thought crossed his mind that he might be the notorious Captain Swing, but that gentleman, if he existed, had never revealed himself before, unless you counted that straw-plait merchant who was already in gaol. And why choose Middleacre? Sir John did not consider himself a bad landlord, better than most for he never interfered in the villagers' lives, most of the time was hardly aware they existed; hadn't he been away over a year? If it had not been for pressing need to increase revenues, he would have left the common alone and let the old rents stand. It wasn't his fault. As for the girl . . .

It wasn't fair that she should upset him so, upset his plans, his marriage, his peace of mind. Was she Tolley's mistress? The man had certainly defended her well. Ruminatively he put his finger to the bruise on his cheek, hardly the thing for a man to display on his honeymoon. Now Laura had issued an ultimatum; either he abandon his hunt and accompany her to London and Italy as they had planned, or she would go with only Annette for company. It was no idle threat, he knew, and what a scandal that would cause. He would be the butt of all the downstairs jokes, the man whose wife went on her wedding tour alone. 'You may join me when you have come to your senses,' she had said. 'But don't leave it too long, for I've other irons in the fire.' He knew she meant it too.

He had no intention of eating humble pie and following on behind, but it was too much to hope that she was already carrying his child and that gave him pause for thought. He was trying to find a way of giving in to her without appearing to do so, when he heard the commotion in the hall. He went to the door to silence it. 'Johnson is that you, making all that racket?'

'No, Sir John,' Fiddy said. 'It's me and I've got the girl. She's a fiery strumpet and no error . . .'

Kate's voice shrilled above his. 'Let me go! Take your filthy hands off me!' A vase crashed to the floor from a spindly legged table and flew into hundreds of shards.

Relief and triumph in equal measure flowed through Sir John as he stood looking down at her. 'Bring her in here.'

Fiddy was hard put to obey because Kate resisted more fiercely than ever, but at last she stood quivering before him, quivering, he realised, not with fear but with rage. She was dressed in the same rough skirt and cotton blouse she had worn the day before, had no hat or coat and her shoes were heavy and mud-spattered. Her hair was bedraggled from the struggle she had put up, but her eyes still defied him.

He turned to Fiddy. 'Get out man, get about your business. I want the man, too, don't forget.'

Fiddy scuttled away and Sir John turned to Kate. 'Now we shall see how brave you are. The whereabouts of the rabblerouser, if you please.'

'Rabblerouser?' Kate was cheered by the news that Matthew had not been recaptured and though she wondered how long he could remain free, she was determined that nothing she said would lead Sir John to him. 'I don't know who you mean.'

'I think you do. The man is not one of the villagers, is he? He isn't even a labourer, anyone can see that; he is stirring up trouble for his own lawless ends. It will go ill for the villagers if they listen to him.'

'Do your worst,' she cried, deciding it was useless to deny his accusations and she might as well be hung for a sheep as a lamb. 'You may be on top now, but the day will come when you will no longer be able to bully and humiliate people as if you own them. Serfdom is dead and it is time you recognised it. The workers will come into their own.'

'Not before I see the rabblerouser hang.'

'Hanged?' she whispered in horror.

'Yes, hanged. He will be caught, make no mistake about that. And as for you . . .' He was coming towards her as he spoke and she backed away, moving round the room, dodging the furniture as if they were performing some strange dance. 'What punishment do you think you merit?'

'None, for I have done no wrong.'

'No wrong! Everything you do is wrong. Your whole life is wrong. You are no more a gypsy than he is a labourer. Do you think I am a fool?'

Wildly looking about her for a way of escape, she did not answer.

'You could make things easier for yourself.'

'By betraying my friends, I suppose.'

'He is not worth the price you are paying – your own liberty, your father's . . .'

Thinking of Pa, she felt a sudden doubt and relaxed her guard momentarily and he reached out to grab her. Ducking, she evaded him and darted to the fireplace, where she picked up the poker and turned to face him, holding it in front of her, ready to defend herself. He moved swiftly and twisted it from her hand, flinging it into the hearth with a resounding crash and turning her about so that her arm was imprisoned behind her and one of his arms encircled her shoulders. She waited for blows, but instead he bent his head and kissed her neck. Enraged, she twisted and sank her teeth into his ear. He yelled with pain and, turning her to face him, held her securely while he kissed her face and neck.

He wanted her, he wanted her so badly he was blind to the consequences. He wanted to break her, to make her cry, to force her to beg; he wanted her on her knees before him, pleading for mercy. She struggled but he had a remarkable strength and held her fast with one hand, while he ripped her blouse from her back with the other. 'I'll have you,' he muttered, bending his head to her bare breasts. 'One way or the other, I'll have you.'

Suddenly he was gone from her, pulled forcibly away, and Kate heard the sound of a slap before she dare open her eyes to see who had rescued her. It was Lady Haddow, white with rage. Her voice, when she spoke, was controlled and icy. 'It would seem I arrived in the nick of time, John dear. How careless of you to put yourself in a position where this peasant could attack you.'

Her husband dabbed at a cut on his cheek made by one of her rings. 'Laura, I thought you were packing.'

'That is done.' She looked at Kate, her dark eyes bright with hatred. 'And now nothing stands in the way of our departure.'

'You haven't got . . .' Kate began defiantly, then paused, unwilling to name him '. . . my friend. He is still free.'

The woman turned to her. 'But not for long. He's bound to come looking for you and then we'll have him too.' She went to the door and called Johnson to go and fetch Fiddy back.

'My dear,' she said to her husband, her voice sugar sweet. 'Don't you think you can leave this affair in other hands now ? You don't need to waste any more time on this hussy, she is beneath your contempt.' She paused and he was left in no doubt of her intentions when she added, 'I have ordered the coach to be brought to the door immediately.' Sir John remained mute and she turned to the door as Fiddy came in. 'Take this . . . this harlot away.'

The bailiff approached cautiously, uncertain of her temper, then looked at his employer, his bushy eyebrows raised in a question.

'You heard Her Ladyship.' Sir John found his voice at last. 'Take the girl to Wisbech and prefer charges on my behalf.'

'What charges, Sir John ?'

'Good God, man, do you need to be told ? Assault, affray, inciting to riot, machine-breaking, arson. Throw the book at her.'

Kate, who had been standing with her arms covering her naked breasts, cried out as Fiddy seized her. 'Not like this! For pity's sake, give me something to cover myself.'

Lady Haddow laughed harshly. 'Let her go as she is. Perhaps it will teach the other women of the village not to meddle.'

Kate was dragged out and taken to the stable yard where a cart horse was harnessed to the tumbril and one of the estate workers ordered to drive it. Fiddy lifted her in and climbed up beside her.

Her cheeks were burning with shame as they left the park by the main gates and trundled through the village at walking pace. She stood upright and stared straight ahead, with her arms crossed over her breasts, mustering every ounce of dignity she possessed, and trying not to shiver, for it was bitterly cold. She would not look to the sides, would not show any sign of being aware of the silent curiosity of the villagers. She knew that Sir John hoped her humiliation would bring Matthew out of hiding, but neither he nor Fiddy knew that Matthew had no real interest in her, that he would always put the cause before her. And he would be right, she told herself; she was unimportant, a nobody, but Matthew was needed if their fight was to be won.

Someone threw a farmhand's smock into the cart and Kate caught sight of Mrs Barber's pale face out of the corner of her eye, but she did not turn towards her, nor bend to pick up the garment; she had her pride and her pride would not let her stoop.

Fiddy picked it up and draped it round her shoulders without saying a word and, once they were out of the village, he allowed her to sit on the floor of the cart and thus they arrived at the door of the Wisbech gaol.

She was reminded of the last time she had been there to plead to see Josiah. What would he say when he heard what had happened? Would he understand? Would she be able to see him now? If she saw him she could explain everything, ask his advice.

Ben Carter was bored. True, there were plenty of people in the gaol but no one of any consequence. All he had to do was feed them and bring them before the magistrates at the appropriate time. He liked doing that; it gave him a sense of power, made him feel important and dignified. What he would really like was to make an outstanding arrest, bring a real villain to justice; petty thieves, drunkards, poachers, they were nothing and their insolence soon collapsed when they found themselves in the dock. Now, if he could capture a murderer or ... His thoughts stopped rambling and he sat up with a jerk, as Fiddy propelled Kate into the room in front of him.

'Lock her up good and tight,' he said.

The superintendent grinned broadly. The girl had given his dignity a severe dent and here she was in his power. 'What's the charge?'

'Rioting, machine-breaking, arson, assault ...'

'Who did she assault?'

'Sir John Haddow.'

Ben Carter looked up at Kate with a gleam in his eye. 'Violent miss, aren't you? Now we'll see who's master. I'll add my name to this.'

Fiddy noticed the look and though he hardly cared what the man did to the girl, he did not want her to have grounds for complaining of her treatment. A sympathetic magistrate might take it into account. 'You treat her proper or you'll have Sir John to answer to, he's taken a particular interest in this one.'

'I can see that.' Ben laughed, looking at Kate's half-covered breasts and torn skirt. He picked up a bunch of keys from the table in front of him. 'Leave her with me. When's she to come up?'

'Tomorrow.'

'That's Mr Gardiner. He's inclined to be soft, but with all she's charged with, he'll do his duty. You may tell Sir John I'll prepare a good case. Unless he wants to do it himself?'

'No, of course not, man, why should he lower himself to prosecute a peasant. Besides, he's off on his honeymoon.'

Kate did not speak as Fiddy left and Ben Carter grabbed her arm, deliberately digging his finger nails into her flesh. 'Come alonga me. Now, you'll learn no one kicks Ben Carter and gets away with it.'

'I'm sorry,' she said, wanting to ask him about Josiah and knowing she had to placate him. 'I should not have done that, but I was so worried about Pa, you see. I still am. Do you think I could see him while I'm here?'

'No, you can't. You're in here to be punished, not to go visitin'.'

Although disappointed, she was hardly surprised. 'Is he well?'

'He does well enough, considerin'.'

And with that she had to be satisfied because they had arrived at the door of the cell which he unlocked, pushing her inside and making a great to-do about locking it again. As soon as his echoing footsteps on the stone flagging had faded away, she sank to the floor, put her head in her hands and wept.

'Cheer up, m'dear. 'Tin't the end of the world.'

Kate looked up to find she was sharing the cell with two other women, who had emerged from the gloom to stand in front of her. They might have been any age, thin as scarecrows and dressed in rags.

She mopped her eyes on the hem of her skirt and smiled weakly. 'I didn't see you. How long have you been in here?'

'Since yesterday. What are you in for?'

'Everything. There was a riot.'

They nodded sagely. 'From Middleacre, are you?'

'You heard about it?'

'Yes. The tale is everywhere. They say Captain Swing was involved. Is it true? Have you met him?'

'No,' she said warily. 'It was just the village men. What are you in for?'

'Taking half a sack of grain that had bin left behind in the barn,' one of them said. 'Half a sack. What good is that to a hungry family? I reckon our lot'll be next for a bit o' rick burning.'

'I don't know that it helps,' Kate said wearily. 'I don't know what does. Some think they should combine.'

'Aye, they've talked of that too, but the risk is too great. If the men are in prison or deported, how will we manage?'

'They get put in prison for burning ricks.'

'If they're caught but you c'n set a rick a-fire in the dead o' night and no one the wiser. If you hev a combination, you hev to tek an oath and stand t'gither in the open. Asides, the justices in't as hard on arson as they be on combinations.'

Kate was glad to have someone to talk to; it stopped her from brooding on her own fate and when night came, she settled down to sleep on the narrow truckle bed, prepared to bear with stoicism whatever befell her.

But her sleep was disturbed by vivid dreams. She was in an enormous room filled with noisy machinery which clanked on and on, so that she could hear nothing else. The heat was so intense it was unbearable and the light was so poor she could see little more than shadows, but there were children there, dozens of them, moving slowly and wearily and they were all silently coughing. She tried to go to them, but was held back, though she did not know who or what it was that held her. And then she was being pulled along and people were shrieking and there were flames. It seemed as if the flames were chasing her and she could not escape them. She moaned and tossed on the thin straw palliasse and then shrieked aloud when she felt a hand on her shoulder.

'It's only me,' one of her cell mates said. 'Best not holler like that, we don't want to rouse the turnkey; he's got a wicked temper.'

Kate breathed with relief. 'I was dreaming.'

'Bad wor it?'

Kate nodded. She lay down again and shut her eyes, but she hardly dare sleep again, afraid the nightmare would return, but instead her dreams were pleasant ones of Matthew tenderly kissing her, and Pa and a lovely lady who bent over her and smiled, and who wore a little gold locket which dangled from her neck as she leaned forward. The dream was still with her when she woke and she knew, as surely as if someone had told her so, that she had once known the beautiful lady.

But she could not dwell on it, there were more important issues

211

to worry her. After a breakfast of lumpy gruel, a turnkey came and took all three women to the hearing.

The courtroom, in a building next to the prison, was packed long before proceedings began and, as more and more spectators crammed into a room not designed to hold them, the air became stuffy and hot. Ben Carter, looking very officious, strode about the open space between the public seats, the magistrates' bench and the dock. He was not wearing his hat and his greasy hair had been carefully brushed; his narrow tailcoat looked neat and his shirt clean. He was obviously very conscious of the importance of his role as prosecutor.

The clerk came out of a side door to sit at a table in the well of the court. He rearranged the papers in front of him, peered into his inkwell and sharpened his quills, then suddenly stood up and banged on the table, calling for everyone to rise. The spectators shuffled to their feet and the magistrates filed in and took their places. As everyone sat down again the chairman called for the first prisoner to be put up and the two women were ushered into the dock. They were dealt with very quickly and let off with a caution and then it was Kate's turn.

She saw several of the villagers, come to gape or support her, she did not know which. There was Fiddy and the village constable, but no sign of Sir John. She supposed he had acceded to his wife's wishes and left for his wedding tour, leaving his fellow justices to try her. She wondered where Andrew was; he might have been an ally, if only a covert one, but he was not in court and she knew there was no one she could count on for support. She was glad that Matthew had not risked coming as she waited in resignation for the charges to be read.

Inciting to riot, they called it, refusing to disperse when ordered to by a magistrate – the magistrate being Sir John Haddow – arson, feloniously breaking to pieces a threshing machine, escaping from lawful custody, assaulting Sir John, to all of which she pleaded not guilty.

Ben Carter rose to give evidence for the prosecution. According to him, Captain Matthew Tolley was the inspiration behind every case of rioting, arson, looting and poaching for miles around and that Josiah Brough's daughter had helped and encouraged him. 'She is the rebel leader's second in command,' he said. 'She was in the thick of the fighting, telling the others what to do. It don't signify that she's a woman, she even dresses like a man in a labourer's smock.'

The clerk had to quell the laughter which rippled round the room before the constable could go on. 'We hin't yet brought Tolley to book, but he'll be took and took soon. In his absence, the prisoner, Kate Brough, the poacher's daughter, is accused of conspiring with him to incite the men to riot.'

Mr Justice Gardiner turned to look at Kate. 'Where is this man, Tolley?'

'I do not know.'

'But you do admit you aided and abetted him in his crimes and that he is the acknowledged leader of the rabble?'

'If by rabble, you mean the sorely oppressed villagers who chose to listen to ...'

'Ah!' Ben Carter pointed a long bony finger at her. 'They listened, did they? They listened when you told them to burn ricks and smash machinery and set fire to Sir John's barn? They listened and obeyed.'

Before she could frame an answer, the magistrate turned to the superintendent. 'If that is so, why are all these people not standing with the accused?'

'Sir John thought it enough to apprehend the ringleaders,' he answered. 'His agent told me he has no wish to punish simpleminded people who have been misled.'

'Simple-minded!' someone shouted from the back of the public benches. 'It's simple-minded we are, is it?'

'No, we're bloody-minded!' shouted another. 'He hen't took us all, 'cause 'e do know we're in the right of it.'

'Down with all landowners!'

'Long live Cap'n Swing!'

Mr Justice Gardiner banged again and again on the table with his gavel. 'I will not have this unruly behaviour,' he said when he was able to make himself heard. 'This is a court of justice.'

'Hark at 'im! Justice!' he says. 'Justice!'

'These proceedings are turning into a farce,' the magistrate went on, amid the uproar. 'I commit this woman, Kate Brough, to the Ely Quarter Sessions, where the court will be able to conduct its business in a proper manner without constant interruptions. Take her away.'

Ben Carter poked Kate painfully in the ribs, indicating she

should leave the dock, and it was then that she noticed Matthew, but a Matthew so changed as to be almost unrecognisable. He was sitting about three rows back among the spectators, dressed in a black tailcoat and wearing a spotless shirt and a neatly tied grey silk cravat, held with a gold pin. His hair was neatly brushed and there was a tophat on the bench beside him. He was fanning himself with a sheaf of papers which concealed part of his face and, although he appeared relaxed, almost indifferent, she could see that his brown eyes were alert and watchful. He caught her glance but gave no sign of recognition and she, realising she would betray him if she continued to stare, looked away to where the Middleacre villagers were gathered. Did they know he was there? She did not think so, but Betty Watson's expression was almost triumphant.

Matthew had not come back to the hut for her as he had promised and now he sat, every inch the gentleman, and watched her being led away. Why had he risked coming to court at all? Was his disguise a sign of cowardice or bravado? Or had he simply reverted to type, become one of the hated enemy? Was one night locked in the harness room enough to make him abandon the people he had come to help? She did not think so but, catching her breath in a suppressed sob, realised it was unlikely that she would ever know for sure. Ely was many miles away and though she had never been there, she believed it was a big, impersonal city. No one would know her or care what became of her and if as a result of her trial there, she were to be deported, what would happen to Josiah? She must not think of that, she must not. She squared her shoulders and tipped her chin upwards as she was led away to a mixture of cheers and boos, but inside she was crying, inside her despair swamped her.

Later that day, Ben Carter took her from the cell to the street where a prison van waited to transport her and three men prisoners to Ely. It was an enclosed box-like vehicle drawn by two heavy horses. The driver was already up on the front seat and, once the prisoners had been bundled inside and shackled to its strengthened sides, Ben Carter climbed up beside the driver and they moved off.

Because there were no windows, they could only guess where they were. Once or twice they slowed to negotiate a particularly bad section of road, at others, they sped along, making the wagon rock from side to side. Kate's bottom became numb. And then just when she thought she would never be able to move again, they stopped so suddenly only her chains held her from being thrown forward. She heard men shouting and their driver cursing, then bangs and thumps on the side of the van and the bellowing of cattle which went on for several minutes and made them fear the van would be toppled over with them chained inside it. The rocking stopped at last and there was silence, then the door was wrenched open and a man climbed in, sorting through the guard's keys. For one heart-stopping moment, Kate thought it was Matthew, but when her eyes became accustomed to the light, she realised that this man was older and heavier, his complexion more swarthy.

'There's vittels out there and a change of clothes,' he said, releasing the prisoners one by one.

'Thanks, mate,' they said, scrambling from the van. 'We're beholden.'

He came to Kate last and unlocked the padlock of the chain which fastened her to the wall. 'Soon have you free.'

Too bewildered even to thank him, she rubbed her wrists and crawled towards the door; her legs had been cramped so long, she could not stand. She was lifted down by another man, heavily built and black-bearded, who showed big white teeth as he smiled at her. He set her on her feet and went to speak to the other prisoners, who were hungrily gobbling up the food they had been given by the third rescuer, a young fresh-faced lad.

Kate looked around her. Of Matthew there was no sign and her wild hope that he was at the heart of her rescue was dashed. The narrow road ahead was blocked by a huge herd of cattle and, in the middle of it, a passenger coach, trying to force its way through, which resulted in a great bellowing and neighing, while the terrified occupants looked out of the windows or hung onto the outside seats. The coach slithered and lurched but, at last, it was through and the driver set the horses cantering.

They stood and watched it go. 'They'll send a welcoming party back to meet us when they get to the next town,' the black-bearded one said. He turned to one of his men. 'Rob, make our friends comfortable in their van. Lock 'em in good and proper and unharness the horses, so's they can graze.'

'You haven't heard the last of this, Kate Brough,' Ben Carter yelled, trying to throw off the man who was tying him up. 'I'll make you pay for it, if it's the last thing I do.'

Kate grinned broadly. 'You'll have to catch me first.'

The head drover turned to the prisoners. 'Get you gone.'

They needed no second bidding and sped away. Kate moved to follow them, though she had no idea where she would go. She was detained by his hand on her arm. 'Not you, you're to come with us.'

'Why? Who are you?' she asked, though she was fairly sure the three drovers were the same ones she had seen from the hut in Middleacre. They wore breeches and leggings and stout boots, but the big one sported a topcoat while the others wore smocks. 'What do you want with me?'

'Nothing, m'dear,' he said. 'My name's Bates and this here's Rob and that ...' He pointed to the boy. 'That young sprat is Tom. We've orders to bring you on, so that's what we'll be doing.'

'Whose orders?' Either Matthew or Sir John was at the back of it, she decided, but it was Sir John who arrested her, so why would he set her free? That only left Matthew or the villagers. Or had they mistaken her for someone else and it was not her they were meant to set free?

'Mr Bates, do you know who I am?' she asked, wishing she knew the answer herself.

'I'm Bates; there ain't no mister to it, and I know who you are right enough. You're the poacher's daughter.'

'Suppose I run away?'

'Where would you run to?'

She had no answer to that; there were no buildings in sight. The road ran straight as so many fen roads did and there was nothing on either side but flat fields, many of them under water, criss-crossed with dykes and dotted with isolated windmills and farms. She could see a few hardy souls out on their stilts, which was the best way of getting about that terrain, but they did not seem in the least interested in what had happened on the road and were too far away to hear her if she called out. 'I thank you for setting me free,' she said, with all the dignity she could muster. 'But I decide where I go.'

He laughed aloud, a great bellow of enjoyment. 'We were told you might be stubborn, but we mean to obey our orders, so you can either come peaceably and we'll not hurt you, or you can travel like that.' And he pointed to Ben Carter and the wagon driver who were trussed up like chickens ready for the oven and being bundled into their own van.

The thought of being tied or chained as she had been for the last three hours, decided Kate; she would rather walk. The drover was big and powerful and his companions were no weaklings; it would be prudent to agree. Besides, she had nowhere else to go and she was curious, in spite of herself, to know who had given the men their orders. 'I'll come with you,' she said, jutting her chin into the air, lest he think she was frightened. 'But only as long as it pleases me.'

'Good.' He chuckled, as Rob rejoined him to round up the cattle and get them moving in the right direction again. 'Now, you'd best settle down to being a drover, and mind you keep up, we've no time to dally.'

They set off with Bates at the rear leading a mule which carried all they needed for a life on the road, and the other two on either side to prevent the cattle straying into the surrounding fields and becoming bogged down. Their busy little terrier ran up and down, doing his bit to keep them all moving. After two or three miles, they left the marsh behind, and turned off the public highway onto a wide grassy track, used since the Middle Ages by generations of drovers.

'Cattle and towns don't mix, so we avoid them where we can,' Rob told her. 'Besides, that coach we saw will ha' told the watch about us.'

'Then you are taking a risk, keeping me with you.'

He shrugged. 'It don' matter and Bates do have his reasons.'

'What are they?'

Instead of answering he hurried forward to stop one of the cows from straying off the road, leaving her to walk alone.

The countryside was damply green and, apart from the shuffle and occasional snort of the animals, it was peaceful and they moved at a slow, even pace. Being on a drove road, they met no wheeled traffic, but now and again they came across a labourer or a shepherd or a child minding geese. They bade each other good-day and passed on.

The life of a drover, Kate decided, must be something like that of a travelling man, such as Pa had been; you were never in one place long enough to be bored by it. But Bates was a taciturn man; he had hardly spoken since they left the prison van. 'You must have a very satisfying kind of life,' she said. 'Free as a bird to come and go and admire the scenery with no master to bully you.'

'Aye.'

'Have you come far?'

'A tidy step.'

'Where have you come from?'

'Scotland.'

'I went there once with Pa. We travelled all over the place before our wagon broke down.'

'That so?'

'Where are you taking the herd?'

'To Norfolk.'

'Why Norfolk?'

'The grazing is good there. It's where we fatten the cattle up after their long walk. We pick up another herd there and take it to Smithfield market in London.'

'London! And you expect me to go all that way?'

He laughed. 'No, me beauty, you'd be wore out walking all that way, now wouldn't you? We'll take you to a place of safety.'

'Where?'

'That depends.'

'On what?'

'What the gaffer decides.'

'The gaffer?' She smiled at him. 'Could that be Matthew Tolley?'

'Who's he?' he asked.

'You don't give much away, do you?'

'Best way,' he said. 'What you don't say can't harm you. Mayhap you ought to have remembered that.'

He left her to force some straggling beasts into line and she walked on alone, adjusting her pace to that of the herd. Her anxiety to know where and why she was being taken was replaced by a kind of lethargy, like walking in her sleep. By dusk she was stumbling with fatigue and wondering how much longer they would keep going, when Rob stopped suddenly and pointed to a red glow in the sky ahead of them. 'That's a rick burning or I miss my guess.'

'We can't drive the herd into that lot,' Bates said, looking round the darkening fields. 'We'll bed down in that meadow.' He opened the gate and turned the herd into the field.

If she had imagined that the coming of night would bring the answer to her questions she was disappointed, but she instinctively knew that as long as she did as she was told they would not harm her. They were probably keeping her until a reward was offered and then they would hand her over. They had not tied her up and she gave some thought to running away but decided against it. There was a great deal of noise coming from the nearby village and there seemed to be more fires flaring up as she watched. The safest place for her was where she was. Besides, she was too exhausted to walk another step, let alone run.

While Bates went to find the owner of the field and pay for the stance and Rob and Tom settled the restless cattle for the night, Kate made a camp fire in the shelter of a ring of bushes and heated the stew they had brought with them. By the time it was ready, Bates had returned. 'There's all hell let loose up ahead,' he said, taking a plate of food from Kate and sitting on the ground to eat it with the others in a semicircle about him. 'They've marched to the poorhouse and forced the governor to give them bread and cheese. They destroyed drills and chaff-cutting machines as well as thresh-ing machines and put householders in fear of their lives demanding money and drink. They dragged the rector through the pond and made him call a vestry to discuss their wages and it seems the farmers themselves are at the heart of it. The yeomanry have been sent for.'

While they ate, they could hear occasional gunfire, the squealing of frightened animals and the yelling of men in the village just ahead of them. 'Lucky we saw it in time,' Tom said.

'Aye, but it means we'll have to make up for lost time tomorrow.'

'D'you think it was Cap'n Swing got here ahead of us?' Tom asked.

'Who is Captain Swing?' Kate wanted to know.

Bates chuckled. 'He's a spirit, a will-o'-the-wisp, he's whatever you like to think he is.'

'He could be a drover, moving around the countryside?'

He laughed aloud. 'He could at that.'

'Or Captain Tolley?'

'Been brewin' long enough,' Rob said when it became obvious Bates was not going to answer her question. 'Flesh and blood can only stand so much and hunger's a powerful weapon.'

'So's argument if it's used well,' said Bates.

'You believe that, do you?' Kate asked.

'Depends. Sometimes you have to stand and fight.' He fetched a blanket from the pack on the back of his mule and handed it to her. 'Now best get some sleep.'

He had spoken flatly and she could not tell what he really thought. The farm labourers' fight wasn't his fight; he had no axe to grind and she supposed his only concern was for the safety of his herd. But he would hardly have waylaid the prison van if that were true. He must have had a reason for doing that and making her go with them. She pulled the blanket round her and lay down to sleep and soon the snores of the men harmonised with the snuffling of the cattle and became a sort of lullaby and, weary as she was, she slept.

The weather changed the next day, becoming decidedly colder with heavy clouds, which built up on the eastern horizon. By midday the sky was almost as dark as night and large drops of icy rain began spattering onto the backs of the animals. In no time it was a deluge. Bates looked up at the sky, muttered an oath, turned up his collar and gave Kate an old sack to put over her head and shoulders. She took it gratefully, wondering what Pa would say if he could see her; he liked to think of her as soft and feminine, someone who could hold her own with anyone, gentry included, yet here she was, soaked to the skin and dressed in rags, with only the rough cowherds for company. If living in the caravan had been beneath her, as Josiah had so often told her it was, then what was this?

The rain turned to sleet and then snow and that added to her misery and it didn't help to know that Bates had no intention of stopping and taking shelter; he was pressing on more determinedly than before towards a village they could see in the distance. 'Stay on the left, there,' he commanded her, ignoring, or not even noticing, that she was in tears. 'Don't let them beasts straggle.'

She did as she was told, moving purposefully alongside one of the steers, which seemed determined to go its own way, but she made up her mind that she would appeal for help at the next dwelling they came to; someone, surely, would listen to her predicament.

Chapter Thirteen

As it grew dusk Bates turned the herd off the road and onto a grassy plain beside the confluence of two rivers and, as if sensing this was the end of the day's journey, the cattle slowed and scattered and lowered their heads to the grass. There was no shelter that Kate could see and she was wondering how she was going to put her plan into action when Bates, having given instructions to Rob about the herd, disappeared in the direction of a light they could see over the fields. He came back half an hour later and approached Kate.

'Come with me.' He started to go back but when she did not immediately follow, turned and added, 'You do want to be dry, don't you?'

The thought of being warm and dry was an incentive she could not resist and she followed him across the meadow to a small village which stood where road and river met. There was a long line of fen-lighters being towed along the river, laden with goods. A barge was tied up to the bank, a lamp gleaming from its interior. Beside the bridge stood an inn called the Dog and Duck and it was to this Bates conducted her. A welcome light shone from its windows and, as they came nearer, she could see a fire leaping up the chimney of the parlour. He opened the door and she needed no second bidding to go inside.

'Wait here,' he said. She stood holding out her hands to the blaze while he spoke to the landlord. 'There's a room ready for you upstairs,' he said when he returned. ''Tis the first you come to on the landing. Go and dry yourself.'

She climbed the stairs and opened the door to find herself in a comfortable bedroom. She stood for a moment gazing at the cheerful fire, the supper laid for two on the table, the big soft bed, heaped with warm blankets, and could not believe her eyes. It was heaven.

The door behind her swung to and shut with a click. Startled, she whirled round, knowing someone had closed it, and found herself looking into Matthew's smiling face.

The wet sack fell from her shoulders as she threw herself into his arms and for several moments he held her close against him without speaking. Then he took her face in his hands to kiss it, tasting the rain and the salt of her tears. Too overcome to speak, she clung to him, forgetting completely her vow not to allow him kiss her again.

'I'm sorry you had such a cold, wet journey.' he said, leading her towards the fire. 'You are soaked through. Come and get warm.'

She found her voice at last, though her teeth were chattering. 'How did you get here? How did you know I would come here?' She stopped and laughed. 'You arranged it all with Bates.'

He smiled, though there was about him a kind of weariness, a sadness, as if the reunion was not all he had hoped for. 'I couldn't leave you in prison, could I? Though what I'll do with you now, I haven't a notion.'

'I'm still a bother to you, then?' The joy left her face.

'You are still a bother,' he confirmed, his voice husky with the effort of controlling his emotions. 'Sit down here, by the fire.'

'I'm sorry about that, truly I am,' she said, obeying. 'I did try to do as you asked and stay in the hut, but when the drovers came, I was afraid ...'

'Afraid of Bates? Why, he's as harmless as a kitten.'

'I didn't know that, did I? I thought he would turn me out of the shelter and he might report seeing me to Sir John.'

'Why should he do that?'

'There's a reward, isn't there?'

'If you thought that, you misjudged him, Kate.'

He had met the drover in London over a year before when he had just returned from India. He needed a new mount and had gone to Tattersalls to buy one. Bates, who had just brought in a string of horses from Newmarket, was there and they spent a pleasant hour or two, discussing horses. From there the conversation had gone on to cattle and farming in general. Bates was unusually knowledgeable about all manner of things and it seemed as though he had been everywhere and seen everything from Land's End to John O'Groats, though he had never ventured beyond the shores of the British mainland. It was Bates who had been partly instrumental in his decision to lead the life of a traveller, to see the country and its people at first hand. They had crossed paths several times since then and had become friends. It seemed providential that Bates should arrive in Middleacre when he did.

'I told him you were there,' he said. 'After I left you I met him coming into Middleacre with his herd and it occurred to me he would be just the one to smuggle you out of the village. But when he reached the stance, you had gone.' He paused to rub warmth into her cold toes, just as he had in William Chapman's living room, but this time she did not draw her feet away. 'By the time he found me to tell me, you had been captured and taken to Wisbech. I heard about the ride in the tumbril. It made me so angry I wanted to dash out and confront Sir John there and then. I think I would have killed him, but fortunately Bates is a level-headed sort and prevented me, though he couldn't stop me going to your hearing.'

'I know, I saw you, and very fine you looked too.' She put her hand out to touch the top of his dark head as he knelt at her feet. 'A real gentleman. But what a risk you took. What did you think you could do?'

He looked up at her and smiled. 'In court, nothing. I had hoped Gardiner might be lenient and let you go, but when you were committed to the Quarter Sessions instead of being sentenced by a magistrate, I realised I had to free you. We knew we would have to take whatever opportunity presented itself while you were on the road and we thought it might be near here, where the road is busiest. I left the details to Bates and his chance came sooner than we expected.'

'Why didn't he tell me this instead of holding me prisoner.'

'Prisoner?' He chuckled. 'Surely not?'

'Not exactly, but he didn't give me any choice.'

The sound of his laughter was like music to her ears. 'I told him not to. I told him how stubborn you can be. And he is not sure that women should be involved.'

'Oh, not that old chestnut.' She paused. 'Where were you while this was going on? Or am I still not to concern myself with that?'

'I had urgent business to attend to in Wisbech. As soon as it was done, I rode across country to make the arrangements for this room, intending to return along the road and be on hand when you were freed, but I was prevented ...'

'Prevented?'

'There was a little matter of a riot and machine-breaking. Someone had to calm them down and negotiate a settlement.'

'And did you?'

'Partially, where the farmers and tythe-holders were reasonable, but in others ...' He hung her wet stockings over the fender and began slowly undoing the buttons at the neck of the smock she wore. 'Where did you get this?'

'Mrs Barber threw it into the cart for me. My clothes had been torn.'

'You like Charlie, don't you?'

'Yes, he was one of the few people in Middleacre to be friendly.'

'Friendly.' He smiled. 'Now I thought it was something more than that.'

She looked at him sharply. 'How do you know that?'

'I noticed how he looked at you, like an adoring puppy.'

'He asked me to marry him.'

So the young man had overcome his shyness. 'And what did you say?'

'I said no.' The smock came off but she hardly noticed.

'Why?'

'It didn't seem right. He's only a boy ...'

He laughed. 'And you, of course, are as old as time.'

'No, but I knew it would not do.'

'Why? Is there someone else?' His touch was gentle as he drew her to her feet and deftly removed her skirt. She stood on the hearthrug in nothing but a pair of cotton drawers. The firelight, glowing on her pale skin, made it vibrant and alive and sensuous. He knew he ought to leave the room, send a woman to help her into bed, find solace in the parlour of the inn with a tankard or two of ale, but how could he, when she looked at him like that?

'You know there is.'

'Do I?' Could he, just for one night, forget the predicament they were in, the men who demanded his loyalty, his doubts about their ultimate success? Could he allow himself to relax his iron self control and hold her in his arms? He groaned and bent his head into her neck, making her whole body tingle. Gone was cold and fear, gone was pride and hate and humiliation, and in its place was an unbounded joy. He held her tightly against him, so that she could hear his heart beat and feel the strength of his arms about her and his warm breath beneath her ear as he kissed the hollow of her neck. He reached behind her to undo the tape of the drawers, stroking a finger down her spine, making her shudder at his touch. The underwear dropped on top of the skirt, leaving her naked.

She reached up without shame and put her arms around his neck. 'Oh, Matthew, I'd have walked to the ends of the earth if I thought you were waiting for me at the end.'

His heart lifted suddenly and as suddenly dropped. 'You don't know what you are saying.' His voice was ragged. 'You don't understand at all.' Gently he disengaged her arms and stood back to look at her. She was gazing up at him, with the firelight flickering on her face, making her more beautiful, more desirable than ever, and his firmly made promise to hold himself in check began to crumble. How could he resist her ? He had asked her to trust him and now that she did, he wished it otherwise. If only she had not become involved in the troubles of the labourers he would not be half out of his mind with worry about her. But if she had not become involved, he would never have known what it was like to hold her in his arms, to feel her body yielding to his, to know the power of a love that had to come before all else, even the selfish desires of his own traitorous body. Did she know what she was doing to him ? 'I ought not to be here,' he said.

'Why not ?' She was puzzled.

'Don't you know that the sight of you, standing there like that, is more than flesh and blood can stand ?' He picked her up in his arms and carried her to the bed, where he laid her gently on the soft feather mattress and covered her with the blankets. 'It's torment.'

'Torment ?' she whispered. 'I don't want to torment you; I want to make you happy.' She reached up and curled her fingers into his hair in an unconsciously sensuous gesture. 'Teach me now, please.'

'No !' he said sharply, realising she would need little instruction; her instinct seemed to be serving her very well. 'You don't know what you are asking.'

'Course I do. I may not be as old as time but I am not a child either.'

He sat on the edge of the bed and gently stroked her cheek with

225

the back of his forefinger. 'No, you are far from a child, my darling, you are a woman grown. But ...'

'Oh, I suppose it's still not the time and the place,' she said with unexpected spirit. 'Beware, Matthew Tolley, when you do decide the time is right, I might have other ideas.'

To refuse her now would be to humiliate her and yet he had to do it. For her own sake, he had to wait. He was a fool to have come. He should have let Bates take her to a place of safety and never seen her again. 'Perhaps that would be best,' he said slowly, watching her face. 'You don't know anything about me, do you? You have no idea what life with me would be like. You deserve something better than that.'

She sighed. 'You know, you are as bad as Pa. He was always telling me I was destined for something better.'

'And so you are. I am not the man for you. To begin with, I am not what I seem.'

'Pooh, anyone with half a brain knows you are not a labourer. You're a captain of Hussars, you told me so, but what has that got to do with what you are, the man inside the skin?'

He smiled wearily. 'The man inside the skin is wanted by the law.'

'I know that. You led the Middleacre villagers and probably a lot more besides, but I don't care what the law says, it was a good thing to do.'

'But it's not just Middleacre, Kate, it's everywhere. I am a stranger in my own home ...' He stopped. Had he been about to tell her about Garforth and Daniel and Amy, and the little boy with the dog? And his conclusion that his two lives could never mix? 'I have brought you to this.'

'No, you haven't. I did it myself. And I'd do it again.'

'Don't say that. You were never meant to be hunted like a fox, afraid, a wanderer, never in the same place for two days together.'

She laughed suddenly and startled him. 'But that is exactly what we were, Pa and I, before we came to Middleacre. Travellers. Some called us gypsies.'

'But you weren't?'

'No, I don't think so.'

'But you are not sure?'

'How can I be sure? No one knows anything about me.'

'Not even Josiah Brough?' He could hardly believe the old man had told her nothing at all.

'He only knows when and where he found me. My life started then, not before.' She paused. 'Oh, I see, it's me that's the trouble. You do not know what kind of a person I am. My mother might have been a gypsy, a whore, or a lunatic. I might have bad blood.'

'What nonsense!' He smiled and put out a hand to twist a tendril of her hair around his finger. When he let it go it sprang into a little corkscrew curl. 'You could just as easily be a princess. Kate, believe me, it is not you that's at fault, it's me. I am not the hero you think I am and the sooner you realise that the better.'

'I don't understand.'

'Kate, I am a soldier, used to commanding men into battle and expecting some of them to be injured, even killed, but when the men you lead are simple labourers and your enemies are your own countrymen, that is different; it becomes insurrection. I am ready to sacrifice anything and anyone for the cause I fight for. Don't you realise that?' He saw her recoil slightly and longed to take her into his arms and reassure her, but this was the best way; it was better to let her think the worst of him.

'Even me?' Her voice was a whisper.

'God help me,' he said, standing up and striding to the window to look out on the fields where Bates herded his cattle.

'I understand.'

'I doubt it.'

'I know how important your work is to you,' she said. 'I realised it when I saw you at the meeting in Middleacre. You were so in command of everything. And at the barn fire ...'

'I let myself down there,' he said, turning towards her with a wry smile. 'I didn't follow my own edicts, otherwise I would not have jumped in so impulsively to defend you and allowed myself to be captured.'

'You did it for me, just as you arranged to set me free from the prison van, so you are not the unfeeling monster you would have me believe.'

'I did that for my own safety,' he said harshly. 'You might have talked, you would not have been able to help yourself. If someone brought pressure to bear, threatened you or promised you freedom, you would have told them what they wanted to know.'

'No, I wouldn't,' she said quickly. 'Sir John asked me for the

227

name of the men's leader, promised to set Pa free if I told him, but I wouldn't.'

'Why not?' he asked, suddenly ashamed and humble in the face of her courage. 'I would not have blamed you.'

'But you were not prepared to take the risk?'

'No.'

'Is that the only reason you rescued me?'

'Yes.'

'Not because you loved me?'

'I am not free to love you, or anyone else. I have nothing to offer but penury.' The words were torn from him.

'Then why did you kiss me?' She was crying silently and the pain it caused him was worse than any sabre thrust.

'Because I am a man,' he said angrily, though his anger was directed at himself. 'I'm flesh and blood and you ... damn it, you were so ... so willing. Why couldn't Josiah have told you about men? Why couldn't he have prepared you for the real world?' He looked across at her, sitting up in the bed with the tears running down her cheeks, and for a second time he nearly threw away his resolve not to give in to the desire which had overwhelmed him the moment she had walked into the room and thrown herself so enthusiastically into his arms. But he could not let her cry. He went back to her, sat on the edge of the bed and took her hands in his. 'Kate, I'm sorry.'

'Pa told me about love,' she said, sniffing. 'He told me when love comes in the door, reason flies out of the window.'

He smiled in spite of himself. 'I suppose that's true, but some of us have to keep our reason.'

'I don't understand.'

'Perhaps one day you will.'

'You are thinking of someone else,' she said, suddenly remembering Betty Watson. It was the only thing she could think of which would account for his sudden change of mood.

'How could I possibly be thinking of anyone else with you lying there like that?'

'Not even Betty?'

'Betty?'

'Betty Watson. Are you still going to marry her?'

She didn't know what she had said that was so funny, but he threw back his head and laughed, as if the joke had released some

228

tension in him, like a spring uncoiling. 'Kate, you'll be the death of me, asking questions like that at a time like this.'

'Well?'

'No one, certainly not Betty Watson, could tear my thoughts from you now or at any time.'

'She told me you were going to marry her and if that's true, you should not be here with me, should you? And you should not have kissed me.'

'What does a kiss matter?' he said, forcing himself to speak lightly. 'Kisses mean nothing.'.

'Nothing?'

'Nothing.'

She lifted her head to look at him, defiant now though the tears still glistened on her cheeks. 'Pa didn't tell me about people like Sir John who take what they want by force, nor about men like you who pretend to something they do not feel. Go on then, keep your reason, be cold and calculating and see how much happiness it brings you. I feel sorry for anyone who marries you, that I do.'

'Kate, I'm sorry. The last thing I want to do is to hurt you.'

'Oh, don't fret yourself on my behalf. I'm only the poacher's daughter, after all – of no importance.'

'Don't talk like that,' he said angrily, taking her shoulders in his hands and shaking her. 'Don't ever speak like that again, do you hear me?'

'Why not, it's true, isn't it? Whoever my real parents were, I have become the poacher's daughter.' She looked up into his eyes, and it seemed her own anger was reflected in them. 'And I am proud of it, proud of Pa, proud of the life we lead, of our independence and our love for each other. I don't care about anyone else, do you hear me? Nothing, not even you.' She was shouting now. 'I don't care!'

'Josiah Brough has a lot to answer for,' he said, getting up abruptly and going to the table to bring a plate of food back to the bed.

'Pa is a good man,' she said. 'And I thought you were like him, kind and strong and giving. I *wanted* you to be like him.'

'I am *not* your father,' he said, truly angry now. She wanted a substitute for Josiah Brough, not a lover; he had been deluding himself if he thought otherwise. 'I am a man with a man's desires and I want a woman, not a child.' He sounded cold and impersonal now, the gentle, caring man of a few moments ago had disappeared, leaving one encased in steel. 'Now, I suggest we end this discussion, because it can lead nowhere and you need to save your energy for tomorrow.' He offered her the plate of food. 'Eat this.'

'I'm not hungry.' She had prayed for a reunion with him and it had come sooner than she had dared to hope, but now they had quarrelled and she had no idea what had brought it about. If he thought he was not the man for her or, more truthfully she was not the woman for him, because she was nothing more than a tinker's daughter and an adopted one at that, then why did he bother with her at all? And why was he so obviously unhappy?

'Nevertheless, you will eat.' He sat down beside her and speared a piece of chicken on a fork. 'You will eat and then you will sleep.' He held the fork to her lips and she opened her mouth like a child, but it took her a long time to chew and swallow the food. Her expression remained childlike, as if womanhood was too much for her and she was rejecting it. He continued to feed her tiny morsels of food until he had satisfied himself she could eat no more, then he set the plate aside and pulled the bed covers over her. 'Go to sleep now, Kate.' He bent over her to kiss her forehead very gently, making no demands, asking nothing but to be with her and protect her. 'Go to sleep and dream of a better life than this. I'll watch over you.'

But sleep came slowly to Kate and when it did it was disturbed by her recurring nightmare of clanking machinery and coughing children and, though she ran and ran, dodging this way and that, she could not escape something unseen that clutched at her, filling her with terror, making her cry out.

Matthew lay down beside her on the top of the covers and put his arm round her and soothed her with quiet words until she ceased to struggle. He remained wide awake and staring at the window, where clouds scudded across the star-filled sky, blowing the wintry weather away. For him, the night was chill, made all the colder by the knowledge that he was soon to part from the girl who slept so trustingly beside him; he had to make things right for her. He had promised Josiah Brough he would.

After leaving her to shut herself in the drovers's hut, he had gone to his lodgings, destroyed the papers which could identify him as Captain Matthew Thorsborough, then packed his belongings, intending to return for her and take her to a place of safety. But

the mystery of her birth came to his mind and would not let him
rest. Before he could ask her to share his fate, unpleasant as it
was likely to be, he had to know, not because he cared who she
was, or what she was, but for her own sake. If there was a
choice to be made, she had to be given the opportunity to make
it and the only person who could tell him anything was the old
poacher.

He had changed from the rough labourer's clothes he had been
wearing into something more befitting a gentleman and gone to the
Wisbech House of Correction, purporting to be a lawyer.

The ruse had worked and he had been taken to the prison
infirmary and into a long ward lined with beds, whose occupants
lay without hope of getting better, or of recovering only to face
long prison sentences. The sickly-sweet smell of decay was overpowering and the turnkey did not stay after pointing Josiah out and
saying, 'There he is, you can have half an hour.'

He had approached the bed and found himself looking down at
the emaciated form of Josiah Brough. He had lost a leg and the
bandaged stump lay on the covers. The putrid smell was sickening.
Kate had said he was a fine figure of a man, but the man in the bed
was shrunken, his black beard was mottled with white and his
weatherbeaten skin was yellow and wrinkled. Only his dark eyes
showed any sign of life.

'Josiah Brough,' Matthew said, sitting on the edge of the bed.
'I'm sorry to see you in these straits.'

'Who are you?' The voice was a whisper.

'I'm known as Matthew Tolley.' He spoke his name softly,
leaning over the old man.

'You're that combination man Kate was talking about?'

'Yes.'

'I'm sorry you ended up in here,' Josiah said, obviously assuming
Matthew had been arrested. 'It bodes ill for Middleacre.'

'Middleacre will be there long after I am gone. Others will carry
on.'

'Don't hold with unions myself.'

'No, I know. Kate told me.'

The old man's eyes lit up. 'How is she? How's my darling girl?'

There had been no reason to distress him with stories of Kate's
involvement with the villagers' cause. 'She is well and concerned
for you.'

'Don't tell her how things are, with me, will you? Don't tell her about the leg. Tell her not to fret, tell her I'm doing just fine.'

'She has a right to know the truth.' He had looked into Josiah's eyes as he spoke, wondering if he would understand the implication of his words.

'Aye,' Josiah murmured and then fell silent. Matthew thought he had fallen asleep, but he suddenly opened his eyes and caught his hand in a grip that was surprisingly strong 'I want ... to talk ... to tell you about Kate.'

'I am listening.'

As the old fellow talked, slowly and breathlessly, Matthew realised he was dying and saw his visitor as his salvation, the key to his peaceful entry into the next world. Josiah had unburdened himself and left Matthew carrying the weight of it. And it was almost more than the young man could bear, made worse by the knowledge that if he had not gone to see him, he would have reached Kate before Fiddy found her. They could have been many miles away.

If what the poacher had told him was true, Kate's whole life would change so completely there could be no place in it for him. But if he said nothing to her of his visit to the prison, she need never know Josiah's secret; the old poacher would take it with him to the grave, but had he – had anyone – the right to withhold her birthright from her? Now he knew the truth, Matthew's feelings for Kate did battle with his conscience just as Josiah's had done all those years ago. He had come back to her intending to say nothing, do nothing, but now he found he could not. Josiah's last words echoed in his brain. 'Do as I ask, go to Middleacre and tell them what I have told you. Then leave her be. She is not for you.'

He had not stopped to argue, the old man was not in a fit state to take in what he said. Besides, what arguments could he use on his own behalf? How could he say that he and Kate were meant for each other and nothing and no one had a right to come between them? How could he say that he would make her happy, when he knew that it would be almost impossible? Now that he had crossed the thin line from lawful negotiator to law-breaker, his life would always be that of a fugitive. He could no longer call himself Matthew Thorsborough because he could never disgrace the family name. But who was Matthew Tolley? He was as much a myth as Captain Swing. How could he ask Kate to share a life like that, even if what Josiah had told him was a lie? It wasn't a lie, in his heart he knew that. The pendulum had swung to its opposite extreme; he was now the one without an identity, not her.

He had left the gaol in a quandary, only to be met by Bates with the news of her arrest. Still in the clothes he had worn to go to the prison, he had gone to her committal. She had been so proud, standing in the dock in borrowed clothes and her lovely hair in disarray. She had done nothing to help herself, had not denied her involvement with him, had not said she had been misled or forced into what she did. But she had been as outspoken as ever. He did not really believe she would betray him, but he could not leave her behind bars, a situation she would never have been in but for him, then having freed her and brought her to this room, he had been overcome by his longing for her and held her naked body in his arms as only a husband had a right to do. She had been like a flower opening to the sun, a child become woman, perfect in her innocence, trusting him, and yet destroying him. The only weapon he had against her was anger and, even then, he had not employed it well enough to make her hate him.

By the time a grey dawn had filtered its way into the room, he had almost convinced himself that Josiah had been lying, or if not lying, then rambling, confusing truth with imagination. There was only one way to be sure and that was to return to Middleacre as he had been asked to do.

He propped himself on his elbow to look down at Kate, not wanting to wake her, but Bates and his men were up and about, he could hear them working with the cattle across the meadow, herding them together ready for the road. He eased himself off the bed and went over to the washstand where he emptied the contents of the jug over his head into the bowl. The icy water served to revive him. He rubbed his head dry, ran his fingers through his wet hair and went to wake Kate. Her arm was flung out across the pillow and there was a faint smile about her lips, as if she was sure of her place in his heart and all the anger in the world could not convince her otherwise. He stood looking down at her for a long time before bending to put his lips to hers and then gently shaking her. 'Wake up, Kate. We must make a move.' He stood up and crossed the floor to ring the bell for a servant, not daring to look at her again. 'There's a new day out there.' He nodded towards the window. 'And Bates won't wait.'

She sat up and stretched like a cat. 'Bates? Are we going with him?'

'Yes, I can see him herding the cattle ready to move.' He went to a cupboard and brought out a pair of breeches and leggings which he put into her arms. 'And it would be best if you went in disguise. If you cut your hair and dress in these and that smock, you could pass yourself off as a boyherd.' He smiled, as if trying to make a joke of it. 'Kit, how's that for a new name?'

'But I must go home.'

'Home?'

'Oh, I know I have no home, but I shall have to find a new one. I must be in Wisbech when Pa is released.'

Pa again! Always Pa. 'That's months away.'

'I will try to be patient.'

Her simple faith tortured him yet again. It had been on his mind to tell her that he did not think Josiah would survive to be released, but he could not bring himself to do it. 'A year is a long time for someone like Josiah,' he said, trying to prepare her. 'You might find him changed. Prison will weaken him and he's not young, is he? And with a wounded leg . . .' He could not go on.

'Then I shall look after him until he is well again, just as he always looked after me.'

'You can't go back now,' he said. 'You'll be arrested on sight and how will that help either of you?' He paused as a servant girl arrived with hot water and breakfast for her. 'When Josiah Brough comes out of prison, you can send a message to tell him where to find you.'

'What are you going to do?'

'I'll walk a little way with you.' He ought to go straight away, not prolong the parting, but he could not. Another day would make no difference. 'Then I must leave you.'

'Why? Where are you going?'

'Back to Middleacre.'

'Back there!' she exclaimed. 'You wouldn't let me go back, so why are you going?'

'It's different for me. There is someone I must see . . .'

'Betty Watson.'

'No, Kate. There is nothing between Betty Watson and me, the idea is unthinkable. She is a foolish girl who wanted to crow over you, didn't you realise that?'

'But I saw you kissing her.'

'What you saw was a silly girl throwing herself at me. I was trying to disentangle myself without hurting her feelings.'

Should that make her feel happier? She supposed it did, but why had he not explained things before? He could have told her when they were in the harness room, or even last night. She didn't understand; all she knew was that she loved him and he was leaving her. 'And are you trying not to hurt *my* feelings now?'

'No. I have hurt you enough.'

'Then why are you leaving me?'

'Would you have the villagers think I've deserted them?' he countered, not yet ready to tell her the other, more pressing, reason for his return.

'But how can you help them now?'

'I don't know. Perhaps I can't.

'Matthew, you mustn't. You will be arrested and I don't think I could bear having both of you in prison.'

'Don't worry, I'll be safe enough but I must go.'

'And I must stay a drover, tramping from one end of the country to the other?'

'No, Bates will take you to some friends of his in Ely. You will be safe there.'

'Can't I go with you?'

'I'm afraid that's not possible,' he said.

'Why not? I can keep up.'

He took her hands in his and looked down into her face, wishing he could keep her by his side. 'Kate, it's not as simple as that. I have things to do, places to go, people to see and I must do it alone. Not even Bates can help me.'

'Will you come back?'

'Yes, I shall return.' One way or another he would return to her. If what Josiah had told him was a lie, then he would know what to do. But if it were true, he would be the one to tell her; he would see her just once more, hold her just once more, before parting with her for ever. He smiled suddenly. 'Nothing but death will prevent me and I intend to avoid that as long as possible.' He went to the door and took his cloak from the peg. 'Here, Bates found this in Haddow woods. You'd better have it. Now hurry up, I'll wait for you downstairs.' He left the room and she heard him clattering down the stairs.

235

It was all too much to take in, and though she thought she understood Matthew a little better now, it still did not explain his behaviour the night before, when he had caressed and kissed her in a way which was a direct contradiction of the unkind words he used. *Kisses mean nothing.* Did he make a habit of taking susceptible young girls into his arms and, when they did not demur, into his bed? The gentry were known for the way they used the lower orders in that way; Sir John Haddow's behaviour towards her had been proof of that. But Matthew had stopped short with her. Why? Had she had a lucky escape? No, she would not believe that; something else was troubling him.

She washed and dressed in the breeches, leggings and smock, then she took a pair of scissors to her curls. Only thinly disguised, she put the cloak over her arm and went downstairs to join him for breakfast. They did not linger over it and in less than half an hour he fetched his horse from the stables and they joined the drovers.

All morning she walked beside him as he led his horse. She did not speak. It was as if doing so would break the thread which bound her to him, the slender thread of love and hope, so fragile it was like a cobweb and would be demolished on the slightest breeze. She had to keep it intact or she could not go on.

She looked up at him now and again, admiring his height, his strength, the way the rough clothes he had resumed wearing fitted him as if they had been tailored for him, emphasising his powerful physique and upright bearing. She tried to fix his features in her memory, the firmness of his jaw, the way his dark hair curled round his ear, the tenderness of his smile when he thought she wasn't looking. She played a game with herself, imagining they were on their way to a new home together – all three of them because she included Josiah – that they would never be parted again, but as the morning wore on it became harder and harder to keep up the pretence.

Matthew seemed preoccupied, but after they stopped for their midday meal and resumed their trek, once again on the public highway, he suddenly seemed to shake himself and square his shoulders, before striding off to talk to Bates, and she realised he had become, once more, the realist, the leader, the planner. She heard him ask Bates where he was taking the herd and how he could be contacted, and moved nearer to hear his reply.

'I'll sell this herd in Norwich and then get together another of fatted beef at Acle,' Bates said. 'I should be at Smithfield in a couple of weeks and, God willing, back here a week later, unless I go straight to Falkirk.'

'Will you pick up my letters while you're in town? I shan't be able to go myself for some time.'

'Aye. I'll leave them at the Dog and Duck. Will that do?'

'I'm much obliged.'

The dread of parting, which had been pushed to the back of Kate's mind, suddenly thrust itself to the fore and her eyes filled with tears, leaving her wondering if she would be able to face it bravely when it came, because that was what she knew she had to do. Whatever was troubling Matthew would not be helped by weakness on her part.

It was mid-afternoon when he stopped and put his hand on her arm to hold her back. The herd moved on. Silently they watched the cattle, the three drovers, the mule and the dog disappear round the bend ahead of them. 'I must leave you now.' he said softly.

She tried to smile. 'How long will you be gone?'

'That's in God's hands, Kate.' In spite of his resolve not to do so, he took her in his arms and held her tightly, cradling her head against his chest and wishing with all his heart that he did not have to leave her. 'But wait for me.'

'Always.' She put her arms around his neck, clinging to him, wanting to hold him captive, not knowing that he was already her captive and there was nothing he could do about it.

Gently he disengaged her arms and stepped back to look at her, drinking in the sight of her, committing it to his memory as if he thought he would never see her again. He took her face in his hands and bent to kiss her lips, very lightly, without passion. 'Now go and catch Bates up before he gets too far ahead and before anyone comes along and wonders why I am kissing a young lad. It wouldn't do my reputation a lot of good, would it?'

She smiled. 'Do I really look like a boy?'

'Not to me.' He turned her to face the way she had to go and gave her a gentle push. 'Now go.'

Unable to speak, she moved away from him and, although she knew he stood at the roadside watching her, she dare not look back because if she did she knew she would break down completely.

'Goodbye, my darling,' he whispered when she was out of earshot. 'God keep you safe, always.' When he could see her no more, he mounted his horse and turned it back towards the Dog and Duck, where he took the turn to Middleacre.

She rejoined the drovers, pretending cheerfulness, and helped to herd the cattle until it grew dusk when they turned them onto a stance beside the road for the night. Bates seemed to know exactly where he could put them, which landowners would tolerate the beasts for a fee and which meadows to avoid, however tempting they might seem.

It was bitterly cold, not the sort of weather to be sleeping out of doors, but the drovers seemed oblivious to it and she was determined not to complain. The next day was like all the others, though the snow held off and the road was reasonably dry. Through hamlets and villages they went, calling a greeting to anyone who watched their passing, crossing bridges, keeping the cattle close together, every now and again taking a short cut across the fields, avoiding those which had been drilled and seeded. The tall spire of Ely Cathedral had been visible for many miles and yet they seemed not to be getting any closer, but on the second evening they rejoined the road just short of the town and it seemed almost within touching distance. In a meadow beside an orchard just outside the city, they stopped for the night.

The next morning as soon as breakfast was over and the fire doused, Bates left Rob and Tom to manage the herd and came to Kate, who was busy rolling up the blanket she had slept on. 'This is where you say goodbye to the herd,' he said. 'Come on, we're going into Ely.'

Ely was not a large town, being about the size of Wisbech, but it was a busy little place. The roads were choked with coaches, farm carts, drays, flocks of sheep and geese, people on foot, some pushing laden handcarts, children with baskets, mothers carrying babies. 'It's market day,' Bates told her.

The place fascinated Kate, if only because the great bulk of the cathedral dwarfed everything else. It had some fine houses about the green, but along its narrow streets there were also odd little shops and tiny cottages, interspersed with ramshackle buildings at whose doors housewives congregated to gossip. In the market place people were going from one stall to another, looking over the produce on offer, from horses, pigs and chickens to cabbages, cooking pans and candles. They were dressed in a wide variety of clothing, from fashionable silks to the merest rags, some well shod, others barefoot.

Bates took her to The White Hart, beside the market, where he left her to sit by herself with a glass of buttermilk while he made a deal with a group of farmers to take their cattle to Smithfield. Then he fetched her and they set off again.

'Where are we going?' she asked. He was loping swiftly ahead, dodging down narrow lanes where washing hung from one side to the other and small children played in the mud; she had to keep pace with him or she would be lost.

'Somewhere safe for you to stay. How d'you fancy working in a store?'

'I'll do anything. But will Matthew know where to find me?'

'He will, though I think he's bein' a damned fool. He has more important things to do than tangle with a wench.'

'Wench! Is that how you think of me?'

He shrugged and lengthened his stride so that she was almost running to keep up with him. 'What I think is me own affair and don't signify. Now come on, we've no time to waste.'

'I love him,' she said breathlessly, tagging at his heels. 'He's gentle and caring, most of the time anyway ...'

'Don't I know that?' the drover said sharply. 'Too soft, he is.'

'You knew him before, didn't you?'

'Before?'

'Before you came to Middleacre this week.'

He laughed. 'You ask too many questions, m'lady. Best keep them to yourself if you want to see your next birthday.' He turned to face her, making her check her stride. 'And for the gaffer's sake too.'

'You can tell me where you are taking me, can't you?'

'To the chandlers. The owner is a good friend of mine, been buying off him for years. We'll see what he can do. But remember, you are Kit Brown and you are no more than fourteen years old; your voice ain't broken yet. Do you understand?'

'Yes.' But she didn't, not any of it.

Chapter Fourteen

With Kate on his heels, Bates hurried down a surprisingly steep hill considering they were still in the fens and along the hythe which opened out onto a quay beside the river. It was sluggish and grey and full of bobbing garbage brought down in the drains from the town or thrown from the river craft and there were a great many of those, from skiffs to barges and strings of fen-lighters.

The store was right at the waterside, for it served the boat people as well as the local population, and was more like a huge warehouse than Kate's idea of a shop. The dusty floorboards and rows of shelves were loaded with produce of all kinds, from sacks of flour and tallow candles, to great rounds of cheese and chests of tea. Sides of bacon hung from the rafters alongside coils of rope; heaps of sailcloth sat side by side with rolls of fine muslin. Oil could be had and butter and beef, boots and shoes, bonnets and shawls.

Three young male assistants scurried about supervised by a very big woman whose arms were as brawny as a man's. She rolled a barrel across the floor and heaved it onto its stand with practised ease. Her hair, pulled tightly back into a bun at the nape of her neck, appeared white, until Kate noticed that it was covered with a fine dust and that underneath it was raven black.

'Good-day to ye, Mistress Fyne,' Bates greeted her. 'Is the master about?'

'He's out the back.' The woman nodded towards a door in the dark recesses of the shop. 'Do you go and find him.'

'That I will. I'd be obliged if you'd see to my usual needs.' To Kate he said, 'Wait here.'

He went off and Kate was left facing the big woman, who looked her up and down, eyeing her from her small brown boots and fustian breeches to her voluminous smock and crop of short blonde curls. 'You don't make much of a drover, do you?' she said, though she was smiling.

'I'm not.'

'What are you doing with Bates then ?'

'He rescued me.' She dare say no more and strangely Mrs Fyne asked for no details.

'Some men are fools.'

'You mean Bates ?'

'Yes. Ten to one, you were in trouble and he's got himself mixed up in it.'

Before Kate could comment, the drover emerged from the dimness of the interior and called to Mrs Fyne to join him.

Left alone, Kate looked around her and found herself being stared at by three sets of eyes. Two pairs belonged to what could be called young men for they were about nineteen or twenty, and one to a boy of about twelve or thirteen. Although he was skinny, he was obviously growing at a pace which made it difficult to keep him in clothes; several inches of skinny leg showed below his trouser bottoms and his bony wrists stuck out of his coat sleeves. In contrast the apron he wore swamped him and she wondered how he managed to walk without tripping over it. She gave him a friendly smile.

'Is it a he or a she ?' the youngster asked his workmates.

'I don't know, I reckon it's an it,' said one and roared with laughter. He was tall and gangly with a long narrow nose and dark hair that fell over his forehead.

'Bates hev got hisself a new toy,' said the other, who sported a gingery moustache in an effort to disguise his spots.

Kate was saved from further embarrassment by Mrs Fyne, who came from the back and cuffed the youngster about the ears. 'What are you gawping at, Archie Carter ?'

'Noth'n',' he muttered, but he was still grinning.

'Then move yourself and make up Mr Bates's order, same as last time, bread, bacon, cheese, tea, biscuits.' To Kate, she said, 'Go out the back, Kit, and meet Mr Fyne.'

Kate was glad to escape the boys. She hurried in the direction Mrs Fyne had indicated and found herself in a tiny office-cum-living room. The two men were sitting on either side of a table which was littered with papers and the remains of someone's lunch. Mr Fyne got to his feet and came towards her. Kate stared at the massive bulk of the man, the huge, hairy hands and bulbous nose. His trousers could hardly have been filled by two normal men and his shirt must have been made from a bedsheet. He laughed as he took her hand and she was immediately at ease, for his laugh was carefree and good humoured and his grip was gentle.

'Kate,' Bates said. 'I've told Jacob your story and he's told his wife, but no one else need know.'

'If you stay here, you'll have to work alonga the boys,' Jacob said. 'There's Archie Carter, David Fincham – he's the tall one – and Jonas Benton. They sleep over the shop, but you'll live in the house with the missus and me. It's down river, away from this stink.'

'Thank you,' she said. 'But I don't make a very good boy and I think the others have guessed.'

'They can guess all they like,' he said. 'They are here to work and not play games and they'll do as they're told and keep their thoughts to themselves. You may as well start straight away and help Archie make up Bates's order. He'll show you where everything is.'

Kate hurried over to where the boy struggled with a tea chest and left the Fynes to seal the bargain with Bates over a glass of ale. She did not know what he had said to persuade them to take her, but she was very grateful; work was just what she needed to occupy her time until Matthew came back for her. And when he did, she would disabuse him of the idea that they were not meant for each other because they were and he must be made to see it.

She was still grateful weeks later when her back was breaking, her feet throbbing and her arms aching with lifting and carrying all day. There was no let up from dawn to dusk, except for the half hour they had for a midday meal and another half hour at supper time. Customers came and went in a steady stream, stock had to be counted and stacked, the shop had to be kept clean and the yard tidy. On top of that, she had her share of chores to do in the house before she could crawl into the little bed in the back room which had been allotted to her. The house was about half a mile downriver; sometimes they made the journey to the store in a gig pulled by Jacob's sturdy little pony, but as often as not they used a rowing boat, which Kate soon learned to handle.

Mr and Mrs Fyne were good to her and she did no more work than anyone else, but the winter seemed never-ending and she became used to working with frozen fingers and hoary breath. The warehouse was so large that it was useless trying to heat it, although there was a pot-bellied stove in the little room which served as an office and a living room for the boys. It was here they would have bread dipped in hot soup for their midday meal. She had become hardened to the boys' taunts and, because they were not exactly industrious, she was easily able to keep up with them, but she could not make friends with any of them lest they discover her secret. She longed for Matthew's return.

She looked for him everywhere, in the streets and narrow rows, among the market stalls when she went to buy fresh vegetables, with every cattle drive arriving on the fields outside the town, on every stage coach which came rattling into The Lamb, even on the boats, plying up and down the river, laden with produce from King's Lynn and Wisbech. Every tall figure, every dark head glimpsed in the distance, set her heart racing, but when she came closer, she realised it was not the man she loved. Bitterly disappointed, she would return to the store, vowing not to look for him again; it only lowered her spirits so that she found her work tedious and that wasn't fair to the dear people who had taken her in, nor the boys with whom she worked. She had to stop brooding and be patient.

Her resolution was hard to keep and every day she hoped for a message to say he was well and still at liberty. The riots had faded with the turning of the year; there were fewer disturbances and those there were merited little space in the newspapers, except for reports of the court cases of those who had been arrested and the sentences they had been given and those varied according to the sentiments of the judges who had been appointed by a special commission to try them. There was no mention of Captain Matthew Tolley or of anyone answering his description. She wished she knew where he was. And she wished she knew how her father was faring in prison, but she could think of no way of finding out.

'Do you think Pa is well?' she asked Jacob one day when they were alone together in the little office. It was her turn to make the soup and he was busy at the table with his ledgers. It was easy to confide in him; he was always so cheerful and ready to listen. He was like her Pa for that; he was like Josiah in so many ways. Kate sometimes found herself looking at him as he worked and wishing a little wistfully that she could have a real flesh and blood father. She had never troubled herself about her lack of kin before, but now, when it seemed to be so important to other people, Matthew included, she wished she had a family and a respectable background and for the first time began to wonder if her Pa had made as much effort as he could have done to find hers. She scolded herself severely for her disloyalty whenever shameful thoughts like this crept into her brain, brushing them away and going at her work with feverish vigour, but they always returned. Her reading had told her that there was a certain class of society to whom breeding was everything. If you were not a gentlewoman, you were nothing. She had dismissed it all as literary nonsense, but now she was not so sure. When Pa came back to her, she would try and get him to talk to her about it. 'His leg will be mended by now, won't it?' She had doggedly shut her mind to Sir John's hints of gangrene; he had only been trying to frighten her.

'It ought to be,' he said. 'And he in't out in the fields having to work, is he? He'll do, don't you fret.'

'Yes,' she sighed. 'I must believe it. But it is so difficult, not knowing. Not knowing about Captain Tolley either. He said he would come back . . .'

'He'll be back just as soon as he judges the time is right,' he said. 'You must learn patience, me lad.'

He always called her 'lad' because they were never sure when any of the boys were within earshot, just as she endeavoured to behave like a boy at all times. But it was very difficult. She did not feel like one at all, though she wasn't sure she felt like a grown woman either. 'Thank you for giving me a home and being so kind to me,' she said, not for the first time.

'You're welcome.' He laughed and patted the top of her head with his huge but gentle hand. 'Now go and call the boys for their dinner afore they complain you're taking too long. Bates will be round again soon and he'll have all the news.'

But Bates did not come and neither did Matthew. Not for the first time, she wished Pa had taught her more about the ways of men and how to understand them, why they said one thing and did another. Matthew's kisses had made her body flare with desire to learn more about herself, about the inner woman who responded so eagerly to his touch, to know more of the man. If he had been insincere, if he had been having a game with her, should she have realised it? Could her mouth and limbs betray her so that, even though her mind told her it was not to be, she still wanted him?

Was it the same for him? Were love and desire two separate things? What had he said to her? *Your Pa has not equipped you to live in the real world of men and women. He hasn't told you the difference between love and desire.* When Matthew came back, she would make him tell her. *If* he came back. She was beginning to think he had not meant it when he said he would return.

It had taken too long, Matthew decided, as he rode his bay into the yard of the Dog and Duck. Instead of being able to confirm Josiah Brough's story in Middleacre, he had been forced to go all the way to Caspertown, and in the middle of the winter, with snow lying deep on the hills; it had taken weeks. Weeks to learn that Josiah Brough had almost certainly been telling the truth. And Kate must be told.

He dismounted and handed his horse over to the ostler before going into the inn, taking off his tall-crowned hat and ducking his head below the lintel. It was over-warm inside and he opened his riding coat, revealing a kerseymere waistcoat, a carefully laundered shirt and starched muslin cravat. Seeing this the innkeeper left off polishing glasses and hurried forward, bowing obsequiously. It was rare for gentry to patronise his establishment. 'What can I do for you, sir.'

'Food and wine, if you please; whatever you've got will do.'

'Aye Sir. Immediately, Sir.'

Matthew smiled; it was extraordinary what a suit of clothes could do. 'I asked for messages to be left here for me,' he said. 'Captain Matthew Thorsborough.'

'Aye, Captain. Bates, the drover, left one a se'n night since.' He disappeared into a back room and Matthew could hear him muttering to whoever was at work there, that they were to produce a meal fit for gentry and open a bottle of the best and where was that letter the drover brought. A minute later he returned in triumph. 'Here 'tis, sir.'

Recognising the handwriting as his sister-in-law's, Matthew held the paper to his nose for a second before opening it. The perfume which usually accompanied her correspondence had been overlaid by a strong smell of cattle. It would be full of family gossip and news of her children, but he didn't mind that any more. She had slipped into her rightful place as a much-loved sister; the torment had gone and he wondered now why he had ever suffered it. The

245

greater torment was what to do about Kate. Would she accept the truth? And if she did, what would be her reaction? That was of tantamount importance and because he wanted to see it for himself, he had told no one where to find her. 'I will bring her to you,' he had said.

He broke the seal and began to read. The message was short and so terse, he knew Amy had written it in a great hurry. 'Matthew, wherever you are and whatever you are doing, come home at once. Papa is fading.'

He read it twice, his mind a whirl of conflicting emotions. He must obviously go home, but what of Kate?

'Not bad news, sir?' The innkeeper's voice broke in.

'What? Oh, yes, I am afraid it is. I must leave at once.'

'But your supper is nigh on ready and your horse . . .'

'My horse is used to changes of plan,' he said. 'As for my dinner, pack it up, I'll eat in the saddle.'

Ten minutes later he was on the road again, turning east towards Norfolk and Garforth. 'Be patient, Kate,' he muttered, realising he had said something like that before, but comforted by the knowledge that she was in no danger if she stayed where she was.

Late the following day he arrived at Garforth Manor to find the house silent and the servants creeping about on tiptoe. Amy, normally so lively, looked pale and her usually bright eyes had lost their lustre.

'Am I in time?'

'Yes. He was determined to wait for you to arrive, but it has been a long struggle. I'm not sure he will recognise you. Go up. Daniel is with him, though he is exhausted.'

He climbed the stairs swiftly and silently, dreading what he would find in the huge bedroom which his parents had shared until his mother's death, ten years before. He hadn't been in there since and now . . . He pushed open the door.

The room smelled fusty because the windows were tight shut and there was a roaring fire in the grate. In the large four-poster bed his father lay, so emaciated he looked like a doll, a wizened male doll with white hair and a snowy beard. His eyes were open, though they appeared unfocused. For one dreadful minute he thought he was too late. Then the hand that lay on the coverlet lifted a couple of inches and dropped again, as if the effort of raising it any higher was too much. Daniel, who had been watching him, saw the gesture and turned towards his brother. His face was drawn; Amy had not been exaggerating when she said he was exhausted.

'Matthew. Thank God.'

I came as soon as I received Amy's message.' His voice was a whisper as he approached the bed and took his father's limp hand. 'How is he?'

'I haven't lost my wits or my hearing,' his lordship croaked testily. 'Ask me yourself.'

Matthew smiled and sat beside the bed. 'How are you, Father?'

'Dying and don't you go denying it. I have enough of that with the others who refuse to let me look death in the face. I ain't afraid.' The effort of saying it was almost too much and he lay back on the pillow and closed his eyes. The clock ticked. No one moved.

'Wanted to see you again, my boy,' he went on after several minutes. 'Wanted you home.'

'I am home.'

'Send him away.'

'Who?'

'Him.' A finger pointed. 'Your brother. Want to ask you something ...'

Matthew looked doubtfully at Daniel but he smiled quirkily and rose to go. 'I've got things to do and if you'll sit by him a while ...'

'Of course I will.'

As soon as Daniel had left, the old man grasped Matthew's hand in a surprisingly strong grip. 'Don't want to feel you are estranged from the family,' he said, fighting for the strength to speak.

'I'm not.'

'Amy's a good girl, did as she was told ...'

'I know. She did right.'

'Can you not live with that?'

Matthew smiled; his father was more perceptive than he had realised. 'I can live with it because it no longer matters.'

'Ah, you have found someone else. I wondered ...'

'Yes, Father.'

'Who is she? Not someone you are ashamed to bring home?'

'No, I am very proud of her. She is beautiful and spirited and caring ...'

'Good family?'

'Yes, she comes from a good family.' He was almost certain that was true.

'Bring her home then.'

Could he? Dare he? There were any number of reasons why it was not a good idea. Kate did not know his real name and he could see storms over that; she would not understand why he had withheld it from her. She had yet to be told the truth about herself and he had no idea how she would feel about it. And there was his work with the labourers. Until he had opened Amy's letter he had been so sure of himself; Matthew Tolley had slipped off the fence and come down heavily on the side of the underdogs. He could not abandon them, but bringing Kate to Garforth would mean that she, too, would have to share his dual personality and he was afraid she would hate it, especially if she also had to come to terms with her own changed identity at the same time. She loathed deception and was so outspoken he could imagine her wreaking havoc with his family's ideas of what was right and proper. Most of all was the fact that he was a wanted man, a criminal in the eyes of the law. It only needed someone to see Captain Thorsborough and recognise Matthew Tolley for the game to be up and his family would be dragged through mire; he was thankful that Andrew had vowed to say nothing. For his father and Daniel and Amy the scandal would be intolerable.

'Well, my boy?' His father's cracked voice forced him to pay attention. 'Is there any reason why you should not?'

'Nothing that cannot be overcome,' he said. 'Now, I think you should rest.'

'I'll have plenty of time to rest later. If you are in trouble I want you to tell me about it.'

'I am in no trouble, Father.' He rose to go, praying he might be forgiven for the lie. 'Now rest and I will come back later to see how you are.' He called a servant to watch over the old man and went downstairs to join his brother and sister-in-law for a silent meal.

Lord Thorsborough died in the early hours of the following morning. His family were at his bedside and the end was peaceful. Matthew felt a terrible pang of guilt that he could not have been the son his father wanted him to be, but relieved that he had not had to reveal his secret existence. But he still had to face Daniel and Amy, both of whom would expect him to give up what they chose to call his roaming life. He could not, though the reason was very different from his original one. After the funeral, which was well attended by family friends and neighbours as well as estate workers, he announced his intention of leaving again.

Amy was appalled. 'Why?' she demanded. 'What is wrong with your home that you cannot bear to be in it more than a few days before you must be off again?'

'Nothing is wrong with it.'

'Papa said you had a young lady.'

He smiled. 'Perhaps I have.'

'Are you going to marry her?'

'I doubt it.'

'Oh. She is married already. Oh, Matthew!'

'No, she is not married, but there are difficulties.'

'Can you not tell us what they are? We will contrive to overcome them together.' She laid a hand on his arm and looked up into his face. 'If she is not ... if she is not quite a lady, we can overlook it if we all try very hard. I am sure I am not one to look down on someone because of something they cannot help.'

He smiled wryly. 'What makes you think she is not a lady?'

'What other reason could there be for hiding her away, if she is single? Matthew, we are your family and we love you and I am sure we will love whomsoever you choose.'

'Thank you, Amy. One day, perhaps I shall be able to tell you everything, but now I must go. Please forgive me.'

He left at first light the next morning, long before anyone was up, saddling his horse himself and taking only his cloakbag.

Winter had gone and spring was well advanced when Bates again visited the warehouse. The floods had gone from the fields beyond Ely, and the grass was lush and green in the meadows where the cattle grazed. The crops were sprouting, flowers grew in wayside gardens; on the river ducklings swam in line after their mothers and yellow and white water lilies pushed their shiny leaves to the surface. The banks were golden with flag and marsh marigolds and the sound of frogs and larks filled the air. For the first time for months the sun had a little warmth and the fenland sky showed more blue than grey. It was a time for hope.

The day's work was done and supper finished and Kate was sitting by the hearth in the Fynes' parlour reading a book of poems she had found on one of the shelves in the house, when the drover arrived, complete with tophat, tangled beard and an overpowering smell of cattle.

'I was beginning to think you were never coming,' she said after he had been greeted by his hosts and taken a seat at the table with a tankard of ale and a meat pie in front of him. 'It's been months.'

'So it has.' He laughed, cupping both gnarled hands round his mug. 'I've been to Smithfield and all the way back to Falkirk Tryst since I last saw you.'

'Was it a good trip?' Jacob queried.

'Middlin' fair, though the weather up in Scotland didn't help. Howsummever, I've a passable herd to sell in Acle.'

'And Rob and Tom, how do they fare?' Bessie asked.

'Well, thank 'e.' He sipped his ale and looked at Kate over the rim of his glass. She made a very effeminate lad and he wondered how she had managed to keep up the deception.

'Have you seen Captain Tolley,' she asked, impatient with the pleasantries. 'Do you know where he is? Is he safe? Is he well?'

'Last I saw of him he was in Wisbech.'

'Wisbech! What's he doing there? He's certain to be arrested if Sir John gets to hear of it. Oh, couldn't you have persuaded him to come with you?'

'I don't tell him where to go or what to do, he is his own master.' He paused to look at her and decided he had teased her enough. 'He said he had some business to attend to, but he should be here about noon tomorrow.'

'Tomorrow!' Her blue eyes sparkled. 'Oh, you don't know how glad I am to hear that. I was so afraid ...' She turned to Bessie. 'Now you will meet him.'

'Seems like it,' she said, then to Bates. 'Is it safe?'

He shrugged. 'As safe as anything else he's done, I dessay.'

'I wouldn't wish him to be in danger on my account,' Kate said, jumping up and moving round the table. She just could not sit still. 'Perhaps he should not ...'

'Then you tell him so,' Bates said tersely. 'See if he'll listen.'

'You'd best calm down,' Bessie told her. 'If the boys see you like that, it'll give the game away.'

'I wish I didn't have to be a boy,' she said, throwing herself into a chair by the hearth and gazing into the flames. They reminded her of the fire in the bedroom of the Dog and Duck, where Matthew had taken off her wet clothes. It was the last time she

had been seen as a woman and she wanted it to happen again.
Except this time she would make him forget all the other things
that had preoccupied him before, whatever they were. But how
could she do that dressed in breeches and smock ?

'You can't change now, you know that,' Jacob said. 'Besides,
you saw the posters they put up when you first arrived. 'Tis Kate
Brough who's wanted, not Kit Brown.'

'Don't you think Sir John has forgotten all about me by now ?'
she asked.

'Maybe,' Jacob said. 'But you've been Kit Brown ever since you
got here and if the boys suddenly saw you in petticoats, their eyes
would pop out of their heads. How long do you think it would take
them to put two and two together, eh ?'

'If I don't go to the shop they won't see me, will they ?' She
lifted pleading eyes to Bessie. 'I can buy a gown with my wages.'

'The captain won't notice what you wear,' Bates said. He didn't
like the situation one bit, he had told Matthew so in his blunt way,
but he could not help being drawn to the girl. She had a refreshing
innocence. If he had ever had time to marry and beget children he
would have wished for a daughter like Kate; his disapproval of her
was entirely on account of the captain. 'He didn't afore, when you
looked like a bedraggled urchin in that cast-off smock and wearing
a sack for a cape.'

She didn't believe that. She wanted to be soft and feminine;
after all she had to compete with the curvaceous Betty Watson,
didn't she ? How could she do that dressed as a boy and a working
one at that, in rough breeches and boots and a smock that all but
drowned her ?

She was still musing on the problem of clothes when she excused
herself and went to bed. She did not hear Bates tell the Fynes that
he thought Matthew was being exceedingly foolish to venture into
the city. Although Sir John had not yet returned from his prolonged
wedding tour, his nephew had increased the reward for the couple
and was actively seeking them.

'His nephew ?' Bessie queried. 'Kate spoke well of him. She said
he had helped them to escape.'

'Seems he had second thoughts. He and his stepmother returned
to their own home after the riot but he came back about a month
ago and it seems he's just as keen as his uncle to lay hands on
them. I warned the gaffer, but there's none so deaf as those who

251

won't hear.' He paused to swallow a mouthful of ale. 'He's becoming more and more reckless, you'd almost think he didn't care what became of him. He's not been hisself since she were took to Wisbech in that tumbril. One minute he says he can't do any more for the labourers on account of he's become too well known as Matthew Tolley and he'd need another new identity, and the next he's talkin' about arguin' the case in a court o' law and lettin' 'em hang him if they want to.'

'What's he coming here for tomorrow, then?' Jacob asked, sucking thoughtfully on his pipe. 'He's not come to give himself up, has he?'

Bates sighed. 'I wish I knew. Mayhap he's coming to say goodbye to the wench.'

'Poor Kate,' murmured Bessie to Jacob, as they went up to bed. 'It will break her heart.'

'Archie, rouse yourself. It's five o'clock.'

Archie Carter shut out the voice and rolled over again but he was not going to be allowed to go back to sleep; the bedclothes were stripped off him. 'Come on, you idle good-for-nothing. It's your turn.'

'No, it in't.' He sat up and grabbed the blanket back from Jonas, who stood over him in his nightshirt. 'I did it yesterday.'

'An' you'll do it ag'in t'day an' ev'ry day 'til you've paid me back.'

Archie owed Jonas two shillings and Jonas had every intention of exacting the last ounce of interest. Archie must be first up to light the fire in the little room behind the stockrooms where they lived and ate, and to draw water from the well in the back yard until such time as the two shillings was repaid. Archie would not have minded so much but the florin had not been in his hand more than five minutes before he lost it in a cock fight. The stupid bird he backed had been more like a tame pigeon than a cock and had dropped dead before the fight had really got under way. 'Gi'e us five more minutes,' he said.

'No. The gaffer'll be here directly with Kit.'

'Kit!' Archie said contemptuously. 'Why do 'e hev t'live up at t'house with the gaffer? Do 'e think 'e's a jin'lem'n?'

'Oh, fer Gawd's sake leave off yar yackin',' David said from the next bed. 'Do one o' you go down and leave a body in peace.'

Reluctantly Archie left his bed, pulled on his trousers and shirt and scratching his head and yawning as he went, descended the steep stair to the warehouse.

It was cold and gloomy and he wasted no time there, though the boys were supposed to be responsible for its security. David had made sure it was all locked up right and tight the night before, so it stood to reason it was still locked. Mr and Mrs Fyne had keys, of course, but they wouldn't be here for another half hour and by then all three boys would have to be ready to begin the day's work.

He was hurrying through to the little back room where they ate their meals, when he heard a sound that stopped him in his tracks. He held his breath, listening. It was only a small sound, a light scuffling.

'Dratted rats,' he muttered to himself. But rats ruined stock; they ate the food and nested in the bales of cloth and if that happened he would be blamed. He picked up an axe which lay with a pile of others on display and crept forward towards the shelves at the back of the building. They were high and were stacked with clothing, breeches, hickory shirts, smockfrocks, small clothes and hose; there were even a few women's dresses and bonnets, which were kept because there were females on the river boats as well as men, and the Fynes never lost an opportunity for a sale. If rats had got into them, he'd be in trouble. He peered round the end of one of the shelves, axe raised, and then stopped and stared with his mouth open. The hand holding the weapon dropped to his side.

Kit Brown was standing there with a spotted blue muslin gown held up to his shoulders and spreading the skirts about his breeches-clad legs. Archie watched as he pulled the dress into his waist and gave a little twirl, smiling to himself. Archie had heard about men who liked to dress in women's clothes, but he had never come across one and now his eyes were popping out of his head. He continued to be a silent onlooker as Kate folded the dress, put it on top of a neat pile of other clothes and took down a bonnet, a yellow straw trimmed with blue ribbon and cornflowers, which she set upon her curls, tying the ribbon beneath her chin in a fetching bow. Archie gasped. Kit was pretty as a picture. And then he noticed other things – the slight swelling of her breasts, the slim waist and rounded posterior and saw what had been staring him in the face for the past four months. Kit Brown was a girl!

'Archie, where the devil are you?' Jonas's voice echoed round the building. 'There ain't no kindlin' fer the fire and no water drawn neither. If you've found a corner and gone back to sleep ...'

Kate, hearing him too, snatched the bonnet from her head and picked up the pile of neatly folded clothes she had selected and dashed along the row of shelves to disappear out of a small door at the back. Archie hesitated, tempted to follow her, but Jonas had found him.

'What are you a-doin' of?' he demanded. 'It's nearly six and time to open up and not a morsel of food ha' touched me lips.'

'I've just seen Kit Brown ...'

'So what? It's time he got here.'

'He's a maid!'

'What squit are you talkin' now?'

'I jes' saw him – her – trying on petticoats and bonnets. I tell you he in't no lad, not nohow.'

'Go on, pull the other leg, why don' you?' Even while he was deriding his workmate, Jonas was thinking. Kit Brown was effeminate and the Fynes did make life easier for him than they did for the rest of their employees, watching over him and letting him live up at the house. The boys had talked about it of course, but they had concluded that Kit Brown was a gentleman's son, come to learn the trade, and not to be subjected to the rough and tumble of communal living. But if Archie was right ... Why should a maid dress as a lad, unless she had something to hide. 'Where did he go?' he asked.

'Out the back yard. And I tell 'e, it's a she.'

'You got to draw water, hen't you? Go and do it and see where *she's* gone.'

Archie obeyed but there was no sign of Kit or Kate. He went back to report his failure.

'We'll have it out with her when she comes in to work,' Charlie said.

But Kate did not come to work that morning. The Fynes came and so did Bates, and the boys were kept busy making up the drover's order and seeing to all the other customers who came to the store and it was mid-morning before they could confer again.

'She came with Bates, so I reckon she'll leave with 'im,' David said, tucking into bread and cheese and washing it down with small beer. 'No doubt she's run away from hoom to be wiv 'im and thass why she do disguise 'erself. I reckon we seen the last on 'er.'

But Jonas, who had never got on well with the opposite sex on account of his spots and a disinclination to wash, didn't think it was as simple or as romantic as that. 'Supposin' she were wanted by the law?' he said.

'Wha' fer?'

Jonas shrugged. 'I don' know, do I?'

'There was a woman what was wanted for them riots,' Archie said. 'Round New Year it wor. I remember cos I went hoom for a day and me cousin Ben told me about 'er. He's the superintendent of the watch at Wisbech. She wor 'elpin tha' Cap'n Swing so 'e said. She'd bin took and got away agi'n.'

'I recall when Kit fust got 'ere,' Charlie added. 'There wor a lot of whisperin' behind closed doors . . .'

'And there wor public notices,' David put in. 'I saw one on 'em on a wall in the city. What was 'er name now?'

'Kate Brown.' Jonas's face was screwed up in his effort to remember. 'No, tha' in't right but it wor somethin' like that. Five feet four, light hair and blue eyes. Thass our Kit a'right.'

'And there wor a reward,' Archie said, thinking about the money he owed. If he could earn that reward he could pay it back and there'd be no more early mornings, not more than his fair share anyhow. 'Ten guineas, it wor.'

'What'll we do?' David said. He needed a new pair of breeks and a shirt.

Jonas turned to Archie. 'How long will it take to get a message to your cousin?'

'I dunno, do I? I hen't ever writ a letter afore.'

'Then you'll hatta go y'self. We'll say yar ma is sick with the ague and you hatta go hoom.'

'What'll I tell my cousin Ben?'

'Fewl! Tell 'im she's 'ere.'

'But she in't.'

'Well, she in't a-goon' far, is she?' David said. 'I reckon she's still up at t'house 'til Bates is done 'ere.'

'Then we'd best 'old 'im as long as we can.' Jonas laughed. 'You c'n get his goods in a rare ol' muddle without even tryin', can't you?'

'Not long enough for Archie to git all the way to Wisbech an' back. It'd take a week by shanks's pony. I reckon 'e oughta go to the Ely watch.'

'But will they pay out the reward?'

No one knew the answer to that. 'You got any better ideas?' David asked irritably.

They had not, but as it happened, the whole discussion was unnecessary. Ben Carter was already in Ely. He had been escorting other prisoners to the Quarter Sessions and was quaffing a quart of ale with his good friend, Amos Howe, one of the Ely bailiffs, when Archie panted up to the Sessions House door. The news his cousin carried brought a wide grin to his face. He had been simmering with anger and humiliation all winter long, not only because of her assault on his person, which Mr Justice Gardiner would not let him add to the charges against her, but because it had been by the merest whisker he had not lost his job over that ambush. And the taunts of his friends had not helped. Now was his chance to live it down, to make amends and earn the undying gratitude of Sir John Haddow and, more to the point, Mr Andrew Carrington-Haddow, who had promised him fifty guineas if he delivered her to him, unharmed. Fifty guineas! What he couldn't do with that.

'Fynes warehouse, you say?'

'Yes, but she's not there and 'sides ...'

'Do you know where she is or don't you? Come on, boy, spit it out.' He paused, realising why his young cousin was prevaricating. 'You shall have your reward as soon as she's under lock and key, so best tell me where I can find her and be quick about it.'

'She didn't come to work this mornin' and I reckon she's up at Mr Fynes' house.'

'Or almost anywhere,' Ben Carter said gloomily. 'She'll have lit out by now.'

'No, she's there a'right. She don' know we know ...'

'Then let's be havin' her. Lead on, Archie, me lad.' To Amos, he said. 'Are you goin' to gi'e me a helpin' hand?'

'That I am. This is my town and my arrest.'

'You can have the drover and his mates,' he said, already out of the door. 'The girl is mine.'

Alone in the house, Kate stared at herself in the mirror in her room and knew she looked her best. Bessie had let her off work, knowing she would not have her mind on it, but Bessie did not know she had taken the spare key off the hook in the hall and hurried to the store on foot while Bessie herself was making an early trip to the market. She had helped herself to a dress and underclothes, not to mention a rather fetching bonnet, and by the time she returned home both Jacob and Bessie had left by boat for the shop. She could and would pay for what she had taken, so it wasn't exactly stealing and Bessie would understand.

It was the first time in her life she had given a thought to clothes as a means to please a man, but as she stood with her hands tight against her tiny waist and saw the bodice of the dress, simply decorated with narrow tucks, curving over her breasts, she knew she had dispelled the boy and was once more the young lady. She laughed aloud and twirled before the glass, watching the skirt billow out to show a tantalising glimpse of cream-stockinged ankle. 'That's one in the eye for you, Betty Watson,' she said and laughed again. Matthew was coming back, he was coming back to her and she meant to make sure he didn't go away again. All she had to do was wait.

But waiting had never come easy to Kate; patience was a virtue which had escaped her and she paced her room until she was almost screaming and then ventured downstairs to pace the parlour. Oh, how slowly the minutes ticked by. Where was Matthew? Was he already in the city, striding purposefully towards the quay? Had Bates told him where to find her? Supposing he had not understood and missed the way? She picked up the bonnet and turned it over in her hand. She didn't know why she had included that in her selection; she was not going out, was she? But it was so pretty and it was a perfect finishing touch. She put it on, standing before the oval mirror in the brick-tiled hall and plucking at her short curls so they framed her face inside the wide brim.

Suddenly throwing caution to the wind, she grabbed a shawl and let herself out of the house to go and meet the man who had captured her heart and, if Pa's edicts were true, had taken her reason.

She sped along the lane to the town, up the hill to the market place where she took up a position which gave her a clear view of the converging roads. She was surprised by the amount of traffic that went by her as she stood watching. Carts pulled by mules or workaday Clevelands rumbled by; coaches clattered into inn yards, vying for space with colourful drays drawn by sturdy Suffolk punches; traps and gigs sped by; riders on anything from thoroughbreds to donkeys walked or trotted and between them pedestrians of every shape and size. She was beginning to wonder if she had missed him or he had come in by another route, when she spotted him riding in on his big bay.

Dressed in breeches and a well-cut riding coat, he sat the animal easily, his hands lightly on the reins as walked the horse along the cobbles of the High Street. She stood, savouring the moment, while her heart gave great leaps and bounds and made her breathless. Whatever Pa said about love, she knew this was it; she had no doubt. And suddenly he caught sight of her. Flinging himself from his mount, he ran towards her, arms outstretched, as if he could not wait to fold them round her. She moved forward and then suddenly his smile was replaced by a look of dismay at something he had seen behind her. She whirled round to follow his gaze. Standing in the middle of the market was the prison van in which she had begun her journey to Ely and coming towards her at a loping run, was Ben Carter, followed by another man. She turned back to look at Matthew, doubt and fear etched on her face.

'Run!' he yelled. 'For God's sake, Kate, run!'

He sprinted past her and threw himself at the two men and though he fought like a tiger, they used cudgels and booted feet to overpower him. Then they dragged him, still struggling, towards the van.

'Kate, run!' he shouted, as they bundled him into the van. She stood frozen to the spot, mesmerised by the suddenness of it all, unable to think for herself. 'Kate, stir yourself!' She could still hear his muffled voice as the two men closed the doors and turned back for her.

Chapter Fifteen

She moved at last. While the driver turned the van in order to pursue her, Ben Carter went after Matthew's mount. It gave her a few moments' start; she sprinted away through the crowds. She ran and ran until she thought her lungs would burst. Darting in and out of alleys which were too narrow for the van, she was able to throw them off. Only when she was sure she had given them the slip did she stop to get her breath, then she slowly made her way back to the Fynes' home by a circuitous route. It was late in the afternoon when she stumbled, exhausted, into the hallway and by then, Jacob and Bessie had returned from the warehouse in order to meet the elusive Captain Tolley.

'In God's name, what happened to you?' Jacob shut the door behind her and ushered her into the parlour, where he helped her into a chair by the fire, calling to his wife as he did so. 'She's back.' He squatted down beside Kate and took her hands in his. 'What happened?'

The horror of it was still with her and for a minute Kate could not speak. She sat staring into the fire, unable to take in what had happened. Matthew had been there one minute, almost in touching distance, and gone the next; it was as swift as that. He had sacrificed himself to save her and when those two men discovered they had a bigger prize than the one they had been after, they would be jubilant. What she could not understand was how Ben Carter came to be there.

Bessie came in from the kitchen, wiping her hands on her apron. 'What's happened? Why are you wearing petticoats? Where have you been?'

'Hold hard, love,' Jacob said. 'She's had a fright, that's evident. Let her tell it in her own time.'

'They caught Matthew,' Kate said dully.

'Who?'

'Ben Carter and another man. They had the Wisbech prison van – at least it looked like the same van. Ben Carter recognised me and they started to come after me, but Matthew ...' She shuddered. 'He threw himself on them to save me.'

'Do you think she was followed back here?' Bessie asked her husband anxiously.

'I wasn't.' Kate's voice was flat. 'I don't think they were bothered about me once they had Matthew.' Overwhelmed by her despair, she put her head into her hands and sobbed. 'What will happen to him? Oh, it's all my fault. If he hadn't come back for me ...'

'Hush, girl,' Jacob said. 'You mustn't talk so. Bessie will make you up some nice warm milk and brandy and then you must rest.'

'I can't possibly rest. Matthew ...' She tried to rise but he pushed her firmly down again.

'I'll go out and see if I can find out what's happened,' he said. 'Wait here. Don't go out again whatever happens.' Then seeing the doubt on her face, added, 'Promise me?'

She nodded. She hadn't the strength to go anywhere even if she wanted to, but she couldn't help wishing she had been taken with Matthew, prison or no prison. And Bessie was obviously very worried, moving stiff-backed about the house and beating the batter for their dinner so energetically Kate thought she would break the bowl.

'I'm sorry,' Kate said.

''Tis no good being sorry now, girl, the damage is done.'

'Yes,' she agreed, but she was thinking only of Matthew.

'Why did you go and take those clothes? Why did you have to go out at all?'

'I was impatient and I'm sorry about the dress.' She looked down at it, torn and mud-spattered. 'I'll pay for it, I promise.'

'It's not just that, is it? There's the boys. You can't go back to the shop now, not as Kit Brown.'

'Do they know?'

'I reckon they do. Archie disappeared this morning. Jonas said he was sick, but he didn't look sick to me when he came back, grinning all over his face and wearing a new weskit. Hideous red thing with brass buttons.'

'He gave me away?'

'I reckon.'

'Then I must leave.' It was always what she intended to do in the end, but not like this, not under a cloud.

'Best wait until Jacob comes back. He'll know what to do, but keep well out of sight. There'll be a hue and cry over this, or I miss my guess.'

When her husband returned, he had Bates with him; the two men had met in the vicinity of the Sessions House. 'I'd arranged to meet the gaffer at The Lamb before coming on here,' Bates said. 'I was waiting for him when I heard a commotion outside the gaol and went to see what it was about. The Cap'n was being taken inside.'

'How was he?'

'Pale and heavily ironed, but he held his head up. The crowd gave a great cheer as he was brought from the van and someone shouted, "God bless ye, Cap'n!". If they could have freed him, they'd have done it there and then, but the gaolkeeper came out and made sure he went in quietly.'

'They'll take him back to Wisbech, won't they?' Kate said. 'We must help him, like you helped me.'

'I reckon they'll keep him in Ely for the Sessions,' the drover said. 'Asides, he told me, not two days since, that if he was to be taken, to let him be. He didn't want rescuing.'

'Why not?' Kate cried. 'Why should he say that?'

'He has a notion to show the world the labourers have a just cause.'

'That's madness,' Bessie said, pouring Bates his customary tankard of ale. 'He'll be convicted and then forgotten. No good will come of it.'

'But good must come of it,' Kate said, remembering what Matthew had said about putting the cause before everything and everyone, even her. She could not compete with that and though it hurt her, she was intensely proud of him for it. 'He is brave and selfless but he is fighting madness, the madness and corruption of Sir John Haddow and others like him, the rottenness of greed and power.'

'They're mighty weapons,' Bessie said. 'An' they don' 'elp us none. Kate can't stay here. We'll have the law down on us like a ton o' bricks.'

Jacob looked at her sharply. 'Where else is she to go, for goodness sake?'

'Back home.'

'This is her home, for as long as she wants it.'

'But the boys know who she is now.'

'They also know which side their bread is buttered,' he said firmly. Usually he and his wife agreed about everything, but when he decided to put his foot down, that was it; no one opposed him. 'If they want to keep their jobs, they'll stay dumb. As far as we are concerned, Kit Brown skit off and he hen't come back. And that's what we say to anyone else who asks questions. We have our niece staying with us for a few weeks. That's my last word.'

Kate was in tears. He was so kind to her and she did not deserve it, not when she had disobeyed them over the clothes and brought all this trouble on them. 'I'm sorry,' was all she managed to say.

'Very well.' Bessie relented and turned her attention to cooking a meal for them all. 'But only for a few weeks, until we know ...' She stopped. They all knew what she was thinking, even Kate. Until Matthew was tried and sentence passed, that's what she meant, and no one could be anything but pessimistic over that. 'And she's to stay in the house, out of sight.'

'When will the trial be?' Jacob asked.

'I doubt a date will be fixed until they've gathered everything they can find against him and that could take some time.' Bates grinned suddenly. 'Some of the witnesses will be a trifle reluctant to testify. The longer it takes, the better, because he'll need to gather a good defence.'

'That'll take a deal of money,' Bessie said.

'Aye, it will, but he has friends.'

'But his friends are all as poor as church mice,' Kate cried. 'It's his enemies who are rich.'

'That ain't exactly true,' Bates said. 'He's not without connections if he chooses to use them.'

'What connections?' Kate asked.

Bates turned to her. 'Didn't he tell you?'

'Only that he had been an army captain and he had been helping other labourers before he came to Middleacre. He wouldn't tell me any more.' She paused. 'But you know, don't you? You know all about him.'

Bates sighed and leaned back in his seat, quart pot in his hand. 'I don't suppose there's any harm in telling you now,' he said. 'It'll all come out at his trial.' He paused to take a mouthful of ale and wipe his straggly whiskers on his sleeve, while Kate sat on the edge of her seat, her attention fixed on his weatherbeaten face. 'Matthew's real name is Captain Matthew Thorsborough, late of His Majesty's Hussars, younger brother of Lord Thorsborough, of Garforth in Norfolk.' He paused and smiled crookedly. 'He is one of the landed gentry you hate so much.'

'I don't believe it,' she said without a second's thought. 'He's not bit like Sir John and his like.' Knowing Matthew was not the cowman he pretended to be was one thing, but to be an aristocrat was another entirely. 'You're teasing me.'

'It's no joke, I can tell you,' he said. 'The captain's brother is one of the richest landowners in the eastern counties. Daniel inherited the estate on the death of their father a se'nnight ago.'

'Will his brother help him?' Jacob asked Bates. 'Can he?'

'Might. If he knew.' He paused to drink again, but Kate, whose mind was in such a whirl of conflicting emotions, hardly heard him as he went on. 'But his family know nothing of his involvement with the labourers' cause. He changed his name to Tolley to protect them. They would heartily disapprove. They are of a mind with Sir John Haddow.'

'No good looking for aid there, then,' Jacob said.

'Mebbe not.' Bates paused before going on to tell them how Matthew had left home and travelled the countryside to become more and more entangled in the cause of an agricultural workers' union when he saw the dreadful conditions under which they lived and worked. When the name of Matthew Tolley became known, he couldn't keep up with the people who were asking for him.

'A good man, then,' Bessie said.

'But why did he lie to me?' Kate asked, trying to make sense of what the drover had said. Why should a gentleman, and a wealthy one at that, bother with the problems of the labouring classes? He had said he cared; did that mean he cared enough to turn his back on his family and his background? Or was there more to it that that?

'Did he lie?' Bates queried.

'He didn't tell me the truth, did he?'

'He daren't tell anyone the whole of it, least of all you, what with your pa being in gaol an' all.'

'But I thought he loved me. You don't keep things from people you love, do you? Pa would never do such a thing.' She was unaccountably angry; angry with Matthew for not trusting her, angry with herself for loving a man who was one of the upper classes, angry with Josiah for giving her ideas above her station, most of all, angry with Sir John who had tried to bribe her. Matthew must have known or guessed he would do something of the sort. 'He thinks I am not good enough for him. I am only the poacher's daughter.'

'Give me strength!' Bates exclaimed, losing patience with her. 'Is that all you can think of when he has just been thrown into gaol on account of you? If it hadn't been for you and wanting to see you again, he'd be safe at home now.'

She was immediately contrite. 'I'm sorry. I just wish I understood, that's all.'

'It's easy enough. He helps the labourers by talking to the landowners on their behalf and often it works, but in Middleacre, you have a tyrant, a man who won't listen.'

'Yes,' she agreed. 'A man I hate with all my heart.' She stopped, remembering something Matthew had said to her: *Don't hate so passionately, Kate. You are a woman made for love not hate.* It was her hate which had embroiled Matthew, not his. 'But why did he go to Middleacre in the first place?'

'He had seen Sir John at the office of the land commissioners. Keeping his eye on the enclosures being put forward was one of the ways he found out where he was needed.'

'And now he's lost everything,' she said wistfully. 'His home, his reputation, the love of his family.' She had lost her family too and though she had, through the years, schooled herself not to think about it, she knew how Matthew must be feeling. She wished she could find some way of letting him know he was not alone, that she was with him in spirit and praying for him.

'It was a risk he was prepared to take,' Bates said. 'He is still taking it.'

'In prison?' Bessie queried.

'He will not defend himself. He will use the opportunity to speak up for the right of the people to a living wage.'

'Will they let me see him?' she asked. 'I must go to him, tell him he is not alone.'

'No!' Bates spoke sharply. 'If you do anything so foolish you will be taken to stand trial with him and he'd take that hard, very hard indeed. You bide here and wait.'

Jacob moved to put his arm about Kate's drooping shoulders. 'Don't you fret, my dear, something will turn up, you'll see.'

She turned her head away so that they would not see her tears. 'I'm going upstairs,' she said, suddenly leaving them and running up to her room, where she could cry in solitude. Captain Matthew Thorsborough. She couldn't think of him as that; to her, he was plain Matthew Tolley. But that was someone who did not even exist. They said there was no such person as Captain Swing. There was no such person as Captain Tolley either. Why couldn't he have told her so? Why the secrecy? Did he suppose she couldn't keep a secret? Bates had related the tale flatly, as if the captain was some distant actor on a stage, out of her reach. And he *was* out of her reach; she could not even go to him; Bates had forbidden it and he was right.

The key rasped in the lock and Matthew, who had been sitting on the edge of the hard bench they called a bed with his head in his hands, looked up as the turnkey threw open the door. Thomas Beeley, his lawyer, had persuaded the judiciary to have his case heard at the Ely Assizes; it was far enough away from Wisbech to make sure he would obtain a fair hearing. Not that he cared about that; he was resigned to his fate. 'Get up and come with me,' the elderly gaoler said, peering down at him in the poor light of the lamp he held. 'You've got visitors.'

The prisoner rose and followed the warder along the corridor wondering who should want to visit him and why they had not been brought to his cell. As soon as he entered the governor's office, he knew the reason. Beside Thomas Beeley stood his brother. Both governor and warder retreated and left the three men in possession of the room.

'Daniel,' Matthew said, refusing to allow himself to be pleased to see him. 'What are you doing here?'

'I would have thought that was self-evident.' Daniel's clothes screamed opulence; figured silk waistcoat, black silk cravat of mourning for his father held by a diamond pin which sparkled in the lamplight, double-breasted frockcoat faced with velvet and dark trousers. The contrast with the dirty black jacket and breeches Matthew wore could not have been greater. 'We must get you out of this mess.'

'We? I cannot see that it is any business of yours.' His voice was brusque, angry almost. 'Go home and leave me to it.'

'Gentlemen, shall we sit down?' Thomas Beeley suggested.

They both turned towards him as if they had forgotten he was there, but then complied.

'For God's sake, Matthew, what have you done?' Daniel asked. 'Surely it is some misunderstanding which we can soon put to rights.'

'There is no misunderstanding. I am being charged as Matthew Tolley for riotous behaviour, destroying a barn and a threshing machine and inciting men to swear an illegal oath contrary to the Mutiny Act of 1745. Enough I should have thought.'

'But you are not this Matthew ... what name was it?'

'Tolley. It is the name I'm known by.' He turned to Thomas Beeley. 'I told you not to go to my family.'

'I did not,' Beeley said smoothly, pulling papers from a small case he carried. 'Your orders were that I was not to approach his lordship; you said nothing of anyone else doing so ...'

'Who?'

'Never mind who. The result was that Lord Thorsborough came to see me.'

'Matthew, I find all this impossible to understand,' Daniel said. 'Tell me you did not do these things.'

'I cannot, for I did. Willingly.'

'Amy said she was sure there was something troubling you when you came home last time, but I thought it was sorrow at Father's passing.'

'Amy is very perceptive,' Matthew said tersely. 'A sweet girl too. I would not for the world, hurt her. Or you. Go home. There is no Matthew Thorsborough and Matthew Tolley is a stranger to you.'

'He most certainly is, but I wish to know him. I want him to tell me what led to this.'

'I doubt you would understand.'

'Try me.'

He did try. He told him everything except his passion for Amy, which was irrelevant now. He told him how he felt when he saw the hardship of the people, how he had compared it with the opulence he could command as a member of the ancient Thorsborough family, how the small amount of help he had at first offered had escalated so that he had become something of a legend in East Anglia. He told him how the death of the little dog had affected him and how the unfeeling attitude of the hunt had sickened him.

And he told him about Kate, mysterious, provocative, delightful Kate. His brother listened but he did not understand.

'Extraordinary!' he exclaimed when Matthew fell silent. 'You must be queer in the attic. The army ... your wound ...'

'My wound was to my shoulder, not my head.'

Daniel turned to the lawyer, who had been listening carefully and taking copious notes. 'Can we get him off? Plead that he didn't know what he was doing? Coercion? Threats?'

'No,' Matthew said sharply. 'Do you take me for a coward?'

'No, of course not.'

'I will not hide behind the smocks of the workers, nor my antecedents either. The name of Thorsborough will never be mentioned by me or by anyone representing me. You need not fear it will be dragged through the mire.'

'Surely if the prosecution want to make capital out of your ancestry, there isn't much we can do about it.'

'They have already agreed not to,' Beeley said.

'On what condition?'

'A plea of guilty.'

Matthew gave a twisted smile. 'I might as well be hanged for a sheep as a lamb.'

'There is no reason for you to be hanged at all,' Beeley said, leaning forward the better to convince him. 'You see yourself as a leader of the oppressed, don't you? What you have just told his lordship illustrates that very clearly. The people look up to you, think of you as a hero.' He held up his hand as Matthew opened his mouth to protest. 'Oh, don't deny it for God's sake, it is your only hope. Even the justices must take note of popular opinion; it is why so many magistrates were lenient over the machine-breaking.'

'If that is the best you can do, then I suggest we employ other counsel,' Daniel said. 'Money is no object. Pay whatever you have to, to whomsoever can do most good. The judge ...'

'Is that your wish, Captain?' Beeley asked, gathering together his notes.

'No. I want no favours obtained with money I have not earned. I am one of the people. I have told them so often enough and now I must prove it.'

Daniel gave a grunt but did not speak.

'Then you agree to the condition?' Beeley asked Matthew.

He did not answer immediately; he was thinking of Kate. His

fate was in the hands of God and those who would try him. But Kate, what of Kate? They could have no future together whichever way it went and he had been foolish to imagine they could. Thank God she had escaped. He nodded his head in agreement. 'Very well.' The lawyer thrust a sheet of paper under his nose and he signed it without bothering to read it.

'What will I tell Amy?' Daniel asked. 'We both love you, but this goes against the grain. It is a betrayal of everything you have been brought up to believe.'

Matthew sighed. He was right, his brother had not understood. 'Tell her the truth, but if that sticks in your throat tell her Matthew Thorsborough is dead. Even if I come through this with my neck intact, I shall leave the country, either because I have been sentenced to deportation or by my own volition. There is nothing to keep me here.' He rose and held out his hand, wanting the painful interview at an end. 'Now go before I make a fool of myself.'

Daniel took the proffered hand in both his own and stood looking at him while the seconds ticked by and Beeley watched impassively, then he grasped his brother's shoulders and drew him to him. 'God bless you, Matthew, and keep you safe. I refuse to say goodbye.' With that he picked up his hat and gloves from the table and strode to the door.

Matthew waited until Daniel had left, then turned to Thomas Beeley. 'I want you to do something for me. I want you to go to Middleacre.'

The wheels of justice ground exceeding slow. Spring gave way to summer and the fields around the town were a patchwork of yellow rape and ripening corn; the eel trappers were out on the fen with their osier baskets and kestrel and harrier hawks floated eagle-eyed above the meadows, ready to swoop on anything that moved. Kate occupied her time doing jobs about the house; if she could not work at the shop, then she would earn her keep in other ways. She cleaned and dusted and cooked. She would have liked to do some sewing but Josiah had not taught her how to do that beyond cobbling together a hole in a pocket or darning a stocking. Bessie had begun to instruct her and though Kate did her best to concentrate, more often than not, her needle would become idle while she dreamed of Matthew and his tenderness and worried herself sick whether he was being fed properly in prison. Jacob, who knew about these things, told her that there were plenty of people ready and willing to provide extra food for him and if food was all he had to worry about, then he must be the most unworried man in the kingdom.

July was unbearably hot and Kate spent her spare time in the small walled garden, sitting in the shade of an apple tree with a wide-brimmed straw bonnet on her curls, reading Jane Austen's *Pride and Prejudice* with a great deal of wry amusement, and William Cobbett's *Rural Rides*. Here was a man who was not afraid to champion the cause of the labourer. There were some who said he was Captain Swing but Kate did not think so. Cobbett would not be one to hide behind a pseudonym; he was all too ready to put his name to his writings and they were far from the illiterate letters that characterised most Swing communications. Besides, he was an old man; he couldn't have been in so many places at once. But then, neither could Matthew.

She was in the garden one afternoon, almost asleep, with the bees droning in the lavender and the quiet swish of the river lapping the bank nearby, when Bates arrived.

As usual he brought with him the pungent smell of cattle and tobacco, but she cared little for that and jumped up to greet him, her spotted muslin skirt swaying as she moved. She looked like a rosebud, he thought, what with that pink dress and the delicate bloom of her complexion. He really didn't blame Matthew for wanting to protect her.

'It's good to see you, Bates,' she said, drawing him into the shade and pouring him a glass of lemonade from the jug at her side. 'Do Mr and Mrs Fyne know you're here?'

'Yes, they're coming to join us any minute. I had to go into the city, do a bit of dealing, but they said they'd row up as soon as maybe.' He looked with distaste at the glass in his hand. 'I'd rather it were a quart of ale,' he said. 'This looks like ...' He stopped suddenly, remembering his manners.

She laughed. 'Come indoors, then, and you shall have ale and eel pie and anything else you fancy.' She picked up her book which had fallen from her lap and led the way into the house. 'How long will you be here?'

'Depends,' he said guardedly, surreptitiously emptying the lemonade onto the flower bed. 'I might stay awhile.'

They arrived in the parlour at the same time as the Fynes, who had left the boys in charge while they came to hear his news. Bates always had news, sometimes good, sometimes bad, but always of interest, be it the price of beef and corn, the doings of the outrageous royals, the latest reform bills or what some idiot had said on some platform in London's parks. Today he had tidings of Matthew.

'The trial's been fixed for the next Sessions.'

'What are his chances?' Jacob asked the question for all of them.

'They ought to be good,' he said cheerfully, accepting a tankard of ale. 'He's got a good defence lawyer, the best there is.'

'And the others?' Kate asked. 'The Middleacre villagers?'

'Seems they're to be left alone, probably because Sir John went off on his wedding trip and there was no one interested enough to charge them.'

'What about me?'

'What about you?'

'Why haven't they arrested me?'

'They don't know where you are,' Jacob said. 'We told everyone Kit Brown had left and we don't know where he went. We made out it was a good joke when the Ely watchman suggested Kit Brown was a woman; we said it was out of the question. We told him to go and tell that Wisbech fellow the only female we had staying here was our neice and she was nobbut a child.'

'But the boys ...'

'I put the fear of God into them. They'll say what we tell them to.'

'I want to go to the trial,' Kate said.

'You can't do that,' Bates said. 'You'll be recognised and nothing the Fynes can do will save you then.'

'I'll go in disguise.' She just wanted to be near Matthew, to be able to see him, to lend him her strength, such as it was. She looked from one to the other, searching their faces, trying to make them understand, but Bates was looking decidedly doubtful. 'If I dress as a man, no one will know me,' she cajoled. 'And there's sure to be a crush and everyone will be looking at the dock and the judge and jury, won't they?'

'And what good do you think your being there will do?' Bessie asked. 'I mind when you went out before and look what happened ...'

She did not need to be reminded that it was her fault Matthew had been arrested. 'You'll keep the boys hard at work that week, won't you? They won't be there. Please, I just want to be near him. I'll sit as quiet as a little mouse, I promise.'

They gave way in the end and at eight o'clock on the morning of the first day of the trial, dressed as a young gentleman of fashion with a roomy frockcoat over her breeches and with her golden curls stuffed under a large, curly brimmed hat, she made her way to the Sessions House.

She was jostled in the crowds who had come to support Matthew or simply to gape and she began to wonder if she would ever get into the building at all, but Bates, who had accompanied her, pushed and shoved on her behalf and at last they found themselves inside and moving along at the direction of an usher to the courtroom where the trial was to take place. Bates, who preferred crowds of cattle to crowds of people, stood at the back but Kate found a seat on one of the wooden benches squashed between a fat woman who was nearly bursting out of her stays, judging by the amount of wobbly bosom she was showing, and a thin little man with a straggly moustache which he continually chewed. With a fluttering heart and trembling hands, she waited for the arrival of the officials and the appearance of the man she loved. If love could support him and set him free, hers would surely do so.

The judge, in full-bottomed wig and red robes, with all his retinue of bailiffs and court officials about him, had arrived in the city the day before when he had taken part in a service in the cathedral and sworn in the grand jury, who had found there was a case to answer and declared a True Bill. Now, on the morning of the trial, looking stern and awe-inspiring, he took his place on the bench and the babble of voices faded. Matthew was called and climbed the steps to the dock.

Although pale and thinner than she remembered him, he looked proud, almost arrogant, certainly not intimidated by the occasion. It's because he's a gentleman, Kate thought; he is as high-born as the judge. But that wouldn't count, she told herself, he had sacrificed his claim to that and chosen to live and be tried as a labourer.

The jury filed in and took their seats; to Kate they were twelve very ordinary men and looked incapable of adding two and two, let alone deciding a man's guilt or innocence. Her spirits sank lower and lower as the indictment was read. He was charged with inciting farm workers to write threatening letters, the swearing of illegal oaths, sheep-stealing, machine-breaking and assault on the person of Sir John Haddow of Middleacre in the county of Cambridgeshire. Kate sat forward, intent on every word, as counsel, acting for the prosecution rose and addressed the jury.

He stood in front of them with his thumbs in his waistcoat pocket and his fingers splayed over his rotund front. 'Gentlemen,' he began. 'It is my painful duty to come before you on this occasion as counsel for the Crown against the prisoner at the bar. You have heard the indictment, but before I put before you the details of the acts which led to these charges, it is necessary to explain the events which led to them, so that you may properly understand the serious nature of the crimes. The events in the village of Middleacre were preceded by threats and excesses in other parts of the counties of East Anglia, on the pretext of the lowness of wages and the high price of food and necessities. This state of affairs was a result in part to the vagaries of the season, but that is no defence, for the rain fell on rich and poor alike.' He paused while a titter went round the court, then continued. 'The problems of the poor were exacerbated, not relieved, by tumultuous assemblies, who intimidated those who wished to go about their lawful business, carrying violence and terror wherever they went. Whether the accused had a hand in such assemblies is for you, the jury, to decide. Suffice it to say the contagion spread to Middleacre, brought by the prisoner at the bar who had arrived secretly in the village and which resulted in an outbreak of violence and destruction such as had never before been seen in what had until then been a peaceful and law-abiding community of people.'

Thomas Beeley, defending the prisoner, rose to his feet and objected to the way prosecuting counsel was addressing the jury. 'He is prejudging the issue,' he said.

'Mr Beeley, you will have an opportunity to comment on Mr Radwinter's remarks in due course,' the judge said and to the prosecutor. 'Please proceed.'

Mr Radwinter bowed to the judge and turned again to the jury. 'I shall bring witnesses to prove that the accused was at the centre of the events of that day, that he led and incited men, women and even little children, to violence.' He went on in like vein for several more minutes before reading a sworn statement from Sir John

Haddow giving his version of events, and then calling his witnesses, men like Silas Gotobed, Bob Hall and Moss, the baker. Kate sat fuming and biting her lip to stop herself shouting out that these men had all taken part in what happened and were betraying the rest.

'And whose idea was it to write the threatening letter to Sir John?' Mr Radwinter asked one trembling Middleacre villager, who had obviously been bribed or threatened to give evidence.

'Cap'n Matthew Tolley's, your honour.'

'And who suggested you should all be sworn to secrecy?'

'Cap'n Tolley.'

'Who set fire to Sir John Haddow's barn?'

'Tolley,' the man replied, with downcast eyes.

Kate gasped and the defence lawyer sprang to his feet, but the judge waved him back to his seat. 'You will have an opportunity to question the witness later, Mr Beeley.'

The questions went on and on, while Kate's eyes remained fixed towards the dock, willing her love to reach out to Matthew and comfort him, though he appeared not to need it; he was so self-contained. He didn't seem to mind the lies being told about him.

At last the judge allowed the defence lawyer to ask his questions. He jumped up and strode to the witness stand. 'Who set fire to the barn?'

'I told you, sir. Matthew Tolley, sir.'

'You actually saw him do it? You saw him put the torch to the straw?'

'No, but others said . . .'

'Others? What others? Name names, if you please, so that we can have them here to testify.'

'I disremember their names.'

'No, because there are no names to tell. No one saw Matthew Tolley set fire to the barn, simply because he wasn't there.' The lawyer turned to the judge. 'My lord, the defendant was in Lowacre when the fire started, he had been there all day. It is three miles from Middleacre. He was seen there by the blacksmith and, with your permission, I shall call him in due course.'

The trial continued with each witness adding his testimony to the others. Fiddy, on behalf of the prosecution, told of the attack on Sir John. 'Tolley pulled him off his horse,' the bailiff said. 'Squire's a good horseman, he'd not come off easy.'

'What happened then?'

'Why, they rolled together on the ground. Tolley laid into the squire very vicious, gave him a black eye and bruised his cheek.'

The judge interrupted to ask if either man had had a weapon.

Fiddy hesitated. 'I disremember. I don't think so.'

Thomas Beeley rose as he had done at frequent intervals throughout the day; he was like a jack-in-the-box, Kate thought, though it didn't seem to be helping Matthew. She longed to add her testimony, but she had promised the Fynes she would sit quiet and say nothing, however tempted she might be, and so she sat with her fists clenched in her lap and listened to Matthew being vilified.

The judge turned to the defence lawyer. 'Do you wish to cross-examine, Mr Beeley?'

'If it please, my lord.' He paused and cast his eye over each juror in turn before addressing the witness. 'Was Sir John armed?'

'No, sir.'

'I do not mean with firearms. Had he a weapon of any sort, a whip, for instance?'

'Bein' on horseback 'til he were unseated, he had his crop in his hand.'

'And what was he doing with that crop when the defendant pulled him from his horse?'

Fiddy hesitated and mumbled something inaudible. 'Speak up, man,' the judge ordered. 'And remember you are under oath.'

'He struck the girl with it.'

'Struck the girl,' the lawyer repeated. 'Then Captain Tolley was acting in her defence?'

'I reckon so,' said Fiddy. 'But she deserved it, she was as bad as all the men...'

'Where is this girl?' asked the judge. 'Is she to be called?'

'She cannot be found, my lord,' the prosecutor said.

The judge turned to the defence lawyer. 'Is she not important to the defence?'

'No, my lord.'

Kate could not understand that. Matthew had been defending her and she could tell them so. She screwed round in her seat to look at Bates. He was shaking his head slowly from side to side and she subsided in her seat. He had only confirmed what she knew already, that she was one of the dissidents herself and no one would listen to her. And by insisting she was unimportant, Matthew hoped to protect her.

She sat on the uncomfortable bench all day listening to the evidence and, at the end, she despaired. Thomas Beeley worked hard, but there was no denying Matthew had done many of the things of which he had been accused, he *had* written anonymous letters, *had* led the combination men and he *had* attacked the squire. How could he escape the penalty the law demanded? And the worst of it was, that if Pa had not gone poaching and she had not asked for his help, Matthew might not have stayed in Middleacre. And if she had not interfered in village affairs and incited the men to march on Haddow Hall, there would have been no riot at the barn and Matthew would never have been caught. He had said he did not want her involved, had said he would rather she were not in the thick of it and she had defied him. If only she had stayed out of it!

At the end of the day, she went back to the comfort of the Fynes' living room to sit over a meal she had no appetite for and tell them everything she could remember of the proceedings. 'It was terrible, the things they said,' she told them. 'Half of it lies or twisted so that it put Matthew in the worst possible light. All the time I wanted to shout out how good Matthew is and how he only did those things to help other people, 'specially me.'

'Thomas Beeley will say it for you,' Jacob said. 'You'll see.'

And he did. After three days of evidence and counter-evidence and a long harangue by the prosecuting counsel, the defending lawyer stood up to address the jury. 'Here you have a young man of good breeding and sound intellect,' he began. 'Yet he stands before you accused of all manner of misdemeanours he had no need to commit.' His voice rose. 'No need, I say, because he is of independent means.' There was a buzz of conversation from the public seats at this news and Kate saw Matthew shaking his head at Thomas Beeley as if disagreeing with the approach he had taken, but the lawyer ignored him and went on. 'Why did he behave in the way he did? Why did he involve himself with the labourers? Did he stand to gain? On the contrary, he had much to lose. Gentlemen of the jury, think of that, think of what his motives must have been. Was he selfish? Was he greedy? Did he long for power? Or riches?

'No, I say, none of these. He did what he did for the people. He could not bear to see the misery, the poverty of the men, women and little children about him. He flinched when they were hurt, he cried with them when they groaned in hunger, he shivered with them when they had no fuel for a fire because their peat meadows had been taken from them. And he looked about him for a remedy ...'

Kate, sitting still and tense in her seat, wished the man were not so flowery in his language, but there was no doubt he held the attention of everyone in that crowded courtroom. He paced about as he spoke, sometimes addressing the jury directly, sometimes turning to the judge, sometimes making his appeal to the spectators squashed closely along the benches. 'He wanted only to help the less fortunate,' he went on. 'He advised his fellows to write letters instead of burning ricks, you must judge which is the greater crime. He urged them not to riot but to combine peacefully. Trade combinations are no longer illegal; they have not been illegal since 1824, in spite of those who would like to repeal the Act and take us back to the dark ages. As for swearing an illegal oath, no one has come forward to tell of taking part in such a rite.'

Someone was heard to mutter, 'Well, they wouldn't, would they?'

The lawyer hardly paused before continuing, striding along the front of the jury box. 'The defendant was not present when Sir John's barn went up in flames. He arrived too late to prevent it. And he had no hand in the killing and stealing of the sheep; my learned colleague has failed to prove his point there.' He paused to allow his words to penetrate, then went on, more strongly than ever. 'Just causes sometimes need strong arguments to convince those who do not wish to be convinced. Until something is done to alleviate the lot of the agricultural labourers there will always be Matthew Tolleys to put their case in the only way they know how. Do not make a martyr of him, for if you condemn him, that is surely what you will do. You cannot stamp out unrest until you stamp out the cause. Matthew Tolley is not the cause, he is the effect. His only crime was compassion.'

A small wave of applause broke out, but it was quickly silenced by the judge who adjourned the proceedings for the midday break.

The room buzzed with conversation as soon as he had retired, but the spectators did not leave their seats; there were others waiting outside to seize them the minute they were vacated and with only the summing up and the verdict to come, interest was as keen as ever. Bread and cheese and currant buns were brought out from their wrappings and consumed amid a hubbub of speculation, and the time, for all but Kate, soon passed. She sat twisting her hands together, her lips moving in silent prayer. She could not even guess at the verdict because the language of the lawyers had been too complicated to follow easily and the judge had sometimes seemed to lean heavily in favour of one and then shift his ground to the other whenever a new argument was brought forward or he found a flaw in an old one. She had no idea what he really thought.

'Gentlemen of the jury,' the judge began on the dot of two o'clock. 'We are not here to decide the rights and wrongs of the labourers' cause, but to decide the guilt or innocence of the defendant of the crimes with which he is charged. You should not ask why he did what he did, but whether what he did was against the law. And if it was, then it is your duty to find him guilty.' He looked directly at the foreman of the jury. 'Do you wish to retire to consider your verdict?'

'No, my lord.'

'Then do you find the prisoner, guilty or not guilty?'

'On the charge of killing the sheep, not guilty, my lord.' He waited until the buzz of comment had died down before adding, 'On all other counts, guilty.'

A gasp echoed through the ranks of the watchers which was quickly silenced. Kate wanted to scream at the jury who were so blinkered they could not see the truth, to dash out and beat her fists against the judge who was so cold and impersonal, to fling Mr Beeley's careful notes all over the courtroom for they had done no good at all. Guilty. It wasn't fair.

The judge turned to Matthew. 'Have you anything to say before I pronounce sentence?'

'Nothing, my lord.'

The judged donned the black cap but Kate was intent on watching Matthew and all she heard of it were the words 'hanged by the neck'. He was so composed, so completely in command of himself; there was even a faint smile playing about his lips. He had told Bates he welcomed the chance to put the labourers' cause to a judge and jury, but he can't have expected this. It wasn't the end, it couldn't be. She would not accept it. She turned to look at

Bates, but his face was almost as impassive as Matthew's. No one moved. It was as if they had all been stunned.

She sprang to her feet, pushing past the thin man beside her who only reluctantly hitched himself back to make room for her. She had to escape from that stifling atmosphere, to get out into the air before she did something very public and very foolish.

It was then that Matthew saw her and, for the first time, his composure cracked. Why was she here and dressed in that ridiculous garb? Why was she still in Ely when she ought to be safe at home with her mother being loved and cossetted? What had gone wrong? She looked so stricken, he longed to comfort her, but he dare not allow himself even the ghost of a reassuring smile. Forget me, Kate, my darling, he pleaded silently, forget me. He turned his face from her lest he give her and himself away. If he had been a crying man, he would have wept.

Chapter Sixteen

'*I*'m sorry the verdict went against you,' Andrew said. 'You'll appeal, of course.'

'On what grounds?' Matthew sat on an upright chair, facing the other man across the table in a ground floor room of the prison where he had been brought to receive his visitor. The two men were similar in many ways, age, height and build; they had had the same kind of childhood and education, but there the similarity ended. Matthew's dark hair was untidy and he had not shaved. He wore fustian trousers and a striped shirt with no collar and his waistcoat was of ordinary drab, the working man's clothes he had chosen to wear for his trial. Andrew, whose toilette was impeccable, wore breeches of supple kid, his shirt was laundered to perfection and his riding coat so carefully tailored it looked as though he had been poured into it. His feet were encased in polished riding boots.

'Surely your lawyer can find something?' he said, apparently oblivious of the difference. 'He seemed a competent chap, a bit theatrical perhaps, but up to the task. It was not his fault the jury were too hide-bound to see the wood for the trees. Changes must be made in the way the poor are treated.'

'I am not the poor.' Matthew did not want to discuss his case; as far as he was concerned it was over and done with. 'And neither are you.'

'True. But you will appeal, won't you?'

'To salve your conscience?'

'No, to save yourself.'

'It's already in hand. But I didn't ask you to come here to talk about my appeal. I want to know what happened about Kate? You told her?'

'No. I couldn't find her.' Andrew smiled quirkily. 'No one would admit to knowing where she was. Her friends are loyal, I'll give her that.'

'Of course they're loyal. But I told you to go to the warehouse down by the river.'

'So I did, but she wasn't there. The man who keeps the place, a great bullock of a fellow ...'

'Jacob Fyne.'

'Yes. He said Kit Brown left the day you were arrested and they had no idea where he went. He insisted he had never had a girl working for him. He even got the other lads to corroborate what he said and that in spite of the fact that it was one of them who betrayed Kate. The boy said he'd made a mistake and I couldn't shake him.'

'You told them who you were?'

'Yes, but that only made matters worse. Goodness knows where she's hiding now. I went back to Middleacre, thinking she might have returned there but no one would admit to having seen her. I even offered a reward, put bills up in Middleacre and Wisbech, but all to no avail, not a single person has come forward. They think it's because I want to see her brought to trial and no amount of argument on my part will convince them otherwise.'

'She was at the trial. I saw her.' He smiled suddenly. 'Dressed like a young buck, in breeches and frockcoat.'

'Was she, by George!'

'You've got to find her, man. I shan't go to my end easy unless I know she is safe with you and her mother. Did you tell Mrs Carrington, by the way?'

'No. She has been disappointed so many times before, it wouldn't have been fair until I was sure and I can't be sure until I have spoken to Kate myself.'

'Give her a good life, Andrew. Make her happy.'

'If I could find her I would willingly do that. Even if she is not who you think she is ...' He stopped suddenly. It would not be chivalrous to hit a fellow when he was down, and revealing his true feelings for Kate would certainly be doing that.

'You love her?'

'How can I lie? Yes, I love her.'

'Then find her. Give her everything I cannot. You must teach her to forget the past, to forget me.'

'But if your appeal succeeds ...'

'It won't. You have only to look at other similar cases to know the landowners daren't show any sign of leniency. I am content as long as I know Kate is being cared for.'

'Then I will redouble my efforts to find her.'

'I'll lay odds she'll go to Wisbech gaol on the day of Brough's release.'

'But he's . . .'

'She doesn't know that, does she? I didn't tell her. She'll need comforting.' He wished he could be the one to do it; he longed to hold her in his arms again, to explain everything, why he had kept his identity from her, why he had not told her he loved her, why he allowed her to go on believing he wanted Betty Watson. But what was the good of sighing like a love-sick calf over what could not be? He forced himself to grin at the man across the table from him. 'I'd do it myself but you see how it is.' And he raised his hands to show the shackles that bound his wrists.

Andrew could not suppress a shudder at the sight of them. He stood up to leave, feeling nothing but sympathy for the man in the chains, but there was also thankfulness that he was able to walk away and that any chains which bound him were of the silken kind. All he had to do was find Kate.

When the appeal failed a vast crowd gathered outside the gaol, chanting the captain's name and demanding a retrial. 'They were threatening to tear the place apart and set him free,' Bates told Kate. 'It got so bad the judiciary didn't dare leave the courthouse. They sent for the militia to escort them all safely home.'

'Will there be a retrial? Can the crowd make them do it?' she asked, hope flaring for an instant only to die with his next words.

'No, m'dear, you can put that right out of your head. The appeal judge upheld the original verdict. He said all the evidence had been heard and the jury were well directed.'

'Then there's no hope?' Her voice was barely more than a hoarse whisper. 'He'll . . . he'll hang?'

For her sake, he knew he ought to tell her there was no hope at all; she would get over it the sooner if she could be made to believe there was nothing to hope for, but he could not bring himself to do it. 'Don't despair,' he said. 'He has friends . . .'

'Friends like his brother who did not raise a finger to help him, men like Sir John Haddow.' She began to laugh hysterically. 'Let's ask Sir John to intercede for him. Let's ask the devil himself. I'd give myself up to him if I thought ...'

'Hush, girl,' he said, gripping her shoulders and giving her a gentle shake. 'What would the gaffer say if he could hear you talkin' like that?'

'I'm angry,' she said, but her voice was calmer.

'I know. And feeling guilty too, i'n't that so?'

'Yes. If I had not involved myself in village affairs, if I hadn't disobeyed the Fynes and gone out to meet Matthew, he wouldn't be in prison at all, let alone waiting to be hanged.'

'There's no need to feel so bad about it,' he said. 'It had to happen, sooner or later, he knew that. The Cap'n doesn't blame you, so don't blame yourself. And you never know, something might turn up.'

He had left immediately to drive a herd to Smithfield, his heart and his feet as heavy as lead, leaving Kate to make of that whatever she could.

She went about her work listlessly, speaking when spoken to, doing her chores in a kind of stupor, and all the time, the words hammered into her brain, 'guilty', 'hanged by the neck'. It was horrible, barbaric and unjust. She could not bring herself to believe that any court of law which was supposed to uphold justice could sentence someone like Matthew to die. He was a good man, a caring man. For the first time she recognised that a man's ancestry or wealth did not make him good or bad; it was the man himself that was important. She had known Matthew less than a year and yet it seemed he had always been there, just as Pa had always been there and now she could not imagine life without him. Each night she cried herself to sleep and then her rest was disturbed by nightmares which threatened her sanity. Matthew was all mixed up with that clanking machinery and the crying children, trapped as she was trapped, and neither could help the other. She saw his proud head, disembodied, gory, with staring eyes. And yet he smiled. That unearthly smile bothered her more than anything. It was as if he had lost the ability to weep.

Then Bates returned, bringing her only crumb of comfort; a petition was being put together for Matthew's reprieve.

'Who is organising it?' she asked. 'You?'

'His friends.'

'His only friends are labourers, other rebels,' she said flatly, refusing to allow her hopes to rise for fear of having them dashed again. 'Some can't even write their own names. Who'll take any notice of them?'

'Now, you mustn't talk like that, m'dear,' Bates said. 'He has connections in all walks of life and a great many of them too.' He was dog-tired because he had returned from London at double his usual speed, hoping to lift her spirits with the news. From resenting her hold over Matthew, he had come to admire her for her fidelity and courage and he wished he could offer more than just a faint hope of life for the man she loved. Freedom was out of the question. 'You never know what can be accomplished.'

'What happens if he is reprieved?' she asked. 'Will he be set free?'

'No, he'll be transported. It's the best we can hope for.'

'Transported?' she repeated. 'You mean sent away to the other side of the world, never to come back?'

'Never is a very long time,' Bessie put in.

Kate turned to look at her and then back to Bates. 'How long then?'

'Life,' he said. 'At least it *is* life. You must be thankful for that.' Then, realising that she must be made to stir herself and look to the future, a future without Matthew, he added, 'What you've gotta do is forget him and carry on with your own life.'

'Forget him!' she cried. 'How could I possibly do that?'

'Bates didn't mean that,' Bessie put in gently. 'We know you won't forget him, but try and remember him with pleasure, a happy part of your life you can look back on without sadness.' She paused, knowing she had to be cruel; it was the only way. 'But make no bones about it, Matthew Tolley has gone from you and you must accept that, whatever happens about the reprieve.'

Kate did not want to listen to them, however well intentioned they were, and she ran from the room and up the stairs to lie on her bed in an agony of grief. But they were right and in her heart of hearts she knew it.

Matthew was reprieved three weeks later on condition of transportation and was sent, under heavy guard, to the hulks in the broad reaches of the Thames, there to await shipment to Australia. When Kate heard this she wished fervently that she was going too, however long and uncomfortable the voyage, however harsh the conditions when they arrived; being with Matthew would be ample compensation. She would have given herself up if there had been any guarantee of being able to travel with him, but Bessie soon disabused her of that idea. 'My dear child, you wouldn't be allowed anywhere near him, and besides, he did not go through that trial in order to have you sent out too, did he?'

Gradually, as the days passed, her natural resilience reasserted itself, her will to live and fight on, came back to her and she chided herself for her lack of courage. She still had Pa. And he would soon be free again. Somehow she found the strength to accept the inevitable and began planning her reunion with Josiah. Perhaps, later, they could both go out to Australia to join Matthew.

'Pa's year is up at the end of the week,' she told the Fynes at supper one evening, when the first cool winds of autumn blew little wavelets in the water of the Great Ouse and stirred the red and gold leaves on the trees in the cathedral park, sending them fluttering to the ground. 'And I must be in Wisbech to meet him when he is released.'

'You can't go there, child,' Bessie said, appalled at the idea. 'You are still wanted for your part in that riot. Sir John will have you arrested as soon as look at you.'

'I wouldn't mind that if it meant being sent to be with Matthew,' she said.'

'Don't talk of it, girl. Don't even think it.'

She smiled to show she was only half-serious. 'When Pa comes out, we'll make plans to go to Australia. He will know how to do it.'

'Australia?'

'That's where Matthew is going, isn't it?'

'That's so, but how do you know your Pa will want to go? It's an awful long way.'

'Of course he will,' Kate said confidently. 'He's a travelling man, isn't he?'

'But if he doesn't ...' She held up a hand to silence Kate who had opened her mouth to protest. 'If he doesn't, you'll come back here to us, won't you? This is your home and your Pa's too, if he wants it. I mean it, girl. We love you and we'd not see you wanting for anything.'

For Bessie, who was not given to showing her feelings, this was a very big admission and Kate was aware of it. She got up from the chair where she had been sitting endeavouring to mend a petticoat, and flung her arms round the big woman. 'Oh, Mrs Fyne, you know I love you too, and Mr Fyne, but I must do whatever Pa suggests. You do understand, don't you?'

'Yes,' Bessie said, wiping tears from her leathery cheeks. 'But you know he's been inside a long time, I expect you'll find him changed.'

'Changed? Why should he have changed?'

'He's not young, is he? And his leg was broke ...'

Kate saw nothing sinister in what Bessie said, nothing she had not already considered many times. If his leg had not mended well, she would be the breadwinner; they would manage. And if close confinement had weakened him, fresh air and good food would soon put that right. She closed her mind to anything more than that. 'I shall look after him until he is well and strong again, just like he always looked after me when I was little.'

'Of course, dear, but you know, you have changed too. You are not the child you were. You have been through so much and grown into a beautiful young lady.'

Kate blushed prettily, but could not or would not understand what Bessie was trying to say. 'That makes no difference. He is still my Pa.'

'I'll go and meet him, if you like,' Jacob said. 'I'll bring him here to join you. It'd be safer.'

'Thank you, but I must be there,' she said. 'It is important, don't you see? The first person he sees when he comes out must be me. It will show I've kept faith with him.'

'Stubborn, that's what you are,' Bessie said, heaving a huge sigh. 'I wonder who you got that from.'

Kate didn't know; she had no notion of the vices and virtues of her parents, whether they were good or bad people, all she knew was that when she needed him, Josiah had been there and now, when he needed her, she would not fail him.

'When do you go?' Bessie said, when she realised nothing she said would change Kate's mind.

'The day after tomorrow, on the morning stage. I must be at the prison door when he is released.'

'So soon?' queried Jacob, stuffing tobacco into his pipe and bending to light a taper from the fire in order to hide his feelings.

She could find no way of thanking them adequately, though she tried, and after a few halting words and a great many hugs and kisses, she left it to them to guess how she felt, taking herself off to bed, looking forward to the future for the first time for months.

Early on the Friday morning, they escorted her to The Lamb where, dressed in a dark blue cloak over a high-waisted merino gown in a soft grey and a fetching blue bonnet trimmed with ribbons and feathers, she was to board the coach for Wisbech. After seeing her basket safely stowed in the boot, they kissed her goodbye and helped her into her seat.

'You will remember what I've said, won't you?' Bessie said, hanging onto her hand. 'Come back here, if things don't work out for you. You'll both be welcome.'

'Aye,' Jacob said, fiddling with his hat brim. 'Come to us.'

As the coach pulled away under the arch, they followed it onto the road, waving until it was out of sight.

Once out of the city Kate sat back in her seat, watching the familiar fen landscape slide past the window, wondering if her Pa really would be changed. Tomorrow, a year to the day since his conviction, she would know. Tomorrow. How much else would be changed, she wondered. What had happened in Middleacre in the months she had been absent? Were things any better for the labourers? On the surface, the countryside through which they travelled seemed quiet. The people were going about their work in the same old way, although now and again she caught a glimpse of a burnt-out rick and a tangle of broken machinery. 'Nothing's been achieved 'cept a whole lot of heartache,' one of her fellow passengers said, noticing her leaning forward to catch a better look at what had once been a barn. 'They'd ha' done better to ha' let well alone.' He nodded towards the ruin. 'Made themselves an incendiary, they did, with sulphur and iron filings. Trouble was it went up on its own and some on 'em couldn't get outa the way quick enough. Two dead and one so burned, you couldn't recognise 'im arterwards.'

'Oh, dear,' Kate said. 'When was that?'

He shrugged. 'Three, mebbe four months ago. 'Tany rate it were arter Cap'n Tolley were took. He'd never ha' let 'em be so fewlish.'

'You knew him?' she asked, trying to keep the eagerness from her voice.

'Met 'im once. Powerful man, he were, powerful big and powerful persuasive. Pity there in't more like 'im.'

'Yes, indeed,' she said with a heartfelt sigh.

'He's gorn now and we've bin put back years by all this. Years.'

And he waved an arm and nearly took Kate's bonnet off. 'Beg pardon, missie, but you mark my words and see if I ain't right.'

'I am afraid you are,' she agreed, setting her hat straight again and retying the satin ribbon beneath her chin. Had she been instrumental in the failure of the labourers' cause? Had her selfishness on her own and Josiah's behalf caused the collapse of the movement? It did not bear thinking about and she was glad when they rattled into the yard of the Dog and Duck for the horses to be changed and her talkative fellow passenger left. But he had set off a train of thought which would not leave her. Matthew had interrupted his crusade to meet her there. It was a night she would never forget, not only for its sweetness but for the strange bitterness which seemed to beset him. It was the last time they had touched each other and the memory of that was something she would savour to the end of her days.

She had paid her fare as far as Wisbech, intending to stay at one of the inns there until the following morning when she confidently expected Josiah would be released, but as they approached the crossroads leading to Middleacre, she decided, on a sudden impulse, to leave the coach and go to see Mrs Barber. She could stay at The Ferryman and go on to Wisbech in the morning.

It was late afternoon when the coach set her down and she was reminded of the day Matthew had arrived in the same way. So much had happened since then, it was difficult to grasp it was only one short year ago; it seemed like a lifetime and she was older by a thousand years. She was no longer the girl who had walked behind him listening to him talking to Jack Watson and becoming aggrieved because William Chapman had given him work. He had been welcomed by the villagers as someone to lead them in their fight against oppression, just as he had been welcomed in other villages up and down the country. He had sacrificed his home and the love of his brother for the cause. Had it all been worthwhile? He might think so, but she could not; the wound was too new for her to be rational on the subject. She remembered him standing in the road, where she was walking now and warning her of trouble if she interfered. If she had heeded him, would it have made any difference? Would she still have loved him? Yes, she decided, because it had been written in the stars.

Nothing in Middleacre had changed, except that this year the harvest had been earlier and many of the fields had already been ploughed. The washes were still dry and cattle grazed on them. From the end of the lane leading to Home Farm she could see the burnt-out barn and wondered why it had not been rebuilt. But the village seemed peaceful, the men were working and the women going about the daily business of looking after their families and hardly seemed to notice her, although she did wonder if anyone would tell Sir John they had seen her. Perhaps it had not been a wise move to come here after all, she should have gone direct to Wisbech.

Charlie, who had been restored to his family, greeted her warmly, drawing her into the family circle, bombarding her with questions. Where had she been? How was she keeping? Why had she risked coming back?

'I'm on my way to Wisbech,' she said, taking the seat by the fire he pulled forward for her. 'Pa comes out of gaol tomorrow. His year is up.'

'So 'tis,' he said in surprise. 'Time do fly. That wor the start on it worn't it?'

'Yes. The day after Captain Tolley arrived.' She accepted the cup of freshly brewed tea she was offered and smiled her thanks. 'So much has happened and yet nothing seems to have been achieved.'

'The Captain was – is – a good man,' Mrs Barber put in. 'I didn't think so at the time, but I do now. It was only after Charlie came out of gaol and told me what the captain said and did and explained everything, I realised he was against the violence. If only they'd listened to him.'

'Yes,' Kate agreed; if only she had listened herself, things might have been different.

'I heard tell he wanted to be arrested so he could fight his case in a court of law,' Mrs Barber went on. 'A proper court, not the trumped up magistrates' hearings we have here with Sir John and his like. Didn' do him any good though, did it?'

'It may not have done him any good, but I believe it helped the farm workers' cause,' Kate said, remembering Bates had said the same thing. 'Everyone is talking about it, even in the towns, and there is some sympathy ...'

'Sympathy!' Charlie said contemptuously. 'What manner o' use is that? It don' put up our wages.'

'No, but it's a beginning.'

'It didn' help the cap'n either. That there Mr Carrington-Haddow do pretend to be sympathetic but when the cap'n went to 'im for 'elp 'e turned 'im down. Cap'n should ha' known the man wouldn't dare go ag'in his uncle. It was a wasted journey.'

'You mean he went up to the Hall, he actually ventured up there?' Kate was perplexed; there had been things going on she knew nothing about.

'No, not to the Hall,' Mrs Barber said. 'Mr Carrington-Haddow had gone home again. Don't know where that is, up north somewhere, I think. Cap'n Tolley rode all the way there in the middle of winter.'

'I saw him when he came back,' Charlie said. 'It were just after I come out o' Bridie. I reckon something happened to him while he was there, he was a different man, bowed down and miserable, the fire seemed to go outa him.' He paused and Kate, who was ready to seize on any piece of news which related to Matthew, found herself holding her breath. 'He came and spoke to us all, told us to keep up the good work. We didn't see 'im any more after that. Then he went to Ely and got hisself arrested.'

'I know,' she said. 'I was there.'

'They didn't arrest you, though.' It was almost an accusation.

'No, I got away.'

'You went to the trial?'

'Yes.'

'Tell us about it. How was the cap'n?'

'Pale,' she said. 'But proud and defiant to the last.'

'Just because he's gone, it's not the end of the fight,' he said. 'We shall gather ourselves again ...'

'Not you,' Mrs Barber put in quickly. 'You've done enough.'

He put his arm about his mother's shoulders and hugged her, but made no promises. How could he? No one had more reason to hate Sir John Haddow and all his like than he had. The six months he had spent in prison had hardened him, made a man of the boy, and he was determined to carry on where Captain Tolley had left off. And now Kate was back. He hadn't expected to see her again. He ought to tell her about him and Betty. He looked at her now, more quiet than she used to be; the lovely eyes were sad but she was even more beautiful. It almost took his breath away. But she had been right; she was not the one for him.

'You think it will start all over again?' Kate asked, wondering what they would do without Matthew to restrain them.

'No doubt of it,' he said. 'And we'll win. There'll be a national farm workers' union, you see. Cap'n Tolley may have gone, but Cap'n Swing lives on. Oh, he won't be called Swing, but what do that matter, the cause will be the same and it'll still be worth fightin' for.'

'Then here's to that,' she said, smiling at him over the rim of her cup.

'But you shouldn't be here,' Mrs Barber said. 'Mr Carrington-Haddow is back in Middleacre and looking for you. He's offered a tempting reward for your capture, very tempting.'

'Mr Carrington-Haddow?' queried Kate in surprise. 'Don't you mean Sir John?'

'No, but squire or nephew, it's all one, isn't it? Sir John came back from his honeymoon as ill-tempered as ever,' Mrs Barber went on, for her son had fallen silent. 'You were foolish to come back.'

'Perhaps, but I have to be in Wisbech first thing tomorrow and I thought I'd come and see how you all were. If anything has changed.'

'Nothing has changed,' she said. 'We're all a little bit older and perhaps a little bit wiser. And Charlie, here, is walking out with Betty Watson.'

Kate turned to look at him. He was scarlet with embarrassment. She smiled. 'I am so pleased for you, Charlie. I wish you happy.'

'Thank you,' he said. 'After ... after ...'

'No need to explain, Charlie, I understand and you are entirely right.'

'You be welcome to stay the night, Kate,' he said. 'You can have my bed, I'll do fine on the settle.'

Kate, declining politely, noticed his mother's expression of relief. The woman was terrified of being caught harbouring her; Charlie's six months of detention had been more than enough to quell any spirit of rebellion she may have had. And there were many others like her, who had lost husbands and sons to prison in England or transportation to Australia and Kate knew exactly how that felt. 'I'll take a room at The Ferryman,' she said. 'I want to be up betimes to go to Wisbech.'

If the landlord at the inn recognised her, he gave no indication of it as he showed her up to the little room he kept for paying guests, who were few and far between; they were off the main road and hardly anyone came to Middleacre for its own sake. It was not a happy place, not since the riots of the year before, nor even before that if he spoke the truth.

It was the room that Matthew had occupied, Kate realised, as she prepared for bed; it made her feel very close to him. 'Where are you now?' she whispered as she climbed between the sheets and blew out the candle. 'Are you still in England or already on your way? Dear Matthew, may you find peace and happiness in that land on the other side of the world. My love and thoughts are with you always. And may God give me strength to look after Pa if he needs it.'

A cock crowing in a nearby farmyard woke her at dawn and she rose almost at once, washed and dressed and went down to the parlour. She was too excited to eat, but she arranged to leave her basket to be collected later, drank a cup of hot chocolate before setting off on foot for Wisbech, just as she had done exactly a year before. But this time she went with a light step for she was going to be reunited with her Pa.

Wisbech was beginning to come to life as she entered the town. People, children, dogs and horses were on the move, doors and windows were being opened, bedding hung out and everywhere was the appetising smell of breakfasts being cooked, but Kate was too preoccupied to think of food. She made her way up the South Brink, just as she had a year before and stopped opposite the gaol, taking up a station on the corner where she could plainly see anyone coming out.

Half an hour passed and then an hour and there was no sign of him. People came and went through the prison doors and each time she started forward, a greeting on her lips, but her Pa did not come. Why was he so long? He ought to have been released by now; didn't they always turn prisoners out first thing in the morning? She had the right date, it was a year to the day since he had been convicted. Where was he? What should she do? Dare she knock on the door and ask for him? She hesitated, torn between her desire to know what had happened to him and the knowledge that there was a substantial reward for her capture. If the Barbers had been telling the truth, and she saw no reason to disbelieve them, the squire, and indeed Andrew Carrington-Haddow too, had not given up the idea of punishing her for her part in the riot and Ben Carter would be triumphant if she walked into his gaol. She would wait a little longer, she was in no hurry, she had nowhere to go. Her hopes, her plans, her life since Matthew's reprieve and transportation, had hinged on the moment when she would see Josiah again, the day when he would, once more, take over the ordering of her life and tell her how to reach Australia.

Another hour passed and then another and despair crushed her. Her head drooped and tears squeezed themselves between her lashes and trickled down her cheeks. At midday, knowing there was no alternative, she crossed the road towards the prison, her vision so blurred she could hardly see where she was going and was almost run down by a carriage, which clattered to a stop beside her. She stood, shaking and bewildered, as someone jumped down and took hold of her arm. 'What are you a-doin' of, girl, I could ha' killed you.' For a moment, she thought it was the squire; it was certainly one of his carriages, but the voice was rough and the accent broad. 'Kate Brough, if it in't the very one I want.'

She raised tear-filled eyes to the weather beaten features of Sir John's bailiff who was grinning triumphantly. 'Now, you come alonga me and this time you won't get away.'

Bowed by disappointment she may have been, but cowed she was not. She began to struggle. 'Let me go! Let me go! I've done nothing wrong.'

'That's for others to decide.'

Still fighting, she was bundled into the coach. He climbed in beside her, calling to the driver to take them back to Haddow Hall. She was too taken by surprise to wonder what Fiddy was doing in the squire's coach and suffered the ride back to Middleacre in silence. There was no point in continuing to plead with him, he would not let her go, and the vehicle was going too fast to risk trying to jump out. By the time they rattled up to the front door of the Hall, she had regained her composure and was ready to meet the squire, or any of his family, with cool anger. She would not let her enemies see how really miserable she was. The coach had hardly come to a stop before Andrew ran down the front steps to open the door.

'Kate, my dear, how good it is to see you.' His voice was unexpectedly welcoming and she had to remind herself that he had wanted her capture, had offered a reward of his own, that underneath he was the same as Sir John and his like. 'I would have met you myself but one of the grooms took a kick from Sir John's grey mare just as I was setting out and I had to wait for Doctor Sissingham. Fortunately it is no more than a very bad bruise.'

'How can you talk of horses and bruises when I am worried sick about my Pa?' she said, shaking off his helping hand and stepping down to face him. 'You have cowed the villagers and taken Matthew from me, is that not enough? Must you also keep me from my father?'

'Don't be a little goose,' he said, taking her hand and holding it fast. 'I'm not keeping you from him.'

'Then let me go to him.'

'No, Kate,' he said, struggling to maintain his hold on her; her work in the warehouse had made her unexpectedly strong. 'Come indoors where we can talk privately. I've something very important to tell you. If you want to leave afterwards, you can. I won't stop you, I promise.'

She subsided, half convinced by his pleading tone. 'I was waiting for Pa and now you've made me miss him and he'll wonder where I am.'

'No, he won't.' His voice softened and he looked down into her face. 'Please, Kate, come inside. You must be cold and hungry.'

She had not been aware of either and was still only concerned for Josiah. 'Why won't he? Where is he? What have you done to him?'

'Nothing. But Kate ...' He took a deep breath and plunged on. 'I am afraid Josiah Brough will not be coming out.'

'Not coming?' Her heart began thumping and she could hardly get the words out. 'What has happened?'

He took both her hands in his own and spoke gently. 'Kate, I have some very bad news and I hardly know how to break it to you. I'm afraid Josiah Brough is dead.'

It was impossible to comprehend; Pa had always seemed so indestructible. Someone had made a mistake. A mistake; that was it. She shook her head from side to side. 'No. No, it cannot be.'

'I am afraid it is, Kate. He died last March.'

'But that was six months ago.'

'Yes, his broken leg never mended properly and the surgeons had to take it off. He was an old man, the shock of the amputation was too much for him.'

She looked up into his eyes and knew with dreadful certainty that he spoke the truth. She had tried so hard to put Sir John's threats and hints from her mind, to pretend he had been lying to frighten her, but in truth she had been deceiving herself.

He put his arm about her shoulders and slowly drew her towards the house. She was too stunned, too benumbed, to resist or even to cry. 'Come inside,' he said gently. 'Come indoors where we can talk quietly.'

'So that the squire can attack me again?' Misery, anger and disappointment in equal measure lent her strength and she almost succeeded in freeing herself. 'No thank you.'

'Sir John is away,' he said, grabbing her again and holding her fast. 'He accepted an invitation to go hunting with the Quorn and Lady Haddow is staying with her sister in Leicester. They are not due back for another two weeks, at least. Please come in and sit down. No one will hurt you or arrest you I promise, but I must talk to you, it's very important.'

'Talk! Is that all you can say when Pa is dead because of what you and Sir John did to him?' She knew she was being unfair to include him but she could not help herself. She wanted to hit out, to rail against the injustice of it, to blame someone and he was the only one on hand. 'You're a monster, that's what you are, pretending to be sympathetic, pretending to help us, when all the time you were on the Squire's side. Pa and Matthew ...' She gulped and went on before she burst into tears. 'Matthew has gone because of you. He came to you for help, didn't he? And you betrayed him ...'

'I didn't betray him,' he said, speaking gently in an effort to calm her. 'And he didn't come to me for help. I'll tell you all about it, if you'll let me.' He was leading her through the hall as he spoke. Almost in a stupor she stood while he divested her of her cloak, gloves and bonnet and handed them to a waiting footman, a man Kate had never seen before. 'Come, my dear. You have nothing to fear.'

Too emotionally exhausted to do anything else, she allowed him to usher her into the drawing room and settle her on a sofa. 'All about what?' she asked dully.

'Josiah Brough and Matthew Thorsborough.'

'What about them?' She was still too dazed to notice that he had used Matthew's real name.

'Later,' he said, going to the sideboard and pouring a glass of brandy from the decanter. 'I'll tell you later, when you have drunk this and calmed down sufficiently to take in what I have to say.'

'I am perfectly calm,' she said, stiffly. This wasn't happening to her, Pa wasn't dead, Matthew wasn't thousands of miles away on the high seas, she wasn't being entertained by Andrew Carrington-Haddow in the squire's own elegant drawing room.

'Nevertheless, drink this. It will warm you.' While she sipped it, he went to the kitchen himself and ordered a meal for her, then poked the fire to make it blaze, before pulling up a stool to sit at her feet. 'Kate, things are not as bad as they seem,' he said slowly, taking her hand. 'In the bad news there is some good.'

'Pa is dead,' she said flatly. And as she spoke the full meaning of the words dawned on her and she put her head into her hands and wept and wept.

He longed to take her in his arms and kiss away the tears but he knew that would be extremely foolish. Instead, he handed her his handkerchief and waited patiently until she was ready to listen.

'I am sorry I had to be the one to tell you, Kate.'

She wiped her eyes, blew her nose and took a deep breath. 'But how do you know? Why have you interested yourself in Pa?'

'Because of something Matthew told me.' He moved away from her as the footman appeared with a tray and put it on a small table beside her. 'I will explain while you eat and drink.' He smiled encouragement as she looked down at the tray. 'Go on, while I tell you a story.'

'About Pa?' Mechanically, she picked up a knife and fork.

'Yes, but also about my stepmother and Matthew too.' She was silent, but he knew he had her attention and went on. 'You know, my own mother died when I was about eight years old. I loved her and missed her terribly but when I was thirteen my father married again and I thoroughly approved his choice. Felicity Wetherby was a very young widow with a year-old baby called Catherine. We were very happy together and we all adored the little girl and spoiled her dreadfully, especially Father. But one day she was taken from us . . .'

'She died?'

'No, she was kidnapped.' He paused but she gave no sign of guessing what he was going to say. 'My father is a millowner and he employs a great many children. He is obliged to because it is the only way to make cheap cloth and cloth is vital to the economy of the area, to the whole country, in fact; it clothes poor as well as rich, it keeps tailors and dressmakers at work when they might be idle and it prevents whole families from starving. It is a way of life in our part of the country.'

She was toying with her food, only half listening for she could not see what any of it had to do with Pa or Matthew; it sounded as if he were trying to justify the kind of life he lived, the reason he was rich and she was poor.

'I don't deny we lived well,' he went on. 'We had – have – a nice house, servants to run it, and a carriage and horses. Catherine had a nursemaid called Bonny to look after her.'

'Bonny,' she murmured. 'That's a funny name.'

'She was called that by her parents when she was very small and the name stuck; she had round red cheeks and such blue eyes ...' He paused, looking closely into her face for a flicker of remembrance, but she appeared to be in a world of her own. 'Sometimes Father used to take Catherine and her nurse to the mill in the carriage when he knew he would not be kept there long. And afterwards, they would ride out onto the moors to gather wild heather and bring bunches home to put around the house. Sometimes, while they were waiting for Father, Bonny would take Catherine to peep into the big room where the looms were and they watched the children ...'

'Children?' Kate repeated. 'In a big room with a lot of noisy machinery? Did they cough a lot?'

'Some did, I suppose.' He did not want to be diverted from the thread of his story.

'What has that got to do with Pa and Matthew?'

'I'm coming to that. Have you heard of the Luddites?'

'No, I don't think so.'

'They were machine-breakers too, only it was not threshing machines they broke but looms. They believed the mills were putting the weavers out of work.' He paused but she made no comment; he wondered if she were even listening. 'One day, sixteen years ago, they gathered in Caspertown. The riots we have seen here in East Anglia were nothing compared to that day. It was a mob, a barbarous, vengeful mob.' He shuddered at the memory of that day. Fifteen years old, he had been, not man enough to take it in his stride, not child enough for him to be screened from it. He had heard the tumult and because no one had thought to forbid it, he had gone out to see what was happening. The things he had witnessed had been imprinted on his mind, like a painting, except that a painting is flat and silent, and his memory was accompanied by the noise of shouting and screaming, of horses galloping on narrow cobbled streets, sabres rattling and guns going off. And fire. He had not known that fire could be so terrifying. His father's mill was well alight and the flames were spreading down the street. The fire company could do nothing for the press of people, most of whom had abandoned all thought of rioting and were fleeing to safety, pursued by the militia, slashing this way and that with their swords, adding blood to the picture, colouring it luridly. He could hear women screaming and children sobbing but he dare not venture any nearer to see who it was that cried so wretchedly. Terrified, he had returned home. 'My father tried to placate them,' he told Kate. 'But they would have none of it. They set the mill alight.'

Kate assumed he was telling her the story to take her mind off her troubles or to excuse his siding with the squire. She would not forgive him for that, however many fairytales he told her.

'Father was forced to let it burn and only escaped being killed when the militia arrived and escorted him home. He found the house in an uproar because Catherine and her nurse were missing.' His calm voice did nothing to convey the panic and distress of everyone at the time, how difficult it had been to get a coherent word out of his stepmother. 'Bonny had gone on a visit to her mother and had taken Catherine, but when the crowds started gathering, she decided not to risk trying to get through the streets back to the house but to go to the mill. She thought Father would be there and would see them safely home. But he never saw them.'

'They were in the fire at the mill?'

'I think it was in the minds of everyone, though no one would speak of it. Father braved the crowds again to find the man he thought was the ringleader, a man called Wates, but he insisted that no one had been on the premises when the fire started; it had never been his intention to risk lives. He said he sent the nurse home with her charge long before then. We went out again, all of us, to try and find them.'

'And did you?'

'Father found Bonny, dying of a sabre cut. She had tried to crawl home.'

'Oh, how dreadful!' She was with him now, living it, her imagination supplying the details. Or was it imagination? Something was stirring inside her, a forgotten terror.

'Wates had sent her home, out into that bloodythirsty mob, and seeing her with the child, who was obviously well fed and well clad, they blocked their way and chased them out into the country.'

'How do you know?'

'Bonny was able to tell us before she died. Catherine was three years old, too heavy to carry for long and poor Bonny was frightened and exhausted. She decided to hide the child somewhere safe and return to fetch my father. She could go more quickly without her burden and would not attract attention and Father would bring the carriage back for Catherine. Unfortunately, she ran into the militia, who were rounding up the last of the troublemakers. She was running, you see and she would not stop when they ordered her to . . .'

Kate had long since stopped even pretending to eat, but now she dropped her fork with a clatter. 'Pa found me on a moorside road.'

'Yes, Kate, I am certain you are my stepmother's daughter, Catherine Wetherby.'

Chapter Seventeen

*K*ate could hardly take it in. Catherine Wetherby. Not a gypsy, not abandoned by poverty-stricken parents, not unloved. But how could he be so positive about it? What proof was there? Are you sure?'

'Yes. Josiah Brough picked you up and looked after you and for that I suppose we must be thankful. He had no idea who you were then and he wanted to keep you, so he moved out of the county. Gangs of men searched the moors for days but there was no sign of our missing Catherine. You can imagine how Mother felt about it; she went out of her mind with worry and grief and she's never been the same since. Father put reward posters up all over Caspertown and the surrounding area and he advertised in all the newspapers, but we never knew what had become of you.'

'But how do you know this if Pa didn't know who I was?'

'Oh, he knew all right.' He tried to keep the anger from his voice for her sake. 'He heard about our search the following year when he returned briefly to the area, but by that time he had come to regard you as his property. He thought his love for you was greater than ours.' He paused, but she did not speak. He went on. 'That wasn't true, Kate, whatever he led you to believe. My stepmother adored her daughter. We all did.'

Her mind was in a turmoil. It was almost too much to comprehend at once, but she could not dismiss it as nonsense because it had the ring of truth. 'I've often wondered about myself,' she said at last. 'I used to wonder what my mother was like, whether she had fair hair and blue eyes like mine or if I had inherited those from my father. I used to paint pictures of her in my mind and ask myself if she had ever truly loved me. That sort of thing. But I never expected anything like this. Are you quite, quite certain?'

He moved over to a small writing desk by the window and took something from the top drawer. When he turned to face her again, he was holding the little gold locket, which he clicked open, revealing the familiar miniature. 'My stepmother found this on Sir John's desk.'

'He took it from me. He accused me of stealing it.'

'I know, but that's why I'm so sure I'm right. This is a picture of Sir John's mother as a young woman, she gave it to Mother herself. Catherine was playing with it on the day she disappeared.'

'It's a picture of the squire's mother?' queried Kate, finding it difficult to believe a man so hateful could have such a beautiful mother. But it explained his reaction when he had first pulled the pendant from her neck; he had recognised it and it had stopped him doing what, until that moment, he had obviously intended. He had accused her of stealing, but she was not the thief, Josiah was. He had kept the locket and her baby clothes, which had gone up in smoke; they were the proof he needed to convince everyone of her identity when he could no longer look after her. He must have had a terrible conscience about it all and yet he had never shown any sign of it.

'My stepmother has been ill with worry all these years,' Andrew went on. 'Sometimes she lives in the past and the present has no reality. The fire at the barn that night triggered off her memories of the one at the mill all those years before, only to her it was not a memory, but the present. She was convinced you were trapped in the inferno. Knowing nothing of the locket at the time, I insisted on taking her home. We were halfway there when she showed me this and said her brother had taken it from a gypsy. She asked me to come back and find the gypsy but the roads were impassable . . .'

'And Pa told no one the truth?'

'Not a living soul until Matthew went to see him in prison and he realised he was dying.'

'Matthew went to the prison?' Was there to be no end to the day's revelations? 'When was that?'

'The day you were brought before the magistrates in Wisbech, the beginning of January. Josiah told him the truth then. But long before that, knowing he was getting old and might one day leave you alone in the world, Brough decided to come to Middleacre so that he could be near when that time came.'

She was suddenly reminded of Pa's comment when the wagon broke down. *Let's be thankful it got us to this place.* It was journey's end as far as he was concerned. 'But why Middleacre and not Caspertown?'

'That was so he could keep you just a little longer, until the very last moment. He had made enquiries and knew that Sir John had made me his heir.' He smiled. 'That was part of a bargain Sir John made with Father over some money and why I added Haddow to my name, but I won't bore you with the details of that. Josiah dare not go back to Caspertown and so, assuming I would one day inherit Haddow Hall, he thought Middleacre was the best place to aim for. He decided he would rather face me than my father.'

'Pa didn't tell me any of this.'

'No, he was afraid he would lose you, that you would choose to come back to us.'

'And if Matthew knew all this, why didn't he tell me?' She felt bewildered and, in some ways, betrayed, used by everyone, an object to be passed from hand to hand. Josiah had saved her life and he had loved her, whatever the rights and wrongs of what he did afterwards. He had been a good father to her, but she should have been told, she should not have been kept in ignorance.

'Matthew wasn't sure Brough was telling him the truth until he had spoken to me. He rode through treacherous weather to see me and he confirmed what I had already guessed.'

'Oh. He didn't come to you to ask for help for himself?'

He smiled. 'No. And he left again almost at once, in spite of the weather. I believe he was on his way to tell you the truth the day he was arrested.'

'Couldn't you have prevented that?' she asked. 'Couldn't you have gone with him or given him a letter, a safe conduct, something like that?'

'I had no power to do so, only Sir John could do that and he was still away. In any case, we could not approach him. And though I would have liked to, I could not go with Matthew. My father had been taken ill with a heart seizure soon after Mother and I returned from Middleacre and I had to run the business.'

'I'm sorry. Is he better now?'

'A little, but he must take care.' He paused to refill her glass. 'It was April before I could get away. I went straight to Wisbech gaol to speak to Josiah Brough but I was too late, he had died, and I thought his secret had gone with him. I made extensive enquiries but they yielded nothing. I returned home in a very dejected mood, wondering how I could break the news to Mother. In the end I took the coward's way and told her we would have to wait until Sir John came back and told us about the gypsy because no one else knew anything about it. She seemed satisfied with that. She thinks that's why I am here now.'

'I still don't understand why it took you so long to tell me.'

'I could not find you. Everyone assumed I wanted you to stand trial for your part in the barn fire and I was met by a wall of silence wherever I went. Matthew told me about Mr and Mrs Fyne. I went to the warehouse but they denied all knowledge of you and would admit to nothing except they had had a boy called Kit Brown working for them who had left.'

'They are dear people and I love them,' she said. 'But they were worried about being implicated, especially after Archie betrayed me for the reward. It was because of that and my own stupidity Matthew was caught.'

'He knew the risks he was running.'

She was silent, remembering that dreadful day when she had disobeyed the Fynes and gone to meet Matthew. They had forgiven her, even though she had put them at risk too. It was her fault, not Archie's. Was it all predestined, right from the day she was born?

'I guessed you would come back to Wisbech to be at the prison on the day Josiah Brough was supposed to be released,' he went on. 'I am only sorry that I could not have been there earlier and saved you that long, worrying wait.'

'Mrs Carrington doesn't know you have found me?'

'No, I dare not tell her until I had spoken to you, it would not have been fair to raise her hopes if I were wrong; we've followed so many false trails before. But, if I know her, she will not sit at home and wait for me to come back with news. She will be here by the time Sir John returns.'

'If what you say is true, it makes him my uncle,' she said suddenly. 'That fiend is my uncle.' She laughed suddenly but it was a hollow sound. 'More mine than yours, it seems.'

'True.'

'How will he take the news, do you suppose? The poacher's daughter is his kin. He will have a fit.'

His smile was a little twisted as he imagined Sir John's reaction. 'He will get over his animosity towards you when he realises how happy Mother is.'

'And what about my feelings for him? I have no love for him, nor ever will have. He took Pa from me and it was his fault Pa died. And he took Matthew ...'

'No, it was the law did that.'

'The Squire is the only law round here, you know he is, and he is a tyrant. It's because of men like him that the people need Matthew, someone who cares.'

'I care,' he said quietly.

'Do you?' She was still uncertain and bewildered, still finding it difficult to believe the news that he had just broken to her, not even sure she wanted to. 'You did not stop them arresting Matthew and you did nothing to free Pa.'

'I did what I could, believe me. Josiah died before I could see him and that may have been a blessing; he would never have been able to face you again and Father would have insisted on punishing him for the years of anguish my stepmother has suffered. And as for Matthew, he rejected my help on the grounds that if he was freed because of my efforts, the labourers would never trust him again. As far as he is concerned I have to remain on the side of the tyrants which is where I was born.' He laughed suddenly. 'It is ironic when you consider that he comes of an even more exalted family.'

'You know that?'

'Yes. I met both Daniel and Matthew at Cambridge when we were all students together, though Daniel was the oldest by a couple of years. The only help I could give was to tell Daniel of Matthew's arrest in the hope he would intercede for him. I believe Matthew rejected his help too.'

'Did you visit Matthew in prison?'

'Yes.' He paused. 'Kate, you know Matthew put the cause he was fighting for before everything ...'

'Yes. Even me.'

'He asked me to look after you and to tell you that he was resigned to his fate. He wants you to be happy.'

'Happy,' she repeated. 'How can I be? What am I supposed to do now? Everything is changed. I am so confused.'

'You will stay with us, of course.'

'No.' Her instinct rejected the idea. 'I don't want to stay here. I don't belong.'

'Of course you belong,' he said, wishing he could erase the frown which creased her forehead and make her smile again. 'You belong to Mother and Father and me. We'll go back home to Caspertown. We built a new house after the riots; it stands on the outskirts of the town away from the mills, surrounded by beautiful country. You'll make new friends and settle down. We'll be happy again and all the wasted years will be put behind us.'

'But look at me.' She spread her hands from the neat wool gown she had been so proud of when she left Ely. 'I'm not gentry.'

'Clothes don't matter, we can soon remedy those. But whatever you wear does not disguise your true station; you already have the grace and beauty of a Haddow. I've always thought so, always been drawn to you. You were never a tinker's child.'

'It's how I feel.'

'That will pass, when you have had a little time to adapt.'

She could not believe that, was not even sure she wanted to. 'And you say your ... my mother will come here?'

'I'll wager she will arrive within the week.' He stood up and took her hand to draw her to her feet. 'Now, I know you must be very tired, so I suggest you rest and we'll talk again in the morning.'

'I left my basket at The Ferryman.'

'We can find all you need for tonight.'

She felt too drained to argue but when he rang for a servant and Bertha appeared, she found herself smiling for the first time that day; Bertha simply stood and gaped in astonishment.

'Yes, it's me,' Kate said.

'Show Miss Wetherby up to her room,' Andrew said. 'The one I told you to prepare yesterday.'

'Miss Wetherby?' The servant made no move to obey and indeed her expression was distinctly disparaging. She would never have believed Kate would have so little regard for her reputation. Mr Carrington-Haddow's mistress and already giving herself airs!

'Yes, that's my name,' Kate said, smiling.

Bertha pulled herself together at last and, with a snort which could have meant anything, conducted Kate up the front stairs, which Kate had never been privileged to use before, to a long first-floor gallery lined with portraits of earlier Haddows. 'I am one of them,' she told herself, but she could not bring herself to believe it.

Andrew followed as they passed through an archway at the end and along a corridor lined with doors. Bertha flung one of these open and stood aside for Kate to enter. 'Here you be, all comfy and cosy as ordered.'

Andrew was about to reprimand her for her impudence, but changed his mind and stood in the doorway as she turned down the bedcovers and made up the fire, then he dismissed her and went to take Kate's hands in his own, holding her at arm's length and looking down at her. 'Go to bed now,' he said, bending to kiss her cheek. 'Try to sleep. You'll find a nightgown under the pillow I believe. We'll meet again in the morning.'

He left her with a smile but she heard the key turn in the lock and knew he was not going to risk losing her again. She was so exhausted, both mentally and physically, she had no desire to run away. And where could she go anyway? But she was angry too, and she did not understand that. She stood in the middle of the luxurious room with her fists clenched at her side, staring at the flames licking up the chimney. He had no right to detain her, no right to put her life in such turmoil just when she thought she was getting used to the idea of being without Matthew. Twelve hours ago, she had been cheerfully optimistic because Pa was coming out of prison. But she was not her Pa; her father was dead. Josiah was dead. But her mother was alive ...

She sat on the bed, trying to put her jumbled thoughts into order, trying to understand the implications of what she had been told. Josiah was dead, she still felt too dazed to absorb that properly, and she had been born one of the gentry. But it didn't make her feel any different, she still felt like the poacher's daughter. Oh, why had Josiah not told her the truth? Or Matthew, when they had spent the night at the Dog and Duck? He must have known then. If he had told her of his visit to Josiah in prison, she could have convinced him she did not want to be a lady, she wanted to be with him, always and always, and if he had renounced his birthright, then so could she.

Then she thought of her mother and her heart was filled with pity. It was funny to think that she had had a mother all these years, someone who loved her and grieved for her. Josiah had been wrong about that. Josiah, whom she had revered and trusted, had been wrong about so many things.

She looked round the big bedroom, at the four-poster bed, the flowered curtains and the polished furniture, the glowing fire and the silken bellrope hanging on the chimney wall. If she pulled that

Bertha would appear and do whatever she asked of her, not cheerfully perhaps, but she would do it. She moved over and gazed at herself in the long mirror near the window. Her hair had come loose and there was a muddy mark on her skirt; she supposed that had happened when she was struggling with Fiddy. Her cheeks were pale but her eyes had a sparkle which could have been caused by tears or, perhaps, hysteria. She didn't know whether she wanted to scream or cry. She felt out of place and ill at ease. Whatever Andrew said, she didn't belong, not up here in the family's rooms, nor downstairs in the servants' quarters where she had been before. She would not stay and she would not let Andrew persuade her otherwise.

But tonight she would take advantage of the soft bed; for once in her life, she would lie in luxury. She found the nightgown, a creamy satin affair, much too big for her, with a faint smell of lavender about it and a smoothness which made her want to stroke it. She undressed and washed and put it on, then she flung herself backwards on the bed with its foot-thick mattress and stared at the ornate plaster of the ceiling.

Luxury like this was hers for the asking. She could sleep on a bed like this every night if she chose, she could wear fashionable clothes, ride in a carriage, order whatever meal she fancied. Now she realised what Josiah had meant when he said she was destined for better things, because he had known who she was. He had deprived her of a mother and a stable home. Could she forgive him for that?

Poor Josiah, he hadn't meant to harm her and he loved her. She had loved him too, all through the years, depended on him, trusted him and, in all but that one thing, he had never failed her. Poor, poor Josiah, she wished his soul in peace. The past was gone, recrimination would not alter it, but the future was there to be lived, with Andrew and their parents or with Matthew in Australia, supposing he survived the long sea voyage and she could go out there and find him. She tried to imagine him on board ship, tried to relive their one night in each other's arms and, in so doing, drifted off to sleep.

Andrew was already at the breakfast table when she went down next morning. He jumped up and hugged her. 'Did you sleep well?'

'Yes, thank you.'

'Have something to eat; there's ham, and eggs and toast. I'll help you to it, shall I?'

How exuberant he was, how anxious to please. She found herself warming towards him. 'Toast and coffee, please. I'm not very hungry.'

'We'll spend the rest of the morning getting acquainted all over again,' he said. 'I shall tell you what a little imp you were when you were small, into mischief the whole day long.' He paused, laughing. 'Nothing has changed, has it? You still have a great capacity for mischief.'

He was easy to talk to and she found herself listening to his description of their life before she was lost and little by little she began to remember tiny incidents, like her visits to the mill.

'I had nightmares about a huge room full of coughing children,' she said. 'And there was a lot of noise and heat and someone was chasing me. I was terribly afraid and woke up in a sweat.'

'That was because the memories of the mill were all jumbled up with the mob and the fires,' he said. 'It wasn't all that bad. Father was never so strict with his workers as some owners were, even before the Factory Act was passed six years ago. He built them a schoolroom and they had an hour's lesson every day and a good dinner too.'

'I remember Bonny now,' she said. 'She had long black hair which she wound round her head in a plait. When I had bad dreams she would take me into her bed and cuddle me. And she gave me sweetmeats. It is sad she died trying to save me.'

'She loved you.'

'And she told you where to look for me?'

'Yes, but by then it was dark and though we searched all night with lanterns and flares and called your name, there was no sign of you. After two or three days, Father became convinced you must be dead but Mother would have none of it. She insisted someone must have stolen you.'

'Pa.'

'Yes.'

'I loved him, you know. You can't take that away, not all the happy years.'

'I wouldn't want to.'

'Where is he buried?'

'In Wisbech churchyard, I expect.'

'I want to see his grave. Take me there, Andrew, please.'

'Why?'

'I want to say goodbye, to tell him I forgive him. You can understand that can't you?'

'Very well. We might as well go at once. Fetch your bonnet.' He left her to go to the stables and order the carriage. The sooner she came to terms with Brough's death and put the past behind her, the sooner she would settle down into her new life. He wondered what he would have done the night he freed the old poacher from the mantrap, if he had known the truth then. So much would have been different. Would he have learned to love her as he did now? Would she have left Brough while he was still alive? Somehow he doubted it.

Josiah lay in an unmarked grave in a corner of the churchyard reserved for paupers. Only the sexton knew which was which, and already the grass was covering the shrunken mound. Soon all trace of the man would be gone. She sank to her knees beside it, unaware that Andrew had returned to the coach to wait for her there. 'Pa,' she whispered. 'I've come to tell you I understand. It's terrible parting with someone you love and I know you loved me. I loved you too.' The tears were coursing down her face now, healing tears. 'I forgive you for what you did and I pray you are in heaven because that's where you belong.' She stood up and remained looking down at the grave for several minutes, remembering the good times, the laughter and the music, the pleasures of the countryside, the satisfaction of work well done, and then, sniffing back her tears, she turned to rejoin Andrew. Now was the time to look to the future.

He did not speak as he helped her back into her seat and she was grateful to him for that. She sat back in her seat, watching the flat fen landscape slide past the window, a land she had come to think of as home. But according to Andrew her home was among the hills and moors of Lancashire, a place she could not remember. Home. What did the word mean to her? A place, or the people in it? A mansion or a tinker's wagon, a crowded cottage with someone like Charlie Barber, or a wooden hut in some land beyond the seas with Matthew?

She became aware that Andrew was speaking. 'I'm sorry ...'

'I was saying we must make plans for you. Quite apart from

clothes and a maid, you must have some schooling. It's a part of your upbringing Brough sadly neglected.'

'He taught me a great deal.'

He laughed. 'To be sure, he taught you to be stubborn and independent and loyal, but not the things a lady ought to know, the social graces, music, conversation, how to behave charmingly to people you dislike.'

'Why should I do that?'

'Sometimes it is necessary.'

'I would rather be honest. You will never turn me into a simpering obedient lapdog, so I shouldn't try if I were you.'

'Kate, my dear, I would never dream of it. But you cannot deny your life has changed. It is inevitable that . . .'

'Andrew, I'm not staying,' she interrupted him. 'I shall never settle. I am not truly part of your life. Inside I am still the poacher's daughter. I am still one of the workers.'

'Nonsense. You are no peasant, anyone can see that, you don't look like one nor talk like one. I give Brough his due for that.'

'But there is a difference between not being a peasant and being gentry. I am neither and it would be better if I left before Mrs Carrington comes. I don't want to be the cause of more heartache for her. It wouldn't be fair.'

'But what can I say to her? She is expecting news of the gypsy.'

'Tell her Catherine is dead, she died over sixteen years ago. The gypsy took the locket off her body.'

'I can't do that.'

'Why not? It could so easily be true. I'll go back to my friends in Norwich until I can arrange to join Matthew. After all, if I had been beside him in the dock, I should have been sent with him anyway. It's only justice.'

'But how do you know where to go?'

'Australia, of course.'

'Australia, my dear Kate, is a vast country, a huge continent.' He spoke with a faint hint of amusement in his voice. 'The penal colonies are dreadful places and the voyage itself is a fearful undertaking; it takes months. The seas are treacherous and the rations poor, even for fare-paying passengers. You could not possibly make that journey alone.' He sighed and covered her hand with his own. 'Kate, Matthew is a convicted felon, a criminal. Whatever you think of the rights and wrongs of that, he would not want you to share his captivity, not after the pains he took to protect you. Why do you think he came all the way to Caspertown to tell me about you? Not to save himself, but so that you should have the kind of life you were born for. He will make a new life for himself, he'll probably marry and settle down out there when he gets his ticket of leave. Kate, he has accepted that and so must you. One day you will find someone else to love.'

'I won't,' she said miserably. 'He's all I want.'

'No one else will do?' He spoke lightly, teasingly. 'Not even me?'

She looked up sharply. 'You are my brother, that's different.'

'No, I'm not, we're not blood relations at all.' He cursed himself for a fool; girls like Kate did not forget the people they loved easily. He sighed. 'But if that's how you want to think of me, I am content.'

'I don't mean to sound ungrateful,' she said. 'You have been kind to me and I know you mean well. But I can't pretend to be what I'm not.'

'You haven't given yourself time. You haven't given us a chance ...' He paused. 'Stay, please. It's what Matthew wanted. We needn't tell Mother who you are, not unless you want to.'

She smiled suddenly. 'Shall I go back to being one of the servants?'

'Definitely not! You are my guest.'

'She will think ...' She stopped and blushed.

'Then let her think it. It won't do any harm, will it? I can act the rejected suitor when the time comes.' He knew he was taking unfair advantage of her ignorance. If she had been used to society, she would have known that what he was suggesting was outrageous. She ought to have a maid and a chaperone but he wanted her all to himself until his stepmother arrived, when he confidently expected all would be resolved. He smiled. 'I could lock you in your room again.'

Kate had glimpsed Mrs Carrington when she had been staying in the house before the squire's wedding and had liked what she saw. In spite of her determination not to stay, she wanted to meet her properly, talk to her, find out the sort of person she was. Curiosity overcame doubt. 'Very well,' she said, as the carriage drew up at the door of the Hall. 'I can hardly leave for Australia today, can I?'

'No. And there is so much to talk about, so much to tell you and so much I want to learn about you.'

'I am not very interesting.'

'On the contrary, I find you fascinating.'

She laughed, too innocent to respond in any way but naturally to this little foray into flirtation. 'What do you want to know?'

And so the morning passed and they were both so absorbed, they were not aware of a carriage pulling up on the gravel outside. Only when they heard the footman go to the door, were they alerted to fact that someone had arrived. Andrew jumped up and ran into the hall, leaving Kate shaking with nerves. She was Catherine Wetherby in the skin of Kate Brough and it felt decidedly uncomfortable.

She stood up as Andrew ushered Mrs Carrington into the room and her firmly made resolve not to stay all but vanished. Her mother was petite and delicate, with a pale smooth complexion and enormous violet eyes, which held all too clearly the evidence of years of sorrow, but now there was wonder there and incredulity. She stood a moment, as if not daring to trust her eyes; she had been disappointed so many times before she could not bring herself to believe that this time it really was her daughter standing before her. But the doubts were swept away as Kate herself moved forward to drop a curtsey. 'Oh, my darling child,' she said, taking her daughter in her arms and hugging her, while the tears ran unchecked. 'I've dreamed of this moment all the years we've been apart. I knew it would come. I would not believe them when they said you were dead. If you had died I would have known, here, inside me.' And she put her hand to her heart.

Kate was in tears too. If this was what having a mother was like, what had she missed over the years? 'But how did you know me?' she asked, turning from her to Andrew, who had left the room to order tea and was then returning. 'Did Andrew tell you?'

'Not in so many words, but he didn't need to. As soon as I saw his face, I knew he had found you.' She paused to dab away her tears with a wisp of handkerchief. 'And when I saw you, I knew you.'

'But it's so many years.'

'Yes, but I have always carried a picture in my mind of what you would be like as you grew up. Each year I added a little height, small changes to your features as you grew from baby to little girl and from girl to woman. Besides, you are the image of my mother.' She turned to her stepson. 'Don't you think so, Andrew?'

'Yes, but even more beautiful.'

Kate blushed and Felicity went on. 'Oh, how I've prayed for this! And now it has happened.' She paused as Hetty came in with a loaded tray. The maid stared at Kate with her mouth open in undisguised surprise and, being peremptorily dismissed by Andrew, put the tray down beside Mrs Carrington and returned to the servants' quarters to report, 'That there Kate do sit beside the squire's sister for all the world as if she was gentry and the poor lady lookin' like the cat what's got the cream.'

'You must tell me all about yourself, where you've been, all the things you've done, every little detail,' Felicity said into the silence that followed the maid's departure. Tell me about that man, the one who . . .'

'Pa?'

'Is that what you called him?' Felicity could hardly keep the loathing from her voice.

'Yes. It's how I thought of him.'

'But now?'

'I don't know what to think. He was good to me. He found me and brought me up, just as if I were his daughter. I was so proud of him and we were happy together until he was taken for poaching.'

'Had you really no idea who you were?'

'None at all. Pa said I had been abandoned.'

'And you believed him?'

'I had no reason not to.'

'He was wrong.' The older woman spoke quietly but vehemently. 'He did me a great wrong.'

'I know.' She had to accept the truth of that, though it hurt her to sound disloyal to the man who had been both father and mother to her. 'But he is dead now and it's all in the past.'

'Yes, we must put it behind us,' Felicity said. 'Oh, life for us all is going to be so wonderful.'

Kate looked up at Andrew, her expression a plea for his help, but he all he did was grin cheerfully. 'She needs clothes,' he said, indicating Kate's plain dress.

She was furious with him. 'I have sufficient for my needs in my basket at The Ferryman,' she said.

'Forget it,' Andrew said. 'You don't need it. You don't need anything from your old life.'

'Oh, yes I do. I can't throw it off like an old petticoat; it's part of me. Don't you understand?'

'Of course we do,' Felicity said gently. 'We don't want to change you. But you must realise you are no longer the poacher's daughter.' She paused, not wanting to hurt her daughter by blaming the old man, but she could not forgive or forget what he had done. 'You are where you belong now, with your family.'

The meeting was not going at all according to plan and Kate suspected Andrew had known it wouldn't. She had been naive to think she could simply walk away from it afterwards. It was not just that it would hurt her mother, but she would find it a terrible wrench herself. She should never have agreed to stay. She should have insisted on going back to the inn and returning to Ely on the very next stage. 'Perhaps, but I don't feel any different. And I still need my friends.'

'If you mean the villagers,' Andrew put in. 'Do you think they will still be your friends when they learn about your changed circumstances?'

'Why not? It will make no difference to me.'

'But it will to them. Kate, you belong on the other side of the fence now, beyond their reach. You belong to the Haddows of Haddow Hall, the Carringtons of Caspertown, the gentlefolk. Class works both ways, you know.'

'Class!' she retorted angrily, feeling her cheeks colour. 'That's just the trouble with people like you, you talk in terms of class all the time; it seems a fashionable word to use just now. Isn't that what all the rioting has been about, those who have nothing against those who have everything? It's so unfair. We are all people, men, women and children, we have the same need for love, for health and strength to do whatever work is asked of us and money enough for comfort ...'

He laughed and clapped his hands. 'Well done, my little Kate, that was a good speech and worthy of Matthew Tolley himself.'

'Matthew Tolley?' queried Felicity, taken aback by Kate's forthrightness. 'Where have I heard that name before? Who is he?'

'He is my ... my friend,' Kate said. 'He is also a champion of the agricultural workers.'

'Your daughter has fallen in love, Mother,' Andrew said in a tone which infuriated Kate. 'Unfortunately, the young man is not one of whom you would approve. He is a convicted felon.'

'Felon?' She turned to Kate in surprise. 'He is a criminal?'

'Of course not,' Kate said, more sharply than she intended. 'He helped the agricultural workers in their fight against oppression.'

'It's too complicated to explain now,' Andrew said. 'Pour the tea, do, for I'm dying of thirst.'

'I'll do it.' Kate jumped up and began arranging the delicate cups on the tray and filling each from a matching china teapot. She was glad to have something to occupy her hands because she felt uncomfortable and on edge. Was it only yesterday her life had changed so dramatically? In the space of twenty-four hours she had gained a mother, a stepfather and a stepbrother, which was how she was beginning to think of Andrew. But none of it made up for the loss of Matthew.

'I can see the young man means a great deal to you,' Felicity said, taking the cup of tea Kate handed her. 'And it is very unkind of Andrew to tease you.' She stirred her tea and sighed. 'But then Andrew has no idea what it is like to be in love.'

'How do you know that?' he asked, laughing. 'How do you know there isn't a beautiful young lady somewhere, breaking my heart?'

'Because you don't act like a man with a broken heart,' his stepmother said. 'And besides, you have never been able to keep anything from me; you would have told me long before now.'

'Perhaps, just this once, I have kept it a secret,' he said, looking directly at Kate.

Kate was glad the subject had changed and she need say no more about Matthew and the labourers' cause, and the conversation went on to more general topics in which she was able to take part without becoming heated.

That evening, Andrew, poking about in the attics, found a chest full of clothes and had them taken down to Kate's room with instructions for her to find something to wear for supper. There were day dresses and morning gowns, underwear and nightwear, all very old and unfashionable, but in perfect condition.

'Oh, they were Mama's,' cried Felicity, pulling them out one after the other and piling them on Kate's bed. 'They must have been packed away when she died; John would never get rid of anything which belonged to her. Look how out of mode they are.' She held up a heavy plum-coloured satin affair. 'This has no bodice to speak of; it's almost indecent by today's standards. No, my dear, you cannot possibly wear that.' She rummaged in the chest and brought out a forget-me-not blue gauze with an underskirt of silk. Its bodice was trimmed with silk rosebuds. 'This is better. Try it on and see how it fits. What a pity the dressmaker hasn't arrived, we could get her to alter it.'

'I can try to do it,' Kate said, pulling off her wool dress and wriggling into the dress. 'Mrs Fyne taught me a little sewing, though I never did it when I was with Pa. There was no one to show me how.'

'How little I know of the kind of life you have led,' Felicity said, standing behind Kate to help her with the tiny buttons at the back of the bodice. 'Was it very terrible?'

'It wasn't terrible at all. I was happy and carefree as a child. It was only in the last year things happened to spoil it.'

'If anyone else were to take you from me, I think I really would go mad, just like they said I was.'

'There is no one to do that.'

'Not even the young man Andrew spoke of?'

'He can't take me from you. He's been sent to the penal colonies, punished for what he believes in.' There was a catch in Kate's voice as she fought back the tears.

Her mother put her arms round her shoulders. 'Kate, I'm sorry I mentioned him, it was very selfish of me. Let's talk of other things. Come to the glass and see how well this gown fits you.'

Kate moved over to the mirror and inspected her image. The dress was comparatively plain and had not been worn more than once, perhaps because her grandmother had not liked its simplicity at a time when ostentation was normal, but on Kate it looked exactly right, setting off the clear blue of her eyes and enhancing the pink in her cheeks and shining blonde hair. Her complexion had a healthy glow not considered fashionable, but her bearing and manner proclaimed her breeding. The little miniature, once more fastened round her neck, provided the finishing touch.

They went down to supper together and were met at the foot of the stairs by Andrew, who stood and appraised Kate for several seconds before he offered the women an arm each to escort them to the dining room. 'She looks exactly like the picture of Grandmama Haddow, doesn't she, Mother? She is every inch the lady and I am rapidly falling in love with her myself.' His tone was light, but

Kate detected an underlying note of seriousness which her mother appeared not to notice, but which filled her with alarm.

'Yes, no one could mistake her now, not even John.'

The mention of the squire deflated Kate and the smile faded from her lips. She had been trying very hard not to think of him, not to remember that she was staying in his home even though he was absent from it, that he was her uncle. It was an abhorrent thought and she hoped she could persuade Andrew to allow her to leave before he returned. She could not face him, not now or ever. He was the one who had separated her from Matthew, who had caused the ache in her heart which never left her, the emptiness deep down inside which only Matthew could fill. Her loathing for the man was as strong as ever.

While Kate toyed with the halibut on her plate, Felicity chatted on about clothes and her plans for Kate's social life once they had returned to Caspertown. Kate felt helpless, as if she were being borne along on a tide, unable to pull herself out of the current and chart her own course. And the longer she allowed herself to drift, the harder it became. Would she do better to settle down to her new life with a mother who obviously doted on her? Could she put Matthew from her mind? It was a silly question. She knew she could not, but each succeeding day would make the decision to leave harder to accomplish. She ought to tell her mother, come right out with it, but she couldn't find the words.

While she was in Middleacre, Felicity liked to visit the sick with food and medicine; it was one of her duties, she told Kate. 'Will you come with me?' she asked. 'There are still so many who need help.'

Kate did not need to be told that and readily agreed; it would be one way to prove to Andrew that he was wrong and the villagers were still her friends.

They went in a light two-horse carriage accompanied by Andrew. Kate was nervous as they bowled along the drive between the trees, now almost bare of leaves, and out of the great iron gates. Would the villagers really reject her? If they did, it would be nothing new; until Matthew's arrival the year before, they had always excluded her and Pa from the life of the community, looked down on her as the poacher's daughter, and now they were expected to look up to her as the squire's niece. She glanced up at Andrew, sitting opposite her with a smug smile which annoyed her. 'It's as bad as the tumbril,' she said, aware of the stares of those who were out on the fields and glad there were not more, for most were in the barns, threshing.

'Your pride sustained you then,' he said. 'Let it do so again. You have nothing to fear.'

'Of course not,' Felicity said, patting her gloved hand. 'I always found the people of Middleacre exceptionally respectful before the troubles last year and now they are over, I am sure they will be so again.'

'Everyone likes you, Mother,' Andrew said. 'So how can they fail to appreciate your daughter?'

But appreciation was not what Kate wanted, though it was all she got; appreciation for good works and a great many guarded looks. They spoke to Mrs Carrington in subservient tones, answering her questions about their welfare and thanking her for the food and herbal medicines she had brought and Kate was reminded of the way Watson had rejected what she took to him from the Hall. There was obviously a difference, but she could not understand what it was.

'You see,' Andrew said as they were bowling back with the empty basket in the boot. 'It wasn't so difficult, was it?'

'No,' she said, catching sight of Charlie Barber coming out of his garden gate. He was standing with his hand on the latch as if turned to stone, his expression clearly told her that he thought she had betrayed him. 'Please stop the carriage,' she said. 'I must speak to Charlie.'

The vehicle came to a halt and she scrambled down and ran back to where the young man still stood, staring blankly after them.

'Charlie' she said. 'Mr Carrington-Haddow didn't want to arrest me after all and he didn't betray Matthew. Mrs Carrington is my mother, he was looking for me to tell me that, not to arrest me.'

'I'm fare glad for you, that I am,' he said politely touching his hand to the peak of his cap. 'Good-day to you, miss.'

It was as clear a dismissal as he could make it and though she stood looking at him a moment longer, he did not add to it, and she turned away. Charlie and Mrs Barber had been her champions before any of the others; if they turned from her, what hope did she have of being understood? She was back where she started, belonging nowhere.

Chapter Eighteen

'Catherine, dear, I do not think you should have done that,' Felicity said gently, as Kate scrambled back into the carriage and they set off again. 'It is not the conduct of a lady.'

'What isn't?' Kate asked.

'Getting out of the carriage and running off down the road like that to speak to ...' She paused, not wishing to hurt her daughter. 'To a young man.'

Kate turned to her in surprise. 'Why not? I wanted to tell him what had happened.'

'There is no need for the villagers to be told our business, Catherine, but even if there is, you should remember your position and act with dignity. If you want to address one of your inferiors, you must sit in the carriage and he or she will come to you.'

'Supposing they don't? Besides, that would be terribly arrogant, don't you think?'

Felicity sighed. 'Oh, dear, I am afraid you have a great deal to learn. When the carriage stops, the groom will indicate to the person concerned that they are to approach. They would not dream of refusing.'

'But why should they come just because someone beckons them? I am sure I should not.'

'No, but then it is not expected of *us*. Now, I think we have said enough on the subject, don't you?'

'I'm sorry if I have displeased you,' Kate said.

'My dear child, you haven't displeased me. Perhaps I expect too much. We will have a few lessons and I will endeavour to teach you how to go on.'

Kate wasn't at all sure she wanted lessons if all she learned was how to stand on her dignity, but she would not distress her mother by saying so.

Next day her lessons began with instruction in what was and

what was not the correct behaviour for a young unmarried lady. It was all a blur of 'you ought to do this' and 'you must not do that'; she must not raise her voice or show emotion, particularly in front of the servants, she must give orders in a pleasant but firm manner, and she must not do anything for herself. On one occasion when she jumped up to open the door for Hetty who was carrying a laden tray, her mother admonished her. 'Catherine, do not do that again. Leave the servants alone.'

'But I was only trying to help.'

'I am sure you were, my dear, but it is Hetty's job to clear the table, you know that. It's one of the tasks she is paid for.'

'But she has so much to do. They all have.'

'If we did the work there would be no servants, would there?' Felicity said patiently. 'And then how would they live? They need us every bit as much as we need them. Now, come and sit down and we will say no more about it.'

Her mother, deciding to change to a less contentious topic, began to talk about clothes. Kate was enlightened about what to wear for every occasion from morning to evening and for everything else she might do in between. It soon became apparent that she would be changing her costume half a dozen times a day and that what she wore for morning calls would certainly not do for evening. The garments Andrew had found in the attic were most decidedly only a stop-gap. 'We shall have such fun choosing everything,' her mother said. 'You have such a beautiful figure. But we must do something about your complexion. It should be pale and I do believe you have the tiniest show of freckles.'

Kate laughed. 'You should see me in the summer. I have hundreds then.'

'I have something that will take care of them.' And from there her mother moved on to explain about lotions and powders and tinctures of this and that, making Kate more bewildered and unsure of herself than ever. It was not that she was slow to learn, it was simply that she did not see the need. She didn't want to lose Kate Brough, but her mother seemed bent on the metamorphosis, of producing the butterfly Catherine Wetherby and consigning the poacher's daughter to oblivion. She could not do it fast enough, though time and again over the next few weeks, she was heard to murmur, 'I must have patience.'

And the day she found Kate in the kitchen, with one of her new day gowns covered by an apron of Mrs Bunny's, learning to make pastry, she was, for the first time, very angry.

'Catherine! What are you doing?'

Kate laughed, something she rarely did in the drawing room, and the realisation of that did nothing to soothe her mother. 'Making pastry, Mama. Mrs Bunny is teaching me.'

'You do not need to learn to cook, Catherine. Mrs Bunny should have known better.'

'It was my idea, Mama. I asked her to show me. I feel so useless, sitting around the house doing nothing.'

'Then do some embroidery or sketching.'

'That's not useful, is it? Besides, I don't know how to.'

'Leave the housekeeper to get on with her work and come back to the drawing room. I wish to speak to you.' She did not wait, expecting Kate to obey at once.

Kate turned to Mrs Bunny with a smile of apology, washed her floury hands at the kitchen sink and took off the apron. 'I'm sorry,' she said. 'I do hope I haven't got you into trouble too.'

The servant smiled. 'Don't you worry about me, Kate. I can look after myself. You just go and make your peace.'

'I'll come again, shall I? If Mama will let me.'

'If she'll let you,' Mrs Bunny said, gathering together the dough Kate had been making and beginning to roll it out. She didn't think for a minute that Kate would be allowed back into the kitchen again. Poor child, she was finding it very difficult to adapt.

Although Kate loved her mother and accepted the scolding stoically, she could not see that what she had done was wrong. Surely it was sensible to know about the work the servants had to do in order to understand their difficulties; you shouldn't ask them to do something you could not do yourself. And she'd rather cook than sew any day. Besides, she liked Mrs Bunny, who had befriended her before; she couldn't just ignore her as if she didn't exist, could she?

Andrew was the only one who seemed to understand. He was attentive and affectionate and she felt comfortable with him. He protected her from the curiosity of the lower servants and the patronising scrutiny of long-forgotten friends and neighbours of Sir John, who suddenly found a desire to call on Felicity and offer their congratulations on her good fortune, sweeping up in their carriages and spreading themselves all over the withdrawing room, drinking chocolate or Madeira and prattling endlessly about nothing of importance. They were shallow and insincere and Kate disliked their posturing.

'Do they think I have two heads?' she asked Andrew after one particularly trying morning. 'Should we not charge an entrance?'

He laughed. 'It won't last, my dear. When they realise you are perfectly able to conduct yourself as a lady and don't eat off the floor, they will tire of coming and things will return to normal.'

But what was normal? Kate didn't know. Had her life been normal when she lived with Josiah? Was it normal when she stayed with the Fynes, afraid to go out in case she was arrested? Was it normal now, when she was cossetted in luxury, her every wish granted – at least, every wish but one? She needed reassurance, to know that she was not being changed out of all recognition and the only people who could do that were her old friends.

It may have been the will rather than any firm evidence, but she had decided she must have been mistaken in her interpretation of Charlie's reaction to seeing her in the Haddow carriage. No one would surely begrudge her and her mother a little happiness when they understood. She would go back into the village on her own and on foot, and explain how it had all come about. She would let the people know she was still at one with them; she hadn't become one of the hated Haddows of Haddow Hall. She would go and see Jack Watson, he was a strong influence on the others.

She had learned enough to know her mother would strongly disapprove, so she said nothing, intending to take the first opportunity which presented itself to go out alone. It was more difficult than she imagined. She was so tightly protected that there was hardly a moment of any day when she did not have mother, maids or Andrew for company.

She accomplished it in the end, one afternoon when her mother, complaining of a headache, decided to take a dose of laudanum and lie down in her room with the curtains drawn. Having assured herself Felicity was comfortable and the headache not severe, Kate waited until Andrew had gone out with his gun and then donned cape and bonnet and set off for the village.

She had not been in the little cottage a minute before she wished she had not come. Jack, who had been working in the fields close by, saw her arriving and returned swiftly to the house where Mrs Watson, completely taken aback by the surprise visit, was gaping at Kate with her mouth open. He hurried to pull a chair forward and asked her to be seated in exactly the obsequious manner he would have used if her mother or Sir John himself had deigned to visit them and Mrs Watson, recovering, bobbed a curtsey and asked if she would care to take tea and then shook so much she couldn't stop the cups from rattling in their saucers.

Betty was the only one of the family prepared to exchange more than polite pleasantries and she was as forthright as ever. 'Come into a fortune, have you?' she demanded, indicating Kate's green silk dress with its fashionably wide sleeves and full skirt, her beribboned bonnet and tiered shoulder cape.

'I've come into a mother,' Kate said sharply. 'All the years I lived with ...' She was about to say 'Pa' but changed her mind. 'Josiah Brough, all those years, I had a family, a real family who loved me and grieved over my disappearance. Mrs Carrington is my mother.'

'So we heard. Charlie told us. It makes you niece to the squire. Kin to that fiend.'

She smiled. 'Yes, I am afraid so, but that makes no difference ...'

'I always did think there was somethin' queer about you. You never did belong ...'

'That's not true and I haven't changed.'

'You won't be able to help it,' Jack said flatly. 'Whether you like it or not, you're one o' the gentry now, not for the likes of us.'

'Not that you ever were,' Betty put in sharply.

'Why should gentry and workers be on opposite sides?' asked Kate. 'Why can't we all live together without fighting, one against the other? It shouldn't happen.'

'No, it shouldn't,' Jack retorted. 'But you tell that to the squire, see if he agrees. He's the one causin' all the trouble, him and his like, even Andrew Carrington-Haddow, your brother.'

'He's not my real brother,' Kate said. 'And he's a good man. He would help you if he could.'

'Then why did he have Matthew Tolley arrested?' Betty demanded. 'Tell me that?'

'He didn't,' she said. It seemed they did not know Matthew's true identity or if they did, they were prepared to overlook it. Perhaps the fact that he had renounced the name of Thorsborough was enough to convince them he was one of them. Was that what she had to do? Somehow she knew that would not be enough. 'Matthew was sent to the penal colonies because of what he did for you and all the other farm labourers; it was none of Andrew's doing.'

'Oh, yes it was,' Betty said shrilly. 'Matthew went up north to ask his help, rode all the way on account of his bein' wanted by the law and not darin' to take a coach. And what happened? 'fore you could say knife, he's in chokey bein' tried for his life. How'd that happen if it weren't for you and that Mr Carrington-Haddow?'

'It wasn't like that. Captain Tolley went to Caspertown because of me . . .'

'There! What did I tell you? You're to blame for all the trouble we 'ad, right from the start. It was your fault.'

'I'm sorry you feel like that,' Kate said evenly, determined not to engage in a verbal battle with the girl, though her anger was quickening her pulse and it was taking all her determination to quash it. 'While you harbour such resentment, we can never have peace.'

'It in't our resentment hinderin' peace,' Jack said. 'It's them buggers up at the Hall, the landowners and the gentry, using them machines and cuttin' our wages, and that includes you now. But we'll rise again, you'll see, and this time we'll win.'

'You mean more threatening letters and more rick-burning? Oh, haven't we had enough of that?'

'We'll ha' had enough when we get our wages reinstated and you can go and tell that to the squire.'

'He's away.'

'He'll be back. Can't stay away for ever, can he?'

'No.' She got up to leave; there was no point in trying to explain that her loathing for the squire was as strong as ever, that, uncle or not, she could not forgive him for what had happened to Josiah nor for taking Matthew from her.

'Matthew would never have married you,' Betty added, almost as if she could read her thoughts. 'He loved me. We'd have been wed.'

'That's not true.'

'Oh, yes it is. He didn't think narthin' of you. Soft, that's what he was. Soft-hearted. Felt sorry for you, see?'

'I don't believe you,' Kate said, but she was not as sure as she sounded. Could it possibly be true?'

'You'll never know now, will you?' Betty taunted, standing so close to Kate the hems of their skirts touched, the green silk and the worn homespun. ''e's gone and we'll none on us see 'im ag'in.'

Kate had no answer to that and turned towards the door, stumbling in her haste to escape.

'Thass right, m'dear,' Betty called after her. 'Go you back to that Mr Carrington-Haddow you're so fond of, he's more your sort.'

Kate hurried away, wishing fervently she had listened to Andrew. He had been right all along; the villagers didn't want anything to do with her. And Matthew? Was it pity and not love which had prompted his actions? What had he said? *I am not the one to teach you.* Betty had been right; she would never know now. Matthew was gone and like it or not, she had become a Haddow and she had to accept it.

But she was only half a Haddow, she told herself, the other half was Wetherby; did that make any difference? She doubted it. Her mother had told her that her father had been quite elderly. It had been an arranged marriage. 'It often happened when I was young,' she had explained, smiling a little. 'The Haddows always lived beyond their means and I had no dowry. Lord Wetherby helped my papa financially.'

Kate's real father had been a peer, more exalted even than Sir John, but since she had learned about Matthew's family, she realised it meant nothing; it was the man behind the title that mattered. 'But you didn't love him?'

'No, though I grew quite fond of him. He was a good husband and a devoted father. You should have seen him when you were born, he was almost like a young man again.'

'How did he die?'

'He had a heart attack one day after a particularly strenuous hunt. You were less than a year old.'

'And then you married Mr Carrington?'

'Yes. That was, and still is, a love match. He has been more father to you than ever Lord Wetherby was. You will meet him soon.'

Kate smiled ruefully as she hurried along the lane towards Haddow Hall; her mother seemed to have forgotten all about Josiah. Haddow, Wetherby, Carrington, what difference did a name make? Matthew was not Tolley but Thorsborough, and she still felt like Kate Brough.

She had just passed through the wrought iron gates which had once displayed the mantrap and the villagers' Swing message when she was almost run down by a post-chaise. It seemed there were yet more visitors come to stare at her. How she hated them all!

Unseen, she slipped into the house and up to her room, where she sat on the bed staring into space. That visit to the Watson cottage had completely unnerved her. She had felt so sure Matthew loved her, had been so determined to join him, even though it meant leaving her mother. How could she do that now? Did she even want to?

A knock at the door made her jump. 'Who is it?'

'Andrew. I want to talk to you.'

She called 'Come in,' without rising from the bed.

'Where have you been?' He strode over to sit beside her. 'I've been looking all over for you. Mother was distraught, I had to tell her I knew where you'd gone and you'd soon be back.'

'Did you know where I was?' she asked dully. If there was going to be this kind of reaction every time she went out on her own, it would be like being in prison.

'No, I didn't.' He didn't tell her that he had been almost as worried as his stepmother. 'You don't know how relieved we were when Susan said she had seen you returning.'

'Did you think I might run away?'

'It had occurred to me.'

'Where would I run to?'

'Friends.'

'I have no friends.' She spoke flatly, as if she had become resigned to the fact.

'What has happened to make you so sad?' he asked, taking her hand in his own and noticing how soon it had lost its workworn look and become white and soft.

'I went to see the Watsons.'

'Why?'

'Because I wanted to. I wanted to explain . . .'

'And they upset you.' He put his arm about her. 'I'm sorry, my dear, but I did warn you. High and low simply do not mix.'

'I can't settle, Andrew. I can't be a lady. I've tried.'

'Yes, you can. You were born to it, it is in your blood, it is only a question of learning and remembering . . .'

'Matthew is in my blood. I should never have let you persuade me to stay. Now, I am so muddled.'

He wished fervently she would get over her preoccupation with Matthew; until she did, he didn't have a hope. 'What has happened to make you say that?'

'Nothing. Everything. Betty Watson said Matthew loved her and would have come back to her, if he had not been arrested.'

He almost laughed aloud at the thought, but then he realised she had put a weapon in his hand. 'My love, he has been sentenced to life a very long way from here. Let the girl believe what she wants. What difference does it make?'

She looked up at him. 'All the difference. I cannot go to Australia if Matthew does not want me. Perhaps he never wanted me.'

'My darling,' he said, treading eggs. 'Why torture yourself? Put it from your mind. Matthew has gone and your future is here, with me and your mother.'

'Do you think so? Do you really think so?' Oh, why couldn't she believe it?

'Yes, no doubt of it.'

'What I can't understand is that Betty is supposed to be walking out with Charlie Barber. He told me so himself. How can she do that if she still loves Matthew?'

He tried not to let her see him smile. 'Sometimes, my dear, we have to compromise, to accept second-best as better than nothing at all. Betty cannot have Matthew, so she has settled for young Barber. He will make her a good husband.'

'Charlie once asked me to marry him.'

'There you are then! He's taking second-best too. But it will work out. Love grows you know, it doesn't always strike like a flash of lightning.'

'Mama told me she did not love my father.'

'What has that to do with anything?'

'I don't want that to happen to me. I don't want to be married off to the highest bidder. It's quite feudal.'

'It won't happen to you.'

'No it won't,' she said sharply. 'Because you will never change me, never turn me into a young lady, saying and doing only what is expected of me. I have a mind of my own.'

He laughed. 'And don't I know it!'

'I'm sorry I'm such a burden to you,' she said, smiling for the first time since he had entered the room.

'You're not a burden. I only wish you were. I would carry it willingly.'

She sighed. 'I'll try to be whatever you want me to be, Andrew, but it is so difficult . . .'

He put his hands on her shoulders and turned her to face him. 'Kate, my dearest one, I would not have you any other way. I love you dearly as you are.' He smiled at her little gasp of shock and put a finger under her chin and lifted her face so that she was looking into his eyes. 'I have loved you ever since I first saw you in that old wagon. I love your beauty, your innocence, your honesty, your fire. I will always love you.'

She was so taken aback she could not speak and simply stared at him.

'Don't look so shocked,' he said, smiling. 'You must have guessed.'

She found her voice at last. 'I . . . I thought you loved me as a sister.'

'No, never that, my darling. I love you as a red-blooded man loves a beautiful woman, as a man loves his wife.'

'But, Andrew . . .'

'Don't say anything now. Just think about it. With me you can be yourself, can't you? We could be married and find a nice little home, just for the two of us, perhaps one or two servants to do the donkey work, but not a great household like this. And there would be no one to lecture you on what is right and proper. I certainly would not presume to do so.' He smiled and dropped a kiss lightly on her forehead. 'You see, I do understand.'

'Do you?'

'Of course I do. You are finding the transition from one life to another very difficult, made more so because you do not want to hurt Mother. I have seen you biting your lip to stop yourself saying what is in your mind. I have seen the tears in your eyes, even if no one else has. It has been too great a jump, it should be done more slowly. We can do it together, step by step at the pace you want. And it will not alienate you from Mother because, believe me, she is finding it very difficult too. She has been building dreams for years and she cannot understand the daughter she lost has become an independent woman.'

'I am a great disappointment to her, aren't I?'

'Perhaps she expects a little too much.'

'I do try, I really do.'

'I know. But if we had a separate home, it would be easier, wouldn't it? Somewhere away from here. Not Caspertown either.'

'But you are Sir John's heir. One day this will be your home.'

'You forget, he has married again for the express purpose of getting himself a new heir.'

'Do you mind that?'

'Not a bit. Now, will you think about what I've said?'

She was very fond of him, but it was a sister's love, and she did not want to hurt him. 'Andrew, I can't,' she said.

'I was afraid you'd say that.' He sighed heavily and stood up. 'No matter, I am a patient man and you will change your mind.'

Before she could answer, there was a knock at the door and he went to open it to admit her mother's maid.

'If you please, miss,' she said with a bob and glancing disapprovingly at Andrew who should never have been in Catherine's room. 'The mistress says will you put on the blue silk and join her in the withdrawing room. And I'm to stay and dress your hair.'

Andrew slipped away and Kate succumbed to being helped on with the dress. She would have to carry on with the charade a little longer, she could not make a scene in front of guests. And she wanted to cause her mother as little hurt as possible, but she must leave, especially now. How could Andrew ask her to marry him knowing how she loved Matthew? Did he think she could turn her love on and off?

'You look beautiful, miss,' Susan said, as she brushed her golden tresses. 'Just like the mistress when she was young and you were a baby.'

'You knew me then?' Kate asked in surprise.

'Yes, miss. You should have seen the mistress when you were first lost, we all thought she'd die of grief. Days and days they searched for you and black days they were. She would never believe you wouldn't be found. All the years, even when her mind was wandering, she held fast to that belief. Such a lovely lady, she is, so good and kind to everyone. It was a terrible thing to take her child away.' She paused and added, 'Beg pardon, miss, it's not my place to say, but if she was to have any more heartbreaks, I do believe she would pine away and die, I do really.'

Kate wondered if the maid could have any inkling of her intentions; it seemed almost like a plea, a warning, and it did not help her confused state of mind. She stood up and went downstairs to meet the company, steeling herself to be pleasant and not to mind their curiosity.

The withdrawing room door was open and the sound of conversation and laughter drifted into the hall and for the first time Kate wondered who the visitors were. Andrew came to the foot of the stairs to meet her, stooping to kiss her cheek and offering her his arm. 'Captivating,' he whispered, then, 'Take a deep breath, my lovely Kate, and try to remember what I said about being nice to people you dislike. And smile, Kate, smile.'

She had no time to wonder what he meant as he led her forward. Standing in the doorway confronted by the bright lights of the chandeliers, it was a moment or two before she could focus on the occupants of the room and then she went weak at the knees; only Andrew's arm about her kept her upright. Sir John was standing with his back to the fire, his hands behind him, lifting the tails of his coat away from the blaze. On one side sat her mother, smiling contentedly, and on the other, Lady Haddow, heavily pregnant. Johnson was moving round with a tray of wine-filled glasses.

Sir John stared at Kate for a full minute, during which neither moved, then he turned to his sister and said, 'You are quite right, Felicity, my dear, she is the image of Mother. In the face of the evidence, who am I to deny her?'

Felicity left her seat to draw Kate into the room, her bright eyes and pink cheeks a reflection of her happiness. Kate could do nothing but allow herself to be led to a chair and pretend to be happy too. But inside her heart was heavy and behind her smiling countenance her thoughts were bleak. How could she make polite conversation and behave like one of the family when all the time there was black hate in her heart and she did not belong there at all?

She sat beside her mother with a fixed smile on her face, deaf to the conversation going on around her. It was too bad of Andrew to inflict this on her. He knew how she felt about the squire and he could have made an excuse for her absence. She didn't like the way Sir John was looking at her either; it was nothing short of lustful. But Lady Haddow was expecting a child and he was obviously as pleased as punch about it.

'We'll have a celebration when my son is born,' Sir John's strident voice penetrated her crowded thoughts. 'You'll stay, Felicity, won't you? And you too, Andrew, you must make the most of your last few days as heir to Haddow Hall.' He looked at Kate before turning back to his sister. 'I want all my family around me when the great day arrives and that includes the poacher's daughter.'

'Don't call Catherine by that name,' Felicity protested. 'It isn't true.'

'Perhaps not, but that's how I think of her.' He was making it very plain he did not mean to address Kate directly, even though he acknowledged their relationship. 'She is one of the rebels and it frustrates me to think I have to refrain from having her arrested on your account.'

'John, how can you say such a thing?' Felicity cried. 'It wasn't her fault. She's a young, innocent girl.'

'Innocent!' he scoffed. 'She's no more innocent than that young stud, Tolley. Witch I'd call her, stirring up the men's passions, goading them into defying me. Goading *me* beyond endurance.'

Felicity, sensing Kate's distress, put a hand on her arm. 'John, let's not talk of such things. The man is halfway to Australia; he'll bother you no more.'

'Halfway to Australia!' He laughed. 'He's not even a quarter of the way there. He's still in the hulks, waiting for a ship to sail – seems they have to wait for a full complement to make it worth their while – and I wouldn't put it past the strumpet to try and spirit him away, even now. I've ordered extra guards and you had better keep a careful watch on her ...' He stopped suddenly because Kate, overcome by the heat in the room and her brimming emotions, had tried to rise and instead had crumpled in a faint.

'Now, see what you've done,' Felicity said, fishing in her reticule for a phial of smelling salts, while Andrew picked Kate up and laid her carefully on a sofa. 'I had almost got her to the stage of forgetting all about that man. She was trying so hard to change ...'

'You can't change her,' Sir John said. 'She's been too long a gypsy.'

Kate opened her eyes to the brilliance of the chandelier immediately above her head and, blinking, turned away. She was lying on the sofa, with her mother kneeling on the floor at her side, clutching a phial, and Andrew was sitting beside her, supporting her head and shoulders. Sir John was standing with his back to the fire again, looking down at her from what seemed a great height. 'She learns fast, that one,' he said with a sneer. 'Swooned like a true aristocrat, all vapours and flouncing petticoats. You'd never suspect, she is naught but a tinker's child.'

'She is nothing of the sort,' Felicity snapped.

'Of course she is. You can't undo all the years of living like a peasant, however hard you try. It's ingrained in her now. Why couldn't you have let well alone, accepted your daughter was dead and got on with your life? It would have been better for everyone concerned.'

Felicity looked down at Kate, cradled in Andrew's arms, and sighed heavily. In appearance her daughter was all she could wish for and the day they had been reunited had been the happiest of her life, but nothing else had been as she expected it. Catherine had a mind of her own, and a very stubborn one it was; it was proving quite difficult to make her conform, but Felicity would not accept what her brother said was true. Breeding was more important than where and with whom you had lived, and breeding would out. 'She was never a peasant,' she said quietly. 'She is half Haddow and half Wetherby.'

He laughed harshly. 'And you can't have a better pedigree than that.'

Kate struggled into a sitting position. 'What do I care for pedigree,' she said, speaking to Sir John, her cheeks pink with anger and her lovely eyes blazing. 'I am *me* whatever my name is. Kate Brough or Catherine Wetherby, it makes no difference. I am not a prize mare to be looked over before buying and I will not be treated like one. It is clear I am not welcome in this house ...' She ignored her mother's cry of dismay. 'I shall find somewhere else to live. I didn't ask to come here.'

'Please, Catherine,' her mother pleaded. 'That is not the way to speak to your uncle.'

'It is not the genteel behaviour of a lady, you mean? I'm sorry, Mama, but I was provoked beyond politeness and you do not know the half of what happened last year.'

Sir John laughed in an embarrassed way and addressed himself to his sister before Kate could tell her mother about that attempted rape. God, she had provoked him then and he could hardly bear to look at her now. He was right about her being a witch. 'My dear, if you want to quell this spirit of rebellion in your daughter, I suggest you marry her off. Find someone to break the mare in, not too high-born or she'll get ideas above her station, but not low enough to make a laughing stock of the family. A sea-going man or an army officer, someone to keep her away from here, so I don't have to look at her.'

'Captain Swing!' Laura laughed at her own wit. 'I heard he was on the loose again and planning more mischief.'

'Or Andrew,' he said, smirking at the young man who still had his arm protectively round Kate. 'They deserve each other.'

Kate twisted round to look at Andrew a question in her eyes; surely Sir John had not put him up to that proposal? He smiled and shook his head slowly from side to side.

'Please do not distress yourself, my darling,' her mother said, placatingly. 'It is only John having his little joke.'

'I do not find it amusing.'

'Nor do I,' Andrew said, producing a loud guffaw from Sir John, which made the young man colour angrily, but he said nothing and Sir John changed the subject.

Kate endured the remainder of the evening in silence while the rest of the company discussed the preparations for the celebrations to mark the birth of an heir, and Lady Haddow preened herself like a fat mother duck. Kate was reminded of the preparations for the wedding which had ended so disastrously. Would history repeat itself? Had Jack Watson been doing more than boast when he said the labourers would rise again? And would Matthew be there to lead them? Was he on his way to the other side of the world or still in London? Could he possibly be set free? Or was Sir John tormenting her because it amused him? Perhaps he would tire of it if she refused to rise to the bait.

It seemed she was right, because the next day he turned his attention to other things. He sent for an army of doctors and nurses to attend his wife's confinement and opened up guest rooms for their accommodation. Invitations were issued, food and drink ordered, changes made to the nursery. It was almost a repetition of the previous year. Fiddy and the outdoor servants were hounded from one end of the estate to the other, ostensibly to make sure the game was plentiful for his guests, but Kate guessed they were sent to uncover whatever they could of any plots in the making. She hoped fervently that they would find none.

'Andrew, I am worried about the villagers,' she told him one day just before Christmas when they were out walking along the edge of the fen. A cool wind was whipping up the water and the reeds lay broken and black with frost but she was well wrapped up in a heavy cape with a fur-lined hood and, in spite of her new way of life, she was still hardy and still liked to be out of doors. 'If they riot again it will be worse than before because this time Sir John will be ready for them.' She stopped to look up at him. 'And this time they have no one to calm them down. Can't you do anything? Perhaps they'll listen to you.'

He tucked her hand through his arm and smiled down at her. 'They would no more listen to me than to the squire himself. Kate, believe me, I would like to help but the trouble is not something you can cure overnight. You can only change things slowly, through caring.'

'And you do care, don't you?' she said softly.

'I care, but my hands are tied. Sir John is absolute ruler here and with the imminent birth of an heir, it is unlikely I will be able to do anything in the future.'

'They need Matthew,' she said. 'They would listen to him. Do you think he will try to escape?'

'No, I don't,' he said firmly, wishing he could take her mind off Matthew. 'Getting out of the hulks is nigh on impossible, and even if he did manage it, he would hardly be so ill-advised as to come back here. After all's said and done, he wanted the trial. He martyred himself. Coming back to lead the people into more trouble would undo all the good he has done, all the public sympathy he attracted. He is not such a fool. Put it right out of your head.'

'He wouldn't come back, even for me?' She didn't know if she wanted reassurance that he would if he could or that he would never risk it. She did not know what she hoped for.

'No, Kate.' He smiled and lifted the palm of her hand to his lips. 'He left you in my care and I intend to care for you, always.'

'Did he know you would ask me to marry you?'

'I believe so.'

'And he did not mind? He did not say you should not?'

'No, he wished us happy.'

'Truly?'

'Yes, truly.'

'Did Sir John know you would ask me?'

'Certainly not.'

'I don't understand men,' she said, once again wondering if Betty had been right and Matthew's feelings for her had been no more than pity for her plight. She didn't want sympathy. 'I don't understand the way they think.'

'No, I don't suppose you do and I don't understand women and the way they cling to lost causes.'

'It's not a lost cause,' she said, misunderstanding him. 'The labourers will win, all they need is a leader who can talk to them and talk to the landowners and make everyone see reason.'

'Perhaps the Lord will provide one.'

'I do hope so.'

'After the baby is born, we'll go home to Caspertown and Father. There you'll learn to forget all this and be happy. And in the fullness of time ...' He stopped; now was not the time to repeat his proposal.

She had to accept what he said, not only about the state of affairs in Middleacre, but about Matthew too. Andrew was so good to her, so understanding; he could almost read her thoughts. And he was right about one thing; she would never learn to be content in her new life while she stayed in Middleacre. Perhaps he was right about other things too, about accepting what you could have and not yearning for something out of reach, about love growing, given time. Could she learn to love him in time? Should she agree to his proposal, ask him to take her away, away from the memories she could not escape while she remained in Middleacre? Perhaps, when Matthew's ship had really sailed and there was no hope of his return, she would know the answer.

'I wish ...' she began and then stopped.

'What do you wish? If it is humanly possible, I'll do anything in my power to grant it, you know that.'

'You can't, not this,' she said. 'I was wishing that I could see Matthew just once more, just to tell him I am thinking of him and wish him well.'

'Oh, Kate,' he cried, exasperated. 'Can't you put him from your mind? How do you think it makes me feel?'

She turned to look at him, surprised by his outburst, then laid a hand on his arm. 'Oh, Andrew, I am so sorry. I didn't think. I wouldn't hurt you for the world.'

'It doesn't matter,' he said, almost brusquely. 'Let's go home. I don't know about you, but I am becoming decidedly chilly.'

They turned to go back, back to a life she could not even begin to like. But for her mother's sake she tried to conform. She learned to embroider, she went shopping in Wisbech for Christmas gifts, took carriage rides to visit well-to-do neighbours, and tried very hard not to provoke Sir John. But because she was preoccupied with worrying about the villagers, which led inevitably to thoughts of Matthew, she felt decidedly unsettled and fidgety. And more and more she sensed her mother's disappointment in her. It was nothing Felicity said, for she was as loving and long-suffering as ever, but she sometimes fell into long periods of silence and hardly heard when anyone spoke to her, as if her thoughts were miles away and Kate guessed that was how she had been when her daughter was lost. She was still lost.

Haddow Hall was full of guests for Christmas, noisy, loud-voiced men and women playing childish games and eating and drinking too much. If her mother had not absolutely forbidden it, Kate would have hidden herself away in the kitchen and helped Mrs Bunny, who slaved away in the kitchens with too little help, trying to satisfy the demands of Sir John and Lady Haddow, who was, if it were possible, even more difficult to please than her husband. And because she was very near her time, every whim must be granted, even to having strawberries brought down from London. One thing Kate was determined on, the villagers would have their share of the food, even if she had to steal out with it as she had done before. And in this she had a willing accomplice in Andrew.

Laden with two carpet bags full of packages of food, they left the house on Christmas night when everyone else was playing charades, and ran through the woods to the little side gate like naughty children, laughing at their own cleverness. One by one they visited the cottages and left little parcels on the doorsteps, until everything was gone and they turned for home. Kate skipped ahead of Andrew, laughing with joy to be out, to be doing some good, however little it was, to be in the company of someone who felt as she did.

'What's the hurry?' he called after her. 'Are you so anxious to be back?'

She stopped and waited for him. 'No. I am happy to be out with you.'

'You are?' He took her shoulders in his hands and looked down into her face. It looked pale in the moonlight and her bonnet had fallen back on its ribbons revealing soft curls which none of Susan's brushing could subdue. Slowly he bent his head and brushed her lips with his own. 'Kate, I love you,' he murmured.

'Kate, not Catherine?' she queried, teasing him.

'Kate,' he said firmly. 'Kate Brough.'

'The poacher's daughter?'

'If you like.' He smiled and then drew her into his arms to kiss her properly. She did not resist. 'Will you marry me soon, please?'

'I have been thinking about it.'

'Have you?' He could not keep the delight from his voice. 'And what have you decided?'

'I have decided that I cannot decide.'

'Oh, I see, an enigma. How is it to be resolved?'

She smiled in the darkness. 'In time, perhaps, when we have left Middleacre and its problems behind us.'

'Then the sooner that happens the better.'

'Can't we go now, tomorrow?'

'I'm afraid not,' he said, cursing Sir John. 'Lady Haddow is in no condition to cope with all the guests and Mother must deputise for her. She needs us.'

'How stupid Sir John is,' she said. 'It's almost as if he must have witnesses to the event like some medieval king.'

'In his own eyes, I suppose he is king.'

'And the labourers are his subjects. No wonder they rise up in revolt.'

'There are good and bad landowners just as there are good and bad kings,' he said. 'It is Middleacre's misfortune it has one of the bad ones.'

'Yes, and I can see no end to their troubles, can you? They need a leader; they need someone like Matthew.'

The mention of Matthew deflated him. Would she never get the man out of her head? Could he endure being second best? Time, she said she needed, but would time make her love him or weaken her attachment to Thorsborough ? He smiled, tucked her hand through his arm and took her home, back to the bright lights and the over-exuberant gaiety.

Chapter Nineteen

*T*he house was quiet when Kate went down to breakfast the following morning. Most of the guests were sleeping off the excesses of the day before, but Sir John and Andrew were in the breakfast room, talking to Fiddy. She would have retreated but Andrew saw her and beckoned her to join them, rising to pull out a chair for her. She smiled at him and slipped into her seat. Sir John ignored her.

'When?' he asked the bailiff.

'Next Sunday, Sir John, the anniversary of your wedding. They're planning to gather with banners and music to march through the village to come here to the Hall. It's meant to be a non-violent demonstration of their solidarity, to remind us that they hen't given up.'

'Let them march,' Sir John said, helping himself generously to poached eggs and ham. 'And the next day they will find they have no jobs to go to.'

'Provided they attend church, the farmers won't put them off for what they do on a Sunday,' Andrew put in. 'And much of the harvest has still to be threshed. They need the men.'

'Not if I offer the use of my new engine,' Sir John laughed. 'It deals with the work far more efficiently and a few trusty men can work one.'

'And I suppose you'll charge for its use?'

'Less than they would have to pay in wages.'

'That's not fair!' cried Kate, unable to keep quiet. 'You're taking the bread from the people's mouths.'

He turned to look at her and although his expression was mild, she could see the anger in his eyes. Even then, he did not speak to her directly. 'Tell the poacher's daughter,' he said, addressing Andrew, 'that if she insists on coming down to breakfast instead of having it in her room as any civilised woman would, she must refrain from speaking unless spoken to.'

'You are inhuman,' Kate stormed. 'Sitting there, stuffing your-self while your own people go hungry.'

'Andrew,' he said coolly. 'Will you please escort your stepsister back to her room.'

Andrew rose at once and went to pull out her chair. 'Come, Kate,' he said softly. 'Do as he says.'

She flounced from the room in anger, her chin in the air, her ringlets bouncing, and Andrew, following, chuckled. 'It's all very well for you to laugh,' she rounded on him. 'You are nearly as bad. And I will not go to my room.'

'Very well, we'll go to the morning room.' He took her arm to guide her. 'But Kate, my dear, you really must learn to curb your tongue. Goading Uncle John does no good at all.'

She sat in a chair near the window where a weak winter sun shone through the glass and picked out the pinks and blues of the carpet, but she hardly noticed where she was; her mind was with the villagers. The so-called peaceful march on the Hall had all the makings of a new riot and needed only a tiny spark to ignite it. 'Andrew, we must do something.'

'What do you suggest?' he asked mildly.

'I don't know. We can't just sit here and let it happen.'

'I don't intend to.' He stretched his long legs and stood up. 'I am going to London . . .'

'London?' she queried. 'You can't do that. We need you here.'

'Do you?' he queried, a faint smile on his face. 'Do *you* need me?'

'You know I do.'

'If you were to say you would marry me, then I would not go.'

'That's not fair! You know how I feel about that.'

'Yes. I am second best to a man you may never see again.'

'I shall see him again,' she said. 'One day. But you are changing the subject. We were talking about the villagers.'

He heaved a melodramatic sigh and bent to kiss the top of her head. 'I'll only be gone a few days. I'll be back long before the march. And then perhaps we can change their minds about it. Look after Mother and try to avoid upsetting Uncle John while I'm gone, will you?'

Then he was gone, leaving her to stamp her foot in frustration. He really was infuriating, but she had become very fond of him and would do as he asked, trying to be patient until his return.

She relied on him so heavily and missed him so much when he was not with her, she began to wonder if, after all, she might be falling a little in love with him. If she could not have Matthew, should she accept second best? She did not doubt they could be happy together. And that was what marriage was about, wasn't it?

The rotting old ship stank. It stank of wet wood and mildewed canvas, of putrid food and unwashed bodies, a great many unwashed bodies. The masts had gone and in their place were ramshackle wooden huts and strung between them were washing lines displaying the ragged remains of clothes which had been dipped into sea water in an effort to clean them. There were men about, some shuffling round and round the perimeter of the ship, hollow-eyed, silent, hopeless men, speaking in monosyllables or not speaking at all. Others were huddled round fires they had lit on the deck and were cooking scraps over them; the flames provided the only colour in the darkness. Still more sat in groups, playing cards. They had few guards; they were not considered necessary. Anyone trying to escape had to dive into the sea and swim for it, and most were too weak to attempt it. Those that did were easily picked off by one or two men with muskets. Land prisons were mansions compared to this and the prospect of hard labour in the colonies was something to be welcomed if you had the stamina to withstand the voyage, but the longer they had to wait for a ship the weaker they became. The majority of those who had been sentenced to the penal colonies for their part in the uprisings of the years before had long since left their native shores, and with the new prisons being built, transportation was an option which was being exercised less often. Consequently it took longer for a full shipload to be gathered together. Most of the men lived for the day when they would set sail; if they were moving, the air would be fresher.

Matthew had tried to talk to his fellow prisoners, tried to interest them in the future, to put some pride and self-respect back into them, but it was hard work and even he was becoming inured to life on board and had lost track of time. How long had he been on this hulk waiting to go? Had Christmas come and gone? If it had, there had been no one to mark its passing.

He thought often of Kate. Carrington must have found her by now. He hoped she was happy in her new life. Would they marry, she and Andrew Carrington? It hurt him to think of them in each other's arms, but what else could he have done? If he could have been sure of a decent life in Australia, he might have been tempted to ask her to wait and join him there; if she had been plain Kate Brough and not Catherine Wetherby; if the verdict of the trial had been different ... Oh, there were too many ifs and he ought to put her from his mind.

He walked slowly round the deck, the only exercise he was allowed before being incarcerated below for the night, where the stench was even worse. The river was inky black, but here and there a wave lapped against a piece of driftwood and for a moment shone silver, before subsiding into an oily calm again. He could just make out the shore and the pin prick lights of a few buildings. Against one of these he saw a boat pulling out into mid-stream towards the hulk and then it was in deep shadow again and he lost it. He moved to the rail, showing no sign of haste.

'Boat ahoy!' The watch had spotted it too. 'Identify yourself.'

'Ship ahoy!' came the answer. 'Ration boat.'

'At this time of night? You should be 'ere in daylight.'

The boat was right alongside now, bobbing just below where Matthew stood. There were two men in it, sitting either side of a large tarpaulin which took up most of the remaining space. One of them stood up. 'Joe's been taken sick of the fever, couldn't come. Sent us in his stead.'

Two guards moved to stand close to Matthew and peered over the side. 'Fever, you say?'

'Aye.'

'I'll send down the rope, but you keep yer distance.'

'We ain't got no fever.'

'No, nor ain't we and we don't aim to get it.' One of the guards turned to Matthew. 'You, help them inboard with the stuff and don't you try any tricks. I'll be aiming this here musket straight at you.'

Matthew moved slowly forward and hauled on the bundle the man had attached to the rope. As soon as it was on deck, the guards moved forward to inspect it. They were soon engrossed in its contents for, instead of rotting potatoes, wilting cabbage and mouldy bread and flour which they had been expecting, it contained meat and pasties, fruit pies and several bottles of brandy. 'What's this 'ere?' they demanded, leaning over the side.

'Food. Ain't it right? Ol' Joe never said what we was to bring, 'e were too sick. There's more.'

The two guards grinned in the darkness and shouted down. 'Send it up then.' They dragged the food to the superstructure which had once been the bridge and which was now their home, leaving Matthew to haul in the next bundle. It was followed by a pair of hands, then a head and shoulders and then by the whole man who hopped lightly to the deck. 'God what a stench!'

'Great Jehosophat! Carrington!'

'What an extraordinary stroke of luck!' Andrew said, chuckling. 'I thought I might have a job locating you and here you are.'

'What do you want me for?'

'No time to tell you now. Get down into the boat. I'll haul the rest of the rations up. Be ready to row for your life when I give the word.'

'What are you going to do?'

'I think these poor fellows deserve a treat, don't you?' He indicated the prisoners who had gathered round them. He turned and pulled the next bundle forward and opened it to reveal more good wholesome food. 'There's a barrel on its way,' he told them, jerking his head towards the rail. Some rushed to the side to pull it in, others crowded round the food, stuffing it inside their shirts before it could be taken from them. Matthew, in the crush, slipped over the side and down the rope, but he was weak from poor food and lack of exercise and he felt his arms being pulled out of their sockets as he tried to control his descent. He could hear the guards now, running across the deck and shouting at the prisoners to stand back from the side. 'Get back! Get back!' And to Andrew. 'Over the side with you, if you don't want to sample our hospitality yourself.'

Andrew appeared against the skyline above Matthew as he scrambled over the side and grabbed the line. Matthew just managed to reach the boat and duck out of sight beneath the tarpaulin as a guard's head appeared over the rail. 'Tell Joe we'll 'ave more of the same next time 'e makes a delivery.' And he laughed and waved one of the brandy bottles above his head.

'Row, man, row!' Andrew spoke to his accomplice as he dropped into the boat and picked up the second set of oars.

They were halfway to the shore when one of the guards realised that the man they had detailed to help haul in the supplies had disappeared. They heard shouts ordering them to return and two or three musket shots spattered the water around them, but by the time the men had reloaded, the little boat was out of range.

Matthew emerged from his hiding place, sat himself on the thwarts beside Andrew and took one of the oars. 'Where are we going?'

'Downstream a bit. There's horses waiting at a spot on the marshes.' He nodded towards the other man, who had not spoken. 'That's Bertie Cotton.'

'I'm obliged,' Matthew said, acknowledging him.

'Bertie's brother was sent to Australia last year and he's going to use the money to buy a passage out to join him. He reckons it'll be easier to set him free and make a new life out there, than wait about in England for his return.'

'That's probably true,' Matthew said, realising Andrew did not want to talk about his reasons for the rescue, nor his plans in front of the man. 'Australia is a vast country and I believe it's possible to make good out there, if you're prepared to work.'

'We'll work,' Bertie said. 'And this gen'leman 'ave given us the start we need.'

Matthew cocked an eyebrow at Andrew wondering just how much he had given the man to help him; he would not have done it for coppers. But why had he done it all? Had something happened? To Kate? He pulled on the oars with all the strength he had left and soon they glided into a little marshy cove surrounded by reeds. Matthew jumped out, wading the last few yards to the shore, while Andrew handed Bertie a small bag which chinked a little. Then he followed Matthew and the boat pulled away again and was soon lost in the darkness.

'Come on,' Andrew said, pushing his way through the reeds and onto a rough path. 'There's a derelict cottage along here. It was once used by smugglers, I believe.'

'They'll be searching for me,' Matthew said, panting to keep up with his rescuer. 'And they'll be looking for my accomplice. I hope you've a good alibi.'

'Why should I need an alibi?' Andrew laughed. 'I am a Haddow of Haddow Hall, your sworn enemy.'

'Then I am thankful for my enemies,' Matthew said. 'But you haven't told me why you did it.'

'For Kate.'

'Kate?'

'Yes.' He didn't want to explain until they were safely away. 'Come on.'

A tiny building with its thatch falling off loomed out of the darkness and Andrew pushed open the door and led the way inside. Groping about he found a lantern and flints and set about lighting it. Then he turned to face Matthew. 'God, man, you look like a tramp and you stink to heaven. There's a jug of water and a bowl on the table, and a change of clothes in that bag.' He indicated a canvas bag on the floor behind the door. 'Be quick with your ablutions. We must get away from the coast as soon as maybe.'

'For Kate? What do you mean, for Kate?' Matthew asked, doing as he was told and stripping off his filthy rags. 'Didn't you find her?'

'Oh, I found her, just as you said I would, outside Wisbech gaol, but nothing else has worked out according to plan.'

'Why not?'

'Because Kate is Kate and not Catherine Wetherby.'

Matthew was astounded but suddenly joyful. 'You mean she isn't your stepmother's daughter, after all?'

'Oh, she's Catherine Wetherby by birth, there's no doubt of that. Even Sir John acknowledges it. But she was too long with the old poacher. She is finding it very difficult learning to be a lady, and the villagers have given her the cold shoulder which is distressing her.' He watched as Matthew drew on the trousers and clean shirt he had left there earlier in the day. 'I have promised to take her away, where she can just be herself but ...' He shrugged his shoulders.

'You've married her?'

'Not yet. I have yet to convince her it's a good idea.'

'You want me to convince her? That's going it a bit too brown, Carrington. I can't plead your cause and you know it.'

'You don't need to sound so cheerful about it.'

Matthew laughed. 'So, what now? Are you going to take me back to the hulk and say it was all a mistake?'

'Don't be an ass.'

'What then?' He was standing fully dressed except for his boots. Andrew fetched a pair from the hearth and stood them down in front of him.

'Daniel tells me they ought to fit, they are yours.'

'Daniel? He's in on this madcap scheme?'

'I consulted him so that he could back up the story of the prodigal brother returning. The search is on for Matthew Tolley, not Captain Thorsborough. And the sooner we get to town the sooner you can be yourself.'

'I promised not to implicate my family.'

'Daniel is your brother, Matthew, your kin, and he can help you more than anyone else.'

'But I never asked for help from him or you. In fact, I remember most distinctly telling you to leave me alone and to get on with your own life. And to look after Kate.'

'Seems she has other ideas. The Middleacre villagers are threatening more disturbances and Kate won't leave with me until she knows peace has been restored. She has this bee in her bonnet that you are the only one who can calm them down.'

'Oh.' He felt deflated. Just for a moment he had hoped that Kate had said she could not live without him, that it was for herself she wanted him back. 'But I'll be arrested again as soon as I put in an appearance.'

'We can hide you.'

'You can't hide me for ever. I'm a wanted man and will be to the end of my days if I stay in England. I can't do that, it wouldn't be fair to Daniel and Amy, or to Kate.'

'Do you want to see her again, or don't you?'

'Of course I do. It wasn't the easiest thing I have ever done, turning my back on her, you know.' It was madness, sheer folly. He was an escaped convict, a wanted man, a fugitive. How could he help anyone, least of all Kate? But the thought of seeing her again blinded him to the risks. Would she have changed? Was the lady any more or less desirable than the poacher's daughter?

'Then let's be off.' He picked up the bundle of clothes Matthew had taken off and went outside with them.

Matthew followed and watched as he flung the bundle as far as he could out across the marshes, where it would sink. Then he crossed the yard to an old shed and led out a couple of horses. 'They're not the fleetest of foot, but they'll carry us,' he said, handing the reins of one over to Matthew. Together they mounted and set off, walking the horses carefully along the rutted track.

They had not been going long when they heard a boat on the water to their left and then sounds of oars being shipped, then running feet and shouts of command. 'Down!' Andrew yelled, pulling the horse off the road and crouching in the tall reeds with it, half submerged by freezing water. Matthew tumbled in beside him. They watched the patrol run past them, muskets at the ready as they made for the cottage.

'Did you leave anything behind?' Andrew whispered.

'No, but they'll know someone has used the place.' There would be footmarks in the dust of the floor and the lantern would still be warm.

'Let's go!'

They returned to the path, hauled themselves into the saddle and set off at a canter, which was as fast as they dare go, considering the terrain and the state of the track. The searchers heard the horses and rushed after them, shouting for them to stop. A couple of shots hit the road behind them. Darkness notwithstanding, they put the horses to a gallop. Another shot echoed behind them and Andrew felt a hot sensation in his arm. 'Dammit, I've been hit,' he said.

Matthew pulled up and looked back. 'Can you keep going?'

'Yes. Don't stop.'

Matthew galloped on, listening for Andrew's horse behind him. At first it came, but then there were more shots and it neighed in terror as it was hit in the rump, going down and taking Andrew with it. Matthew wheeled about and rode back. Andrew was scrambling to his feet, holding his arm with his other hand. Their pursuers were gaining on them.

'Leave me.'

'I'll do no such thing. Get up behind.' He held out his hand. Andrew hesitated only a second before pulling his pistol from his belt and shooting the horse, then he grasped Matthew's hand in his own uninjured one and hauled himself up. Even before he had settled himself astride the horse, they were galloping away again.

Several minutes later, Matthew pulled up. 'I think we've lost them and we'd best walk the horse, if we don't want him dead too.' He slid off its back and led it forward, leaving Andrew to hitch himself forward onto the saddle. He felt weak and dizzy from loss of blood, but they couldn't stop; they were not yet safe and, besides, there was no habitation anywhere where they might ask for help.

Half an hour passed in silence. Matthew was busy discarding one plan after another. It was all very well for Andrew to set him free and he was certainly grateful for it, but it was only the beginning. What of all the other days and nights to come? Where would he be safe? Not in Middleacre, that was certain. Nor at Garforth Manor; it would need only one person who had known him as Matthew Tolley to set the cat among the pigeons. And what of Kate? He had given her up for her own sake. Were his reasons not just as valid now as ever they were? The fact that she apparently did not want to marry Andrew did not necessarily mean she would, or should, share the life of a fugitive.

He swivelled round to look at his passenger. Andrew had grasped a handful of his coat and was clinging on determinedly; his other arm hung by his side, bloodied and useless. 'Can you hang on?'

'Yes. Keep going.'

A few minutes later they joined a made-up road and as dawn came up behind them entered a small town and Matthew pulled up at an inn.

The innkeeper, who was standing in his doorway, looked them up and down, as Andrew all but fell from the horse's back. Two men coming in off the marshes at this ungodly hour was suspicious enough, but when one of them was obviously wounded it was doubly inauspicious. They could be revenue men or escaped convicts, or part of a press gang, all equally unwelcome, but they were too well-dressed and well-mounted to be any of those.

'Duck-hunting,' Matthew said, helping Andrew into the parlour. 'I am afraid I accidentally shot my friend. Can you do something for him?'

The man called to his wife, who came and sat Andrew in a chair by the table and ripped away his sleeve. 'It's only a flesh wound,' she said. 'I'll put some salve on it and bind it up and he'll be as good as new in no time.'

'Did you shoot his horse as well?' the innkeeper asked, watching his wife and wondering what the outcome of this day's work would be. Blame or praise? A reward perhaps?

'What?' queried Matthew, then laughed. 'I'm afraid in my anxiety to get my friend some help I galloped it too hard. It stumbled in a hole in the road and broke its leg. I had to shoot it.'

'A chapter of accidents.' The innkeeper made no effort to hide the fact that he didn't believe a word of it. 'You'll be hungry.'

'Starving,' Matthew said, which was nothing but the truth. 'But

I need to get my friend to a doctor, so if you'll be good enough to pack something, we can eat in the saddle.'

As soon as Andrew was bandaged and the pain dulled with a little laudanum, they set off again. They rode double in silence, keeping a careful watch for pursuers or anyone on the road viewing them with suspicion.

'I'll take you to a doctor as soon as we reach town,' Matthew said, after a long silence.

'Are you mad? We'll be arrested as soon as we put our heads round the door.'

'But your arm needs seeing to properly.'

'Let me worry about that.' He paused to grip Matthew tighter about the waist. 'I'll take the stage back to Middleacre. You go to your brother's town house and follow in a day or two when the heat has died down.'

'It'll never die down, you know that. I have to think of the future and make some plans.'

'And Kate? Will you include her in your plans?'

'Will she want that?'

'I don't know. You must ask her yourself.' He had set the man free because until the ghost of Matthew was laid, Kate would never settle down. It was the biggest gamble of his life and one he had little hope of winning. 'She told me she wished she could see you just once more before you leave and as making her happy is the one aim I have in life, I have to try and grant her wish.'

'Mine too,' Matthew murmured, but he doubted the other man had heard him. And they were not out of the wood yet.

On the day before the planned demonstration, when Andrew had still not returned, one of Sir John's newly arrived guests complained of being held up by a herd of cattle filling the road into the village. 'Ought not to be allowed on the public highway,' he said, ignoring the fact that half the drove roads no longer existed. 'We had to sit and wait twenty minutes surrounded by stinking animals and three equally smelly men.'

Bates! It was Bates, Kate was sure of it, and he would be staying in the drovers' hut. He might be able to talk the villagers out of that march.

Hiding her impatience, she managed to spend the rest of the day in her mother's company being the dutiful daughter, endured a long-drawn-out dinner which began at five and ended at eight, and then, without Andrew to lighten the atmosphere, sat in resignation to listen to Lady Haddow's endless grumbling. It was gone nine o'clock before she dare plead tiredness and retire to her room. But going to bed was the last thing on her mind. She changed into the least cumbersome of her new gowns, found an old sturdy pair of shoes abandoned in a cupboard, took down Matthew's black cloak and crept out of the house by the back stairs.

It was a cold, windy night and as she hurried across the park and into the wood she was reminded of the night Josiah had been caught in the mantrap. She was glad she knew the path well and was careful not to stray from its centre.

The clouds parted as she reached the meadow where the herd was gathered and moonlight shone on hundreds of dark backs, here and there picking up the gleam of horn or eye. She could hear their shuffling, smell their animal warmth and it took her back just a few short months to the time she had spent with the herd. The three drovers were sitting by the fire outside the hut, the empty tin plates from their last meal on the ground beside them, pots of ale in their hands. They turned as she approached, petticoats rustling.

'It's me. Kate Brough,' she said, as Tom and Rob scrambled to their feet.

'Is that what you call yourself still?' Bates asked without rising.

'It's how I think of myself, though my mother calls me Catherine.'

'What are you doing out at this time o' night? And all alone too.'

Kate squatted down to be on his level; his pointed discourtesy was lost on her. 'I want to talk to you.'

'What can you possibly hev to say to us? Smelly, we are, and dirty, fit only to live with cattle. Go back home to your new family. What would they say if they knew you were out talking to peasantry like us?' He tamped down the tobacco in his pipe with a grubby forefinger, as if the conversation had ended.

'They won't know I've even been out.' She looked round at the others. 'Tell me all your news. Are you well? Is business good? Have you seen Mr and Mrs Fyne?'

'We're well as ever,' Rob said, laughing at her eagerness. 'And so were the Fynes when we saw them last.'

'Are you going to Norwich next?'

'Mayhap.' Bates said.

'I wish I were going with you. I wish it was like it was . . .'

'You can't put the clock back, Kate.'

'I know, but the villagers are trying to. Did you know they are planning to march on the Hall tomorrow?'

'Are they now? What's it got to do with me?'

'You were Matthew's right hand man. You always helped him, didn't you?'

He laughed. 'Just cos I did him a favour and fetched you out of that prison van . . .'

'It was a very big favour. And I know you did other things. You told him where there was trouble brewing in places you passed through so that he could do something about it.'

'I hope you hin't bin spreadin' such rumours.'

'As if I would! But the villagers need a leader, someone like Matthew . . .'

'He's been sent to the colonies, you know that full well.'

'Has he gone? He's not still in London?'

He laughed and gulped beer from his pot. 'Where did you hear that?'

'At the Hall. Sir John was taunting me with it.'

'That's all it was, taunting. You shouldn't let him rile you.'

'Oh.' She paused, her disappointment plainly showing. 'I thought perhaps he might have been set free. I thought he might come . . .'

Bates's voice softened and he put out a rough brown hand and laid it in her arm. 'Kate, put him from your mind. Go back home. ''Tain't fittin' for a lady to sit on the ground in the middle of a herd of beef, now is it?'

She managed something approaching a smile. 'I'm no lady and never will be. I've tried. For my mother's sake I have truly tried, but I can't be what she wants me to be. Pa didn't foresee that, did he?'

'No. Nor he didn't foretell the uprisings and Sir John marrying ag'in and the cap'n coming, and the barn bein' set on fire. Nor you bein' so mixed up with it all.'

'I'm still mixed up with it.'

'No, you in't. Not any more. An' you must make the best of what you've got, same as we all have to. You'm luckier than most.'

She supposed he was right, but how difficult it was. 'But what about the villagers? Sir John has said they will all lose their jobs if they march and for many that will mean their homes too. They will be playing right into his hands. We can't let it happen. Can't you talk to them? They'd listen to you. They won't take any notice of me.'

He laughed suddenly. 'Are you surprised?'

'No, I suppose not.'

'Go home and leave the villagers to solve their own problems, young lady.'

Reluctantly, she scrambled to her feet. 'Very well, I shall go back, but if you have any influence with the Middleacre men, then I suggest you use it to save them from themselves.'

She set off for the Hall feeling very dejected. She could not call it home; it would never be that. Halfway across the meadow she saw a tall figure striding towards her and for one heart-stopping moment she thought it was Matthew, simply because she had been thinking and talking of him, but as he came nearer she realised it was Andrew.

'I thought you were in London,' she said as they came within speaking distance and then noticing that his coat sleeve hung empty. 'What have you done to your arm?'

He lifted the heavily bandaged arm from inside his coat. 'A slight accident when I was cleaning my gun. Nothing to worry about. What are you doing out so late and unaccompanied too? Mama will not be best pleased.'

'I came to see Bates.'

'The drover? What did you want to see him about?'

'To ask him to use his influence with the villagers to stop them causing more trouble.'

'And will he?'

'I don't know. I don't know if he can.'

'Why are you so worried about them?'

'They are my friends,' she said simply. It didn't make the slightest difference that they had scorned her; it was simply that they did not understand.

'Kate,' he said softly. 'Can you not accept your place is beside me now? Marry me, my darling, and I will devote my life to making you happy. You'll learn to forget the old life, the poverty, the unhappiness.'

'I don't want to forget,' she retorted. 'Memories are all I have.'

'Then I will endure the memories if you will only say yes.'

If she had not gone to see Bates, if seeing him had not reminded her of all Matthew had done for her and the risks he had taken to set her free, she might have agreed. If she had been the sort of girl who could accept second best, she would certainly have said yes because he was a fine man, a loving, caring man. He merited the very best; he deserved a wife that adored him and nothing less was good enough for him. 'Andrew, I can't do it to you. I would make you miserable.'

'Let me be the judge of that.'

'Please Andrew, don't make it difficult for me, don't make it so we can't even be friends. If I can't marry Matthew, then I will not marry at all.'

He sighed. 'I was afraid you'd say that.'

They emerged from the trees and could see the great house across the park. Every window was ablaze with light, shining out over the gardens, eclipsing the moonlight.

'Something's happening,' he said, hurrying forward.

Kate followed him through the front door and into the hall, where several servants bustled to and fro carrying bedlinen and trays of crockery. A nurse pushed past them and went upstairs, followed by the weeping Annette. Kate and Andrew looked at each other and hurried up to Felicity's sitting room.

'Catherine, where have you been?' she demanded. 'You said you were going to bed early. I went to see if you needed anything and you had gone. You must not go off like that without a word to anyone and all alone too, you really must not. Anything could have happened to you.'

'I'm sorry, Mama, I had a headache, I thought a little fresh air would help.' She looked at Andrew, defying him to contradict her.

'Kate did not go beyond the park, Mother,' Andrew said. 'And I soon found her.'

'We'll say no more about it then,' Felicity said. 'But do try and be a little more considerate in future.' She paused as sounds of people hurrying along the corridor outside the room intruded. 'You know Laura has started her baby?'

'So it seems,' Andrew put in. 'There are people dashing up and down stairs and getting in each other's way. You'd think there were a dozen babies about to be born instead of just one.'

'I believe things are not going smoothly.'

'Where is Sir John?' Kate asked, moving over to the window

and looking out across the park to the woods. Out there Bates and his men were sleeping; down in the village the labourers slumbered, and somewhere, over the horizon there was the ocean and Matthew. She could not imagine it.

'He is in his room,' her mother said. 'Sit down, both of you, we'll have a glass of wine and amuse ourselves for an hour or two. I don't suppose anyone wants to sleep.' She paused and inclined her head to listen. 'There! I can hear someone else. I'm going to ask how things are.' She stood up and went to the door, almost colliding with a white-aproned nurse carrying a bundle wrapped up in a sheet. 'Has the child been born? Is that it?'

Before the astonished nurse could prevent it, Felicity had taken the bundle and begun feverishly undoing it. 'Don't you know better than to wrap the poor little thing up like that? You'll suffocate ...' She stopped speaking, but her mouth remained open. The bundle had no life; if it had ever breathed independently, it did so no more. The angry nurse snatched it back and continued down the corridor, while Andrew put his arm round Felicity to steady her.

'I thought ... I thought it was Catherine,' she whispered, sagging in his arms. 'It took me back to the dark days ...'

'I know, Mother, I know,' he said softly. 'But Kate is here beside you, a full grown woman, a baby no longer.' He turned to Kate, who was looking worried and perplexed. 'Mother has never been able to look at a dead child without thinking of her lost daughter,' he explained. 'It was seeing the still-born baby of one of Father's employees soon after you were lost that triggered off her confusion of mind.'

Kate took her mother's hand and leaned forward to kiss her. 'I am here now, Mama.'

Sir John came from his room and stood looking at the little group, then, with a snort of derision, he turned on his heel and marched to his wife's chamber.

'Well?' he demanded of the senior physician who was washing his hands in a bowl at the table. The water was red and blood was spattered all down the long white apron he wore. 'Well? Why did no one come to fetch me?'

'I was coming,' the doctor said wearily, 'Just as soon as I had cleaned up. The child did not live. It was a boy.'

'What? You have let my son die?'

'It was stillborn.'

'Why?' His face was purple. 'You have been negligent. You said there would be no difficulties, you told me my wife was strong and would have no trouble . . .'

'I cannot see the unforeseeable. It is God's will.'

'God's will!' shouted Sir John. 'God's will I should be deprived of an heir? God's will I should marry twice and have no progeny?' He stopped suddenly. 'Is my wife well?'

'She will recover, but she is extremely fatigued. She will need rest and a very careful diet.'

'Yes, yes, of course,' he said impatiently. 'She will have everything she needs. But in time she will have more children?'

'I think not.' The doctor finished drying his hands and left the room, followed by his assistant and the second of the nurses. For the first time Sir John looked at his wife, who was pale and exhausted, but his expression did not soften. Without a word, he turned and left the room.

Fate had decreed he would never have a son. He had not married well for all Laura's good looks and money; he should have picked a sturdy peasant girl to bear his child, someone like that little wretch, the poacher's daughter, who still haunted his thoughts. It was a pity she had turned out to be his own niece, for she was a spirited young thing with the body of a goddess. Even now, he could not trust himself near her.

He went down to the library, where he poured himself a glass of brandy and sat in an armchair to drink it. He swallowed it almost at a gulp and got up to fetch another. He took a step towards the chair with his refilled glass, changed his mind and went back for the decanter. An hour later, very much the worse for drink, he discovered the decanter was empty and rose unsteadily to ring for another. Instead he stumbled over to the window and stood looking out across the park.

The moon was full, although there were a few clouds, and the wind was whipping through the topmost branches of the big trees. It was a poacher's night. They would be out in force in his woods, getting rich on his game.

'I'll catch me a poacher,' he said thickly, weaving from window to door, knocking himself against the furniture as he went. He crossed the hall and went into the gunroom. Moonlight streamed through the window and he needed no light to reach down his gun

and find powder and shot. Then he left the house by the front
door, leaving it wide open behind him.

Kate slept late. No one came to wake her with hot water as they
had done each morning since her arrival, but remembering what
had happened, she was hardly surprised. After such a disturbed
night, it was no wonder everyone had overslept. She sat up,
stretched like a supple cat, then padded across to the window to
draw the curtains.

The day was bright and frosty, exactly as it had been a year
before and the church bells were ringing for morning service; they
carried clearly on the cold air. She opened the window and leaned
out. Above the sound of the bells she could hear shouting and
cheering, and then a drum, beating out the rhythm of a march.
The rumours were true; it was the anniversary of Sir John's
wedding and the villagers were intent on their demonstration. She
washed and dressed hurriedly, then, snatching up a shawl, raced
down the stairs and out of the front door, hardly noticing that the
house was unusually quiet.

She was breathless when she reached the village green where the
villagers were gathered, forming themselves into ragged lines, carrying banners proclaiming, 'Middleacre Combination of Farmworkers', 'Long Live Captain Swing', 'Down with all Landowners'.

She ran to the head of the column where Watson stood, with
Charlie Barber and Betty hand in hand beside him. 'Please don't
do this. Sir John will only punish you.'

'Outa the way, m'lady,' Jack said with heavy emphasis on the
title, as he pushed her to one side. 'You hen't no business here.' He
turned to the villagers crowding behind him. 'Ready? Then let's
march!'

The handful of amateur bandsmen began a ragged marching
song and they moved off, singing and cheering. She ran alongside,
dodging between them. 'The squire's baby was born last night,' she
told them. 'It was dead. You can't march to the Hall now. Have
some pity for Lady Haddow.'

'I ha' lost two little'ns,' Nat Green said. 'And nobody give a
thought to my missus. She wor out in the fields next day.'

Kate stopped and watched helplessly as they marched past her
and round the bend in the lane towards the Hall. But she couldn't
give up. She ran across a field with ice crackling beneath her feet,

over the bridge which spanned the dyke which surrounded it, along the bank of the river where icicles hung from the willows, through a small spinney to the perimeter wall of the estate. Her lungs were near to bursting but she stumbled on, wishing the skirt of her gown were less full and her shoes less flimsy, until she came to a spot where subsidence of the peaty bed on which it had been built had made a section of the wall collapse. She clambered over the rubble into the grounds and ran on, arriving at the main gates only a minute ahead of the column. The gates were rarely shut and they were heavy and stiff, but at last she managed to move them.

'Leave them gates be!' shouted Green, when he saw what she was trying to do. 'We're a-comin' through!'

'I won't! If the squire sees you he will make sure you all lose your jobs, he said so . . .' She was talking to them through the bars now and they were banging on them with the implements they carried, making a deafening noise.

'We're only a-goon to talk to 'im peaceable,' Chuckley said. 'We hatta remind 'im he in't done narth'n about our wages. He do have a new family, mebbe that'll mek him more reasonable.'

Charlie, younger and more agile than many of them, clambered on the shoulders of another and scrambled over the top of the gates, dropping lightly down beside her.

'Charlie, don't do this,' she pleaded. 'For everyone's sake. Think of your mother, think of Betty . . .'

He turned to look at her and eyes that had once seen her as one of the oppressed, someone to be adored for her courage and tenacity, saw her now as a betrayer, a turncoat. 'It in't narthin' to do with you any more, Kate. Go back where you belong.' He pushed her aside and opened the gates. The men swarmed in, regrouped and then set off along the estate road towards the house. Defeated, Kate sank to the ground and watched them go, knowing Fiddy and all the estate workers were waiting for them and the chances of it remaining a peaceful demonstration were nil.

A minute later a sound made her look up again. The villagers were returning, but they were not singing and cheering as before; their banners had been discarded and they were running pell-mell before a herd of stampeding cattle. Some of the men ran across the grass, making for the trees, but most headed for the gates. Charlie, almost last, was pulling Betty along by the hand and the girl was sobbing.

Kate scrambled to her feet and cowered behind the half-open gates as they passed her and made for the road into the village. The leading animals, hooves thundering, were almost on her when she realised she had it in her power to stop them. Without thinking of the consequences, she pushed one gate shut and then the other, leaving the herd on the inside and Charlie and Betty and most of the villagers, on the other. But she was trapped.

She stood with her back to the closed gates and shut her eyes as the herd bore down on her. They could not stop and those coming from behind careered into those in front as they tried to turn, clambering over each other's backs, snorting and bellowing. She screamed as she was tossed over their heads and then felt herself sliding down between them, among the stampeding hooves. She heard someone shouting her name as a merciful darkness enclosed her.

Chapter Twenty

'She's alive, thank the good Lord.' Andrew's voice seemed to be coming from a great distance.

Kate, on the edge of consciousness, felt someone feeling along her legs, up over her body and arms to her shoulders and neck. Then a second voice, saying, 'And no bones broken either, which is a miracle.'

'I'll fetch a carriage to take her back to the house.'

'No, I'll carry her.'

Then she was being lifted and carried by someone with broad shoulders and strong arms and a long firm stride. She opened her eyes and shut them again quickly. She must be dreaming; it couldn't be. She ventured another look and his face came slowly into focus. His hair was very long and he sported a thick dark beard, but it was Matthew just the same. She reached up and linked her arms round his neck clinging to him. 'Matthew! Oh, Matthew!'

Now she could hear other sounds, bellowing, snorting, stamping hooves and, above it all, the strident voices of Bates and Rob and young Tom as they rounded up the herd, and everything came back to her. 'You mustn't go to the house,' she murmured. 'It's not safe. Sir John . . .'

She heard him chuckle, then felt his lips brush her cheek, like the touch of a butterfly, before she drifted into unconsciousness again.

Andrew led the way through the stableyard to the kitchen door and pushed it open so that Matthew could enter with his burden. Mrs Bunny was alone in the kitchen.

'Captain Tolley! And Kate! What has happened?'

'There's been an accident,' Andrew said. 'Show the Captain up to Kate's room by the back stairs, will you? Help him to look after her.'

'Of course, sir.'

'There's no need for anyone else to know he is here.'

'I understand.' She opened the door to the passage and made sure no one was about before beckoning Matthew to follow her. 'What happened? Is she badly hurt? Poor child, she has had such a difficult time of it. Have you come to stay?'

Andrew heard her string of whispered questions and Matthew's gruff responses fading as they disappeared up the back stairs then, with a heavy heart, he turned in the opposite direction and went to search out his stepmother.

She was sitting in her room, looking out across the park, where Bates was busy rounding up the cattle. She held her handkerchief screwed up in her hand and there was evidence of tears on her cheeks. 'She's run off again, Andrew,' she said as soon as she saw him.

'No, she hasn't. She's in her room.'

'She wasn't there a minute ago. I've looked everywhere for her. She is like a wild thing.'

'A bird, mother, a beautiful bird who can't live in a cage.'

'She doesn't live in a cage.'

'I expect it feels like it to her.'

'Why? She has much more freedom than ever I did as a child.'

'Yes, but you must not forget she is used to being out of doors, being able to go where she pleases, running barefoot with the wind in her hair.'

'What am I to do, Andrew?' And the tears began to flow afresh. 'It has not been anything like I had hoped. Catherine is my daughter, but she does not behave in any way as I expected. Oh, she tries, I know she does, and that makes it worse.'

'Perhaps you are too close. Perhaps if she were to marry ...'

'You? Oh, I would not mind that ...'

'Not me, Mother.' He gave a wry smile. 'I love Kate dearly, but I cannot hold her. There is only one man for her.'

'This man Tolley. Isn't that his name?'

'Yes.'

'But he has been transported. And he is not at all suitable, you said so yourself.'

'Oh, he is eminently suitable, Mother. He is brother to a peer and though he is not wealthy, he is certainly not impoverished. It was my jealousy speaking. And he has not been transported. He is here, in this house.'

'Good heavens! How did that come about?'

'I brought him to her.'

'You mean they are alone together? How could you encourage such indelicate conduct Andrew? I must go to her at once.'

Andrew, putting out a hand to detain her, laughed, but it was a hollow sound. 'Forget the conventions for a moment, Mother, I fancy you would be too late anyway. Listen to what I have to say, please.'

She sank back into her chair, her face white and drawn and listened as he told her about the villagers' grievances as told to him by Kate herself. 'She can be very persuasive,' he said with a wry smile. 'She won me over in more ways than one.' He went on to describe Matthew's fight for the villagers and his arrest and trial. He told her of the injustice of it, of Kate's loyalty to the people of the village and to Matthew, all of which she had known to some extent, but not in the fine detail he was telling her now, trying to make her understand. 'You must set her free, Mother, just as I have had to do.'

'But I do not want to part with her again.'

'It won't be like it was before, will it? She won't be lost, she will simply be an ordinary dutiful daughter who has married and set up home with her husband. Every mother has to accept that sooner or later, if her daughter is not to become an old maid. You don't want that for Kate, do you?'

'No, of course not, but I had hoped to have more time.'

'So did I,' he said. 'But it seems it is not to be granted to us.'

'And I must accept this?'

'You could try persuasion; you could pull at her heart strings, appeal to her conscience and I expect she would stay, but it would be a hollow victory. You would have her physical presence, but not her heart.' He had learned that sad truth himself and he had to make her see it too. 'You must let her go in order to keep her. You can understand that, can't you?'

'Yes, I suppose so,' she said, still reluctant. Kate would never become the daughter she had longed for because that daughter did not exist. Years ago she had lost a baby, a child called Catherine, but Kate was not Catherine, not the person Catherine would have been if she had never left her side. She was still her daughter, but a different one, one she did not know, one she was very unsure of; not even to herself would she have used the word disappointed.

Perhaps they did need a little time apart to adjust, to come to a true appreciation of each other. 'But is the man not wanted by the law?'

'He is.'

'Then are we not taking a dreadful risk, having him in the house?'

'It's the safest place. Besides, Kate was hurt by the stampeding cattle and he carried her home.'

'Hurt?' Felicity sprang to her feet. 'Why didn't you tell me straight away?'

'It's all right; it's only a few bruises. And Mrs Bunny is looking after her.'

'But I must go to her.'

'In a moment. I want to talk to you first.'

She subsided into her seat. 'What was she doing anywhere near those smelly cattle?'

He smiled. 'She was trying to stop the villagers making fools of themselves. She didn't know Matthew was coming. We must give them a little time.'

'If John finds him ...'

'He won't go to Kate's room, will he?'

'The man can't stay there!' she exclaimed, appalled by the thought.

'No, but there are plenty of attic rooms. He'll be safer here than anywhere until they leave.'

'When will that be?'

'Let's go and ask them, shall we?' He rose and held out his hand. Almost like a child, she took it.

When Kate came to her senses again, she was lying on her own bed and Mrs Bunny was very, very gently removing her torn and muddied clothing. She felt so weak and bruised it hurt her to breathe. She had a dreadful headache and couldn't be sure exactly what had happened. Had she imagined Matthew was there?

Mrs Bunny turned to a bowl of warm water on the table at her side and wrung out a cloth to sponge the mud from her face and arms. 'You know, most of this is dirt,' she said. 'It's not nearly as bad it looks. The angels must have been watching over you.'

'Matthew ...' She tried to lift her head.

'He'll come back directly. I've sent him into the dressing room until you're fit to be seen.' She stood up and set the bowl on the washstand and picked up a nightdress. 'Now, let's get you into this and tuck you into bed, then I'll let him in.'

Kate dutifully held up her arms and the nightgown was slipped over her shoulders and eased down over her aching limbs. Matthew was here. It wasn't a dream.

'You can come back in now, Captain,' Mrs Bunny called, pulling the bedclothes up around the girl's chin.

Kate looked towards the door as Matthew strode into the room and fell on his knees beside the bed to take her hand. 'How do you feel, my love?'

'I ache all over.'

'I'm not surprised. It's a miracle you haven't broken any bones.' He leaned over to kiss her very gently so as not to hurt her. But it was not pain she felt, but a great welling up of love and desire and her bruised body tingled with pleasure. 'When you are better, I shall have to scold you severely for the fright you gave us. What you did was suicidal.'

'I wanted to stop the herd getting into the village.'

'You did that all right and nearly killed yourself into the bargain. If I hadn't caught a glimpse of you among all those cattle before you fell ...'

Her mind was a whirl of questions, all tumbling about in disorder and she didn't know which to ask first. 'Oh, Matthew, I can't believe it's really you. Have you been pardoned?

'No, I wish I had.'

'You escaped? Sir John said you might. If he catches you ... Oh, Matthew, you must go at once.'

For a brief moment he remembered that attempted rape and his jaw hardened. 'Sir John doesn't come to your room, does he?'

'No, of course not.'

'Then I am safe enough for the moment. Mrs Bunny is just outside the door, keeping watch.'

'How did you escape? Everyone said it was impossible from the hulks.'

'It is without help, but I had a very able accomplice in Carrington-Haddow.'

'Andrew?'

'Yes, Andrew. He hired a boat and smuggled me off. All we had to do was row ashore.' There would be time enough later to tell her their adventures and how they had both been so nearly caught when the tavernkeeper had told the searchers their direction, and Andrew had sent him off on the horse while he ran the other way, drawing their pursuers after him. Matthew had not even been sure he had got safely away until he saw him in the middle of the stampede, trying to turn the herd away from Kate. Like everything else the man had done, it was an act of selfless courage. 'He told me about the villagers' plan to march on Haddow Hall, so I had to come. I was afraid you would be embroiled in it as you had been before. And I was right, wasn't I?'

'Someone had to stop them and Bates wouldn't listen.'

'Oh, he listened all right.' He smiled, bending to kiss the tip of her nose. 'He heard the music and shouting and hurried to the village, but he was too late, they were already on the march and you with them. There was nothing for it but to go back to the herd. I was there by then.'

The herd. It had scattered all over the park. 'How did the cattle get into the grounds? There's a wall all round.'

He laughed. 'Not quite all round. Down by the stance, where the woods are thickest, there is only a brook to mark the boundary, you should know that. They came through there.'

'But how?' she asked again. 'Bates is far too good a stockman to let that happen.'

He laughed and shrugged. 'Let's just say he was a little careless on this occasion, though if I had known what you would do ...' He stopped speaking to look down at her. She had a small bruise on her temple which would heal but otherwise her lovely face was unmarked. 'Do you know how close you came to being killed? A herd of beef is no light matter.'

'I had to do something. I couldn't let them crash through the village; they would have trampled everything down. Someone might have been killed.'

'Yes, you.'

She winced as she tried to move. 'I was caught on the wrong side of the gates, that's all.'

'You fell into a small depression in the ground at the base of one of the pillars; it protected you. We must thank the good Lord for that.'

'Why didn't Andrew tell me he was going to try and free you?'

'I expect he wasn't sure if his scheme would work.'

'But why didn't he give me just a little hint you were coming when he came home last night?'

He laughed, making her look fearfully towards the door, worried he might be heard. 'I think he still hoped to persuade you to marry him. When the herd stampeded and he helped to rescue you, he finally conceded defeat.' He stopped speaking to take her hand and put it to her lips. 'You know, my darling, it was a great risk he took and an even greater act of self-sacrifice because he knew success would mean he would lose you.'

'Oh, Matthew, we have so much to thank him for. How shall we ever repay him? Do you think he is very unhappy?'

He was sanguine about that. 'I've no doubt he'll recover.'

'But why did you refuse his help at the trial?'

'It would not have served, my love. If I had publicly accepted his help it would have destroyed my credibility with the labourers.'

'But, surely, once you had been arrested, that no longer mattered.'

'Oh, yes it did. I had to leave something behind for them to hold onto, a model if you like, something that even the most diehard sceptics could accept.' He paused and stroked her hair away from her face, revealing a purple bruise. 'Besides I was in the throes of a dilemma.'

'What to do about me?'

He grinned. 'What had I to offer you? Oh, it would not have been so bad if you had been a tinker's daughter, but after I discovered who you really were ...'

'You saw Josiah?'

'Yes, I saw him.'

'How was he? Did he suffer much?'

'No, I don't think so,' he said, not wanting to distress her any more than she had been. 'They gave him something to deaden the pain. He was more concerned for you than himself.'

'He was always like that. He took great care of me, right up to that last day. I am so sorry I could not have been with him at the end.'

'He wouldn't have wanted you there, my love. He wouldn't have wanted you to see him so weak and helpless when he always thought of himself as the strong one. He told me to tell you he loved you dearly and begged you to forgive him for what he had done. The pain of losing his leg was nothing beside the suffering he endured over that.'

'I have forgiven him,' she said. 'I pray he can rest in peace over it. But why didn't you tell me that night at the inn that you had seen him?'

'Because I was too cowardly, I suppose. I knew that if what Josiah had told me was true, then I had no right to keep you. I had put myself outside the law. And later when I was arrested, it seemed to be the end of any hope we could ever have of being together. I knew Andrew loved you and he had so much more to offer you than I had. He is rich and he does not have the stigma of being a convict. I thought he would make you a good husband.'

'I decide whom I marry,' she said, miffed. 'I am not a child, though everyone seems bent on treating me like one. I have a mind of my own, you know.'

'I know that!' He smiled briefly. 'It was the hardest decision I have ever had to make, believe me. But when Andrew got me out of the hulks and told me you had not settled down here as he had hoped and had refused his offer of marriage, I changed my mind. I had to come and hear it from your own lips.'

'And now you have, what are you going to do?'

'I'm going to carry you off and marry you.'

'Is that a proper proposal?'

'Oh, very proper.'

She began to laugh but stopped suddenly when it hurt her ribs. 'I can hardly believe you are here, in this room, that I am talking to you like this. I was afraid I'd never see you again.'

'I'm not so easy to dispose of,' he said laconically.

'But it wasn't fair to keep things from me,' she said. 'It's almost as if you didn't trust me.'

'I trust you with my life; I told you that right at the beginning.'

'So you did. But I didn't understand then.'

'And you do now?'

'I think so.'

'I think I began to love you the first day I came to the village and watched you walking down the lane with your head in the air. You were so angry because I had usurped the place of one of the village men.'

'So you had.'

He chuckled. 'William Chapman never paid me, it was just a cover, but I couldn't tell you that at the time.'

'Why not?'

'We all knew you would do anything to free Josiah and we couldn't be sure you wouldn't tell Andrew, if not Sir John, about our plans.' He paused, caressing the back of the hand he held with his thumb. 'I guessed he would use Josiah as a lever. The trouble began when our plans went awry; I had difficulty in persuading the Lowacre villagers to come in with us and then Charlie went and killed that sheep, and you all went to the barn. Oh, I was so angry about that ...'

She laughed. 'I know, and mostly with me.'

'When I saw Sir John raise his crop to you, I lost all control. I lashed out at him without stopping to think. I was angry with myself, not you; angry for not being there earlier, angry for not being able to control hotheads like Green and young Barber, angry because I knew that once the squire realised who I was and why I was in the village, my usefulness to the farm labourers would be over.'

'And you're not safe now, are you? It's exactly like it was before and if Sir John finds you here, he'll have you sent straight back to prison and they'll take care you don't escape again. I couldn't endure that.'

'You are right, my love and I must make a move.' He left her side and went to the window. 'Andrew has undertaken to occupy Sir John while we make our plans.' He chuckled suddenly. 'But with the cattle roaming all over the park and Bates needing the help of the estate workers to round them up, I should think he has enough to keep him busy for another hour or two at least.'

'That's not all,' she said, reminded of the events of the previous night. 'I had almost forgotten about the baby. Had you heard what happened?'

'Andrew told me.'

She sat up and swung her legs over the edge of the bed and gingerly tried to stand. She was weaker than she realised and suddenly the room seemed to spin round her and she fell back with a little cry of dismay.

He ran to help her back to bed. 'Lie down, my darling. You must rest until you recover from the shock and those bruises heal.'

'But I must come with you.'

'So you shall, sweetheart, but we don't have to go today. This house is big enough to hide a small army, let alone one man, and who would think of looking for me here?' He looked at her with an expression of infinite tenderness as he bent to kiss her. 'You are not ready to travel yet.'

'Where are we going?'

He sat on the edge of the bed and took her hand. 'Does it matter where?'

'Not at all, just so long as we are together.'

'Even Australia?'

'Australia? But ... Oh dear ...' Her thoughts flew to her mother; she had said she would go mad if anyone else took her daughter away. How could she do it to her? But how could she let Matthew go without her? Oh, it was a terrible, terrible decision and she could not face it.

'It is where the law has decreed I should go and in England we should never be safe. We would be forever looking over our shoulders, always afraid. I'm told Australia is a wonderful country with endless opportunities for someone with ambition.'

'But what about your brother? Your home?'

'Matthew Tolley has no home. As for Matthew Thorsborough, perhaps, one day, he will return on a visit. I saw my brother two days ago and said my goodbyes.'

'And the labourers? Must they fight on alone?'

'My work for them is done. Andrew will carry on where I left off. He told me he means to stand for Parliament and it's there the changes must be made. As a convicted felon, I could never do that.' He paused and looked at her intently. 'It's a big step to take, my darling, and you, too, will be giving up a great deal. Are you sure you want to go?'

It had to be faced, that terrible decision. 'It's such a long way from Mama. She has been through so much and I don't want to hurt her all over again.'

'She will understand. I'll go and find her and we can talk about it.'

She sat up in alarm. 'No, you might run into Sir John ...' She couldn't go on for the picture such a possibility conjured up. 'Mama will come herself soon. She never leaves me alone for long.' It was almost a complaint. 'I'm surprised she hasn't come before;

she must have heard the commotion. And yet, the house is very quiet ...'

'I expect Andrew explained everything to her and they are simply being tactful.'

Kate didn't think so. Her mother would be appalled by such indecorous behaviour. 'Ask Mrs Bunny to fetch her.'

'Very well.' He went to the door and listened, then, hearing nothing, opened it and stepped onto the landing.

Kate sank back onto the pillows and shut her eyes, unable to believe she wasn't dreaming. Now she was alone, she realised how much her bruises throbbed and how weak she felt. Matthew had been right; she was in no state to travel. As usual her impetuosity had caused him endless trouble; instead of being well on his way, he was creeping stealthily about the house, afraid of being discovered. But oh, the joy, of having him back! Nothing must part them ever again, and if there were hardships to face, then they would face them together.

She heard voices and a flurry of petticoats as Felicity hurried into the room ahead of Matthew.

'My darling girl,' she said, crossing the room to sit on the side of the bed. 'Andrew told me what happened. I wanted to come to you at once, but he would not allow it. Are you badly hurt?'

'A few bruises, that's all.'

'It's a miracle, but you should not have done it, truly you should not.'

Kate smiled, reaching for Matthew's hand. 'Mama, this is Matthew.'

'So I understand, and wanting to carry you off to the other side of the world. Are you quite sure you want to go?'

'Yes.' She paused, trying not to hurt, but knowing she could not avoid it. 'Mama, say you do not mind. I could not bear to hurt you. Say you understand.'

'Yes, I suppose I do.' Felicity sighed. 'And Andrew has said it will not be for ever; I could not endure that. He tells me he intends to work hard for a free pardon for Matthew. Then you'll be able to return. He says he has already made a few tentative enquiries and the prospects seem hopeful.'

'Oh, that would be wonderful!' Kate exclaimed. 'How long will it take?'

'It might take some time,' Matthew said, realising Andrew had raised Mrs Carrington's hopes in order to persuade her to agree, but he didn't want Kate to be deceived into thinking they would soon be back. 'Until then I must go into voluntary exile.'

'Then I must go too,' Kate said. 'Oh, Mama, you will give us your blessing, won't you?'

'If this young man is the only one who can make you happy, then you have it,' she said, noticing Kate's eyes. It was the first time she had seen them really sparkle since the day they had been reunited. Andrew had been right and it was breaking her heart, but she managed a watery smile. 'Papa and I will come and visit you when you're settled.'

'You won't tell Sir John Matthew's here, will you?' Kate said. 'If he finds out . . .'

'No, of course I won't tell him, but didn't you know? He has disappeared.'

'Disappeared?'

'Yes. He went out of the house last night and didn't return. The front door was left open and his gun gone from the rack.'

'You don't suppose he meant to harm any of the villagers?' Kate turned to Matthew in alarm. 'He wouldn't, would he?'

'There was an empty decanter on the floor by his chair,' Felicity said. 'He was upset and angry about the baby and no doubt drank too much and didn't know what he was doing. He's probably sleeping it off somewhere.'

'I hope you are right,' Kate said.

'Everyone who can be spared is searching for him.'

Matthew sat on the edge of the bed and took Kate's hand. 'Now, my love, we have plans to make. You are not too tired? Shall we leave you to sleep?'

'I'm not tired at all,' she assured him, reaching out her other hand to grasp her mother's.

Fiddy found the squire's body in the middle of the afternoon, lying beside a little-used path through the wood, shot by his own gun. His death could have been caused by a poacher's trap, tripping him and making him fall on his gun, but he was too close to the path to have found any of those. Fiddy knew where they were and the knowledge had remained undivulged. Ever since the squire had returned from his travels just over a year ago, and told him to round up every poacher he could find, ever since he had, on orders he dare not disobey, set fire to Josiah's caravan, he had felt differently about poachers. The roaring flames had troubled him as he watched; he had felt the injustice of it in his bones. He had never said a word to anyone, he had simply left the small-time poachers alone and concentrated on the organised bands who made a lucrative business out of it. Sir John could have been murdered by one of those, or he could have died by his own hand, but his gun was lying just out of his reach and the ground around him was broken up and trampled, as if a great herd had passed over it.

He heaved the body over his shoulder and took it back to the Hall. Andrew would know what to do, he was the squire of Middleacre now; he must look to Andrew for orders.

The whole household was stunned, but gradually the realisation dawned that the tyranny had ended. Andrew was where he belonged and the whole village would benefit from his fair-minded attitude and love of justice. And one day, Kate thought, he would find someone to love and marry, and he would come to look on her as a much-loved sister.

The effect on Kate and Matthew was more immediate. It meant their departure had to be delayed because Andrew insisted she stay to attend the funeral. He wanted the villagers to see her by his side as a kind of symbol that the unrest was over. 'You and Mother will be on one side of me and Lady Haddow on the other,' he said. 'She has lost her husband and her baby and we must do all we can to support her.' He had said her ladyship was welcome to stay as long as she wished and that he would have the old dower house refurbished for her. It had not been lived in for years, not since Sir John's first wife had died and his mother had moved back into the main house, but it was a solid dwelling and Laura could direct the operations to her own taste. She had haughtily declined, saying she hated the fens, a cold, wild country, she called it; she would go back to London and civilisation just as soon as the funeral was over.

Felicity had imposed her own conditions; Kate could go with her blessing, only if she were married first. The wedding, to be held in secret, would follow the funeral service.

The three days between finding the body and the funeral were spent on tenterhooks by all who shared the secret of Matthew's presence in the house, particularly Kate. She saw danger round every corner, betrayal on every face, and lived in continual fear

'Be easy, my love,' Matthew said, as they stood side by side in his attic room looking out of the high dormer window across the park to the village, where all but the church spire was hidden by trees. The most dangerous time would be when he emerged from the house to make his way over to the church, but by taking a route through the woods and across the drove road, he could avoid the funeral congregation. 'I haven't been seen by anyone except you, your mother, Andrew and Mrs Bunny since I returned and the housekeeper is completely loyal, you know that.'

'But you know the villagers gather whenever something happens in Middleacre and they won't want to miss seeing Sir John's coffin go by and they will all be out and about.'

'My darling, even if they do catch sight of me, no one will tell the constable and even if he saw me, he would not do anything for fear of reprisals from the villagers. You are worrying unnecessarily.'

'All the same,' she said. 'I shall be glad when we are on our way.' She smiled suddenly. 'Even in death, Sir John has managed to make things difficult for us.'

'It will be the last time. After tomorrow, you need think of him no more.' He took her in his arms to kiss her longingly before sending her downstairs to take her place with the family and guests at the supper table, guests who had come for a birth and stayed for a funeral – two funerals if you counted the still-born child.

After tomorrow, she mused, as she endured the muted chatter at the table, she could breathe freely again, but supposing something went wrong? Supposing the funeral cortège was late leaving the church or someone stayed behind to gossip? Supposing their carriage broke a wheel or one of the horses went lame? Supposing, just supposing, every catastrophe she could think of actually happened, what then?

She spent a sleepless night, pacing the room, rehearsing every move, not daring to look further ahead than the wedding ceremony itself. The next morning she rose early, packed a small valise and put it in the closed carriage Andrew had given them for their journey to London; she dare not trust anyone else to take it. Then she returned to prepare herself, first for a funeral and then for a wedding.

By wearing Matthew's sombre cloak over her gown, she would appear to be in mourning but after everyone had left the church, she could discard it. There had been no time to have a wedding dress made and, in any case, it would not have been seemly, but Felicity had helped her to choose something from her new wardrobe, a duck-egg blue satin, almost stark in its simplicity, but beautifully cut and trimmed with ermine. Grandmama Haddow's wedding veil was made into a small parcel, to be carried beneath the cloak until the moment came to put it on. It would not be the wedding she had dreamed of, but she was happy there was to be a marriage at all and would gladly have settled for less to be with Matthew.

The funeral service seemed interminable and Kate, standing with head bowed between Andrew and her mother, hoped fervently that the Reverend Cox would not take long over the marriage ceremony when every minute counted. She glanced up at Andrew and he allowed himself the tiniest smile to reassure her, before he led the congregation out to the graveyard behind the coffin bearers. Kate did not follow, but remained behind in the quiet church in silent contemplation, waiting and praying.

She heard a light step behind her and looked up to see Matthew, who had slipped in unnoticed, coming to take his place at her side. He gripped her hand and smiled. 'No one saw me,' he whispered. 'Except Andrew. He and your mother will be back in a minute.'

'Do you think they will be missed when everyone gets back to the Hall?'

'Not for a time and Andrew will make their excuses.' He paused and looked into her eyes, eyes which met his, clear and uncompromising as they had always been. 'Are you sure you want to go on with this?'

'I am sure,' she said firmly, as she removed the cloak and draped the veil over her blond curls.

'Good, because here comes Andrew to give you away.'

She turned towards the back of the church as Andrew, one arm in a sling, made his way towards them. He had a bright, fixed smile on his face and though he walked steadily enough, Kate knew he had been drinking. She touched his good arm and smiled up at him as he took his place beside her. 'Dear Andrew,' she whispered, as her mother and the Reverend Mr Cox followed him in and took their places. 'Thank you.'

'Be happy,' was all he said.

The parson looked uneasy, but his living was in the gift of the squire of Middleacre and for that reason he had acceded to every whim of the late squire and would bow to every wish of the new one. He would not ask why the marriage had been hurriedly arranged for the same day as Sir John's funeral, nor why there was to be no congregation. He moved to the altar, genuflected and turned to face the young couple who stood together before him. 'Dearly beloved,' he began . . .

Just why he was so sure the girl now living at Haddow Hall was Kate Brough, Ben Carter could not say. But who else could it be ? A young lady who had been brought up as a gypsy and who turned out to be the long-lost niece of the squire of Haddow Hall, it was almost too fantastic to credit. But he had been assured of it by no lesser person than Mr Justice Lawson, who had actually been and seen her himself. It could not be anyone else but the girl Ben thought of as the poacher's daughter. Ever since he had heard the rumour, he had been fuming with frustration. He could not go up to the front door of the Hall and arrest her, could he ? Sir John would not allow her to be taken. But if Sir John had forgiven her, the law had not. And certainly Ben Carter had not. And that very morning he had heard from his superiors that Matthew Tolley had escaped and was to be watched out for, though they doubted he would dare return to Middleacre. Ben didn't doubt it. The man had risked all for the girl once before, he would do so again ; she was the perfect bait and now there was no Sir John to protect her. He would bag two birds with one stone and not even Mr Carrington-Haddow would dare try to stop him. Oh, it would please him no end to prove that it was not a case of one law for the poor and a different one for the rich ; the fact that the poacher's daughter had turned out to be gentry would only add a piquancy to his final triumph. He pushed his top hat to the back of his head and smiled as he drove the prison van into Middleacre village, listening to the sombre tolling of the church bell denoting the end of the interment.

The ring was hardly on Kate's finger when there was a noise at the back of the church and they turned to see Jack Watson hurrying towards them. 'Ben Carter's comin',' he said breathlessly. 'He ha' brung the prison van.'

Matthew paused in the act of taking his wife into his arms, reluctant to give up the pleasure.

'There ain't time for that, Cap'n,' Watson said bluntly. 'Get you gone. Right now.'

Matthew took Kate's hand and turned towards the vestry door, just as Ben Carter burst in. Andrew stepped forward to speak to him and delay him long enough for them to escape. Felicity just had time to put the cloak about Kate's shoulders and drop a swift kiss on her cheek, before Matthew pulled on his bride's hand, and led her through the vestry and out of a side door. They skirted the newly covered grave and scrambled over the low wall which gave onto the lane behind the church. They could see the carriage waiting a little way off and dashed towards it.

Kate was still feeling the effects of her encounter with the herd and her feet stumbled. 'Go on,' she cried. 'Go on, Matthew. Leave me. It's you he wants.'

His answer was to sweep her up into his arms and run on. They could hear Ben Carter's shouts behind them, but he was being hindered rather than helped by the villagers, who seemed adept at getting in his way in their enthusiastic efforts to chase the couple. Matthew reached the vehicle at last and put Kate on the seat, calling to the driver to make all speed as he climbed up beside her. He had no sooner pulled the door shut behind him than they jolted into motion, just as their pursuer appeared in the lane behind them. But he was on foot and could do nothing but watch and curse as the horses were whipped into a gallop and the vehicle disappeared round the bend of the lane.

Matthew did not speak until they had covered several miles and the horses were tiring, then he ordered the driver to slow down and turned to smile at her. 'Well, wife?'

In spite of the fact that she was still trembling uncontrollably, Kate managed to laugh. 'Will we ever be safe?'

'Not while we're in this country, I'm afraid. I was right, there is no future for us here.'

'But in Australia?'

'Oh, yes, there our future is as bright as the morning star.'

'I shan't feel easy until we are on board ship.'

'And that will be tomorrow evening. Our berths are booked on *The Prince*; we have only to walk on board.'

'When did you do that?'

'While I was in London, after escaping from the hulks.' He chuckled at her mystified expression. 'I spent the time between gaining my freedom and returning to Middleacre laying plans. I am now the owner of a parcel of land just outside Sydney. I'm going to learn to become a proper farmer – with your help, of course.'

'And what name did you give?' she teased. 'Could it have been Captain Swing?'

He laughed and drew up outside an inn for their first change of horses. 'Captain Swing? Now, who might he be?'

As each mile passed under the galloping hooves, Kate's anxiety receded and slowly she began to relax, though she would not feel truly safe until they had left the shores of England. That night they stayed at a wayside inn. It was not palatial but she hardly noticed; her eyes were only for her husband as he slowly undressed her, caressing her naked body, gently, tenderly, making her arch towards him, filling her with a fire of longing and desire which could not be denied. She was still sore, but her bruises were forgotten as she put her arms up and round his neck, pulling his head down and finding his lips with her own. The kiss lasted a very long time as his mouth explored hers, and she was not aware of him removing his own clothing, until she felt the warmth of his naked thigh close against hers. A little shiver ran through her as he knelt over her. 'Oh, Kate, my love, my only love.'

'The time is right, isn't it?' she whispered. 'And you are the man to teach me?'

'Yes, my darling.' He lowered himself onto her, afraid of hurting her, but she felt none of the bruises, either to her body or those she had sustained to her spirit. All had fled in the face of a love which could not be denied.

The next evening, just before sunset, she found herself standing at the ship's rail taking her last look at England. Then, and only then, with Matthew's arm encircling her waist, did she dare to begin looking forward to the future, a future which Matthew had told her was as bright as the morning star.

Historical Note

*A*ll over England in 1830, bands of agricultural labourers rose up in protest over enclosures, low wages, the employment of outsiders and the new farm machinery which they maintained, was putting them out of work. Driven to desperation, they pulled down fences, destroyed threshing machines and set fire to ricks and barns. Their actions, for the most part, were not directed against the farmers who employed them, but against the landowners and clergy, and were often preceded by a warning letter signed *Captain Swing*. No one knows why this particular name was used, nor if such a person ever existed. The use of the name was widespread and led many people to believe the riots were co-ordinated by one man, although the fact that they were so far apart and apparently spontaneous seems to preclude that.

Because of the numbers involved and suspecting that magistrates might be too lenient, the Government ordered special commissions to conduct trials in the counties where the uprisings were most proliferate. By the time the disturbances were over, 644 rioters had been sent to prison, 505 sentenced to transportation (481 actually sailed), 19 were hanged (two from Cambridgeshire), one was whipped and 800 were acquitted or bound over. The proportion sentenced to transportation was unusually large, even for those times, and many small communities were devastated by the loss of a whole generation of their young men.

A National Agricultural Labourers' Union was not founded until 1872.

All Orion/Phoenix titles are available at your local bookshop or from the following address:

Littlehampton Book Services
Cash Sales Department L
14 Eldon Way, Lineside Industrial Estate
Littlehampton
West Sussex BN17 7HE
telephone 01903 721596, *facsimile* 01903 730914

Payment can either be made by credit card (Visa and Mastercard accepted) or by sending a cheque or postal order made payable to *Littlehampton Book Services.*
DO NOT SEND CASH OR CURRENCY.

Please add the following to cover postage and packing

UK and BFPO:
£1.50 for the first book, and 50P for each additional book to a maximum of £3.50

Overseas and Eire:
£2.50 for the first book plus £1.00 for the second book and 50p for each additional book ordered

---

BLOCK CAPITALS PLEASE

name of cardholder ....

address of cardholder ....
....
....
....
        postcode ....

delivery address
(if different from cardholder)
....
....
....
....
        postcode ....

☐ I enclose my remittance for £..............................

☐ please debit my Mastercard/Visa (delete as appropriate)

card number ☐☐☐☐☐☐☐☐☐☐☐☐☐☐☐☐

expiry date ☐☐☐☐

signature ....

prices and availability are subject to change without notice